The One Who Ghosted Me

Fontaine Family Series
Book 1

Erica Devon

Alpine Aura LLC

First edition 2026

ISBN 979-8-9900071-3-0 (Digital EPUB)

ISBN 979-8-9900071-4-7 (Digital PDF)

ISBN 979-8-9900071-5-4 (Paperback)

ISBN 979-8-9900071-6-1 (Audio)

For my Family

Chapter 1

Amelia

Austin, Texas. Five years ago.

WHAT'S the statute of limitations for receiving a response before you know for sure you're officially ghosted? A week or a month? Does it matter if you're sure he's your soulmate?

A year ago, Amelia Preston believed she was on the right track when she accepted a summer internship with Gateway2-Green in the mapping department.

After graduation, she'd left Florida to take the job. It was the perfect stepping stone into a geology career. Her new boyfriend, Jonathan, was her second-biggest supporter. Only her mom, Rachel, was more excited.

A long-distance relationship was tough, but they were going to make it work.

> AMELIA: They assigned me a mentor, and I like her. Feels like I'm drinking from a firehose, but I'm learning so much.

JONATHAN: You're a rock star. You've got this! Being apart is rough, but I'm proud of you. Will call u tonight.

For her birthday he'd sent a beautiful bouquet of lilies, and they'd made plans for their next monthly visit.

Then, a week before their first-date anniversary, his last message to her had arrived.

JONATHAN: I'm sorry, but I can't come to Austin next month.

AMELIA: I can fly to Florida to see you for a long weekend. I'll spend some time with my mom, too. I haven't seen her in months. She'll be thrilled.

JONATHAN: No, I won't be available for a while. I'm sorry. It's complicated.

AMELIA: What? Why?

A brief metaphorical middle-finger text. The cold dismissal made her wonder if she'd imagined their entire relationship.

Then came the radio silence. *Who does that?* Their relationship had evaporated. A real breakup would have been easier to accept, or at least easier to understand. Her stomach sank deeper every time she thought about his vanishing act.

After a month with no response, sleep vanished. Food tasted like cardboard. She checked her phone compulsively, a hollow ache spreading through her core with each empty notification screen.

She'd hoped it was temporary, so she waited. And waited some more before she tried calling and texting a few last times. But her resolve ran dry, and the hurt seeped in as weeks passed.

He wasn't going to respond. Not now, not ever.

Now she searched for distractions, ways to escape the pain and find an outlet for her anger. Extra projects at work. Late nights at the office. Hiking get-togethers with a new group. Anything to avoid her silent apartment.

* * *

"A trainer will be with you in a few minutes. Please have a seat." The gym receptionist handed Amelia a colorful brochure. "Nate will go over everything on your tour."

An expanse of weight machines and treadmills extended beyond the reception area. Machines swished and balls thudded rhythmically from the indoor sports courts.

Amelia took a seat on the couch and stuffed the brochure in her purse. Of course, she'd already reviewed all the gym's facilities and amenities on its website before scheduling a tour: a pool, state-of-the-art weight machines, basketball and pickleball courts, martial arts, and exercise classes.

It was expensive, but after getting a full-time job offer, she wanted to treat herself with a membership.

Pouring her heart and effort into working long hours was a decent distraction from Jonathan's ghosting and wondering what the hell happened with him. Getting sweaty and learning to lift weights a few times a week would be even better. As much as she loved getting outside and hiking, she was ready for a new challenge.

"Hi there. Amelia?" An enormous shadow swept over Amelia, and she glanced up from her phone.

"Yes. And you must be Nate." His solid, muscular legs fit snugly in his workout shorts. Her gaze continued upward, where his black gym t-shirt accented his firm chest and broad shoulders. The trainer had short, dusty-blond hair trimmed close to his head and gorgeous ice-blue eyes, which focused on her.

Just wow. She blinked twice and swallowed hard. *Now there's a distraction.*

"Hi. I'm Nate." The trainer extended his hand and Amelia smiled. *Right, the tour.* She shook his hand. His hold was comforting, self-assured.

"So," he said with an easy smile, "tell me about your fitness goals."

Chapter 2

Amelia

Rainmere, Washington. Present day, early March.

WITH HER CLIPBOARD tucked under one arm, Amelia stepped into the chilly March morning and tried to overcome the familiar twinge of anxiety in her chest. Six weeks in this unexpected refuge, and she was still waiting for something to go wrong.

Ken's call from the security gate had been routine—a delivery truck arriving as scheduled—but routine felt foreign after the last year of upheaval. She took a steadying breath of pine-scented air and headed toward the gravel drive.

A few minutes later, a delivery truck turned and backed toward the house.

A man hopped down from the cab, smiling as he approached.

"Good morning, miss. We're here to start your kitchen rebuild. I'm Pete, your installer, and this is my partner, Mack," he said, nodding toward his colleague as he opened the back doors of the truck.

"Nice place you have," Mack said.

It wasn't hers, but for one year, the sprawling estate was hers to manage.

"I'm grateful for every day I get to live here," she said.

She glanced up at the security camera mounted discreetly on the corner of the garage. The surveillance was reassuring each time delivery men came and she had to greet them alone. Between the cameras, gated entrance, and round-the-clock security, the place felt almost like a fortress.

Behind her, the mansion towered high like a castle from a European fairy tale, with ivy-covered stone and towering chimneys, even an old carriage house a short walk up the hill. So many places she had yet to explore.

Six weeks ago, when William Jewell offered her the on-site assistant position with rent-free housing included, she'd accepted without hesitation. She'd worked as his virtual assistant for several years, long enough to trust his professionalism. The side gig offered minimal pay but beautiful accommodations and her own space after the months she'd spent squeezed into her friend Audra's apartment.

She'd been exploring the century-old house room by room, though something about the uppermost floor made her uncomfortable. Too many shadows, perhaps, or the way certain stonework felt warm under her fingertips when logic said they should be cold.

"After we unload, I'll install your appliances," Pete said.

She took pictures for Mr. Jewell while they unloaded items from the truck: appliances in large boxes, counter backsplash tiles, and light fixtures.

The men worked efficiently, the truck's hydraulic lift whirring as they lowered a stainless steel refrigerator. Pete grunted as he and Mack maneuvered it onto a dolly. They unloaded the dishwasher next, then boxes of clinking cabinet hardware.

Amelia's phone buzzed.

> AUDRA: Hey BFF, the apartment is lonely without you! When can I see your new place? I'll bring pasta.

Her mouth curved into a small smile. Audra, her bestie since college, had convinced her to move to the Seattle area. For over six months they'd shared Audra's "cozy" apartment, but the cramped space had posed a challenge for both of them.

> AMELIA: Soon. I promise.

> AUDRA: Is there a blind date on the horizon? Melanie has a hot lead for you. Did you see the pic she sent? He's got that whole "I rescue puppies in my spare time" vibe.

> AMELIA:

Tsk. Amelia shoved her phone into her jeans pocket. Dating again was the one thing she planned to put off indefinitely. Love was always a lie or an enticing, shiny lure, but never hers to keep forever.

She led the delivery crew through the house and into the kitchen. The antique clock on the wall chimed at the top of the hour. Only thirty minutes to go before she had to leave for her day job in town. The installers would complete the job after she left, but she'd examine everything thoroughly after she got home that evening.

Pete confirmed the installation plans with Amelia, as she diligently reviewed the work checklist provided by Mr. Jewell. Each page bore the bold header *WJ7 Inc.* at the top.

After she'd taken some unboxing pictures in the kitchen,

Amelia's cell phone rang. A picture of her mom flashed on the screen.

"Hey, Mom," she said. Amelia never ignored a call from her mom.

"Hi, honey. Did I catch you before work? I can never keep track of the time difference."

"It's okay. New kitchen stuff is being installed today. After the contractors get started, I'll be heading into the office." Fortunately, she'd negotiated a flexible schedule with her boss, Lydia, at NorthSound Timber. The lumber company didn't have many geologists on staff, and they were willing to accommodate her rather than risk losing a good contractor.

"I found a crack along the side of the house this morning," her mom said. Sam's barking echoed in the background. "Hush, Sam."

Amelia's stomach dropped. Ugh. Another repair. Another expense her mom couldn't afford. "How bad?"

"You sound stressed," her mom said. "Everything okay up there?"

She'd failed to mask her worry. "Just busy. Mr. Jewell keeps adding projects." The gradual renovation plan he'd promised was becoming anything but gradual.

Recent additions to his list included sending photos of the attic and detailing its contents—which meant doing a thorough inventory—as well as receiving a new hallway chandelier delivery on Friday afternoon. With every email from Mr. Jewell, her part-time side gig was becoming less and less "part-time."

"Overloading yourself is an intentional distraction, Amelia. Filling every moment of your life with tasks won't fill the emptiness in your heart."

"I enjoy being busy. The crack, Mom ... how bad is it?"

"It runs up one corner of the house. I'll send you a picture if I figure out how."

Her mother was technology-challenged, beyond making a phone call or sending a few texts. "Great, snap a few photos," she said. "After I get home tonight, I can walk you through how to send—"

Muffled barking over the line interrupted Amelia. She followed Mack back through the house and outside to the driveway.

"What about that friend of Melanie? Leo?"

Amelia closed her eyes. She should never have mentioned Melanie's matchmaking attempts. "Mom, I'm fine. Really."

"You're twenty-nine, honey. I know last time didn't work out, but you can't give up. You deserve—"

"I deserve peace," she said. "I'm not ready for ... complications." Her voice softened. "I have friends, and I have you."

Mack passed her as he headed toward the truck's driver's door. He scrambled in, and the engine thundered to life. She took one step backward.

"Bye, Mom, talk to you again soon. Love you!" Amelia ended the call.

"Hey, Mack, wait!" Pete shouted from behind her. As he rushed toward the truck, he bumped Amelia's shoulder. She swayed.

Amelia's phone popped out of her hand and skittered across the gravel toward the truck's back wheel.

"No!"

But the tire found its target with a sickening crunch.

She stared at the mangled device, glass scattered like tiny accusations over the gravel. Another thing broken. Another thing lost.

Pete rushed back toward her. "Oh, jeez. So sorry about that," he said.

Her hands trembled as she collected the pieces, careful to avoid the sharp edges. Nothing good lasted.

With a deep sigh, she composed herself.

Mr. Jewell expected pictures—lots of them. Her personal phone had doubled as a work phone, and now she was without a camera.

The thought of asking Mr. Jewell to replace the phone gave her instant heartburn, but it was damaged on the job. She hated asking for money, even when it wasn't her fault.

Once back inside, she glanced at her hiking boots by the door with a sigh. Too bad there was no time for an excursion today.

Her laptop chimed with an incoming email from her boss at NorthSound Timber. The merger had been generating endless administrative emails, most of them routine updates about personnel changes and project reassignments.

Amelia glanced at the clock and closed the laptop with a snap. Time to go. She'd catch up on emails at the office.

Chapter 3

Jonathan

Jonathan Fontaine slid into the seat behind the cab driver, next to his fiancée, Paige. "Seattle-Tacoma Airport," he said as he shut the door.

As the driver adjusted his GPS, Jonathan appreciated the cab's immaculate interior. No coffee stains on the seats, no worn patches in the leather.

He was relieved to be going home to Atlanta, back to his friends and lazy weekends on his fishing boat. Those weekends wouldn't last forever, though. Eventually he'd trade them for the life he really wanted: coaching his future kids' soccer team, talking his best friend Drew into building them a treehouse in the backyard. The kind of stable family life he'd grown up without.

Tall trees intermixed with office buildings whisked by the window behind a steady drizzle of raindrops. He was a creature of habit, and a week in the Pacific Northwest had been more than enough.

Paige covered his hand with hers. The familiar contact was comforting.

"I had a conversation with my boss about giving me the promotion next month," she said.

"That's your third ask this quarter," Jonathan replied. It was a gutsy move, one he admired. "You're incredibly persistent."

"You should do the same. There's no shame in climbing the corporate ladder," she said.

By age thirty, Paige Whitlow was fast-tracked as the youngest of five managers in the East Coast division of Whitlow Forest Resources, and no one could deny that she deserved it.

"Have you discussed it with your father? There's got to be a perk to being the daughter of the company's owner."

"He'll have less control under the merger agreement." She leaned back in her seat. "If it goes through. More importantly, I'm holding that card in reserve for the future."

In reserve for what? Then again, maybe it was best he didn't know.

"I'll be a regional VP in three years if we play things right," she said.

We? His brows squeezed together. "I have my own plans, Paige." Which didn't involve ladder climbing.

"You know if I want something, I go after it." Her fingers drummed against her handbag, a familiar strategizing *tap-tap-tap*.

"I like that about you," he said. It was true. A woman who knew exactly what she wanted was attractive. "But how much of that drive is to please your father? He's molding you to take his place someday."

"I'm pursuing my desire, which, fortunately, aligns with his goal. And, despite my father's position in the company, I've achieved my success on my own merits."

Paige hesitated. In his peripheral vision, Jonathan noticed her staring at him, eyes narrowed, the way a curious parent would scrutinize her child for hints of an emerging prodigy.

"But he's always made it clear he expects me to have an equally qualified partner."

She was sizing him up. The side of his mouth twitched. *No, she was challenging him.* His chest tightened with irritation. He didn't like playing games, and he certainly didn't like being tested.

"It's time for us to find an apartment near the Atlanta office," she continued. "I'll start looking at a few places, and we can tour the best ones together."

Jonathan rolled his shoulders to release the tension.

"You should ... wait awhile."

He enjoyed having a significant other, as long as the relationship was easy. His relationship with Paige had always been straightforward: no fighting, no drama. At least until recently. Their engagement, or more precisely the lack of movement on wedding plans and living arrangements, had become a point of strain between them.

"You know I don't like to wait," she said. "We've been together two years."

Jonathan stiffened. She spoke about their future as though it were a business plan with strategic moves, calculated outcomes, and forecasted deadlines. But relationships weren't mergers.

Jonathan's phone buzzed. *Steve-Boss* flashed on the screen.

"Hey, boss."

"You aren't on the plane yet, are you?"

"On our way to the airport," Jonathan said.

"The plan has changed. Don't get on the plane. I need you on the merger assets project team."

"What? The asset assessment work at the local office? Isn't Simpson taking that one?" He protested, knowing he would ultimately agree but still not happy about it. He could stick around for a few days to help get the team up and running. Not his first choice, but he could deal with it.

"Simpson fell down a flight of stairs last night. He's in the hospital with multiple leg fractures and a minor head injury. He's going to be out of commission for at least a month."

Fuck. He knew what was coming next.

"You were always my top-choice candidate for lead geologist, Jonathan. It's a high-profile project that needs your expertise. I respect your aversion to away assignments, and Simpson was a suitable replacement. But now he's out, and I don't have another good backup. You're it. Tomorrow, you report to the Rainmere office."

"Christ. How long, Steve?"

"Review the assets for the merger and come home. You'll be back in Atlanta in three months, maybe sooner. I promise."

"Three months?"

He leaned back on the headrest and closed his eyes. How the fuck was this happening?

He groaned quietly. Three months in Rainmere sounded like an eternity.

He really wanted to go home. Life was comfortable in Atlanta. He could grab a beer with Drew after work, help his mother with her latest garden project, or take his kayak out when he needed to think. Three months in Rainmere meant three months away from everyone who actually knew him.

"I'm reassigning two timber management specialists from our Seattle corporate office. NorthSound Timber is providing two techs and a geologist," Steve said.

"Who's the local lead geologist? Anyone I've heard of?"

"Probably not. She's a contract mapper they picked up a year ago. Name's Amelia Preston."

Amelia? What the hell was Amelia doing here in Washington?

The name landed as a total shock. It had been five years since he'd walked away from her, from the best thing that had ever happened to him. Then she'd moved on, and it had crushed him.

Ghosting her was the biggest regret of his life. He couldn't change what had happened between them, but maybe this was an opportunity to explain. If she'd listen.

Maybe this was the universe offering him a chance to apologize. Though the odds she'd forgive him weren't good. How absurd. Taking an assignment he didn't want in order to face the woman he'd wronged by making a choice he'd thought was right.

With a sigh of resignation and a touch of curiosity, he decided not to push back on the assignment. "Okay. I'll do it."

"Good man," Steve said. "I'll have Julie send you the address and access code for one of the corporate townhomes. Call me back this afternoon after you're settled so we can go over the project objectives."

"Will do," Jonathan said as he clicked to end the call. He turned to look at Paige.

"That was Steve. Simpson is in the hospital. I won't be going home today."

"I heard enough to catch the gist of it," she said, covering his hand with hers. "Now I wish I could stay longer."

The cab pulled into the passenger drop-off area. Jonathan opened the door for Paige, unloaded their suitcases from the trunk, then paid the driver. He'd get himself a rental car later.

A boy holding a Nintendo Switch exited the next cab with his parents. He didn't look up from his game as his thumbs flew over the controls.

"Ah, shit," Paige mumbled when she saw the gamer. "I forgot to buy a birthday gift for Jake." Her nephew was turning nine, and Paige's sister had an elaborate celebration planned at the Jump Spot for Saturday afternoon. "Maybe I can find something in the airport shops."

He unzipped his carry-on bag and pulled out a pirate ship

model kit. "Here. I bought this yesterday. I was going to give it to him, but you can take it. Tell him it's from you."

Jonathan loved boats, especially fishing boats. Model building was his go-to evening relaxer, along with a glass of scotch.

He handed her the kit. It was a replica of a boat he'd seen once in a museum, the kind built for deep water and rough crossings. Every boy needed to build a ship in a bottle.

"Thank you," Paige said as she opened her handbag and placed the box inside. "You'd make a wonderful dad, Jonathan." Her expression softened, and she gently stroked her fingers along his forearm. "So, when are you going to tell your family we're engaged?"

He felt his throat tighten beneath his shirt collar. He'd been procrastinating discussing it with his family for nearly two months.

Two months of dodging that conversation. How could he tell his family he was engaged when saying yes had been less about loving Paige and more about wanting a family of his own? And was that reason enough to commit to a lifetime together?

"Let's go," he said, as he checked his watch then grabbed the handles of both their luggage bags. "You need to leave now, or you'll have to sprint through the terminal. I'll walk you to check in before I head to the rental car desk."

* * *

An hour later he slid into the driver's seat of a rental SUV.

For the next three months, he'd focus on finishing the project and getting back to Atlanta.

And on making amends with Amelia.

Amelia. She must still hate him for disappearing like a total asshole, even if he'd done the right thing by keeping her safe.

What am I thinking taking an assignment with her? Working with Amelia meant facing what he'd walked away from. And pretending five years hadn't changed everything between them.

His phone buzzed with an incoming text from his brother.

> BRANDON: It's time to discuss the transition. Let's review the accounts when you're back in town.

He shoved his phone into his pocket and put on his seatbelt. At least now he had a legitimate excuse to postpone working with his brother and the family charity organization.

As he exited the airport, he turned on the radio. A talk show host was rambling, "...the difference between settling and choosing. When you settle, you're avoiding something. When you choose, you're moving toward something."

He clicked it off. Some wisdom came too late to be useful.

Chapter 4

Amelia

"AMELIA," the receptionist called without looking up from his computer. "Lydia wants to see you ASAP."

ASAP is never a good sign. Amelia hurried down the hallway, her mind racing through reasons for the urgent summons. She should have kept a closer eye on the administrative emails from Lydia.

She knocked on Lydia's office door, then entered at the muffled "Come in."

"Have a seat," Lydia said, gesturing to the chair across from her desk. "I've given you access to the merger assets project."

Amelia dropped into the chair in front of Lydia's desk with a frown. "Merger assets. Why?"

"It was in my email."

"I'm sorry I missed it. My phone got run over and—"

"I noticed you didn't respond." Lydia's tone was neutral, but Amelia flinched. Being unprepared wasn't like her, and they both knew it.

"I know. I'm sorry," Amelia said. "The phone situation caught me completely off guard. Would you fill me in on the details?"

"The merger negotiations with Whitlow Forest Resources are going well, but they want us to take part in a joint project to review all lease holdings before they'll agree to the final merger terms."

Amelia hesitated. She was only a contractor for North-Sound Timber, not a full employee. "Isn't that out of the scope of my contract?"

"Technically, it's not. There's a provision for reassignment as needed." Lydia leaned back in her chair, studying her.

"Three months, Amelia," Lydia said. "You'll be working with the Whitlow team from Atlanta to evaluate our subsurface mineral leases. Determine what the new company should keep or divest. It's exactly the type of high-visibility work that leads to permanent positions."

A permanent position. Amelia's eyes widened. These were the words she'd been waiting to hear for months. A down payment on a house. More income to help her mom. A chance to rebuild the savings she'd drained paying off the loans she'd co-signed for Nate's failed business. Security. Things always a little out of reach.

"If this goes well, and I have complete confidence it will," Lydia said, "I'll do everything I can to make your job here permanent."

This was it. Her chance. "Yes," Amelia nodded. "I want the assignment. Absolutely."

"Good." Lydia's smile returned, satisfied with Amelia's recovery. "The Atlanta team arrived early this morning. They're setting up in a conference room." She stood. "Come on, let's make introductions. You'll be working closely with the project lead for the next three months."

Amelia followed her boss down the bright hallway, mentally scrambling to shift back into a professional, settled mode. She could handle this. She was adaptable, competent, reliable, even when life kept knocking her off balance.

Lydia pushed open the conference room door, and Amelia froze.

Jonathan Fontaine stood with his back to them, hands tucked into his pockets as he studied a wall map, but she'd recognize his back view anywhere. The confident stance and the way his short dark hair barely touched his collar. It was him.

Five years dissolved in an instant.

Her breath caught somewhere between her lungs and throat. *No, no, no.* This couldn't be happening. Not now, when everything was finally falling into place.

Time stood still.

He turned.

Those eyes. God, those inviting brown eyes that had haunted her dreams. He was still the most handsome man she'd ever met. The same devastating smile that softened when he saw her. It was her Jonathan.

"Amelia, this is Jonathan Fontaine, the project lead," Lydia was saying, her voice sounding far away, as though underwater. Lydia motioned toward the two technicians. "You already know Patricia and Gavin from our tech department. Jonathan, this is Amelia Preston, our geological specialist."

Preston-Levi, his lips formed silently. She saw the exact moment he registered the missing hyphen and the confusion that flashed across his face. So, he didn't know how things had ended with Nate. Good.

"Amelia." Her name on his lips sent an unwanted shiver through her. "It's been a long time."

Five years and two months. "Yes," she said. "It has."

He stepped forward, extending his hand as if they were strangers meeting for the first time. Like he hadn't once traced every curve of her body with those same fingers.

"Did you know about this?" The question escaped before she could stop herself.

"I found out yesterday." His hand hung in the air between them. "This project wasn't supposed to be mine."

Of course it wasn't. Jonathan Fontaine had become very good at avoiding her.

Memories flooded over her: Jonathan's apartment, poring over college textbooks together, and the way he'd look at her like she was everything.

"Are you sure?" he'd whispered against her lips, and she'd nodded, threading her fingers through his hair, pulling him closer. His kisses had been desperate and wild. For a perfect year, she'd believed in happily ever after, even if it had been long-distance.

Then nothing. Radio silence. Like she'd never existed.

Her gaze landed squarely on him. *Still hot. And I still hate what you did to me.*

But Lydia was watching, so she took his offered hand. Walking away wasn't an option, and she was a professional, damn it.

His fingers closed around hers, warm and inviting and completely unfair. Her pulse skipped—a Pavlovian response she'd thought she'd buried.

"You two know each other?" Lydia's eyebrows lifted with interest.

"We were..." Amelia pulled her hand free, the skin still sensitive where he'd touched her. "We knew each other in college. Briefly."

Briefly. As if a year of believing she'd found her forever person could be summarized so simply.

Jonathan's jaw ticked. "Briefly, yes."

His validation stung, but Amelia forced her expression to remain neutral. She wouldn't give him the pleasure of seeing her upset.

"Is that going to be a problem?" Lydia asked, glancing between them.

Yes. "No," Amelia said quickly. "No problem at all."

"None whatsoever," Jonathan echoed. He kept looking at her, searching her face, as though looking for answers.

Liar. She straightened herself and inhaled slowly. They were both liars.

After the other team member introductions, Jonathan said, "I'll get us some coffee." He gave a half smile, the one that had once made her forget her own name. "A hint of cream, right?"

It annoyed her how he remembered. No latte machines here. "That's fine."

When he left with the technicians, Lydia touched her arm. "You sure you're okay with this? There seemed to be some ... tension."

That was one way to describe it.

"We have a history," Amelia admitted. "But it's in the past. We'll be fine."

Lydia nodded and headed for the door. "I'll let you get settled. The project files are on the shared drive."

Alone in the conference room, Amelia sank into a chair and pressed her palms against her forehead. *Holy shit, Jonathan Fontaine.*

She had to work with him for three months, pretending she didn't remember how his laugh had once been her favorite sound in the world. Three months of pretending she'd forgotten the way he'd ghosted her so completely she'd fallen apart and rebounded in the worst way possible.

But she needed this job. Needed the security, the benefits, the chance at a real future. And she'd survived worse than Jonathan Fontaine.

She just wasn't sure she'd survive him twice.

Chapter 5

Jonathan

An hour later, Lydia led Jonathan and the technicians to the front desk to get their badges.

He'd expected Amelia to still hate him for ghosting her.

After he took the merger assignment, he'd considered texting her to let her know he was coming to Rainmere, but she'd long ago blocked his number. He'd tried emailing her, but either she didn't read it or she'd never opened it.

Her expression when she'd seen him was devastating. She'd tried to hide her feelings, but he'd seen the hurt and betrayal simmering in those green eyes. He'd been prepared to see anger, but he hadn't expected how deeply he'd feel it.

He wanted to make peace with her and complete the project expeditiously so he could return home.

After completing the security routines, getting paperwork and photos taken for his access badge, then working with the IT guy to get access to the appropriate digital files and project folders, Jonathan made his way back to the workroom.

The workroom was typical of NorthSound's bright aesthetic, with white walls and standard office carpet, and eight workstation desks arranged in a rectangular formation. Large windows overlooked a mix of businesses and a nearby park, lined with a thick expanse of trees.

Jonathan chose the desk directly across from Amelia's and plugged in his laptop. The proximity felt both fortunate and torturous.

Gavin and Patricia were already busy reviewing project files.

Jonathan began unpacking the box he'd had shipped by overnight courier from his Atlanta office. Just the bare necessities: a tablet bound in a leather portfolio his mother had given him, a small, framed photo of the Atlanta skyline over a lake, and a few laptop accessories.

Amelia kept her eyes focused on her own desk arrangements. Her auburn hair brushed the cream-colored jacket at her shoulders, catching glints of light from the windows.

She'd always been beautiful in an understated way, though more polished now: subtle makeup, hair slightly longer, professional clothes that replaced the casual college style he remembered. Those green eyes could flash with intelligence, or, like now, careful reserve. She tucked a strand of hair behind her ear, and he smiled faintly at the familiar habit. What else had changed, and what hadn't?

"Amelia," he said cautiously. She looked up at him. Her expression was blank.

"Could we go somewhere and talk privately ... over lunch?" He sat in his desk chair.

"I have lunchtime plans." Then she lowered her voice to a whisper. "And I don't want to talk with you privately. Our relationship is purely professional, Jonathan."

A brunette dressed in a crisp skirt suit entered the workroom, scanning the group, clearly at ease.

"There you are," the woman said as she approached Amelia.

"You weren't in your office. And you didn't answer my texts. Are you hiding from me? It's yoga time. Let's go."

"Not hiding." Amelia nodded toward a small stack of papers on her desk. "I need to file these, then we can go." She opened a drawer of files. "I got assigned to a merger project. This workroom *is* my office for the next few months. And my phone died a horrible death this morning, crushed under a delivery truck tire."

The well-dressed woman laughed softly. "That's different." Her gaze settled on Jonathan, and she looked half curious and half speculative.

He nodded. "Jonathan Fontaine, nice to meet you."

"I'm Melanie Foxx."

"Melanie's a lawyer," Amelia said, her tone warming noticeably for the first time since Jonathan arrived. "An excellent one. Fortunately, she works for us."

"Please relay that message to Foxx, Katz & Foxx," Melanie said. "I'm sure my parents would be thrilled to send you a rebuttal on both points."

"Whatever. Total nonsense." Amelia waved her hand in dismissal, then continued with her filing.

"And who exactly are you again?" Melanie's eyebrows rose skeptically as she evaluated Jonathan.

"Just in from Atlanta," Amelia said with a scowl. "He's the lead on the asset project team. And as of this morning, I'm on the team now, too."

"He's your new boss?" Melanie said.

"No, I'm not her boss," Jonathan said. "I'm just leading the project work."

A sly grin swept across Melanie's perfectly oval face as her attention turned back to Amelia. "Don't think for a second that I'm going to forget what day it is."

Jonathan typed in his password and opened a spreadsheet for review.

Amelia closed the file drawer, then stood and grabbed her purse from the back of her chair.

"Monday? Trash day?" Amelia tilted her head with a cute smile that made Jonathan wish it was for him. She reached under her desk and pulled out a gym bag and a rolled yoga mat.

"Cute," Melanie said. "You're avoiding Leo."

He stopped typing, his fingers frozen over the keyboard. *Who the fuck is Leo?*

Jonathan looked up as Melanie crossed her arms and tilted her head with the expression of someone who wasn't finished with her argument.

"Do we have to talk about this *right now*?" Amelia looked back and forth between Melanie and Jonathan. She looped her free arm through Melanie's. "Come on. Class starts downstairs in fifteen minutes, and we still need to get changed."

They disappeared down the hall toward the restroom, gym bags in hand. Jonathan tried to focus on his spreadsheet, but curiosity—and something uncomfortably close to jealousy— gnawed at him. He'd lost his appetite for lunch.

A few minutes later, he gave up pretending to work and headed for the break room.

"...it's the perfect day to call him." Jonathan heard Melanie's voice carrying from the restroom as he approached the break room. "I know you've got this whole anti-dating thing," she continued, "but he's a really nice guy ... Leo is perfect for you. Plus, you lost the bet, fair and square."

At the counter just inside the break room, he reached for the carafe of lukewarm coffee. *Anti-dating?* His jaw tightened as a familiar knot formed in his stomach.

"If you'd just texted me back about the blind date..."

"It's a miserable idea," Amelia said.

"Leo is great. And if it doesn't work out, then at least you'll have gotten your feet wet and put yourself out there."

He blinked as he absentmindedly stirred his coffee, trying to sort the pieces of the conversation that made little sense.

"I'm too busy for dating ... I'm on this merger project that's potentially going to suck up a lot of my time. And I need to complete an inventory of the attic, as well as start on landscaping upgrades as soon as possible. And now my mom's house is falling apart—"

"One evening, for one simple date. Think of it as an adventure," Melanie said.

He caught a glimpse of Melanie as she and Amelia exited the restroom in yoga clothes and turned in the direction of the elevator.

"Using the A-word was a low blow," Amelia said.

His eyes narrowed. Exactly what kind of "adventure" did this Leo have in mind?

"Lawyer's purview," Melanie replied with mock innocence.

Then realization hit him. *Dating ... not married.* He'd been so busy getting oriented in the new office that the implications hadn't sunk in.

He leaned across the doorway, just far enough to see them. His eyes dropped instinctively and searched Amelia's left hand for verification as they neared the elevator. *No ring.*

Amelia and Melanie entered the elevator as Jonathan's phone vibrated in his pocket. Drew. He left the break room and found a private place to talk to his best friend.

Jonathan always found time for Drew Slater. He'd helped his friend start his construction business in Atlanta, and they shared a bond of mutual support. "Hey, Drew."

"How's the West Coast treating you?"

"I know you didn't call to check up on me. What's up?"

Drew laughed. "Actually, I did just call to check up on you."

"So far, so good. Remember Amelia, my ex from grad school? She's here, working at the lumber company. I found out the day I accepted the job."

Sitting down on a bench in the empty hallway, he leaned back against the wall and gazed out at the park, visible through the building's large windows. "We're working on the same project," he said.

The line was silent.

"And ... she's not married anymore. I had no fucking clue," Jonathan whispered. He paused for a moment. "Why aren't you saying anything? Wait a minute..." His eyes narrowed as he stared out a window. "You knew. You *knew* she was here, didn't you?"

"I knew she was there," Drew said slowly. "Through Audra. Why did you still take the assignment after you found out?"

"Steve didn't give me much choice in the matter. But I didn't push back either. I thought maybe I can finally explain what happened and apologize. Steve gave me her name as Preston, without Levi on the end and ... I ... blew it off as a mistake." *Fuck.*

"Audra told me what happened with Amelia and Nate."

"Why the hell didn't you tell me?"

"When I told you Amelia got married," Drew said, "you told me you didn't want to hear anything more about her. By the time Audra told me Amelia and Nate had split, you'd started rebuilding your life. You said things were good with you and Paige, and I took you at your word." Drew paused.

Jonathan leaned his elbows on his knees and dropped his forehead against one palm. He hadn't been completely open with Drew about his relationship with Paige.

"And it wasn't my story to tell," Drew said.

Drew was right. When he'd heard Amelia had gotten

married, he'd wanted to escape from all his feelings and memories of her.

"She still hates me," he said. He knew Amelia had every right to hate him.

"That wasn't your fault, Jon. You had to keep quiet," Drew said.

Five years ago, his part in the international sanction violations investigation had torn his world to shreds, including his relationship with Amelia. Being an informant was the right thing to do, but it had led to so many unforeseen consequences. "I hope she sees it that way."

"She will."

"How long since she and Nate—"

"The split with Nate was over a year ago. I don't remember exactly when, and I wasn't given details."

"I'm trying to wrap my head around the idea that she's single. And her friends are trying to hook her up on a blind date. It sounded like she was trying to avoid it." Jonathan straightened himself with a deep inhale. "I don't want to repeat what we went through in college. Watching Amelia date someone else again would suck."

"Not your business, dude." Drew cleared his throat. "How are things going with you and Paige?"

Jonathan groaned. "You're a nosy shit." He hated how Drew so easily drilled down to a core point. "I have to figure out what I'm going to do about Paige. Something is just ... off." He cared about Paige. But he wasn't sure he should have agreed to *marry* her.

"If you have to figure out what to do, it means you already know in your gut what you need to do."

Jonathan sighed. "I'm not ready to act on a gut feeling. I need to be absolutely sure." He needed more time to sort everything out in his head.

They said their goodbyes and Jonathan ended the call.

Drew was right. Amelia would eventually start dating, and while it made him uncomfortable, he had a fiancée and it wasn't any of his damn business. He shifted position and rolled his tight shoulders.

Damn. He was stuck in a box of his own making, caught between a past he'd walked away from and a future he wasn't sure he wanted. The familiar weight of regret seeped into his chest.

First things first, he decided. He needed to figure out what he was going to do about Paige. And after Paige, he needed to check in with Whitlow management about the program. He'd been away from Atlanta too long. The launch timeline was tight, and he couldn't afford to let momentum slip.

But as he walked back toward the workroom, he couldn't shake the image of Amelia's smile, the one she'd given Melanie, the one he wished she'd meant for him.

Chapter 6

Amelia

THE ANGER from being ghosted surged through her again, tangled up with the jarring shock of actually seeing Jonathan after all this time. Wave after wave of conflicting emotions. Amelia needed backup. The second she got home, she opened her laptop to the group chat with Audra and Melanie.

> AMELIA: Emergency besties meeting tonight.
> 7pm housewarming party at my place.
> Who's in?

> MELANIE: I'll bring drinks.

> AUDRA: Woo-hoo, finally get to see the mansion in real life! I've got the food covered. I'll be DD.

> AMELIA: Kitchen renovations ongoing. Limited appliances 😶

Amelia took a quick shower and changed into comfy sweats and a warm cotton shirt. Her laptop chimed, alerting her to a text in the security app, also bearing the *WJ7 Inc.* label from the guard gate. She clicked to approve entry.

As soon as Audra and Melanie arrived at the door, Amelia greeted them with hugs, then gave them a quick tour of the lower floor as they made their way toward the kitchen.

"Holy shit, this place," Audra said. "The pictures do not do it justice."

"You live in a castle," Melanie added. "The stonework on the outside is gorgeous and looks ancient."

"It is. I'm guessing the house is at least a hundred and fifty years old. There are old paintings hanging everywhere. Some portraits in the dining hall and the foyer have plaques with late-eighteen-hundreds dates on them. I need to ask the owner for more details about the house's history. The electrical and plumbing are pretty new, though."

Amelia opened the set of double doors beyond the foyer and switched on the lights. "This is the library, and the door behind you leads to the dining room."

Melanie admired the massive room lined with floor-to-ceiling mahogany bookshelves. "Whoa. I could spend years in just this room."

"Me too. It's one of my favorite spots in the house," Amelia said.

Leather volumes filled the shelves, stretching toward the vaulted ceiling. Late afternoon sun rays illuminated dust as it danced above the reading chairs.

"I'm not sure I'd like living all alone in a place this big," Audra said. "Even if it is beautiful."

"It was weird at first. I turn on some music when it gets too quiet. But I feel safe with the security guards on property, and there are cameras all over the grounds."

"You're being watched?" Melanie said cautiously.

"Mm, the guards monitor the grounds and perimeter fences.

There are a few indoor cameras, mostly monitoring the doors. I control those recordings, so it's fine."

They moved into the kitchen, where fresh sawdust scented the air. New honey-colored wood cabinets lined the walls, but plywood still covered the countertops.

"The kitchen cabinets are installed. Still waiting for the new countertops. Later this month, there's another contractor crew starting on bathroom renovations."

"So, the guy who owns this place ... have you met him?" Melanie said. "What's he like?"

"I've never met him, and I know very little. I realize it's odd ... he's been my client for over six years, but he's secretive. His name is William Jewell, and he owns a security company, WJ7 Inc. But I don't even know what he looks like."

"Ah, so that explains the high-tech security gate and all the cameras," Audra said.

"Have you searched the internet for him?" Melanie asked.

"Yep. Just company stuff online. No photos. He's so private I figured maybe he's someone famous? Lately I've nicknamed him Mr. F-O, for Famous Owner."

"Okay, now that we've had the mini tour," Audra said, "what's the emergency?"

"Let's talk while we eat," Amelia said. "I'm starving." Best to settle in with food and enough alcohol to feel comfortable discussing the Jonathan bomb.

Amelia began unpacking Audra's bags. "There's a ton of food in here. Are we expecting other guests?"

"Stress cooking," Audra said, pulling out containers. "Keeps my hands busy when work solitude gets overwhelming."

Audra sighed, then continued. "So there are lots of leftovers." She assisted Amelia with the food containers. Homemade pasta, fresh bread, and vegetables with garlic and herbs.

"My job isn't as fun as I'd hoped it would be. Marine geology is fascinating, but working in the lab full-time is so isolating."

"Yeah, tell me about it. I'm ecstatic about the possibility of getting a permanent job, but the next three months are going to be challenging." Amelia folded the empty bags and put extra items in the refrigerator. She didn't dare start mentally counting all the carbs. "You're lucky you've got that hummingbird metabolism."

They carried plates of food to the dining room and sat at one end of the long wooden table. The oak table could seat twelve. Crystal stemware behind a glass cabinet caught light from the overhead chandelier. Tall windows overlooked the darkening gardens.

"Did you see my text? When are you going to call Leo?" Audra said.

Amelia sighed. "That's not part of today's emergency."

"Leo is good-looking, *and* he has his life together," Melanie said in a bright tone.

Amelia was ready to push back. "Even if I wanted to date—which I don't—I have too much to do. There's the new project at work, my mom's cracking home, plus the renovations on this enormous house."

It was easier to list excuses than admit the truth: she'd tried dating a few months ago and failed miserably. Ten minutes into dinner, her chest had tightened and her throat closed around the appetizers. The guy had been perfectly nice, but all she could think about was Nate—the lies, the debt, the guilt.

She'd bolted before the entrées arrived. The embarrassment came later, sitting in her car, hyperventilating. She'd told her mother the date hadn't gone well but she'd never mentioned the panic—not even to Audra and Melanie.

"This isn't a house," Melanie scoffed. "It's a full-scale estate."

"With all that on your plate, you're going to need an occasional night of fun," Audra countered. "Some casual sex might be exactly what you need."

"You would say that," Amelia said with a smile.

"Am I wrong?" Audra grinned.

"No," Melanie said. "You're absolutely right. Oh, speaking of avoiding fun—a very hot guy transferred into the office today. Amelia's been assigned to work with him, and she barely acknowledged his existence."

She was right. Jonathan was still very hot.

Amelia let out a long breath. "Jonathan Fontaine. From college. You remember him?"

"Uh, yeah," Audra said. "How could I forget your sexy ghoster?"

"The hot guy from Atlanta that I'm working with," Amelia said. "The same."

"No way," Audra whispered. "*That's* the emergency. Oh my god. What's he doing *here*?"

Melanie's eyes widened. "You two acted like you didn't know each other. Why didn't you tell me?"

"I was still absorbing," Amelia said.

"Did you date him?" Melanie's tone sounded as though she were questioning a witness.

One side of Amelia's mouth turned downward. "Late in my senior year, I got together with Jonathan."

Back then, Jonathan had made her feel like she could take on the world.

"After three terrific weeks together, I packed up and moved to Austin to start my internship. Jonathan stayed in Florida to finish graduate school, but we agreed to keep the relationship together. A year later, *bam*, he suddenly ghosted me. He just vanished, and I was blindsided."

Too bad the hurt and anger couldn't erase the chemistry between them.

"And then I met Nate. It took nearly a year for me to let my guard down with him, but he seemed so … right. He loved the outdoors and talked openly about his feelings and commitment. It took me another year before I said yes. And still another year to make sure he wasn't going to ghost me. And after all that time and caution, he turned out to be lying about everything. The marriage, the love, all of it. He was just telling me what I wanted to hear."

Melanie poured herself another drink and topped Amelia's glass. "I get why you haven't mentioned Jonathan." Her expression turned mischievous. "Sounds like the perfect reason to go on a blind date while you're working with the ghost-man."

Amelia shook her head with a half chuckle and turned toward Audra. "Hey, you're still talking to Drew, right? Did he mention Jonathan was coming here?"

"No, not a word. I think he would have told me if he'd known. I'm surprised, though, because Drew and Jonathan are still tighter than biscuits and honey."

"So, the four of you were friends in college?" Melanie pointed her fork at Audra. "Did you date Drew?"

"We were all geology majors. Drew Slater and I are just good friends." Audra dipped a piece of bread into the dish of olive oil. "Drew's the flannel-shirt-and-work-boots type, a far cry from my skinny-surfer-dude type. We were drinking buddies at field camp, lab partners later, and always just friends."

"You seem very determined to emphasize the *just friends* thing," Melanie said, with a mildly accusing tone.

Audra twirled pasta around her fork. "Just the facts. Besides, he has his life in Georgia, running a construction business, and I have my life here." She looked at Amelia. "But we're not talking about me. How are you going to play this? I mean, cutting you off like that was brutal. And now you have to work together like everything's okay? After Nate, you deserve some smooth sailing, but this is kind of messed up."

"It *is* messed up. And I don't know. Honestly, it hasn't sunk in, and maybe I'm trying to ignore how I feel. But I need the job. I need that permanent position. So despite what my gut is telling me, I've got to make it work."

Audra refilled their glasses as Melanie broke off a piece of bread.

"Still," Melanie said. "You lost the bet, and the agreement was a blind date. I'm telling you, Leo is great."

Amelia took a big swig of wine. "My mom is on your side, too. Every time she calls, I get peppered with questions about dating. She's pretty old-fashioned. I don't think she can get her head around the fact that I'm turning thirty without a husband and two point five kids. But I know she just wants me to be happy."

"Well, maybe Rachel has a point," Audra said.

They finished eating and cleared their dishes. As Amelia made her way to the kitchen, she tried to envision getting dressed for a date.

Would it really be so bad to go on *one* date?

But the thought of trusting someone new felt impossible.

I never loved you. Nate's ugly words slammed into her head.

She'd never expected her husband to say those words. The lies and deceit led to utter brokenness.

A throbbing sensation formed near her right temple, and the pain traveled down to the pit of her stomach. Nate had stolen so much of her confidence.

There was no way she'd go on a blind date. No way.

"Pick another consequence," Amelia said. "I'm just not ready for a date. I'm not ready to have a man anywhere in my life again, wondering if he's honest or a liar, and knowing how bad I am at telling the difference. And I don't want to put my emotions out on a limb like that again."

She blinked, and a tear escaped down her cheek. "Realizing you're unloved is worse than losing a love that was real," she said. "Maybe I won't ever be ready."

Audra and Melanie exchanged glances, their expressions shifting from concern to protective determination. Both of them wrapped Amelia in a tight hug.

"This needs to stop. You will never know if you are ready if you don't try," Melanie said, squeezing her tighter.

"Or I might crash and burn because I'm completely not ready."

"How about a double date?" Audra said. "You'd have one of us there to take some of the pressure off."

"A double date would feel less like an obligation and more like meeting a new friend," Melanie added.

"That would help," Amelia said with a small smile and a sniff. "But I'm still going to delay this for as long as I absolutely can."

Audra laughed. "We know."

When she was younger, being asked on a date had been exciting, another kind of grand adventure. That was then. Now, a dating adventure sounded like a doomsday mission. Where was the eject button when she needed one?

Chapter 7

Amelia

AFTER WORK, Amelia settled on the living room sofa with wine and her laptop.

The main living room showcased Mr. F-O's contemporary taste. A sleek charcoal sectional wrapped around a low walnut table, and abstract art on the walls that had probably once held family portraits. The space felt beautiful but impersonal, like a high-end hotel lobby rather than a home where generations had lived.

Her day at NorthSound had been mercifully Jonathan-free. She'd mostly avoided him for three days by working out of her office instead of the team workroom, but Monday would force more face-to-face encounters.

Several times, she'd caught herself listening for his voice in the hallway, which was ridiculous and annoying. Thinking about those warm brown eyes watching her with that steady, knowing expression made her pulse race and stirred irritation at the same time. Ugh. *Focus.*

She reviewed Mr. F-O's latest exhaustingly thorough to-do list.

1. *Bathroom renovations, select matching colors and styles of accessories.*
2. *Receive delivery of art decor on Friday at 9 a.m.*
3. *Photograph, clean, and inventory the east-wing attic.*

The list continued. She made a mental note to order supplies before next Friday's art delivery, then copied the items into a new shared spreadsheet.

The attic. She'd been curious about that stairway since moving in. Stairways led upward from the second floor at opposite ends of the mansion, but that was the one area she hadn't investigated yet.

Something about the smell drifting from beneath the attic stairway door—old wood and mustiness mixed with something faintly metallic—made her pause each time. She'd stand there, hand on the doorknob, then shake her head and find another task that seemed more urgent.

Time to check it out. Amelia grabbed her new phone off the coffee table and pushed it into her pocket. She'd asked for a simple camera, but Mr. F-O sent her a brand-new phone with a high-tech camera, explaining that her old phone needed an upgrade for security reasons. She smiled to herself.

When she opened the east-wing attic door, Amelia flicked on the flashlight she'd found in the kitchen drawer. That smell again, musty wood and something metallic she couldn't place. She gripped the railing. The circular staircase creaked underfoot, and cobwebs brushed against her shoulders like ghostly fingers.

The confined space pressed in from all sides. Unfortunately, the maids refused to clean the attic. Next time, she'd bring replacement bulbs for the overhead fixture and a vacuum.

The top of the stairs opened into a large space, heavy with decades of silence. She drew a deeper breath, the oppressive feeling from the stairwell lifting as cooler air touched her face. Dust floated in the flashlight beam. The stillness felt expectant, as if the room had been waiting. Along one wall, opaque windows allowed moonlight to form strange, shifting shadows.

More dust lay in a thick blanket across the piles of furniture and stacks of odds and ends across the room. Any treasure here was covered with years of grime.

Amelia sighed and ran a finger along the top of an old wooden trunk, leaving tracks in the dust. Beneath the dirt, she could make out intricate brass corners and a leather binding around the edges. The metal was warm under her touch, noticeably warmer than the chilly attic.

She brushed her dusty fingers over her jeans. The clutter was inconvenient, but the beginning of an adventure lay somewhere underneath. The space felt personal, as if it held secrets meant just for her.

She was eager to investigate further, but the cleaning chores would have to wait for another day.

Amelia snapped a few photographs of the attic from different angles, enough to give Mr. F-O an idea of the current state of affairs. After making a mental note to order heirloom boxes and extra cleaning supplies, she moved quickly through the narrow stairwell.

The musty metallic smell made her eager to reach fresh air, and the creepy claustrophobia of the dark stairwell had her skipping the last few steps. The attic door clicked shut behind her with satisfying finality. She breathed a sigh of relief. Ridiculous. It was just an old staircase.

Satisfied with the attic visit and with her initial photographs, Amelia emailed Mr. F-O with the link to the shared spreadsheet and the photos of the attic before she settled onto the couch with a blanket and a second glass of wine.

* * *

The next morning, Amelia called her mom while preparing her breakfast eggs and toast. "Hey, Mom. How's your morning?"

"I've had better days," her mother said, her voice filled with concern.

"What's wrong?" Squeezing her phone between her cheek and a shoulder, Amelia opened a jar and spread raspberry preserves across her toast.

"You first, honey. You called me."

"Okay, I'll make it quick. Exciting news to share. I told you the lumber company is in the middle of a merger. My boss assigned me to handle an important merger-related project. Lydia told me that if it goes well, she can offer me a permanent job, with full benefits and better pay than my current contract."

She sat on a barstool, set her phone to speaker mode, and took a bite of eggs.

"Amelia, that's wonderful! But it also sounds like more work."

"That's true; it means more work. But it'll be okay. I've got a lot of things to do at the mansion, but the rent is free," she said, reaching for her coffee cup. "A permanent job is important too, because this virtual assistant project won't last forever and I need something more stable than being a contractor. I need to make it all work."

Amelia scooped another spoonful of soft eggs. "Your turn. What's going on?"

"A sinkhole opened up over on Oak Street near Silver Pond last night." Her mom's voice carried exhaustion and worry. "It's all over the news."

In the background, Amelia could hear the local news anchor's urgent tone and Sam's anxious whining.

Amelia's fork clattered against her plate. "That's only a

block away." Shit. Sinkholes could swallow entire neighborhoods without warning. "Mom, that's why your house is cracking!" The mental image of her childhood home being sucked into the earth made her stomach clench. "You need to leave. Today. You should come live with me in Washington."

"What? Oh, honey, I don't know."

"We've already talked about your moving to Rainmere. This isn't a new idea."

"Honey, you know I'd love to be with you, but starting over? At my age? I'd lose everything I've built here. There's not much left of Sam's investments, so what I bring in from teaching makes a big difference. Plus, I can't abandon my students right before their spring piano recitals." Her mother's voice carried a familiar note of stubborn independence that meant she'd already decided.

"I'll make it happen, Mom, I promise." Amelia's protective instincts took over. "Once I've got a permanent job, I can pay to move you here."

Amelia's dad, Sam Preston, was her hero, and he'd taught her the importance of taking care of family. It's what he would have wanted. She missed him. They both did. Mom missed Dad so much that she'd named the stray German shepherd pup that showed up on her doorstep after him.

A dog barked. "See, even Sammie thinks staying is crazy," Amelia said.

"I'm going to call some friends today," her mom said, "and ask if anyone has a room to rent. I don't want to leave my teaching business behind."

She set down her fork. "There are music students here who need piano teachers, too, Mom."

"I'd have to start completely from scratch." Her mother's voice grew smaller. "The thought terrifies me."

"You could come to visit, explore the area and see if you'd like to move here," Amelia said.

"Are you seeing anyone?" her mom said, shifting the topic.

"Mom, you know how I feel about that."

"Is it because of Nate? It's been over a year since your marriage ended. Don't you think it's time to move forward?"

"I don't want to talk about him." Dammit, she did not want to talk about him. Thinking too often about Nate always resulted in a pounding headache. She ate the last bite of her toast and carried her dishes to the sink.

"You're about to turn thirty. Don't you want that kind of relationship?"

Amelia groaned. Despite the wreckage of her marriage, she missed intimate conversations and holding hands, and she missed sex. Those would be positives for dating again. But the memory of the panic attack was still fresh and raw.

"Mom, I can't promise anything about seeing anyone. And you know I'm very busy. So please don't get your hopes up."

Her mom chuckled and let out a small sigh. "I can't help it; that's what moms do. I just want you to be happy."

"I know. I love you, Mom."

After ending the call, Amelia finished getting ready for work.

How could she convince her mom that she'd still be able to have a successful teaching business in Rainmere? Understandably, her mom wanted to rescue her from a loveless life, but her mom's actual sinkhole was a hell of a lot more dangerous than a dating drought.

She needed to find a way for her mom to quickly re-establish her business. And she needed enough money to help her mom move.

It was more important than ever that she stay on the project with Jonathan. Moreover, she had to ensure the project was a success, which meant no more hiding from Jonathan in her office.

Opening her phone to the chat with Audra and Melanie, she dictated a message.

> AMELIA: I want to convince my mom to move to Washington, and I need some ideas for jump-starting her teaching business here. Plus, maybe some courage. Help, please!

She hesitated, staring at the message. Asking for their help twice in one week seemed like admitting defeat. But with sink-holes opening, her mom's stubborn independence, and Jonathan's unavoidable presence, maybe it was time to stop trying to fix it all herself.

She hit send.

Chapter 8

Jonathan

Monday. Week two.

AFTER THEIR MORNING MEETING, Jonathan watched Amelia close applications on her laptop before she got up to leave. He sighed. She'd avoided the workroom all last week, choosing her office over collaboration. Today would test whether that pattern continued.

After he'd had to cut ties with Amelia, he'd had other girlfriends, but mostly for companionship and physical satisfaction. He'd dated Paige for eighteen months before she'd surprised him with the proposal, taking charge the way she always did. The move was gutsy and honest, and he admired her for it. But did that mean he loved her or that they would be happy together? The more he thought about it, the less likely it seemed.

Over the weekend, he'd tried calling Paige to end their engagement. She didn't pick up Saturday night—unusual for her. His text had gone unanswered too. Instinct told him she knew what was coming.

He returned to his desk and unlocked his workstation. Both

NorthSound Timber and Whitlow Forest Resources held underground mineral leases that needed evaluation. The team's job was determining which mineral assets the merged company should keep or sell.

Later in the afternoon, Amelia finally appeared with a cart of moving boxes. "Today I'm transitioning the last of the Johnson County project to Gary," she said, not looking at him. "I'll be in the workroom full-time now."

After she sat and turned on her computer, he moved around to her side of the workspace and pulled a chair next to hers.

"I'm glad you're here. Patricia and Gavin reviewed more of the project files and added to our inventory list," Jonathan said. "We've now got about a hundred assets to evaluate in three months."

"I made a first pass of the review priority based on previous value assessments," she said.

"Great." Jonathan smiled and nodded in approval. "The techs can gather and assemble the map and metadata portfolios we need to begin our analysis."

They divided the assets between them, then Jonathan moved back to his desk.

Amelia's desk phone buzzed, and she put on her headset.

"Hey, Melanie." From a small moving box, she unpacked a framed family photo and laid it on her desk. In the photo her family stood on a beach with golden sand and frothy ocean water swirling around their feet. They smiled happily, arms wrapped around each other.

"I'm moving some stuff from my office to a workroom," Amelia said into her headset. She sat in her chair and set the photo upright. "No, I don't want you to call Leo for me."

Jonathan's chest tightened. He scowled at his monitor.

"Yeah, this weekend is too soon. Look, I'll let you know

when the time is right," Amelia said. "I need to get back to work. I'll catch up with you later."

Jonathan tried to concentrate on his screen. Melanie was organizing blind dates. How much longer before Amelia caved from the pressure?

Feeling uncomfortable with eavesdropping, and even more uncomfortable with the topic of her conversation, he repositioned himself in his seat and tried to block her out.

He considered his choices. Like Drew said, it was none of his business. He should just stay out of her situation, especially the dating quagmire.

Watching Amelia date someone else in college had been agonizing.

That was then. But if he truly loved Paige, if he was meant to marry her, he wouldn't feel like his world was sinking at the thought of Amelia dating some stranger.

Leaning back in his chair, he closed his eyes and exhaled. He should be rooting for her. But he wasn't. It was more proof that he needed to end his relationship with Paige. And the sooner the better.

Instead of doing nothing, he could ask Amelia out so her girlfriends would let her off the hook for the blind date obligation. A small warning knot formed in his chest. She'd insisted their relationship was only professional.

It could be one simple outing, not even really a date. More like a substitute date ... and he'd get the chance to explain the things he wished he'd been able to tell her years ago. No strings attached, just a smooth icebreaker that would let him explain why he made the asshole move to ghost her. He could finally apologize.

Since it wouldn't be a genuine date, there wouldn't be a conflict with his relationship with Paige. Especially if his relationship with Paige ended soon.

Amelia struggled with a heavy box on her cart. Jonathan quickly moved around the desks to help.

"I can do it myself," she said.

"Let me help." He took the box and set it on her desk, then stayed close. "I heard your conversation with Melanie."

Her eyes narrowed. "You were eavesdropping?"

"Not intentionally." One side of his mouth twitched. "Look, I know you don't want to go on this blind date. What if you and I go out together instead?" He swallowed against the lump forming in his throat. "Consider it a ... substitute date."

Amelia's eyes narrowed again, and her expression hardened into a steely glare. "Substitute? You mean a *fake date*? With *you*?" She tilted her head.

A "fake" date sounded disingenuous and a little gross. *Shit.*

"Just ... as friends. Old lab partners catching up. Melanie gets off your back, and you avoid an awkward evening with a stranger."

"Friends?" Amelia's voice was ice. "We are not friends, Jonathan." She crossed her arms defensively. "You can't just waltz back into my life and pretend things are normal between us."

The words hit like a physical blow, but he'd earned every bit of her loathing.

She stepped closer, lowering her voice. "Have you forgotten that you ghosted me? I haven't."

"Because I want to explain—"

"Sorry to interrupt." Lydia appeared at the workroom entrance. "Amelia, I need you for a few hours on the Harrison lease technical review."

Amelia turned toward Lydia with visible relief. "Right behind you." She grabbed her notebook and coffee, leaving Jonathan standing there.

Fuck. That did not go well.

Jonathan sank into his chair, running his hands through his hair.

She was right. They weren't friends. Not after what he'd done.

But he wasn't giving up. He had to tell her the truth about why he'd disappeared. About the choices he'd made, about the biggest regret of his life.

She deserved to know.

He wasn't fool enough to think an explanation would fix what he'd broken, but maybe—if he was lucky—she'd stop hating him. Maybe they could find their way to something like mutual respect, even if that might be all they'd ever have.

Chapter 9

Amelia

A FAKE DATE. What a ridiculous idea. Amelia hastily grabbed the cleaning supplies. The bucket clanged against her leg.

That evening, Amelia reviewed Mr. F-O's weekly to-do list and decided to begin with the attic. In a storage pantry off the kitchen, she'd found everything she needed: a vacuum, a bucket of cleaning supplies, and spare lightbulbs.

She paused at the attic door, that faint musty smell seeping through. Her hand hesitated on the knob for just a moment before she shook her head and pulled it open. Just an old staircase. Nothing to be nervous about. The stairwell felt less oppressive than before, though that faint metallic smell lingered as she hauled the vacuum up the narrow steps.

After replacing the dead bulbs above the staircase and in the attic, she vacuumed the layers of dust that coated everything and cleared cobwebs from the corners and walls.

There was a row of shelves lined with old books and a small sofa that might have been brilliant green long ago but had darkened with age. Amelia carefully vacuumed the sofa and tried not to think about Jonathan, but the way his sexy smile melted her insides invaded her mind.

Ugh. The guy ghosted her after they'd made a long-distance relationship work. Now, five years later, he suddenly wants a fake date? How cocky and insulting.

If she didn't need the job so badly, she'd march straight to Lydia's office and demand a different assignment. But bills didn't pay themselves, and she couldn't help her mom move if she didn't have a permanent position.

She continued her dusting, making mental notes of the attic contents for an inventory sheet. Mr. F-O had requested she donate anything useless and choose some unique family heirlooms to decorate the library, subject to his approval, of course. Boxes of pictures needed to be moved into heirloom containers.

She removed the dirty cloth coverings from all six windows. With them gone, actual sunlight would reach the musty corners.

Because I want to explain, he'd said. She stuffed the window coverings into a bag. Right. If he needed to talk to her, why didn't he do it five years ago instead of vanishing?

She stopped her work and sank down onto the small sofa with a deep sigh. As much as the ghosting had hurt, part of her really wanted answers. And that made her angrier with herself than with him.

But a fake date?

Unless ... what if fake dating was different? Practice without pressure. A controlled environment to test whether she could make it through dinner without panicking.

Still, any dating could lead to talking. She didn't want to talk about her Nate experiences with Jonathan or Leo or anyone else and relive the humiliation and unworthy feelings.

She wasn't ready to rip off that Band-Aid.

A twinge of regret nibbled at her heart. Despite the ghosting, she wasn't looking forward to turning Jonathan down. She'd accepted he was gone, but she'd never completely gotten over him. She knew her anger was a cover for the hurt. *Ugh.*

Enough lingering in the past. She pushed herself off the sofa to resume her work. From her bucket of supplies, she found a clean cloth and began wiping dust from the nooks and edges of the furniture and bookcases.

One row of books stood out from the rest. There were no titles on the spines, just initials. They looked like journals with softer covers in various shapes and colors. Folded papers poked out between the pages of some of them. One bulged in a way that Amelia guessed might be from a pressed flower in the book.

Mr. F-O had given her explicit instructions to sort through everything. If she wasn't allowed to read anything, he absolutely would have told her. So satisfying her curiosity wasn't being too nosy.

He'd also said that the stuff in the attic was fragile and some of it valuable. She carefully slid a reddish-brown book from the shelf and gently eased the cover open. The pages were full of detailed hand-drawn flowers and plants, each with locations, notes, and dates. Hmm. A botanist's journal? Most of the locations were towns in Washington.

Another journal appeared to be a politician's diary, detailing regional events from the 1920s.

Her gaze caught on a thick, brown, leather journal, with the initials RJ on the spine. Something about the well-worn book drew her in. It seemed so ... treasured.

The first page was titled "Rebecca Jewell" above a deliberate, hand-drawn spiral. Not a careless doodle, but something deliberately crafted. Each curve carefully drawn, flowing into the next with intentional precision. Amelia turned the page.

14 March 1849

Thomas mentioned the Oregon Territory again today.

He wants to leave New York, to escape the sadness of the last year, and I do not resent him this wish.

There are many opportunities for a carpenter of his skill. I see the pain in his eyes when he looks at ten-year-old Everett, so much like his dear mother. Thomas needs to escape these memories of his beloved sister's death, and I understand. But to leave my family and everything I know, especially now with the baby coming ...

He says he could go alone, that other men do. But my heart would not survive it. Still, the journey terrifies me. What kind of life awaits us in such a wild place? What if something happens to our child?

Rebecca's fears tugged at Amelia's heart and made her already raw emotions bubble to the surface again. Had Rebecca lost her love?

Amelia's phone buzzed with a group chat alert. She gently closed the old, weathered book and placed it back on the shelf.

> AUDRA: The housewarming party last week was fun. I've got some business ideas for Amelia's mom. Also need to discuss a double date. Let's get together soon!

Amelia winced. She wasn't thrilled at the thought of talking about the double date concept, but she could use some business ideas for her mom.

> MELANIE: I'm out of pocket until the weekend. Working extra hours on a case.

> AMELIA: Saturday works. And I definitely want to hear these business ideas for Mom. Plus, I need girl time that doesn't involve work drama.

She shoved her phone into her pocket. Leaving most of the supplies in the attic, Amelia gathered the bags of laundry and made her way downstairs.

Had Rebecca found the courage to leave New York with Thomas? Did Thomas leave without her? Sometimes people just walked away and created new lives. She sighed. Losing a loved one wasn't anything new.

A few minutes later, she climbed back up the attic stairs, drawn to the journal like a magnet. Her fingers traced the worn leather cover, and unexpected warmth spread through her—a quiet sense of rightness, as if she'd been meant to find this. Amelia tucked it against her chest and turned to head downstairs again.

Had Rebecca gone with him? Surely Thomas hadn't left Rebecca behind.

Chapter 10

Jonathan

WHEN JONATHAN ARRIVED in the morning, Patricia and Gavin were discussing the pros and cons of different database software for organizing lease information. The morning sun streamed through the windows, highlighting Patricia's color-coded filing system spread across her desk.

A black privacy divider stood on Amelia's desk, blocking his view of her. Or was she blocking her view of him? Either way, the message was obvious.

Another hurdle, one he'd built himself. Every barrier between them could be traced back to his decisions, his silence, his disappearing act.

He needed to find a way to ease back into her good graces. Explaining why he'd been an asshole and dropped out of her world would be a good start, but it might take a while before she would listen to anything he had to say.

He shouldn't have suggested the fake date. It had been a gut reaction. Normally, he wasn't the impulsive type, but with Amelia, he had a track record of trying to move too fast. Some things hadn't changed.

As he straightened himself in his seat, he saw her face over the top of the divider. She glanced up at him, and their gazes caught for a split second.

Her deep green eyes held a glimpse of wariness. Like she was trying to figure out what he wanted from her and whether she had the energy to deal with it. Then she looked away again.

Okay, trying to avoid him, but not exactly succeeding. There was hope. Assuming he didn't screw it up again.

After the heated discussion about ghosting and his disastrous fake date proposal, he'd shifted his priorities and had tried to call Paige several times. Breaking up with someone was never easy, but he was ready. It wasn't about Amelia; it was about righting his life on an even keel. Breaking up with the company owner's daughter probably wasn't his smartest career decision, but staying engaged to the wrong woman was an even worse *life* decision.

He should have realized sooner that he couldn't marry Paige. He'd texted her several times over the last few days, but she hadn't responded.

> JONATHAN: Call me tonight after work. We need to talk about our plans.

> JONATHAN: I tried to call you. Call me. Please.

> JONATHAN: I think you're avoiding me, and I'm getting concerned.

Paige wasn't answering her phone either. But he'd checked her social media and seen a few new posts of her with friends, so he knew she was still alive. He would circle back to that later.

Diving into his work, he spent several hours researching the first asset on his list, though the black shield was distracting.

Later in the morning, Lydia gathered Jonathan, Amelia, and the technicians for an impromptu meeting. Her expression was somber. She handed him a thick envelope. The words *Project Scope Update* were plastered on the front.

"I know all of you are just settling in," Lydia said, "and had well-defined expectations of the project." She shifted in her chair. "But ... upper management met yesterday and decided that the plans have changed. More assets have been added to your project for evaluation."

As Lydia continued to explain the situation, Jonathan's stomach sank. Their workload had doubled overnight.

Amelia's face paled.

Gavin clenched a hand firmly around the arm of his chair, and Patricia anxiously nibbled the edge of her lip.

"Unfortunately, the duration of the project remains the same—three months. For this month, we're not adding any more people to your team. Adding more later is still under discussion. I understand it's a lot to digest, but I also have complete confidence in this team." Lydia smiled, and her expression brightened. "You were each assigned to this project because you're the best at what you do. If you work together, I know things will turn out well."

Jonathan glanced toward the privacy screen on Amelia's desk. It was a hindrance to communication and information flow. Any barrier between them would slow down the project, and they weren't working well together. At least not yet.

The workroom fell silent except for the quiet hum of computers. Jonathan scanned the surrounding faces. Gavin pressed his lips tightly, Patricia continued to shuffle through the papers Lydia gave them, and Amelia tapped one foot silently.

Three months had felt condensed before. Now it seemed impossible.

After answering a few last questions, Lydia wrapped up the meeting. She left the workroom while the team continued to discuss ways to distribute the extra load.

"We'll need a single set of files we can all share," Amelia said. "It'll reduce any duplication or reconciling of formats when we're done with the initial analyses."

"Pat and I can create a repository," Gavin said. "We've both got database experience."

"I'll send you the first template I put together this morning," Jonathan said.

Amelia nodded. "Great. I'll send what I've been working on as well."

Patricia and Gavin excused themselves to sketch out a database design for the asset information. One shared repository. No more separate spreadsheets.

"We need more collaboration than simply a shared database. Working in our silos isn't a luxury we can afford anymore," Jonathan said. "The work has increased, and for now, we aren't getting more hands to help." He caught her gaze and held it. "To stay on schedule, we'll need to work faster and ... more closely."

Amelia's brows drew together and she paused for a beat.

"I ... agree," she said reluctantly. "We'll need to coordinate everything if we want to finish in three months."

He needed to bridge the gap between them without making it seem personal, though it *was* at least partially personal.

"We'll also need to review each other's work more often," Amelia continued, clearly thinking through the logistics. "Catch problems earlier instead of at the end."

"Exactly." Jonathan saw his opening. "Which brings me to another thought. What if Gavin and I switched desks? It would put the techs together and help us coordinate quicker if we can easily see each other's computer screens."

Amelia's shoulders dropped in surrender as she exhaled a long breath. Hints of frustration swept across her face. He could see her weighing the practical benefits of having to sit next to him all day, and whether it was worth making her life harder in ways that had nothing to do with work.

"Yeah." She clearly wasn't happy about the rearrangement, but she nodded in agreement. "It's a good idea."

Yep, he had a lot of work ahead of him to smooth things over with her.

* * *

After work, Jonathan sat in his rental car in the parking lot of his townhome. He adjusted the rearview mirror, avoiding his own reflection, then opened his phone to text Drew.

JONATHAN: You were right, and I'm going to follow my gut. Now Paige is avoiding me. I think she knows what's coming.

DREW: Good decision. But watch your back, dude. She's not the type to leave quietly.

JONATHAN: Yeah, I didn't do myself any favors by accepting her proposal and then taking so long to end things with her.

DREW: You've gotta do what you've gotta do.

He tried Paige's number again. The soft click caught him off guard. He hadn't expected her to pick up. Why would she?

"Hello?"

Chapter 11

Jonathan

"Hello?" Paige's voice was cautious. "Jonathan?"

Jonathan held his phone in one hand and gripped the steering wheel with the other. His heart hammered. He'd rehearsed leaving another voicemail, not having an actual conversation.

The sun was setting, casting deep shadows over the parking lot. Perfect timing for this conversation. Nothing like breaking up with someone at the end of a long day.

"Where are you?" On the East Coast, it was three hours later. He assumed she was home, but there was talking in the background. If she was having a late dinner with clients or friends, the breakup conversation would need to wait until later.

"At home." She sounded tired. "I took a shower and then I turned on the TV. Thought I'd catch up on some episodes tonight. I've been so busy with management meetings lately that I need to relax before going to sleep."

He turned off the engine and got out of the car.

"Look, I'll be in Seattle next week for business," she said. "I'm planning on staying the weekend to see you. I've already booked my flights."

So that's why she answered the phone.

"You were here two weeks ago. Why another work trip so soon?" He walked up a short flight of stairs, picked up a delivery box from the doorstep—a decorative piece he'd ordered for his work desk—and unlocked the front door.

"The VPs are having ongoing discussions to smooth out a few transition issues. Blending of corporate culture, growing pains, some technology problems, etcetera. I got tagged for a committee that's meeting often and mostly in person."

"You're a good choice for the group." From the refrigerator, he grabbed a beer and a box of leftover Chinese takeout.

"I'll be pretty busy, but Friday after work let's go out," she said. "We can explore Seattle's nightlife."

"Paige—" He popped the top off his beer bottle and set the food on the coffee table in the living room.

He'd called her multiple times over the past few days, knowing this conversation couldn't wait. But now that she was actually on the line, the moment felt tougher than expected.

"On Saturday, let's be touristy together," she said. "You love art. How about the art museum or the pop culture museum? Then dinner at some fancy place."

He didn't want to drag this out for another weekend, but he also didn't want to get into a heated argument.

"Paige, listen to me. I don't think we should make weekend plans." He cleared his throat as he sank down onto the couch. "The thing is, I don't want to get married."

"What do you mean?" she asked. "You don't want to get married to anyone, or you don't want to get married to *me*?" There was a tense pause. "No, wait. I don't want you to answer that now. We haven't sent out invitations or booked any venues, so we can wait six months ... or a year, if that's what you need." Her voice was edgy and her words spilled out faster. "I know I've been pushing you on the wedding plans, but we can slow things down. A lot. There's nothing wrong with a long engagement."

Slowing things down would not solve his problem.

"I've given it a lot of thought, Paige." He set down his beer. He didn't want to hurt her, but he needed to be honest with her. "I've had doubts about us for months. I kept thinking it was just cold feet and I'd get over it. But I'm not getting over it. I'm sorry. I'm breaking the engagement, and I think we should end things completely."

He waited for the information to sink in.

"What exactly are you saying, Jonathan? Is this the end of *us*?" Her tone sharpened.

"Yes," he said. "I've been having doubts for a reason. This isn't going to work. We want different things, and we both know it. Don't you want a husband who's thrilled to be getting married? You deserve that and a lot more. I ... can't give that to you, and I can't pretend that I would."

"Don't you dare try to make this about what's best for me. I'm not the one who can't figure out what he wants. You are such a coward, Jonathan."

Click.

He stared at the dark phone screen and sank deeper into his couch. She'd hung up on him. He couldn't blame her.

He took a long pull of his beer and swallowed hard. She'd never walked away from a fight, especially one she hadn't won. This conversation was far from over, but at least he'd said what needed to be said. For the first time since accepting her proposal, he felt like he could breathe.

Chapter 12

Amelia

AMELIA ARRIVED at work the next morning still thinking about yesterday's meeting dynamics. She set her coffee and binder on her desk, determined to focus on teamwork rather than avoidance.

Jonathan and Gavin had already switched desks, and Jonathan sat next to her, looking devastating in that effortless way that had always made her knees weak. She could feel the pull of attraction despite every wall she'd built against it.

Collaboration. She needed to do her part for the team.

Amelia frowned at the privacy divider. It needed to go. She couldn't keep trying to avoid Jonathan.

The large divider bumped her chair as she attempted to fold it.

Jonathan stood and grabbed one end. "Here, let me get that for you. There are some advantages to having a large wingspan."

She relented with a quick nod. "All yours. Thanks."

With him standing so close, she could smell his pleasant musky aftershave and see his biceps flex and stretch under his shirt as he closed the frame. They exchanged glances, and he gave her an inviting grin.

Her cheeks warmed and her skin prickled along her arms. *Oh yeah. Still sexy-hot.*

Her eyes trailed Jonathan as he finished folding the divider and stowed it in the workroom supply closet. The gesture was a reminder that he was a cinnamon-roll kind of guy.

But then there was the ghosting.

Why would a nice guy like that just vanish? The same question had tormented her five years ago. His embrace had been warm ... until he was gone. His laughter had made her feel alive ... until silence replaced it.

She was relieved he hadn't brought up the fake-date question again, but she also needed an explanation to reconcile the past.

With the barrier gone, she could see Jonathan's workspace clearly. Beside his laptop sat project notes in his neat handwriting and a small stack of manila folders labeled with asset numbers. A clear tube of rolled survey maps leaned against the desk. Organized but lived in.

He returned to his seat and took a paper bag from under his desk. He handed it to Amelia. "This is for you."

"What is it?"

"I thought you might appreciate some workspace inspiration. I found these online, and they came as a pair. The second one seemed meant for a fellow geologist."

Accepting the bag, she looked inside. Polished granite stones. Black and white swirls shaped into flattened oval disks. "Oh. I do like it," she whispered. *Another thoughtful gesture.*

She traced the smooth surface of the top stone with her fingertip. A cairn. The balanced stones reminded her of past promises, stirring memories she'd tried to forget.

* * *

The last time Amelia had seen a cairn was a year ago, just before her second wedding anniversary, at a secluded resort in Sedona. Before Nate's accident. Amelia had registered them for a couple's retreat that had promised to "bring you and your partner together in harmony," and a cairn of white stones had been their symbol for a pathway forward.

She'd had no idea how to form a stronger connection with Nate, but she had wanted it. She was desperate to find something, anything, to fix their relationship.

They'd sat facing each other on yoga mats in a room with floor-to-ceiling windows that looked out toward towering red rock cliffs.

"Now," the harmony guide said to the group, "take turns telling one another an important story from your past, when you first dated each other. Give as much detail as possible, sharing exactly how the situation made you feel. Remember why you went out with each other."

Nate winced. Amelia wished she hadn't seen his discomfort, but there was no way to unsee something like that.

"I'll go first," she said.

His shoulders relaxed in relief.

"When I first met you, I thought you were a strong and gorgeous light of confidence that collided with my world," she said. "Meeting you broke me out of my grief-bubble, and I couldn't wait for my next trip to the gym to see you. You made me feel special, like I was a celebrity, when you shined that light on me. I was hoping, dreaming, that you'd ask me out, and I was so excited when you finally did. It was only three weeks after meeting you, but it seemed like it took forever."

"I remember those days." He paused, licking his lips while he searched for words. "I was ... lonely," he said, his voice flat. "You were there. You made things easier." A long pause stretched between them before he shrugged again. "And honestly, I thought your career potential could help bankroll my business plans down the road." His eyes were cold as he delivered the final blow. "I never loved you."

Deception laid bare.

His words had broken her heart, but he'd also broken the shackles that bound her to him. Every fiber of her being had screamed that she'd be better off alone.

* * *

"Amelia?" Jonathan's voice cut through the painful memory. She blinked twice and forced herself to look at him. The concern in his expression was so genuine, and so different from Nate's indifference—but could she trust it?

"Sorry. Lost in thought," she said.

I never loved you. How many times had those awful words echoed in her head? How did someone get past such a crushing blow?

She peered into the bag again. One way to move on was to create a new memory, a pleasant memory, to replace the old. She set the cairn on her desk. "It's gorgeous. Thank you."

She ran her fingers over the smooth, delicate cairn. The symmetry of the stones soothed her. Though she hadn't forgotten that Jonathan had abruptly cut her out of his life, she felt her anger toward him subsiding.

She still wasn't ready to date, but she *was* ready to replace an unpleasant memory or two.

Chapter 13

Jonathan

Friday. End of week two.

When Jonathan exited the elevator and rounded the corner into the cafeteria, the air carried the aroma of grilled hamburgers and rich lasagna meat sauce. He spotted Amelia seated at a table near a wall of windows, eating lunch and reading a book.

He bought himself a hot meal at the food counter and made his way toward her.

"Would you mind if I joined you?" He smiled when she looked up.

"Oh." She nodded. "Okay." She closed her book and set it aside.

Relieved she'd agreed, he sat down opposite her and set a napkin in his lap.

"What are you reading?" He nodded toward her book. The faded, plain brown leather cover offered few clues.

"Mm ... a very old journal I found in an attic." Amelia laid her hand on the book as her expression softened. "It's about a woman who crossed the country in a covered wagon. Her story sucked me in."

"If you'd rather read, we don't have to talk," he offered. Though he hoped she wanted to talk.

The low buzz of nearby conversations created a backdrop to their careful words.

"No, it's okay," she said. "I just finished an entry; the rest of Rebecca's story can wait."

"I've been wondering how you ended up working for North-Sound Timber." He forked a large bite of pasta. "The last I knew, you took that job in Austin after graduation."

"That's complicated." She paused, seeming to weigh how much to share. "Austin was great at first. I loved the town, and the job was solid." Her gaze dropped to her plate. "But ... then life dumped a pile of shit on me about a year and a half ago."

She reached for her water bottle and took a slow sip, then shrugged. "None of it was work-related, but I needed a fresh start."

He assumed Nate was part of the pile of shit.

"I wanted to start over somewhere else," Amelia continued. "Anywhere else. Audra convinced me to take a leave of absence from Gateway2Green and stay with her for a while. Six months later, I'd found contract work here and decided I didn't want to go back. So I quit the Austin job and stayed in Rainmere." Her gaze dropped toward her plate.

A succinct summary. It wasn't much, but at least it was more than she'd told him before.

He changed the subject and asked about Audra and her job, then moved on to asking how they became friends with Melanie.

"Is Melanie still trying to hook you up with a blind date?"

"Yeah. My friends and my mother are still bugging me to date again." She ate a spoonful of her soup. "I know they mean well, but I'm not ready. And even if I were, I've got a lot of things going on outside of work."

"I understand." He nodded as his thoughts flashed to memories of her college routines. "You always liked to keep busy." *Busy* was her trademark.

Amelia chuckled softly. "Yeah, it's partly a desire to do everything and partly a coping mechanism. Both good and bad, I suppose."

"I heard you moved out of Audra's apartment into some big place that needs lots of repairs." He'd gotten more details from Drew in the last few days. "I'm guessing that's some of the 'lots going on'?" And it probably had an attic, too.

Amelia's eyes narrowed.

"Audra talks to Drew, and Drew talks to me ... but not about everything." Drew had notably left out some critical details.

"Ah, I see," she said. "I had a side gig in college, working as a virtual assistant. I intended to quit once I got a full-time job. And mostly I did. But I had one client who offered to pay me double to continue. Not long after I moved to Washington, he hired me for a local job at his family estate. It was a very lucky break."

Between mouthfuls of garlic bread, she filled him in on her coordination of the mansion restorations for the mysterious Mr. Jewell.

"Money was tight, and he sent me photos of this giant old mansion."

Amelia pulled out her phone and thumbed through pictures for him. There were massive stone facades with tall windows and what looked like acres of forest surrounding it.

"Between not having to pay rent and the adventure appeal, I couldn't turn it down," she said.

"Very impressive place. I get it," he said.

She continued to swipe through photos of the interior: high ceilings, crown molding, old portraits, intricate woodwork.

"Looks remote," he said. "Is it safe with all the contractors coming and going?"

"The estate is sprawling. So yeah, it covers a lot of area. But the owner is serious about security." Amelia forked a bite of salad. "There's an on-site guard round the clock; sometimes they're both on duty, and there are cameras everywhere. I also took self-defense classes a few years back, so there's that."

"All good stuff. It might be overkill, but have you thought about getting a dog?"

"I considered it after the owner suggested I might want some company." She scooped a spoonful of tortilla soup. "The mansion does feel a tad empty sometimes," she said. "But I'm not sure I'd be the greatest pet owner."

Her comment was out of character. He frowned. "Why not?"

She'd always been meticulous in her work and studies. And so confident. Of course she would be a good pet owner. A terrific pet owner. Why couldn't she see that?

The focused, ambitious woman he'd known in college had built walls he could almost see. She measured her words now, held herself differently. More careful. More protected.

Amelia shrugged.

He reached for her hand to comfort her. She stiffened slightly and drew it away, tucking both hands in her lap. He should have expected that.

"There's a possibility we'll need to visit an off-site map storage location on Monday," he said to change the subject. "I'll call you this weekend if I get the final go-ahead. You still have the same number you had in college?"

"No, I got a new one."

Jonathan waited, but she didn't elaborate. "I'd appreciate it if you'd send it to me." He hesitated. "If you're comfortable with that."

"I'll need your number." She looked him straight in the eyes. "I deleted it after you disappeared."

After I ghosted her. "Okay. That's fair." He recited his number as she typed it into her phone. Then she sent him a hello text.

"Work-related only," she said firmly.

For now, he wanted to say. "That's fair, too." He paused. "Look, I don't want to pressure you, but I want a chance to talk about what happened back then. To explain why I had to disappear."

"Had to? Why would you *have* to ghost me?" Lines of doubt spread over her face. "Ghosting is childish, and, frankly, it was … cruel." Her words were biting, but her voice remained calm.

He pushed one hand through his hair. "It's kind of a long story and I wasn't allowed to talk about it when it happened. Believe me, I didn't want to hurt you."

"So, let's hear it," she said with a tinge of irritation. "Right now. And while you're at it, you can tell me why it took you five years to get around to explaining yourself."

"It's a legal matter, and it's complicated." He shifted in his chair. "I couldn't explain at the time without putting you at risk."

"A risky legal matter?" Her expression relaxed as she leaned back against her chair. "Well, that was unexpected."

He looked around at the crowded cafeteria, at the tables of people working only a few feet away. "I'd like to discuss it privately," he said. "Have dinner with me. Call it a date to satisfy your friends if you'd like, and we'll have time to talk it all out."

"Privately." Amelia paused, as though unsure if she was comfortable with the idea. "If I agree to this dinner at some point, and that's a big if, am I going to be more or less upset about it afterward?"

He let out a breath and locked his gaze on hers. "I can explain and apologize. It won't fix the past, but you'll know why it happened."

"I appreciate the honesty," she said. "I really do. And maybe someday I'll be ready to spend time with you beyond a cafeteria lunch. But ... definitely not yet." Amelia stood, tucked the book under her arm, and picked up her tray. "I should get back to work. The conversation was nice. Thanks."

He watched her return her tray and leave the cafeteria. Her movements were smooth and deliberate. And she kept looking forward.

He'd made progress today. Small steps. She was still guarded and hurt, but she had talked to him. Openly talked to him.

The careful way she'd withdrawn her hand told him everything he needed to know. She couldn't trust him. Not yet. And knowing he'd caused that hesitation filled him with regret.

Chapter 14

Amelia

Saturday.

THE HOUSE WAS quiet without contractors or maids. Amelia finished loading the dishwasher and wiped down the granite countertops as she waited for Audra and Melanie to arrive for a girls' lunch.

Audra wanted to test a new recipe, and Amelia wanted help with Mom's business-move problem. In the few minutes of quiet before they arrived, her phone buzzed with a text.

JONATHAN: Monday's map facility visit is set for 9am. Bringing Patricia and Gavin to help with inventory.

AMELIA: Sounds good, see you then.

Tired from her chores, she curled up on the living room couch to read more of Rebecca's journal.

The stories detailing Rebecca's four-month crossing on the Oregon trail, all the way from New York to the eastern shore of Puget Sound, enthralled her. Knowing they'd all traveled together—Rebecca, Thomas, and Thomas's orphaned nephew, Everett—and survived the arduous trip gave Amelia hope for Rebecca's future.

Rebecca's entries were less frequent once they'd established their farm.

21 October 1851

It seems like a lifetime since I last saw New York, though it was only late spring of last year. Liza is now two years of age, walking and chattering in complete sentences, and we welcomed Little Mary this past July. Between caring for two small children and the endless work required to establish our farm, I find little opportunity to take up my pen.

On our small plot of land, Thomas built for us a modest cabin and the beginnings of a barn.

Life here is difficult, though the seasons are mild and the forests are lush with giant trees blanketing the earth in every direction. We are close enough to the sea to smell salt on the breeze or walk to the shore in under a quarter hour.

Thomas works as a skilled carpenter near a lumber mill. With the seed I brought with us from New York, I planted a small vegetable garden.

Everett is nearly twelve now and growing strong. Working with a neighboring farmer, he's learning to tend the animals and grow crops in exchange for fresh meat and more seed. We make ends meet, but we have little more. Despite the hardships, I want to make the best of this life.

From Everett, I am learning what I can of tending animals. I am finally confident in taking care of the three chickens Thomas purchased during our first months here.

It's been nearly a year since Thomas sold Belle, my

favorite of the oxen, at market and returned with a milk cow and three ewes. I miss Belle dearly, but with the children growing and winter approaching, we had greater need of milk and wool than another beast for plowing.

Thomas and I have weathered much hardship. Love alone cannot protect us from all of life's trials, but it gives us strength to endure them.

A yellowed, folded paper loosened from somewhere between the later pages of the journal and fell onto her lap. Amelia carefully opened the paper.

A map! Why hadn't she noticed it before? She eagerly studied the markings.

The map, or more like a sketch of a property, was dated 1877, twenty-six years after the beginning of Rebecca's journal.

There was a small square labeled "Cabin" and a dashed line … for maybe a path? And a few other squares for "Barn" as well as a cross symbol with the notation, "Everett's Chapel."

Her pulse quickened. *Everett's Chapel.* A chapel named after the young boy from Rebecca's entries.

Amelia's phone buzzed with an alert from the WJ7 Inc. security app. Audra and Melanie had arrived. She granted them access then hastily tucked the journal with the map into her work backpack.

* * *

Audra heated the soup and preheated the oven for the homemade rolls. "Tinkering with a new recipe is a great way for me to relax." She ladled soup into bowls. "And I'm thinking about taking cooking classes or maybe even cooking night school."

"Cooking classes? That's a great idea," Amelia said. "Which means more leftovers, right?" she teased.

"You'll have zero social time, especially for dating, if you're working and going to cooking school," Melanie said. "What does Drew think?"

"Actually, speaking of dating and Drew..." Audra grinned. She slow stirred the soup again. "We agreed a long time ago. If neither of us is married by age thirty-four, we're going to marry each other."

"Why thirty-four? That's so random."

"No, it's not. Fertility plummets after that," Audra said. "It wouldn't be for love. It would be a best-friends match."

"You've thought about having kids with Drew?" Amelia smiled and gave Audra a knowing look. "Just friends, my ass."

Melanie opened a cabinet and reached for the plates. "Mm ... you said he's older than you, right? Or did I imagine that?"

"Ha, yeah, he's thirty-two. We still have a few more years to go before the clock runs out."

"Tick, tock..." Melanie said as she set three plates on the counter.

They sat on stools at the kitchen bar as Audra served their food.

Amelia filled them in on the latest news about her mother's house and the sinking neighborhood. "She's far enough away from the sinkhole that I don't think she's in immediate danger, but long-term it's not a good idea to stay."

"Why? I mean, the hole isn't on her property." Melanie said.

"Sinkholes spread," Audra said. "And new ones frequently open up nearby as water levels decrease in underground caverns."

"Her house might be fine for the next twenty years. Or it might not," Amelia said.

"Would she be able to sell the house?" Melanie asked. "Are buyers going to want the risk?"

"It'll be tougher to sell now," Amelia sighed. "She'll probably have to lower the price on it, and she's already worried that she can't move her business. So, about that. Let's talk business. If I can come up with sound suggestions for quickly re-establishing her business here, or for supplementing her income until she can establish a new base of students, then I'll have a much better chance of convincing her to sell and move. I loved the ideas you texted me. You're both exceptional, by the way. Thanks for that. But we'll have to flesh those out or I'll never convince her."

They discussed several possibilities for Rachel: recording piano tracks for vocal performers, music translation services, creating teaching videos and a virtual class or a correspondence course for her existing students or new students with transportation issues.

Thirty minutes later, Amelia had a good list for her mom to consider.

"Would Mr. Jewell consider taking on other renters?" Melanie said. "Your mom would like it here. Anyone would be crazy not to fall in love with this place. It's gorgeous. And there are several schools and a college nearby with opportunities for her to pick up students."

"He hasn't said much about his plans," she said. "Though I think he's moving here soon. He asked me to research potential shipping companies to move a car and some furniture from Denver to Rainmere. But I don't think he's planning on taking more renters. And it won't last forever for me. Our contract is only for one year." Her chest tightened at the thought of moving. "I've got a goal to buy a house for myself after the year is done. Unfortunately, I'm getting a little too attached to this place."

Melanie set down her spoon. "I'm hearing a lot of stressors but not a lot of stress relievers. I think you need to get out and have some fun."

"Yep, that," Audra agreed.

"Speaking of getting out, last week I went to that gallery event downtown," Melanie said. "I met an interesting art curator, Jason." Her expression turned hopeful. "We talked for hours over wine and appetizers. I'm thinking about calling him." She paused, then turned to Amelia. "Actually, should I arrange a double date? You, Leo, me, and Jason?"

Amelia winced. The blind date again. Heat crept up her neck as she remembered Jonathan's unexpected offer. Should she tell them? They'd have strong opinions about it.

"Jonathan asked me out on a date. I think it's just to keep me from going on the blind date with Leo." She hadn't meant to blurt that last part out. Though, whether it was a fake-date suggestion or not, he *had* asked her out on a date.

"What the hell?" Audra plopped down on the couch. "That's a ballsy move. I mean, he had his chance with you, but he ghosted. I hope you gave him the middle-finger salute."

"I told him the same thing I've told both of you," Amelia said. "I'm not ready for a date."

Audra frowned. "That's a far nicer reply than he deserves, honey. I mean, dinner and personal conversation with him? That sounds way too intimate for someone who ghosted you."

"He's been trying to smooth things over. I've been resisting. He said he wants to explain what happened. Part of me really wants to know why he disappeared. I deserve an explanation. But another part of me is still angry and scared of getting hurt all over again."

"I'd probably feel that way too," Audra said. "Between Jonathan bolting and Nate's awful exit, you've had a shitty couple of years with relationships."

An image of Nate's funeral flashed through her mind. If he'd agreed to sign the divorce papers before the accident, things would have been much easier. No funeral plans. No bill collectors. No probate court.

A familiar nerve in her temple started to pinch. She'd blamed herself after the crash. The guilt wasn't logical, but she couldn't shake it. He probably wouldn't have driven so recklessly that day if he hadn't been so angry with her.

Melanie nodded in a slow, confident lawyer way. "It's time to move on from Nate. What happened to him wasn't your fault. And it's not good to let fear dictate your romantic life ... or the lack of one."

Amelia wasn't convinced.

"She's right," Audra said. "When you first arrived in Rainmere, you said you'd like to find love again, eventually. What changed your mind?"

Panic attacks will do that. "I'm not saying *never*," Amelia said. "But not now."

"I think you're afraid of trying again. That's not healthy," Audra said. "You've gotta dip a toe in the water."

"One date is not a relationship commitment," Melanie added.

"Look, I make time for the two of you because you're my best friends. I need you. But even if I were ready to date, I'm too busy to start a relationship. My boss just doubled our workload with the same timeline and no additional help." She paused, meeting each of their eyes. "I appreciate that you care. I really do. But I need you to trust that I know what I can handle right now. When I'm ready, you'll be the first to know."

Melanie and Audra exchanged glances. "Okay," Audra said. "We'll back off."

"For now," Melanie added with a small smile.

Amelia felt her shoulders relax. She knew they'd revisit this eventually—they cared too much not to—but for now, the pressure had lifted.

Chapter 15

Amelia

Monday. Week three.

Amelia buckled her seatbelt, then typed the address of the off-site map storage location into her phone. The route loaded as a blue line stretching south.

Jonathan turned the key, and the engine rumbled. "Tacoma, here we come."

She glanced toward the back seat. Patricia and Gavin huddled close over a tablet, engrossed in watching training videos, with a set of shared earbuds connecting them. Their forearms pressed together as they leaned against each other in a familiar way.

"Tsk," she murmured, a corner of her mouth curving upward. Clearly something was going on between them, something they hadn't admitted out loud. Not wanting to pry, she turned to face forward again.

As they merged onto the interstate, Amelia took in the scenery: thick patches of towering evergreens and the jagged peaks of the Cascades in the distance shrouded in low, gray clouds. The mountaintops were dusted with remnants of winter snow.

The soft hum of the car tires on the road created a low, rhythmic sound beneath Gavin's occasional keyboard taps or a quiet "go back" comment from Patricia.

Jonathan's hands rested on the steering wheel, thumbs absently brushing the leather. She noticed the way his dark hair curled slightly at the ends, and the faint crease between his brows deepening as he concentrated on driving.

He always looked so put-together, but there was a slight edge to him now. The hint of stubble along his jaw and the way his shirt stretched slightly over his forearms when he adjusted his grip on the wheel.

A rush of heat curled in her stomach.

Flashes of memory hit. Her hands threading through his hair. His warm breath whispering against her skin. The weight of him over her. The way he looked at her with those honey-brown eyes, like she was the only thing in the world that mattered.

She shifted in her seat and forced her gaze back toward her window. Focusing on the passing scenery, she tried to ignore the heat still sweeping through her stomach. That was years ago. A different time and place. A different version of them.

It's a legal matter, and it's complicated. Whatever Jonathan's reason for ghosting her was, it was too private to discuss while Patricia and Gavin were within earshot.

Later, looking for a distraction, Amelia thumbed through a paper copy of the asset inventory list. Last night she'd made a few notes to herself, highlighting details on the larger assets. "There's a lot on this inventory list. How accurate do you think this is?"

Jonathan frowned, keeping his eyes on the road. "No clue. But Lydia thought we'd find more assets in the map storage than what's on the official inventory. Some of the paper maps are likely forty years old or more and hand-drawn."

Pre-computer age. "Lydia's probably right," Amelia said. "I don't think many of the older maps have been digitized. It might take us all day to complete the inventory."

Her phone buzzed. "It's my mom," Amelia said. "She always forgets about the time zone difference and thinks she's calling me at lunchtime." She answered. "Hey, Mom. I'm on a day trip for work. Can I call you back later?"

"It's nothing urgent," her mother said. "Call me when you can. Love you."

"Love you, too. Bye." Amelia clicked to end the call and tucked the phone back into her bag.

Jonathan smiled and kept his gaze focused straight ahead. "It's nice that you're still so close to your mom. How's she doing?"

"Mmm ... she's not exactly young, but her health is decent." Amelia paused as her shoulders tensed. "Her house, not so much. A sinkhole opened in her neighborhood just a block away, and she's got some cracks starting along several walls."

"Shit. That's not good." His voice had a serious edge.

"No, it's not. The area is prone to sinkholes, but this one is so close to her place. I'm worried. I'm trying to convince her to move, preferably near me. Since I'm her only child, it makes sense in the long term to be in the same city. But she loves her teaching business and doesn't want to start over."

"Have you considered moving back?"

"I have," she said slowly. "But I left Florida because there were better mapping opportunities elsewhere."

If she'd stayed, would he still have ghosted her? *Ugh*. She couldn't afford to fall into that rabbit hole. Moving away had been the right decision.

"Speaking of family, how's your sister?" Amelia said. "Last I heard, she was going into business with your mother?"

"Jess is in Atlanta, working at my mother's design company. But we haven't talked in a while."

"Oh? I thought you two were still close."

He let out a slow breath. A hint of something long and thoughtful swept across his face. "She wants to reconcile with our father. Jess and I argued about it last year. I don't think I'll ever forgive him, so Jess and I are at an impasse."

Amelia didn't begrudge him the lack of forgiveness for his cheating father.

"I've never had the pleasure of arguing with a sibling," Amelia said. One of the few perks of being an only child.

"I'm used to arguing with Brandon, but it's the first big disagreement I've had with Jess."

Brandon? She thought back to their conversations in college and realized he'd said so little about Brandon that she'd forgotten he even had a brother.

"You didn't mention Brandon much back then."

Jonathan let out a small laugh. "Probably not. We get along okay, but we butt heads sometimes. Well, maybe *more* than just *sometimes*. Brandon drives me crazy, sometimes, but, even with the drama, family means everything to me, and I'm glad we live near each other. Atlanta's home. My friends, my favorite spots, everything that matters to me is there. When the work here is done, it'll be good to go back."

He'd be happily going back to Atlanta when they finished the project. Her heart dipped. Why was the thought bothersome? Amelia turned away from him to stare out the window again at the passing green of the trees and the overcast skies.

* * *

Half an hour later, Amelia opened the door to the off-site storage facility. The map area occupied a secured floor in a modern high-rise. The temperature and humidity were precisely controlled for preservation. Rows of old wooden cabinets lined the walls, their long, thin drawers housing delicate paper maps, while taller steel cabinets held modern hanging files.

Scents of old paper and ink lingered under the soft glow of recessed lighting. In the center of the room, two large tables offered ample room for reviewing materials.

"Feels like a library," Patricia said, running her fingers along a cabinet.

"A very expensive one," Amelia replied, scanning the inventory list on her tablet.

They split into pairs. Patricia and Gavin handled the hanging files while Amelia and Jonathan tackled the long drawers. The work was meticulous, checking what paper maps existed and identifying anything that wasn't on their inventory.

The quiet was filled by the rustle of paper and occasional taps on a tablet.

Jonathan's methodical approach complemented her attention to detail. And once, when their hands accidentally brushed while reaching for the same document, neither of them immediately pulled away. After realizing she wanted to look up into his eyes, she pulled her hand back and busied herself with the next drawer. But she couldn't keep her gaze from wandering sideways and watching him move confidently from drawer to drawer.

Then Jonathan stilled. "Wait a second."

He pushed the top drawer closed, then reviewed another midway down the cabinet. He pulled out a thick bundle of maps, frowning as he flipped through the pages. Swearing softly, he repeated the process with the next cabinet.

"These aren't on the inventory list. Two entire cabinets of maps."

Amelia moved closer, scanning the contents. "Oh, no. No."

Patricia and Gavin glanced over.

"What is it?" Patricia asked.

Jonathan found paper inventory packets for each of the cabinets and laid the documents on the central table. "More maps, more asset files. And our digital list doesn't account for any of them."

Amelia exhaled as she absorbed the magnitude of the situation. "That means we have way more to process than we planned."

Gavin let out a low whistle. "So, I don't suppose we can pretend we didn't find them?"

Patricia shot him a look. "Tempting, but no."

Amelia rubbed her forehead. "We expected to find more stuff, but not this much. This is going to throw off our timeline completely."

After they documented the existence of all the additional map areas, Jonathan leaned over the table, bracing his hands against the edge. "Our team isn't staffed for even half this workload," he said flatly.

"Maybe management would hire a few contractors," Patricia said.

Jonathan considered it. "It's an option, but we'll lose time in hiring and training them."

"We could ask Lydia to release two people from the Amherst project," Amelia offered. "The lead hasn't advertised it with management, but I heard they're overstaffed. It would be faster than hiring contractors."

Gavin grumbled as he thumbed through the inventory packets Jonathan had set on the table. "Either way, there's so much here we're still looking at mountains of overtime."

No solution was ideal. They'd be stuck with extra work no matter how they handled it.

Jonathan didn't answer right away. His gaze stayed on the table, jaw tight with frustration. The way he stood, the tension in his shoulders, the way his fingers absentmindedly tapped against the binder, made her insides twist.

She wanted to lay her hand over his to show her solidarity, to calm his concern. *Ugh.* Amelia shook off the thought. "We've been here for hours, and we have what we came for. Let's get out of here. We'll figure it out later."

They gathered their things and headed for the door. Amelia turned to grab her bag, but her foot caught on the base of a cabinet and she stumbled.

Jonathan's firm hands caught her waist, and he drew her into his chest.

"Oh," she said. They were too close. His firm chest was against her hands, the alluring scent of him, the way his hands fit perfectly at her waist. It all felt terrifyingly right. For a moment, she wanted to stay there, to sink into the safety of his arms like she had years ago.

There was a look in his eyes. Protective, possessive, and ... she swallowed, her pulse skittering. She pushed off of him and looked away.

What was that?

Slowly, she met his gaze again. That same intensity. That same pull between them from long ago. Slow heat wove a dance through her core.

This was too risky.

A slow smile spread across Jonathan's face. "It's been a long time, but it still feels nice to hold you, Amelia," he whispered.

She stepped back a little farther. "Thank you," she said, her voice softer than before. "For catching me," she added nervously, needing to make sure he understood she wasn't thanking him for embracing her or for making her feel … things.

"You okay?" Jonathan's gaze swept her body then lingered at her ankle.

Amelia gently rotated her ankle from side to side. Nothing broken, and no blood. She nodded silently, but the moment hung between them.

Patricia cleared her throat. "If you're okay, we should probably head out."

As they walked out, Amelia's thoughts tangled between how completely right it felt to be in Jonathan's arms and how wrong everything had felt after he'd gutted her heart with silence.

You've gotta dip a toe in the water.

No matter how much she wanted to ignore it, the truth was clear. She still felt something for him. And if she went on the blind date with Leo instead of spending time with Jonathan, what would that mean?

She'd never gotten closure after he vanished. Maybe that's what she needed—a chance to understand what happened, to finally close that chapter. Or maybe she was just making excuses because part of her wanted to say yes.

She didn't want to say no to him. But she still wasn't ready to say yes either.

Chapter 16

Jonathan

Saturday afternoon.

JONATHAN KICKED back on the sofa to unwind after a grueling week. The team had spent days poring over inventory from the map storage, dividing workloads and researching asset histories.

From the moment he woke that morning, he'd been thinking about Amelia, first at the gym while he lifted weights and again through his shower after his workout. How she felt when he caught her in his arms, soft and warm against his chest. The way her eyes had widened when she looked up at him, not with fear but with a hint of longing. How her breath had caught, and for just a moment, she hadn't pulled away.

The way her waist fit so perfectly under his hands had his brain in a snarly knot. Not even the meticulous neatness of his apartment could soothe his tangled thoughts.

His space was clean and precisely arranged; everything was in its place. It was a temporary place for him. He'd purposely kept the decor impersonal, which usually cleared his mind—no family pictures and no art on the walls.

The book he was reading, *The Vanishing at Piedmont Park,*

sat on the coffee table. Nearby, two unassembled ship models still in their boxes and his current project lay on the small table he'd recently purchased for the main living area.

After turning on an aviation documentary, he sat at the table to work on the miniature Viking ship he'd begun assembling the previous weekend. Even with his large fingers, the tiny wooden pieces slid easily into place as he meticulously followed the guidebook.

As he moved the pliable wooden pieces, his mind wandered back to Amelia and how the way she looked at him was softening. *Baby steps.* One side of his mouth turned upward.

Fifteen minutes later, his phone buzzed with a text from Paige. She'd been at the local office the last few days, but between the asset project heating up and her schedule of back-to-back meetings, their paths hadn't crossed long enough for anything more than an awkward hello.

> PAIGE: Stopping by your place in 10. Left my scarf last time.

Jonathan frowned. She hadn't left a scarf behind, or anything else, and he certainly hadn't invited her.

As he reached for the door, he reminded himself of his goal: to walk away without hostilities.

When he opened the door, Paige wasn't alone.

The guy standing next to her was almost as tall as Jonathan and handsome in a preppy-boy kind of way. He exuded confidence. Jonathan recognized him as someone he'd seen near the elevator at the office. He probably worked for another company in the building.

Paige plastered on a casual smile. "We were in the neighborhood. I figured I'd retrieve my scarf and introduce you two." She gestured toward her companion with a broadened grin and looped her arm around his elbow. "This is Cameron. We've been spending a lot of time together since I arrived."

Don't give her the reaction she wants. Play along. Stay neutral.

Cameron thrust out a hand with an affable grin. "Hey, good to meet you. Paige mentioned you two work together."

I bet she did.

Jonathan nodded and shook hands with Cameron. "Come on in." He kept his tone pleasant and even.

As she crossed through the entrance, a quick flash of annoyance swept across Paige's face, then disappeared. Yep, she'd realized he wouldn't take the bait.

"I haven't seen your scarf, Paige," Jonathan said.

"It's got to be mixed in with your things, somewhere." She set her bag on the entry table then casually began searching the townhome while talking past him to Cameron.

"It's supposed to rain soon," Jonathan said. "You might want to make it quick." He could hope, at least.

"Remember how we got completely lost walking in town last night? And the rain, oh my god. I want to do it all over again, only next time we'll bring an umbrella. One wrong turn heading back to the car and I was soaked through for the night! You should've seen us, completely drenched from the rain, searching for the car."

Cameron stood with Jonathan. "But the pasta was great," he said.

"It was the best I've had in this town." Paige continued her sham of a search by running her hand between the couch cushions. "And," she said in a silky lilt, "the company wasn't bad either." She glanced at Cameron with a practiced smile. "It's nice being with someone who doesn't overthink everything."

Whatever. Jonathan let out a quiet breath of boredom and resolved to get them out of there as quickly as possible.

"Jonathan used to be too serious about things," she called out from the bedroom. "Jonathan, remember Newark? That storm?" She laughed lightly. "You were so worried about a little rain."

Interesting. She was trying to put him on the defensive in his own home.

A few moments later, Paige emerged from the bedroom empty-handed.

He remembered the fight all right. *Too serious, my ass.* Trying to keep her from doing something dangerous was more like it. A walk in the rain was one thing. Walking in a thunderstorm with lightning was stupid.

Jonathan didn't flinch. He nodded politely and let her talk.

"Maybe it isn't here after all," she concluded.

"It was worth a look," Cameron said. He gave her a simple smile and placed his arm around her shoulder.

She ran her fingers along Cameron's forearm and leaned in close to him, then stole a glance toward Jonathan to gauge his reaction.

He would not bite.

"You two seem like a good match," Jonathan said. Indifference was easy; he didn't even need to pretend.

Paige stiffened. Then she moved her hand to Cameron's waist and squeezed herself against him.

Jonathan considered the situation. They worked for the same company, so he didn't want to fight with her, but he definitely wasn't jealous. He needed an exit plan to send her on her way.

"I was just about to return a call," Jonathan said. "I'm working on a tight project deadline with someone."

"Someone?" Her eyes narrowed. "Or *Amelia?* Lydia mentioned you two have a ... shared history."

Jonathan casually shrugged. *Let her think whatever she wants to think.*

Paige extricated herself from Cameron's side and crossed her arms. "Well, I guess you moved on fast." Her eyes sharpened as her tone cut colder. "You always had a way of compartmentalizing things, didn't you?"

Jonathan met her stare with an empty gaze. He would give her nothing. "You're the one who showed up at my door with a date, Paige. I don't think you get to be offended."

She smoothed her expression, smiling again, but this time, it was calculated.

"You know ... things are shifting at work. Big changes are coming with the merger." Her warning was a subtle but dangerous pivot.

Observing him closely, she tapped a manicured nail on the entry table then picked up her bag.

"I just hope you're making the right choices, Jonathan."

Jonathan understood immediately. This wasn't about the breakup anymore. It was about control.

She stepped closer, lowering her voice just slightly. "Keep your options open, Jonathan. You know how quickly management decisions are made. I'd hate to see you end up on the wrong side of those decisions. Especially when there are so many variables to consider."

Was she threatening him if he chose Amelia?

Jonathan opened the door for them. "Have a pleasant flight home tomorrow, Paige." He lifted his brows and tilted his head toward the outside.

Then he shook hands with Cameron. "It was nice meeting you, Cameron."

"You too," Cameron said. He handed Jonathan a business card with a friendly smile. "Hit me up if you ever want to grab a beer or play some pickleball."

"Thanks, man," Jonathan said. Naïve, but nice. Too bad Paige would shred him into tiny bits before he had any indication of what was coming.

Paige flashed one last conniving smile in Jonathan's direction and left with Cameron in tow.

He shut the door.

Leaning against the closed door, he considered his position. Paige had just declared war. She'd wanted to see his reaction. And when he didn't take the bait, she wanted to gauge his attachment to Amelia and deliver her warning. Typical Paige.

Her threat had been delivered professionally. Not unexpected, but disappointing. So much for a clean break.

Keep your options open.

Paige wasn't the type to make empty threats. Her father ran Whitlow Forest Resources. If she wanted to complicate his life, she could do it. And knowing Paige, she absolutely would.

She could do more than make his work life difficult. The Career Recovery Program had his name all over it. He'd been the one pitching it to management, recruiting the other companies, building the framework. If Paige wanted to sabotage that, she knew exactly where to strike.

Worse, she'd picked up on Amelia's name. If Paige felt vindictive enough, she might use her influence in the merger decisions to hurt Amelia's career prospects. He'd need to check in with Steve on Monday, make sure everything was still on track, and warn him about potential interference.

He'd made an enemy. The question was how far she'd go to prove it.

Chapter 17

Amelia

Amelia's alarm sounded early on Sunday. Morning sunlight peeked through the shades and bathed her bedroom in a soft glow. Yes, adventure time!

Ever since she'd discovered the map in Rebecca's journal, she'd been speculating if Rebecca had eventually lived here. The first house Rebecca described couldn't have been this one; the Jewell residence was too far from the coast and the lumber mills. But twenty-six years later? And Everett's chapel?

What if she found the echoes of Rebecca's life here on the estate? It could be proof that Rebecca's and Thomas's love survived.

Besides, how could a mapping expert *not* follow a map? Adventure was calling, and she needed a distraction from the whirlwind of Jonathan, noisy mansion contractors, the asset overload, and her mom's house situation.

With only a few hours to spare before she needed to attend to more attic cleanup and make a list for a lighting consultant, Amelia was eager to explore the grounds to the north and see if they matched the map from Rebecca's journal.

She pulled on a pair of faded jeans and a thick sweatshirt to cut the chill of the morning. After scarfing down a bowl of overnight oatmeal and a cup of coffee, she laced up her hiking shoes and grabbed her backpack with the journal tucked inside.

Before leaving the mansion, she opened the security app and sent a message to the guards to let them know where she was going and when she'd return.

Last night, she'd compared Rebecca's map to the one Mr. F-O had provided of the estate. If her hunch was right, the pathway notated along the western border of the old map corresponded to the service road to the northeast of the mansion.

If her assumption was correct, Mr. F-O's map covered a much larger area than Rebecca's. His map showed no sign of a chapel or a cabin, and the area east of the service road was shaded in gray yet appeared to be part of his property. It was a logical place to search. Why would he gray out that section?

Amelia set a two-hour timer on her watch, then headed for the path behind the mansion that she knew led northeast and eventually intersected the eastern service road.

Moist from yesterday's rain, the air held fresh, earthy scents of early spring. The soft dirt trail beneath her feet gently sloped upward. She quickened her pace through the dense pine forest, keenly aware that she might not have time for adventures like this one in the coming weeks. Because of the additional assets they'd discovered at the off-site facility, the luxury of free time would likely disappear for the foreseeable future. Disappointing, but necessary.

Perhaps it was just as well. She'd have another solid reason to postpone a blind date or a fake date. A fake date. The memory of Jonathan catching her as she stumbled over a map cabinet flashed across her mind. The look of concern on his face and the strength of his arms as he held her were vivid. Warmth and desire stirred in her core and whipped through her body.

Focus. Focus! She tried to shake off the memory by training her thoughts on her footsteps and finding the service road.

The trail let to a wooden bridge crossing over Cedarbend Creek. Glints of early morning sunlight shone through the trees, lighting the path and the mossy-green ground cover hugging the edges of the trail.

Ten minutes later, Amelia emerged to find the service road stretching to her left and right. A heavy-duty barbed-wire fence along the opposite side of the dirt road blocked her access to the forested area beyond. Exactly where she intended to go. Shit.

Amelia walked north along the road. Tiny gravel crunched under her feet. Oddly, the sturdy fence looked new. She spotted two security cameras along the fence and knew there were probably more she hadn't noticed.

Eventually, she found an unlocked gate with a posted sign:

Property of WJ7 Inc.

It made no sense. The entire mansion estate was the property of WJ7 Inc., and this was inside the security boundary. Why bother sectioning off the area with a fence but leaving the gate unlocked?

On the other side of the gate, the trail continued northeast, through more forest and away from the service road. She checked Rebecca's map. Not much farther to the chapel. It would be north of the two cabins; she was certain of it. Amelia put Mr. F-O's map into her backpack, since it had no information in the gray zone, and closed the gate behind her.

She followed the narrowing dirt trail as it led upward, inhaling cool air filled with scents of pine and damp earth. The forest was quiet except for the rustling needles and branches and the occasional calls of nuthatches and chickadees.

When she reached the top and crossed a narrow road, she found the small, sturdy chapel of weathered stone standing in quiet solitude. Its edges were decorated with creeping ivy and green moss. It really existed. She'd found it!

The arched wooden door, dark with age, was secured with a robust digital lockbox. Amelia smiled and exhaled a small huff. Mr. F-O's security was everywhere.

Beside the door, a brass plaque reflected the dim forest lighting:

Everett's Chapel
Property of WJ7 Inc.

Skimming her fingers across the rough stone as she walked along the side of the building, Amelia listened carefully and with reverence. She felt something shift inside her. This place felt safe, like shelter from a storm she couldn't remember. It was as if the wall still held echoes of whispered prayers and the weight of the past.

Her curiosity was partially satisfied, but she was disappointed that her boss had locked the chapel. Amelia made her way back to the narrow road nearby.

Ah, it must be the other private drive noted on Mr. F-O's map.

She walked south along the dirt road, hoping it would lead to the creek and the two cabins marked on Rebecca's map.

She passed a large rectangular lot, freshly cleared, with surveyor's stakes marking precise distances. A small digging machine sat beside a stack of treated lumber posts, the kind used for permanent installations. Moments later, the sound of rushing water from the creek grew louder as the cabins appeared ahead of her, nestled among the trees.

Her phone timer chimed. One hour down, one to go. The perfect time for a rest. Amelia sat on a low stone wall.

She opened the group chat. In a short video, Melanie posed in a black cocktail dress with a red sash tied around her slim waist. Black stockings and black stilettos accentuated her long legs, and sparkling ankle bracelets finished the look. Very Melanie.

> AUDRA: OMG, you are stunning, honey! Send a close-up of the ankle bling, please!

> MELANIE: Wednesday I'm going on a date with Jason. Dinner and a play. Amelia, want to make it a double with Leo?

> AMELIA: I get you think I need to date again. But you seem too eager to hook me up with Leo. What gives? Maybe you should date him instead of Jason?

> MELANIE: I wasn't going to tell you, but you called my bluff. Leo's my cousin. Our families have been tight since I was a kid. He's like a brother to me. Guess I'm sort of biased. Truthfully, he's terrific, and you know I wouldn't hook you up with a dud.

Amelia stared at her phone. Well, that made more sense. No wonder Melanie wouldn't let go of the idea. She shook her head. "Tsk." Clever trick, lawyer Melanie.

> MELANIE: He's been away for special forces training for the last several years.

> AUDRA: Holy crap. How did I not know that?

MELANIE: Just got back last month.

AMELIA: I might accept Jonathan's date offer.

The realization hit her the moment she hit the send button. She hadn't just said it to get Melanie off her back. She *was* considering accepting his fake-date offer. Maybe she'd lost her mind. And she couldn't even blame it on her friends' pestering.

His sincere efforts to smooth things over had eroded her deepest fears. And wanting to know what happened, wanting to know why he felt he had to ghost her, was chipping away at her resolve.

The sharp feelings of hate toward Jonathan were wearing smooth.

Besides, Jonathan would be gone in two months, on his way back to Atlanta, where he belonged. One fake date. She'd hear him out, then they'd go back to the status quo, finish the job, and never see each other again.

Never see each other again. Amelia winced.

AUDRA: What??? OMG.

MELANIE: You'd choose a known ghoster over my cousin? That's harsh. I think I'm horribly insulted.

AUDRA: You were devastated. He. Ghosted. You! I'm still mad as a hornet at him for putting you through that nonsense.

AMELIA: He said he had to do it for legal reasons. And he wants to explain and apologize. I wasn't ready to hear him out before, but I think I'm almost there. I want to know what happened to him and to us.

AUDRA: You still like him, don't you? Even after everything that's happened.

Amelia hesitated, her finger hovering over the question. *Do I?*

AMELIA: Maybe?

MELANIE: A legal matter? Damn. Without knowing exactly what it was, I don't think I can argue against that point. Well, if you go out on a date with him, do it quickly. If it bombs, you'll still have a chance with Leo, at least until someone else discovers him.

AUDRA: I will twist Jonathan's balls into an excruciating knot if he hurts you again.

AMELIA: If I decide to go through with it, I'll let him know.

AMELIA: I found the chapel and the cabins! But they're more like cute cottages. Rebecca's map shows two, but I see four. Two on either side of the creek.

The cabins appeared well maintained, with doors and shutters newly painted a deep blue, contrasting against the off-white stone. Maybe two more were built later?

Standing on the creek bridge, she snapped a few photos of the small houses and the creek below, then added them to the group chat.

AUDRA: Whoa. I'm seriously in love Is anyone living there? I don't see any cars.

AMELIA: Nobody here.

Her mom would love this quiet spot. It was perfect for practicing piano with the windows open. If only there were a way for them to be closer together.

AMELIA: The stonework is gorgeous. Matches the main house. The grounds could use some garden cleanup, but at least from the outside, the cabins look like they've received a lot of updates and TLC.

MELANIE: "Cabin" is an understatement. You could ask Mr. F-O if he's considering renting them. But it looks isolated. Is it okay to be out there by yourself?

AMELIA: I'm still on WJ7 Inc. property. There are cameras everywhere. I saw some along the fences and under the eaves of the cabins, too. Mr. F-O has a fortress of security. And I told the guards where I was going.

What was it like inside? Blinds in the windows, all closed, hid the interior from curious eyes. Had Rebecca lived here? Amelia's gaze swept from one cabin to another to another.

She turned and made her way north along the dirt road, back to the trail. The air grew cooler as the trees closed in around the narrow trail. Her adventure was about over.

Could I make a home here, too? She'd tried putting down roots in Austin with Nate and failed miserably. An empty marriage, with roots that rotted, had caused her life to topple when winds blew strong.

She attempted to shake off the memories. It was time for a new future and a solid home.

You still like him, don't you?

Realizing she was no longer emotionally detached from Jonathan was a hell of a wake-up call. She hadn't forgiven him, yet the layers of hatred were gradually peeling away. What remained underneath was raw and vulnerable to the touch.

But other things needed her attention too. Her mom had to get out of that house, before it sank underneath her. Determined to move her mother closer, she decided to ask Mr. F-O about the possibility of renting a cabin. What was the worst he could say?

Chapter 18

Jonathan

Monday. Week four. Lunch hour in the gym.

Jonathan pulled the rowing handle toward his chest as his legs pressed solidly against the platform. The whirring rhythm of the flywheel drowned out the clanks of weights, pounding shoes on treadmills, and the distant drumbeat of background pop music.

The rowing machine repetitions usually soothed his mind. Pull back, release forward. Pull back, release forward. A controlled, even burn spread through his legs and arms.

The movements should've been satisfying, but they weren't. His mind was stuck in his recent conversations with Paige. *I'd hate to see you end up on the wrong side of those decisions, Jonathan.* Pull back. He didn't want to give in to her veiled threats, but he couldn't afford to ignore them, either. Release forward.

Paige's father had actual power at Whitlow Forest Resources. One word from her could derail his entire career. But giving in to her manipulation would be worse than any professional consequences. Pull back.

Canceling the engagement was the right decision. Wanting to be married and have a family was one thing, and he wanted it. But he needed more than just someone convenient to marry, and that's what his relationship with Paige had been: convenient. Release forward.

He should have followed his gut months ago and refused Paige's proposal. *Damn.* That mistake was squarely his.

At least he hadn't moved in with her. He still had his Atlanta apartment to himself. With a grunt, he gripped the handles harder as he drew his arms toward his chest. Pull back, release forward.

Breathing hard, with sweat dripping down his neck, he let the rower glide to a stop. Atlanta. He missed spending time with Drew and his friends in the fishing club. And he missed the warmth of the southern spring, where everything turned greener in March and fishing in the morning didn't require heavy gear to keep out the chill. Only two months to go, he reminded himself.

But instead of energizing him, the deadline felt like a burden he wanted to delay. What was wrong with him? Was this place growing on him? He looked out the window toward the low afternoon clouds, hovering dark over the mountains and the icy rain. The deciduous trees were still barren. He shook his head. *Nope.* That part was not growing on him.

Zipping his jacket, Jonathan stepped out of the gym. A blast of cool air hit his face. The drizzle had morphed into sheets of rain. His phone buzzed with a call from Drew, and he paused under the doorway overhang to answer.

"Hey, how's it going in Washington?" Drew said. "Are you going to make it back to Atlanta for this month's golfing?"

"Yeah. I'm coming in for a long weekend." He leaned against a wall and slipped in his earbuds. "The timing sucks because work just exploded, but I committed to a family media interview before everything went sideways."

"Is Brandon in for golf?"

"Yep, Brandon is in." His brother never missed their monthly game.

"How'd it go with Paige?" Drew asked. "Did you officially break up with her?"

"Ah, so that's why you really called. You wanted dirt," Jonathan said with amusement. No reason to hurry to his car. He might as well dish for Drew. "Yes. I broke the engagement and ended the relationship."

Drew laughed. "How did she take it?"

"About as well as expected, I suppose."

"So, she sliced your nuts?"

"Not yet," Jonathan said. "But she's back in town this week for more in-person meetings. She stopped by my place with a new boy toy."

"Seriously? Would not have expected that play."

"She was trying to make me jealous, which went nowhere. So, she switched tactics to threatening me on the professional front."

"Threats I can believe; that's more her style. I'm surprised the two of you stayed together as long as you did. She's a looker, but that 'get what I want at any cost' streak of hers ... just wow."

"I've seen hints of it before but never aimed in my direction," Jonathan replied. He'd rather forget what Paige had said, but downplaying her warning could be a fatal mistake. "I'm bracing myself for her next move. And, changing the subject to something more appealing ... I asked Amelia out to dinner."

"A *date?*" Drew took a long pause. "I thought she was still furious with you for—"

"Not a date, really. An opportunity to explain to her about the investigation and why I disappeared. And as a substitute for a blind date she didn't really want. She was getting pressured by her friends." He took a breath and paused for thought. "I hoped it would make it easier for her to spend personal time with me and overlook being ghosted if I could be her escape from the blind date. We won't be on an actual date. I made that clear."

"A *fake* date? I don't know, man. Look, I get being jealous of a potential blind date, but you're leaving in two months. You sure you're not setting both of you up for more hurt here?"

Was Drew right? Had he made a mistake in proposing a date?

Jonathan winced as he searched his pocket for his keys. "Yeah, I was jealous. But I also need to explain what happened five years ago. She deserves to know the truth."

Drew huffed a quiet breath. "I bet that didn't go over very well."

As the rain slowed back to a drizzle, Jonathan avoided several puddles and made his way across the parking lot. "At first she hated the idea."

"You're playing with fire," Drew said.

He opened the car door. "It'll be a platonic dinner between old friends, assuming she ever agrees to it. I'll have the time I need to explain what I couldn't tell her back then."

"Come on, man. You and platonic don't belong in the same sentence with Amelia. You were a total fucking mess when she married Nate. What makes you think you can handle just being friends now?"

Fuck. Drew might be right. He had a lot to lose if he opened up to her and got hurt again. And he didn't want to put Amelia through any more turmoil.

No. He could handle this. Just a simple fake dinner date for appearances, if Amelia decided she wanted it. Old friends catching up.

"I'm going to keep things on a friends level. I have to," he said. *For both of our sakes.*

Rain drizzled down the windshield as he settled into the driver's seat. He wasn't staying in this rainy, rolling hills forest, and he wasn't going to start anything serious with Amelia.

The smart thing was to focus on his Atlanta life. His real life. The job, his friends, his family. Everything that mattered was back there.

But as he started the engine, he couldn't dismiss the sense that maybe the smart thing wasn't what he wanted anymore.

Chapter 19

Amelia

ALONE IN THE workroom at her desk, Amelia forked a bite of roasted sweet potato from the grain bowl Audra had left in her freezer. The earthy flavors reminded her how lucky she was to have a friend who actually enjoyed cooking.

She glanced at Jonathan's empty seat. He'd left to catch a short workout at the gym. The workroom felt too quiet without him.

Patricia and Gavin had invited her to join them in the cafeteria, but Amelia opted for some quiet time reading Rebecca's journal.

She examined the delicate cairn beside her computer screen and smiled. The polished stones soothed her and softened the old, ugly memories of the couple's retreat.

Moving aside her empty food containers, she carefully opened the journal.

After the entry she'd last read, Amelia discovered a letter tucked between the next pages:

2 December 1851
Beloved Sister Rebecca,

I hope this letter finds you well. I worry about your health and the struggles of settler life with your young family. To that end, I have a proposition for Thomas.

Have you heard, California is now a hub of the rush to mine gold? There is much money to be made in service of the mining efforts. The Traub family, also of New York, plans to open a dry-goods business in California. I am of the mindset that I should invest in this new company to expand our own dry-goods business. The new company will open in less than two years' time, in the spring of 1853. It is an exciting venture, is it not?

Would Thomas serve as my liaison in California and oversee my investment in the new company? I need a man I can trust, and I would pay him well. Sister, this would be good stable income for Thomas and your family.

Fondly, your elder brother,
James

Amelia replaced James's letter then began reading the next entry in Rebecca's journal.

7 December 1851

After much discussion with Thomas, I replied to my dearest brother James. While thanking him for his generous offer, I wrote that Thomas has decided to remain here, and we shall keep trying to better our lives.

Despite our struggles to grow crops, missing my family in New York, and suffering an agonizingly long labor of birthing our second child this past July, I am not ready to give up on this dream of creating a stable life for ourselves on this beautiful, forested coast. Thomas says he will always take care of me, and I trust in his deep affection. Better we should remain together and face familiar hardships rather than venture into unknown perils.

And we have faith that our situation will improve. In August, more settlers arrived in Seattle to work in the mills. They will no doubt hire Thomas to build pieces of furniture in the spring, as he is the most skilled carpenter on the shores of Puget Sound. In early November, Thomas and Everett finished a small room addition to our cabin for the children. And there is even talk that this part of the Oregon Territory may soon become the Washington Territory!

Amelia closed the journal carefully. Rebecca had trusted in Thomas's love rather than chase her brother's opportunity for financial security.

Amelia hoped Rebecca hadn't made a mistake by turning down her brother's offer. Sometimes fortunate opportunities fell into your life, and you had to be brave enough to grab them before they vanished.

She glanced at the stones again. Rebecca had continued to endure with Thomas's love and support. Maybe she'd been right to place her hope and reliance on love. Rebecca's relationship had been so different from Amelia's own marriage to Nate. She sighed.

New memories, she reminded herself, to replace the old.

It still feels nice to hold you, Amelia.

She'd realized it felt good to be held, too. After the shockingly brief "honeymoon phase" had worn off, Nate's touch had become demanding, like she owed him something. But Jonathan's arms had felt safe and protective. Like she could finally stop bracing herself against the world.

Her phone buzzed, interrupting her thoughts. Amelia set the journal aside and opened her email, hoping for a response from Mr. F-O about renting a cabin above the creek. Wanting to secure a place for her mom that wouldn't leave her scrambling to pay the bills, she'd sent him a note before work. She sat up straighter when she saw who'd emailed her, then clicked to open the message:

I'll lease Cottage #3, on the north side of Cedarbend Creek, to you for your mother.

Yes, yes! Amelia clenched her fists and pumped the air.

But the roof has two holes, and I don't have the funds available for the repairs. I'm fully extended with the main house upgrades. There are temporary patches in place, but I can't lease it in its current condition, and I have plans for the other cottages. If you fund the roof repairs for cottage #3, I'll let you have the cottage rent-free for three years and reduced rent after, for as long as you lease it, as compensation for your investment.

Investment? Amelia sank back in her chair with a long exhale. Three years rent-free was too good a bargain to dismiss, but how could she afford a new roof?

She thought back to her visit to the cottages along the banks of the creek. How did she miss seeing the temporary patch coverings? She regretted she hadn't thoroughly examined the cottages from all sides.

A quick mental calculation made her stomach drop. Even a basic roof replacement would cost at least fifteen thousand dollars, maybe more if there was structural damage. That was half her entire house down-payment fund—what little she had left after paying off the shared business loans Nate had left behind.

What other repairs would the cottage need? Maybe she should apply for a loan. But that would require collateral.

Why couldn't Mr. F-O pay to fix the roof himself? She frowned and nibbled at the edge of her lip. Something wasn't adding up. A man who could afford private security, huge mansion renovations, and designer furniture should be able to handle basic roof repairs for a cottage. An uneasy feeling settled in her chest.

Voices and soft laughter drifted in from the workroom entrance. Gavin and Patricia were returning from lunch. Amelia stuffed her lunch containers and the journal into her desk drawer then typed an email reply to Mr. F-O:

Thanks for the offer. I need to get an assessment of the damage and figure out if I can afford the repairs. There's a padlock with a code on the door. Can I get access?

After she hit send, her gaze drifted to Jonathan's empty chair, again, and a soft heat spread through her chest. The cabin roof wasn't the only thing requiring a leap of faith.

Chapter 20

Jonathan

ALONE IN THE BREAK ROOM, Jonathan poured himself some coffee, then turned to lean against the counter. Fragrant steam escaped from his cup. The rich coffee aroma mixed with a hint of cinnamon coffee cake.

As he waited for his beverage to cool, he mentally reviewed the progress of his team since the off-site trip. Over the past week, they'd integrated the additional assets discovered in storage into their plans, discussed how to divide the extra workload between them, and worked themselves ragged to meet the impossible deadline. To say no one was pleased would be the understatement of the century.

He was concerned. They were all putting in extra hours to figure out which of the assets required deeper evaluation, but he needed to request more staff.

Amelia's familiar light laughter floated in from the hallway.

Engrossed in conversation, Melanie and Amelia entered the break room. Amelia wore a soft burgundy top that highlighted her green eyes.

"Did you ask Mr. F-O about renting the cottage?" Melanie asked.

Amelia exhaled with a sigh. "Yes," she said. "It's a long story. I'll get back to you on that one."

"Hi Jonathan," Melanie said.

Amelia flashed him an easy, warm smile as she passed by. His chest squeezed. *Beautiful.*

She followed Melanie toward the middle of the room. They sat at a table, and Amelia retrieved two bagels from a paper bag bearing the logo "Brenda's Best Bagels."

Jonathan stirred his still-steaming coffee. Not cool enough yet.

Melanie placed her portfolio on the chair beside her. "I've got a teleconference in fifteen, so I can't stay for long," she said, her voice slightly irritated.

"A difficult client?" Amelia said.

"Two lawyers representing a potential company client. They're both based in Atlanta." Melanie opened her bagel and slathered a layer of cream cheese on one side. "I might need to visit in person to complete the contract negotiations. Typically, we can resolve issues through virtual meetings, but we're encountering difficulties. Some in-person discussions might make for a better outcome."

"You like to travel, so isn't it a good thing?" Amelia said.

"Travel for vacation? Yeah, I'm all in. Travel for business, meh, not really my thing. But conversations over dinner can definitely improve relationships with colleagues, and I need to close the deal soon, so I'll likely request the trip."

Jonathan stirred his coffee again. Confident it was cool enough to drink, he snapped on the portable lid and sat at a table near Amelia and Melanie.

"Speaking of dinner ... Leo asked for your number," Melanie said. "Jason and I are going out again this weekend, and it would be great if you two joined us." Her exuberant attitude grated on his nerves. "Honestly, I've told each of you so much about the other that it almost wouldn't be a blind date anymore."

Jonathan's stomach dropped at Melanie's enthusiasm. He set down his coffee and looked toward Amelia, though her back was turned toward him.

"I think I'll pass," Amelia said. "I'm sure he's great, but ... I've decided to take my chances elsewhere." She turned slightly in her chair and locked her gaze onto his. She gave him a slow, genuine smile, and his panic dissipated.

It had been a long time since he'd seen that effortless, warm glow on her face. Too long. His pulse quickened, and he felt a familiar pull toward her. He'd forgotten how she could affect him, how that look of hers never failed to create an immediate surge of desire through his body. He returned the smile.

"Jonathan, do you still want to take me to dinner?" She tipped her head and looked up at him, eyebrows raised expectantly.

Platonic. Yeah, right. What had he been thinking? This was going to be fucking hard. Was it all a show for Melanie? Or was there a hint of honesty in Amelia's eyes?

Unsure what to think, he hesitated.

Amelia's eyes widened, and her expression morphed into ... pleading.

"You know I do," he said casually, with a slight nod.

Melanie gasped. "But ... he's not sticking around."

"Gotta dip my toe in the water, right?" Amelia said, turning back toward Melanie. "Just a simple date," she whispered. "I'm not signing up for a commitment."

Melanie's gaze swept toward Jonathan, then back to Amelia. "And that's my cue to head to my meeting." She stood, gathered her belongings, and shook her head with a soft chuckle as she headed for the door.

Amelia changed tables and sat across from Jonathan, close

enough that he caught the subtle lavender scent of her shampoo. After Melanie was out of earshot, Amelia added, "Don't think this means I've completely forgiven you. I'm just ready to hear what actually happened. And I admit I'd like to put some distance between myself and the whole blind date concept."

"Not an *actual* date," he said tentatively. "Our secret."

"Our secret," she agreed.

Jonathan's chest relaxed slightly. She was willing to talk, which was more than he'd hoped for an hour ago.

One side of his mouth lifted. "You were the one who asked me out," he said with a playful wink. "I like it."

"Tsk," she said with a wave of dismissal. "So, where are we going for our non-date *date*?"

"How about Russo's on Thursday? Seven o'clock?" He observed her neutral reaction.

"Perfect," Amelia said.

Chapter 21

Amelia

AMELIA FLIPPED ON THE LIGHT. As she made her way upward to the attic, she wrinkled her nose at the now familiar but less noticeable metallic smell.

She had done it. That afternoon, she'd crossed her own no-date line and asked Jonathan out. Rebecca's journals had given her the strength to try. If she could maintain hope for things turning out for the best, despite all her hardships, certainly Amelia could, too.

Nerves fluttered in her stomach. A thousand questions ran through her head. Should she dress to impress? Would he make her laugh and treat her with the care he once had? Did she want that?

She turned on the attic lights.

An image of Jonathan in a sexy black suit flashed through her mind as heat unexpectedly rushed through her chest.

Ugh, that's ridiculous. It's a fake date!

She shook off the date thoughts and admired her work.

The thick dust and corner cobwebs were gone. She had removed boxes of broken toys, ancient camera equipment, and unsalvageable pieces of small furniture. The window coverings were freshly laundered and rehung, while newly purchased heirloom boxes for the older books and photos were half filled.

She placed her clipboard and phone on a small side table and began inventorying. The first large oak trunk held vintage dresses and matching shoes wrapped in yellowed tissue paper. Two identical trunks and several shelves of books would need to be catalogued for Mr. F-O's review.

In a corner of the trunk, she discovered a small painting. A couple sat on the grass, cuddling under a broad shade tree on a sunny afternoon. Was it perhaps Rebecca and Thomas? A faint smile tugged at the corners of Amelia's mouth.

The scene was nothing extraordinary, yet it touched on a deep longing she had suppressed since Nate died: the desire for intimacy she'd buried on the day he confessed he'd never loved her.

After meticulously listing the contents of the trunk, Amelia carefully repositioned the painting in its original place and closed the lid.

As she turned her attention to itemizing a shelf of books, her phone vibrated, and her mother's picture flashed on the screen. It was Wednesday, their regular check-in evening. She clicked to answer the call and set the phone to speaker mode so she could continue working while they talked.

"Hey, Mom," Amelia said. She flipped over the inventory sheet and, at the top of the page, penciled in, "Bookshelf 4."

"I lost two more students this week. A big music chain opened nearby, and they're charging half what I do. I can't compete with those rates and still pay my bills."

"I'm sorry, Mom," she said.

She told her mom about the cottages and Mr. F-O's rent offer. "Three years rent-free is a tremendous opportunity. I'm waiting for a structural assessment report from Mr. F-O for the cottage, and I'm going to look inside this weekend. The cottage would be *perfect* for you, Mom. I think it has stone floors. Can you imagine the acoustics? Your piano would sound beautiful."

"That sounds wonderful, sweetheart, and you know I'd love to live close to you. But how could I possibly start all over again?"

"I've been thinking a lot about this." Amelia sat back on her knees, taking a break from sorting through the stack of old books. "There are several schools and a university nearby for finding new piano students. Or you could teach. And there are ways to make ends meet while you establish a group of client students in Rainmere. You could record piano tracks for vocal performers or even create a virtual correspondence course for your existing or new students. I can help with the technology."

"That all sounds a bit overwhelming."

"Your business is already struggling, Mom. It's a good time for a change."

"I'll think about it, dear." Her mother's tone was gently resistant. "Please don't worry about me so much. You've got enough going on in your own life."

"I know, but I can't help it," Amelia said. She set a hand on the couch as she stood up from the floor, then brushed a few spots of dust from her jeans. "I love you, so I worry when your house is too close to a sinkhole and your students are leaving for a cheaper teacher in a big company." She left out the part about her mother being older than most of her friends' parents. "You worry about me, and I worry about you. That's just what we do." She blinked and hastily brushed away a few tears sliding down her cheeks.

They exchanged another round of I love yous before saying goodbye.

After ending the call, Amelia sat on the faded green sofa, leaning back into the cushions to stare at the ceiling. The competition was threatening to put her mother out of business.

Her house could collapse into a sinkhole. And yet her mother refused to consider moving her business.

She must be missing something about the situation.

She wiped her eyes and looked around the dusty attic. Perfect. Nothing said *I've got my life together* like crying in a musty attic. At least there were no witnesses.

Deciding to take a longer break, she opened the group chat with Audra and Melanie. She explained about the leaky cabin roof, Mr. F-O's offer, and her mom's reluctance to move her business.

AUDRA: Your mom might warm up to the idea. Give her some time, honey.

AMELIA: I hope you're right. Mr. F-O sent me the cottage access code, so now I need to check it out. If she doesn't take to it, I think I could be happy living there while saving up for buying a house.

MELANIE: Okay … there's something important you haven't mentioned yet!

AMELIA: lol. I should know never to keep a lawyer waiting. Yes, Jonathan and I are going on a date tomorrow night. I'm ready to hear what he has to say.

AUDRA: I'm not exactly warming up to that idea. But I hope you get the answers you're looking for, and I'm proud of you for taking a step forward. Nate and that sour aftertaste don't deserve another nanosecond of your present or your future.

AMELIA:

> MELANIE: I'm disappointed you didn't choose Leo. But I hope you have fun with the hottie ghoster. I'm going to want details! And if it doesn't work out with Jonathan, you can still go on a date with Leo.

Ugh, Melanie clearly wasn't ready to give up on the Leo front.

> AUDRA: Hey, look at the pic I found in my memory box!

Whoosh. Amelia grinned when a college group photo from a cave tour popped onto the screen. Happy, carefree times! Despite her love-hate relationship with caves, Jonathan had planned a fun adventure. They'd taken the picture just before they'd entered the cave ... before Audra's bat freakout and before they'd gotten lost.

> MELANIE: Love the orange hard hats 😜 Jonathan on the left? And the brawny lumberjack blond guy with an arm around Audra? Gotta be Drew. Just like you described.

> AUDRA: Yep, all four of us. My guy-bestie was my hero that day.

Amelia stared at the photograph with its cheerful grins and arms casually wrapped around each other. Audra had been by her side through thick and thin. They'd shared everything back then. No secrets.

What would her college-self think about keeping this secret, about faking a date? An uneasy feeling sank to the pit of her stomach. Still, she *was* determined to resolve the past, and she was certain her younger self would understand those feelings.

How would Audra and Melanie react if they discovered

she'd lied about the date with Jonathan? Or that she hadn't told them about the panic attack? They could hardly blame her. After all, she'd clearly told them she wasn't interested in dating yet.

She exhaled a large breath as one side of her mouth turned downward. *It's just one date.* A controlled experiment, a way to see if she could even handle a dinner date without panicking, but with zero real stakes. *I don't have to tell my friends everything.* Some things should remain private, and this was one of them. She didn't owe anyone an explanation if it wasn't anything serious. And it wasn't.

Amelia again stared at the photograph. Her gaze lingered on Jonathan's soft brown eyes, and her heart melted into a puddle.

There lay the naked truth. The actual harm of the fake date was how real it already felt. Was she lying to her friends or lying to herself?

Chapter 22

Amelia

Thursday evening.

AMELIA STOOD in front of her bedroom mirror, applying a final coat of mascara.

She'd changed her sweater twice, settling on the soft white one that brought out the green in her eyes. Her hair fell in loose waves past her shoulders. She'd resisted the urge to style it further. *This isn't really a date*, she reminded herself, but her reflection suggested otherwise.

When Jonathan appeared at the front door, his greeting died on his lips. "You look..." he started, then cleared his throat. "Ready for this?"

The car wound along the narrow streets, uphill toward town. Typical of the end of March, the days were still cool and mostly overcast.

"How do you like Rainmere so far?" she said.

He let out a gentle, barely audible huff. "I'm not sure I could ever get used to the nonstop rain. But I'm about to go home for a long weekend. It'll be good to catch a little Atlanta sun. The timing is bad considering our hectic workload, but I promised my mother I'd be there to take care of some family business."

"This weekend?" she asked.

He nodded. "I fly out tomorrow. At least I can get some work done during the flights."

They passed the old brick library on Ridge Street, with towering cedar trees. The branches dipped, heavy with new spring growth and still dripping from the afternoon rain.

She chose to save the ghosting talk for dinner. They might both like a drink before that discussion.

"Will your sister be there?" She was curious how long he would keep his grudge as a barrier between him and Jessica. When they were dating, he'd often talked about Jessica and how much she meant to him.

"Last I heard, she's traveling," Jonathan said. "So I don't think she'll be there."

"I know you don't empathize with her desire to reconcile with your dad," Amelia said carefully, "but it's far too easy to believe that the people you care about are going to be alive forever." She often wished she could spend one more day with her dad. "You never know when they might suddenly be gone."

Jonathan frowned without taking his eyes off the winding road.

"I'm just saying I wish I had a chance to talk to my father again," she said. "And I often wish I had a sibling to talk to or stay up late watching movies together."

"I see your point," Jonathan said, as his expression relaxed. "Maybe I have taken it for granted that Jess would change her mind and give up on Roger."

"Talk to her while you still have a chance," she said, "before it's too late and you regret leaving things broken between you for too long."

He took a deep breath then exhaled slowly. "I'll think about it."

A step in a good direction. Amelia's heart warmed.

She watched the streetlights slide past for a moment. "Then what's next for you? Career-wise, I mean."

Jonathan hesitated, his jaw tightening slightly. "I have a lot left to do at Whitlow. But eventually, I'll take over the family foundation from Brandon. Form to Function Fund. It's my mom's charity. Brandon's been running it, but the plan's always been for me to step in." He paused. "In a few years, though. Not yet."

"In Atlanta?"

"Yeah, it's based there. At the family estate, actually. My mom's design business and the foundation are pretty intertwined." He shifted in his seat. "The foundation does good work. I believe in the mission, but I'm not ready to leave Whitlow yet."

"Being full-time in Atlanta is what you want though," she said. "So that will be nice for you."

The side of his mouth twitched.

"Do you have any weekend plans?" Jonathan asked, changing the topic.

"I have to pick up an order of plants for Mr. Jewell," Amelia said. "When I asked to borrow her truck for the errand, Melanie mentioned she'll be in Atlanta, too. Client meetings there early next week? Or something like that," she said.

Jonathan nodded. "Melanie's been working with our HR group. Some of NorthSound's clients overlap with ours. My boss mentioned they're having trouble booking a hotel room anywhere near the office for her. Apparently, there's a high-profile fashion convention in town, so I mentioned to Steve that she could stay at our family home. It's close to the offices, and we have extra rooms."

"I didn't know she's staying with you," Amelia said.

Jonathan grinned. "Steve put the offer out there. She's probably still searching for an alternative."

Amelia smiled to herself. "You're not Melanie's favorite person right now, and she prefers doing things her own way." She hesitated. "Speaking of getting her way, did I tell you the guy she wants me to date is her cousin?" She sighed and shook her head. "He must be a favorite."

"I guess that explains some of the pressure."

"Their persistence is intense sometimes, but Melanie and Audra genuinely believe they have my best interests at heart, wanting me to rejoin the dating scene and move on from my marriage shitshow with Nate. It's a long story."

A very long story. Moving forward would be easier if she could finally forgive Nate and forgive herself for allowing him to hurt her. It was probably a substantial part of the reason for the panic attack. But forgiving Nate meant trying to understand his perspective, and despite her best efforts, Amelia had never found a reason for his deceptive nature.

She tried to steer the conversation in a different direction. "Are you looking forward to your trip home?"

"Yeah, I love Atlanta," he said. "All my friends and family are there. Weekends, I'm usually fishing or golfing. And there's always something going on. Dinner, live music, that kind of thing."

Evening dates?

"Is there someone special waiting at home for you?" He didn't seem the type who would ask her out, even on a fake date, if he already had a girlfriend. But given her history, it didn't hurt to ask.

"No," he said, shaking his head. "There was someone, but not anymore." His grip on the wheel tightened and loosened several times, then he turned the car into the restaurant parking lot. "I recently ended it."

He was leaving things unsaid.

* * *

After seating them at a table near a window, the waiter took their drink and appetizer orders. They discussed her mom's house and the mansion projects. She told him about the attic cleanup, the cottage discovery, and the leaky roof situation.

As a large group sat at two long tables nearby, Amelia explained her mother's hesitation about relocating her business. The next table erupted with loud talking and laughing.

"Beyond the challenge of convincing her to move the business, why not find a place that's ready to move in? A roof repair could be a significant undertaking," he said.

"I know. I'm concerned about affording the repairs, even if I get a loan. But one of the major draws to the cottage is its size. It's a lot bigger than what we could afford in other rentals. Also, the schools and university nearby offer a lot of potential students for my mom. It's just too good an opportunity to miss."

She scooped cheese pâté onto a garlic cracker from the appetizer plate. "And maybe I'm being naïve, but I'm hoping the assessment will say that the roof only needs minor repairs and not a complete replacement."

"I hope it works out," he said.

Then Jonathan leaned closer to her. "I had planned a fine dining experience, but the noise is killing the mood."

The giggling grew louder. It didn't seem like a place to bring children.

"We could ask for another table," Amelia said. "But there is a wait list. It might be a while."

Jonathan pointed out the window to a small shop with an outside patio. "What do you think about leaving and trying the pizza place next door instead?"

Amelia nodded with a smile. "Mm, I was eyeing it, too. Let's go!"

Chapter 23

Amelia

JONATHAN PAID THE BILL, and ten minutes later they were seated on the outdoor patio of Maddie's Pizza. Scents of garlic and fresh basil wafted from the kitchen, carried on the cool breeze.

When Jonathan draped his jacket around Amelia's shoulders, it still held his body heat, and she caught a hint of his cologne—woodsy and clean—that made her want to lean closer.

They shared a loaded pizza with pepperoni and bell peppers; the cheese stretched in long strands as they lifted each slice. The Chianti was smooth and full-bodied, warming her from the inside.

"This is really good," Amelia said.

"Honestly, this is perfect," he said, raising his glass to toast with her. "But it's not quite what I'd imagined for our first date."

"Not a date. And *definitely* not our first," Amelia said with a knowing glance. She touched her glass to his.

"All right, all right," he conceded with a few humble nods.

"Maybe we should start talking now about what really happened five years ago. You abandoned me," she said, her inflection tinged with accusation, "with no explanation and nothing to hold on to."

Jonathan hesitated, then locked eyes with her. "I inadvertently got caught up in something bigger than either of us." He took a large swallow of wine, then glanced over his shoulder.

"No one else is out here," Amelia said. "It's just us."

He nodded. "Unfortunately, it's important not to broadcast my story. I still reflexively check who's nearby before I talk about any of it."

Amelia frowned. *Privacy*. He'd mentioned it before.

"The graduate program I was in partnered with a foreign company. Unfortunately, the foreign company was involved in illegal activities," he said, his fingers tapping lightly against the table.

"What kind of company?" Amelia asked.

"They were helping us source rare materials for geological research. But I discovered they were falsifying inventory documents." He glanced at her briefly. "I reported it to the department chairman."

"That sounds like the right thing to do."

"It was more complicated than I imagined." Jonathan's jaw tensed. "The company was bypassing international sanctions, facilitating restricted purchases from embargoed nations. When we reported the violation, I became a key witness in a federal investigation and ended up in protective custody with limited outside contact."

Amelia's eyes widened. "A federal investigation?" It hadn't occurred to her that his legal reason might have been so serious.

"Complete secrecy was required. I was cut off from everybody and not given any way to contact anyone except one five-minute phone call a week to my mom to reassure her I was alive. I couldn't tell anyone. Not friends, not the rest of my family." His voice dropped, and his gaze fell away. "Not you."

"Oh my god," Amelia said. Her hand moved to cover her mouth.

"Since my involvement as a research assistant made me privy to critical details, I became a key informant, and they couldn't risk either my safety or my being pressured via friends or family ties."

His gaze returned to hers. "You were about to start a new job, a new life. You were building something important, standing on the edge of everything you'd worked for. And if anyone had connected you to what was happening with me, you could've lost it all. I couldn't risk dragging you into an investigation and jeopardizing your safety or your career."

"I realize you thought you were protecting me, but I should have had a say in the decision, Jonathan." Amelia was torn between forgiveness and irritation that he had made decisions about their future without her. "Why didn't you trust me enough to include me?"

Jonathan struggled visibly to find the right words. "I know how it sounds. Maybe it is unforgivable. But back then, I couldn't give you half the truth without putting you in danger. Even giving you a hint of what was happening might also have put you at risk. And not just your reputation or your career, Amelia. Real physical danger."

"What kind of danger?"

He lowered his voice. "It's over, but even now, I still can't reveal everything. At the time, there wasn't a safe version of the truth. No way to protect you and still hold on to you. Ghosting you was the ugliest choice I've ever made, but it was the only one I could see that kept you clear of it. Completely clear. Final. Cold enough that you'd walk away from me and never look back. And believe me, I hated myself every damn day for it."

She reached for the wine bottle and refilled her glass.

"It destroyed me to walk away from you," he added quietly.

"But I would do it again in a heartbeat if it meant keeping you safe. So now you know about the mess my life became. I spent two years off the grid in protective custody, then the next two finishing up grad school and putting my life back together. Only in the last year have I finally become free of it."

"It must be an immense relief," she said.

"Yes," he said. "But the fallout was hard. My whole life got derailed for two years, so I've been attempting to make up ground ever since."

"You look like you're doing pretty well making up ground. A lead for a Whitlow merger team isn't so bad."

He nodded, looking a little self-conscious.

"Part of making up ground has been working on something meaningful—a program to help other professionals who end up in situations like mine," he said. "People whose careers get put on hold or damaged for doing the right thing when they report unethical or illegal corporate actions. Whitlow agreed to sponsor it a few years ago, and we're close to launching."

He hesitated. "I've struggled with how much I lost by walking away from us." He paused for several moments. "Losing you was the hardest part," he said. "And you were married long before my life became normal again, so I didn't expect I would ever get a chance to fix it."

He hadn't wanted to ghost her. The breakup had been hard on both of them. Questions swam through her mind. The most pressing was what to do with this new perspective.

"I had no idea. I was so caught up in my disappointment and loss that it didn't occur to me you could be in any danger. Are you sure you're completely safe now?"

"As sure as I can be. There are no complete guarantees. But I can't hide forever."

Amelia sat quietly for a moment, processing the magnitude of what he'd endured. No wonder he'd vanished so completely.

Jonathan leaned forward and gently loosened his collar. "So," he said slowly. "About the long story and Nate … is he still part of your life in any way?"

Another difficult topic from her past.

Amelia hesitated, contemplating how much to tell him. "He's gone. About a year ago, I discovered our relationship wasn't what I thought it was, and it crushed me. So, I filed for a divorce. Then, Nate died in a car-racing accident. It was all so sudden and horrible. He hadn't even signed the papers yet when the crash occurred, so technically, I'm a widow." Which still felt strange, and … unresolved.

She blinked, and the tears she couldn't control slipped down her cheeks. It still hurt to talk about it.

"Without an official divorce, I feel like I never really got closure. And, if all of that wasn't stressful and traumatic enough, the police spent months investigating whether the crash was really an accident." She paused, choosing her next words thoughtfully. "There were questions about whether Nate might have caused it deliberately."

"I'm so sorry, Amelia," Jonathan said. "I can't fathom what that must have been like for you."

"Not knowing took a heavy toll on me," she said.

Even with the official determination, Amelia wasn't entirely certain. Even after telling her he never loved her, Nate still wouldn't agree to the divorce. They had argued loudly and often in the last days leading up to the crash. She'd wanted him out of her life, but she hadn't wanted him to die.

After his death, she discovered why he hadn't wanted to divorce her: he'd still been using her credit, opening new accounts in her name without her knowledge.

"I'm sorry you had to suffer through that experience."

They sat in silence for a few moments. Amelia poured the last of the wine into their glasses.

As she set down the bottle, her gaze drifted over Jonathan again. Maybe it was the alcohol spinning through her veins, but he was gorgeous in the sunset's glow.

"Let's take a walk," she said, downing the last swallow of her drink. "There's a park across the street." She needed to walk off her buzz and move on from the past.

Jonathan set cash on the table for the tab, then stood and held out his hand for her.

"We're holding hands now?" she said curiously.

"Audra and Melanie," he said with a slight grin. "To your far left. Looks like they're on reconnaissance."

She whipped her head to her left. Across the street, Audra and Melanie sat on a bench at the edge of the park eating sub sandwiches with a large paper bag wedged between them. They cheerfully waved at her.

"Oh my god," Amelia said with the start of an eye roll. "What are they, teenagers?"

Jonathan's grin widened as she rose from the table. "Fake date calls for fake PDA, don't you agree?" He took her hand in his, surrounding it in a soft, inviting embrace.

When their fingers intertwined, Amelia felt the familiar shock of awareness she'd experienced five years ago. His hand was larger than she remembered, but his touch was exactly as gentle as it had always been.

She squeezed his hand in return and nodded. "Fake PDA," she echoed, plastering on her best smile and feeling proud she'd made it through dinner without a panic attack.

As they crossed the street, away from the spot where her friends continued their spying picnic, Amelia felt a wave of comfort. She tightened her grip on his hand, and they slowly made their way along a path that hugged the street.

The warmth of his palm against hers felt anything but fake.

Her pulse quickened, and she matched his stride naturally, as if he'd never left her side.

"Since it'll be getting dark soon, we shouldn't venture too far," he said.

"You know, Melanie won't give up easily on the idea of me dating Leo, especially when I tell her this date is one-and-done—"

Jonathan turned sharply and cupped her face with a gentleness that stole her breath. He brushed his thumbs lightly over her cheeks, his touch steady and achingly intimate.

"You want to make this look real, right?" he whispered. He glanced briefly toward Melanie and Audra. "They can still see us. Let's give them something to talk about."

Her heart skittered in her chest. *Fake PDA.* Just for show. But the way he was looking at her and the way her heart melted under his touch felt anything but fake.

"Can I kiss you? Just for your friends," he said, leaning his head down toward hers. "Only if you're okay with it," he added softly, still holding her face.

Amelia's mind screamed that this was purely a ruse, with a man she had barely forgiven. But her traitorous, eager heart whispered something entirely different.

She gave a tiny nod.

Jonathan's mouth lifted into a mixture of relief and hunger. And then he closed the remaining distance between them.

His hands drifted down to her shoulders, and his lips brushed hers with soft, cautious pressure, as if giving her one last chance to pull away. She didn't. Instead, she wrapped her arms around his waist and leaned into him, driven by a need she'd almost forgotten existed.

He responded immediately and deepened the kiss, slipping from staged and careful into what felt like a deep need of his own.

Amelia gasped against his mouth, and he answered with a low note of pleasure that vibrated through his chest. He drew her closer to him, nothing polite this time, but as though he needed to anchor himself to this moment.

The kisses tasted like wine and possibility, like coming home and falling off a cliff all at once.

When he finally pulled back to rest his forehead against hers, they were both breathing deeply. "I ... expect they bought it," he said. His voice was low and gruff.

"I'd say so," Amelia said with a faint laugh, her pulse still sprinting. "That was the intention, right?"

As she stepped away, she didn't want to believe that the kiss meant nothing. *It wasn't real.* But if it wasn't real, why did it feel like the start of something she wasn't prepared to lose again?

"Now I'm going to have trouble convincing them that this date didn't lead anywhere." She gently pressed one hand onto his chest and took a deep breath, trying to calm herself. "Did you have to kiss me like that?"

A smooth grin slid across Jonathan's face. "Like what?"

Like a hot fireball explosion. He still had his arms around her.

"Like you had an intention of impressing me." She hadn't forgotten what it felt like to kiss Jonathan, but this one hummed, like *you're mine* rather than fake PDA. She took a slow step back, uncurling from him. No need for him to know he'd succeeded in impressing her.

"We could continue dating," he said nonchalantly. His expression became matter-of-fact. "Dinner dates, maybe some weekend activities. Nothing too serious, but visible enough that your friends back off about the blind date situation." He paused. "And maybe I can start making up for how I handled things five years ago."

"This would be purely for show?" she asked, not sure if she could handle either answer.

"That's what makes the most sense."

But even as he said it, the space between them still sparked with an afterglow of their kiss.

He curled an arm around her shoulder and motioned to her to walk toward a nearby bench along the path. "Besides, I enjoy spending time with you. And I'd prefer not to go full hermit while I'm in Rainmere for the next few months."

They sat together on the bench, Jonathan's arm still resting around her shoulder.

"What do you think?" he said casually.

Companionship, conversations, and an activity partner? She wanted temporary cover to avoid blind date pressure, and his reasoning sounded logical. They'd have a mutually beneficial arrangement. But, wow, the reality of that kiss had been intense, and the lingering excitement was undeniable. Of course, that meant his suggestion was anything but simple.

More space between her and blind date Leo would be a gift, though spending more time with Jonathan would also mean further compromising her openness with Audra and Melanie.

What exactly would fake dating be like?

Ugh. She was tired of thinking too hard about everything, of scrutinizing every potential action.

"Okay," she said.

He tilted his head slightly and raised his eyebrows. "Don't you want to think about it?"

"No, I don't," she said. "Maybe it's the wine." *Or maybe it was the knockout kiss.* "But I don't want to overthink it. I'm not angry about the ghosting anymore. I wish it had never happened, and I can't say it didn't leave scars, but I understand why you thought you had to do it. And if casually fake dating means I get space from the blind date for the next two months, I can do it."

So much for just one casual dinner to get closure.

Still, she had made it through tonight without panicking. No chest tightening, no need to flee. Was that because the stakes were fake, or because it was Jonathan? Was this real progress or just a fluke? Another few dates would tell her if she was actually healing.

"But I *will need* clearly defined relationship boundaries." She wasn't about to put her heart too far out on a limb or get ghosted twice.

"I'm good with that," he told her.

Amelia stood from the bench and held out her hand to shake on the deal. "Let's do it."

Chapter 24

Amelia

Friday afternoon.

AMELIA PARKED Melanie's truck near the entrance of the nursery lot and cut the engine.

Despite the cushy seat, she felt uncomfortable. Jonathan's suggestion to continue the dating ruse had seemed reasonable yesterday. Today, the plan felt as sound as trying to build a fence around quicksand. Where exactly do you draw the line when nothing is supposed to be real?

Thick, earthy scents of mulch, sweet roses, and citrus flowers filled the air.

"Thirty rose bushes?" Audra said, squinting at the receipt. "I thought you said we're only picking up a few."

Amelia grimaced. "Apparently, Mr. F-O and I have different ideas about the definition of *a few*."

The contract landscapers were backlogged, so he'd asked her to pick up the order to avoid delaying the project. All she had to do was keep them alive for a few weeks until the gardening crew showed up.

Thirty rose bushes, all needing TLC to survive transplant-

141

ing. Like relationships, she supposed. Provide some careful attention, or they'd wither when moved to new ground.

"Did I tell you I really appreciate your help?" Amelia said. "Because I do. You're a rockstar."

A nursery employee checked the receipt and nodded toward a row of large plastic pots stretched beyond the main door. "The ones he ordered are here," she said. "They're all just starting to break dormancy, no flowers yet. But you can check the tags for the colors against your purchase order."

They found a flatbed cart. Amelia pulled out a pair of work gloves from her bag and gave Audra another pair before inspecting the tags.

"Holy crap, this is a lot of buckets." Audra picked up a bucket and set it on the cart. "Too bad Jonathan's not here to help lift," she teased.

"He's in Atlanta this weekend. Family commitments," Amelia said, ignoring Audra's innuendo.

Despite the cool air, she was soon sweating from lifting the heavy pots. Her arm strained as she pulled the first cartload toward the truck.

"And Melanie's there too?" Audra said. "She mentioned she's staying at his family's place. That's not weird at all." Her expression twisted as she hefted another pot, grunting slightly with the effort.

Amelia lifted one of the heavier pots into the truck bed. "All the decent hotels close to the offices were booked and she didn't want to stay in creepy motels. Melanie isn't too happy about the situation."

"Mm. And ..." Audra leaned over a coral-pink bush with a smirk. "How was your date? Melanie and I expected immediate detail texting. What gives?"

Amelia returned the look with a gentle headshake. "I still

can't believe you two were spying on us." She shifted a few pots to organize them by color.

Audra laughed. "Best picnic entertainment ever! You looked like you were enjoying yourselves." She flashed a quick, knowing wink.

"We were," Amelia said, a tad too rushed.

They loaded and unloaded the cart several times with buckets of roses.

"It reminded me of spending time with him in college. I've missed it," Amelia admitted. "He explained a lot. About how he was a whistleblower over a mess at the university, how he spent time in protective custody, and how he ghosted me to shield me from the fallout."

She explained more of the details while they continued loading the truck.

As they loaded the last of the bushes, Audra stretched her back. "Okay, now the most important question. How did the date end? Did you sleep with him?"

"No," Amelia said, snapping the tailgate shut. "We shared a cab, and that was the end." Her voice was calm, but her pulse thudded in her ears.

The memory of his hand on her back during the cab ride surfaced before she could stop it.

Audra's eyes narrowed as she studied her. "You're being weird about this. I mean, you skipped the best part! Usually, you tell me everything."

"There's nothing weird about wanting some privacy," Amelia said.

She'd considered sleeping with Jonathan for all of about two seconds. But she wasn't about to sleep with a fake date. He'd suggested they continue to pretend ... not to have an actual relationship.

"Hey, I had to ask," Audra said. "That kiss was hot, and you know it." She raised her hand for a high-five, and Amelia grudgingly matched it. "And you have that post-date glow, you know?"

Amelia sighed softly. "It wasn't like that," she said. But Audra was right. The kiss *was* hot. What else could she say? If it *had* been an actual date, she'd be texting photos and spilling everything by now. And Audra could offer her much-needed advice.

"You're allowed to have fun," Audra added, climbing into the passenger seat. "On another note ... I heard from Drew yesterday. Apparently, they're golfing this weekend. And he sent me a pic of his living room and some paint swatches, asking which color would make it look less like a rental. He's such a DIY nerd."

"You miss him," Amelia said as she started the engine. "A guy bestie is a cool thing. I'm glad you have each other."

"Hm..." Audra smiled faintly. "I guess I do miss him. Sometimes I think about the fun times we had in college, and the cooking shows we attended together."

* * *

Amelia let out a small breath as they merged onto the road. "I applied for the cottage loan this morning."

Audra turned to her. "Wait, seriously?"

The paperwork sat in her laptop bag, every signature reminding her she was betting on futures that might not exist. Just like the fake-dating arrangement.

"I checked out the property again," she said with a brief nod. "If I can get approval and find a contractor, it might work."

"I think that's a brilliant move. Your mom would love it out here."

"I hope I can convince her." Amelia's throat tightened. She

paused. Her employer's "investment" offer had seemed generous until she read the fine print.

"Though Mr. F-O's requirements are strict," Amelia said. "He called it an *investment*. I'm not sure I can afford all of it."

"Maybe run the numbers by Melanie; see what she thinks. She's good with that kind of stuff."

Amelia nodded, grateful for the idea, then added quietly, "Jonathan's going back to Atlanta when our project's done."

Audra looked at her, mouth turned slightly downward in empathy. "Well, at least you're getting your feet wet again. That's something."

Amelia swallowed. She wanted to tell her friend the truth. That she hadn't dipped her toe into anything, that she was faking it. That the kiss hadn't been for fun, it had been for show ... mostly.

But she nodded, pretending to agree.

They rode in silence for a while before Audra said, "You okay?"

"Yeah. I just ... there's a lot happening right now. I totally intended not to overanalyze it, but I'm not succeeding. At all." She chuckled. "I never learn."

"Don't beat yourself up about it," Audra said. "Thinking things through keeps you sane and out of trouble."

* * *

By the time Amelia dropped Audra at her apartment, unloaded the last rose bush bucket, and stepped into the empty hallway of the estate-house, she was exhausted and thoughts were spinning in her head.

After years of hating him for ghosting her, kissing Jonathan shouldn't have made her feel anything. But it had. And that alarmed her more than she wanted to admit.

Pulling out her phone, she opened the email draft she'd worked on the night before. The subject line stared back at her: *Fake-dating agreement.* The words looked clinical on the screen, nothing like the way her stomach had flipped when he'd suggested the arrangement.

She texted Jonathan to request his personal email address and he replied quickly.

He was leaving in a few months, and they had a project to complete. She had a cottage to fix and a mother to move. Moreover, her heart had already been hurt too many times.

This wasn't about playing games; this was about setting boundaries. She needed the rules, and she needed the grounding reminders, because this wasn't real. It couldn't be.

Too bad she couldn't show the contract to Melanie without getting laughed out of the room.

Amelia hesitated. What was she defending herself against? The possibility that something might become real, or the possibility that it wouldn't?

She typed Jonathan's name in the address field and pressed send before she could change her mind.

Chapter 25

Jonathan

Late Friday afternoon, Jonathan steered his rental car into the tree-lined calm of his mother's neighborhood. Atlanta sunshine filtered through dogwoods in full spring bloom as he turned onto the estate's curved drive.

The house stood serenely under a sweeping arch of magnolia trees. His mother and brother were out meeting with charity donors.

Despite the planned family weekend and impending interviews, it was easy to breathe in Atlanta. Slower.

He'd rather be at his apartment, but it was on the outskirts of town, and staying at his mother's place was more convenient for a brief family-business trip.

He parked under the carport and grabbed his phone from the console. A new text had come in.

> AMELIA: Would you give me your personal email address?

His heart skipped a beat, and his mouth tipped into another smile. There was something intimate about that ask. Maybe this wasn't entirely fake after all.

> JONATHAN: Of course. Why now?

He texted her the address.

She didn't reply right away. Then the bubble popped up.

> AMELIA: So I can send you the agreement I created last night. Rules for our fake-dating situation.

A contract? He stared at the screen, reading her message twice to make sure he'd understood correctly.

> JONATHAN: A contract??

> AMELIA: I know I said I wouldn't overthink things, but I couldn't help it. I started thinking about boundaries.

The PDF landed in his inbox moments later. Rules, terms, and conditions, all formatted with legal precision. Some made sense: keep work separate, no social media posts, no overnight stays. Others made his chest tighten in frustration.

The no-romantic-gestures-in-private clause came with a side note about avoiding mixed signals. And the honesty clause stopped him cold. If either of them developed genuine feelings, they had to disclose it and end the arrangement immediately.

His throat went dry. He leaned his head back against the headrest.

She was asking him to promise honesty about feelings while he was already hiding the fact that he had them. Not the complicated, messy, marry-you kind. Or at least, that's what he told himself. The kind that made kissing her feel like touching a live wire: electric. Yet also timelessly familiar and utterly inevitable.

He hadn't planned to fall back into anything serious with

Amelia. And she clearly didn't want that. This was her way of keeping control. Setting the limits to prevent either of them from getting hurt.

She'd drawn a line in the sand. He respected that.

He walked inside, dropped his bag in the guest room, and sat on the edge of the bed, staring at the contract again.

Through the window, he heard a neighbor's lawn mower and the distant sound of traffic. Everything felt surreal, sitting in a luxury guest room in his mother's house, reading relationship terms from the woman he'd loved but walked away from five years ago.

Could he do it? He thought of her smile at dinner, the way she'd fit against him when she stumbled at the map facility, how kissing her had felt so right.

If this contract was what Amelia needed to feel safe enough to try again, he'd take it. Rules were better than nothing.

He opened the file, clicked the signature field, and typed his name: Jonathan Fontaine.

No strings attached. Just enough closeness to remember what they'd lost. And hopefully enough boundaries to keep from losing it again.

His phone buzzed with another text.

> DREW: How are things at your mother's place? Please tell me you're not brooding with a scotch.

> JONATHAN: Info not for sharing—I just signed a fake-dating contract. Your move.

Three dots appeared immediately.

> DREW: I take it back. Brood away.

Chapter 26

Jonathan

JONATHAN STOOD at the counter slicing zucchini into uniform half-moons with a rhythmic motion of the knife against the cutting board. Lemon zest and oregano fragrances filled the kitchen.

Tomorrow's magazine interview had necessitated this family gathering. Edge Global Today planned to feature Charlotte Fontaine's design empire in next month's magazine edition, and she'd insisted all three children be included in the photos.

A skillet hissed on the stove while Brandon flipped chicken thighs with indifferent precision, his soft gray shirt sleeves pushed to his elbows. Behind him, their mother, Charlotte, uncorked a bottle of wine with a quiet pop and moved with her usual serene command. She set the table with linen napkins and pale ceramic plates she'd designed herself.

The house reflected her style, sleek and modern, with neutral tones, rich accents, and organic textures. The space looked staged, yet lived in. A wall of windows overlooked the lawn, where pink and white azaleas bloomed beneath a stand of pines.

His mother moved from stovetop to table as though she were

hosting a gala instead of a casual dinner. She wore a flowing green scarf with matching earrings and a fitted brown jacket over wide-leg pants. Charlotte Fontaine was always composed and intentional. Stylish even when there were no guests to impress.

"Mother's been rearranging furniture all week. You know how she gets when the press comes calling," Brandon said as he handed Jonathan a bowl for vegetables. "Glad to be back?"

Jonathan shrugged. "Yeah. Good to escape the rain and the chill for the weekend. And the townhome they assigned me? It's a drab, monochrome nightmare. I'm considering taking a few small paintings from the studio storage to spruce it up."

Charlotte smiled without looking up. "Take whatever speaks to you, darling," she said. "Oh, and I also added some new pottery to the studio last month. The new sage pieces would be perfect. There's nothing worse than beige walls sucking the life out of a room."

Jonathan nodded, tossing the zucchini with olive oil.

He wondered what Amelia would think of his mother's art collection. She'd probably have pointed questions about the glazing or clay composition. The thought made him smile, then pause. When had he started wanting to share random details of his life with her again?

A few weeks ago, all he'd wanted was to wrap the project and return home. Now that he was enjoying Amelia's company, he wasn't so sure.

Huh. The awareness surprised him.

"Don't get too comfortable in Washington," Brandon said as he checked the oven.

"Eh, not a chance in hell," Jonathan scoffed. "Besides, I wouldn't get to beat you at golf so often."

"In your wildest dreams."

"Give it time," Jonathan said. "Eventually you'll win one—maybe in about thirty years."

The amiable tone didn't quite cover the tension between the brothers.

Brandon made no secret of the fact that he wanted Jonathan to take over his role in the charity organization sooner than they'd agreed. Much sooner. They'd quarreled about the timeline more often than Jonathan cared to admit.

Brandon set down his wine glass. "Speaking of timing, the board wants to know your transition plans. I told them you're reconsidering."

Jonathan tensed. "What? I'm absolutely *not* reconsidering. We've discussed this. My commitment to Washington is for two more months, and our original agreement on when I would join Form to Function wasn't until another two years from now."

Then again, maybe he should get comfortable in Rainmere and put a bigger wrench in Brandon's transition plans.

Charlotte turned from the prep counter. "Jonathan, how's Paige?"

He kept his focus on the vegetables. "Let's talk about that later."

She didn't press, and the conversation shifted.

They moved into the dining room, Charlotte at the head of the table. She passed the open wine bottle to Brandon, who filled their glasses.

The meal started with shared dishes passed around the table: roasted vegetables, lemon-herb chicken, and rice with almonds. The simple, elegant food Charlotte preferred.

"I know asking you to come home for the interview and photo shoot was short notice," Charlotte began, "but having the family in the photos was nonnegotiable for me. The magazine wants to showcase the personal side of the business. How design runs in our blood."

Jonathan sighed. Here he was, about to be photographed as the perfect family man for a national magazine, while the only woman he'd ever truly wanted to build a family with was three thousand miles away, bound to him only by a fake-dating contract that felt more real than anything else in his life right now.

"But I also want to hear your thoughts about something more important than the latest color palettes," Charlotte continued. "I'm contemplating purchasing properties to expand the business. I think it's time to consider expanding the geographic footprint of Studio Charlotti. Maybe to Europe or perhaps Asia." She paused, swirling her wine thoughtfully. "Brandon mentioned the Pacific Northwest tech market has potential; Jessica's been fielding inquiries from Seattle and Portland clients. I want both of your perspectives, not just as professionals, but as family."

Jonathan took a sip of wine. "Shouldn't Jessica be involved in this kind of conversation?"

Charlotte's expression tightened. "She's visiting friends in Seattle. At least, that's what she told me." She leaned back in her chair. "But I think she's looking at graduate programs. She's been hinting about stepping away from the business to pursue an MBA."

Jonathan set down his fork. "Seattle? She didn't reach out to me."

"She provided her input before she left," Brandon added. "And visited the photographer for photos."

"Convenient timing for her trip," Jonathan muttered.

Brandon gave him an annoyed look. "Come on. She's allowed to make her own choices about *her* relationships."

Jonathan didn't answer. He couldn't bring himself to explain why her decision to contact Roger still bothered him.

Charlotte sighed. "I know things between the two of you are

strained," she said to Jonathan. "But she's still your sister, and I don't begrudge her desire to reconcile with her father. I'm no longer angry with Roger. I warned her that your father might not be open to a relationship going forward, but I don't object to her trying. At some point, to keep myself sane, I had to let the hurt of his abandonment go." She straightened the silverware beside her plate. "I hope you'll reconcile with Jessica," she said without looking up from her task.

Jonathan nodded slowly, turning the wine in his glass. He understood his mother's position. Charlotte had found her peace with Roger's abandonment years ago. But forgiveness wasn't on his agenda. Not when he still remembered Jessica's tears the night their father left and how she'd made Jonathan promise they'd always stick together.

He pushed back his plate, his appetite gone.

"I'll reach out to her," he said finally. "Do you have her itinerary?"

Charlotte's eyes softened. "She's not due back for a week. I still have the address where she's staying with her friends."

He nodded. "Good. I can try to catch up with her while she's still in Seattle."

He leaned back in his chair and let his shoulders sink. His mother was right. And Amelia was right. He needed to talk to Jessica and to fix what had gone so wrong between them.

They finished the meal with quiet clinking of forks and casual conversation. Talk turned to the magazine shoot, the opportunities to expand the business footprint, and Brandon's arrangements for the charity organization's upcoming events.

* * *

Later that night, after Brandon and Charlotte were already in

154

bed and the house had gone quiet again, a car door slammed in the driveway.

A few minutes later, Jonathan greeted Melanie at the door. She had a black roller bag and wore a tired expression. Jonathan let her in and led her through a long side hallway.

"This place is huge and gorgeous," she said, as he led her out to the guest suite. The private apartment had its own entrance, sitting room, and oversized bathroom. Charlotte did nothing halfway.

"Thank you for the room. I'm sorry I haven't seemed more appreciative, but I am," Melanie said.

She studied his face. "You look distracted. Everything okay?"

"Just family stuff. The magazine interview tomorrow has everyone on edge."

"That's not it." She tilted her head. "You've got that look, like when someone's working through a problem they can't solve."

Jonathan hesitated. Scary how right she was.

"Would you like something to eat?" he said, redirecting the conversation.

"I'll pass, thanks. Travel is exhausting. I'm going to call it a night and go straight to sleep," she said. "See you in the morning. But not early."

Jonathan chuckled with a slight nod. "My brother, mother, and I have midday interviews here at the house with a magazine reporter. Afterward, there's a photo shoot in the gardens. If we're occupied when you get up, help yourself to breakfast and make yourself at home."

As he walked back through the house, his mind cycled through tomorrow's obligations. Between the magazine interview and family commitments, he'd need to carve out time to check in with Steve about the Career Recovery Program. The other participating companies were waiting on Whitlow's framework revisions, and with less than six months until launch, he couldn't risk any deadline slippage.

He climbed the stairs, and his thoughts drifted to Amelia's terms-and-conditions contract. He let out a short, amused breath. *Tsk.*

He considered texting her to playfully tease her a bit about all the rules, or perhaps to simply say goodnight.

He picked up his phone again and typed *Hope you're having a good weekend,* then deleted it. Then typed *Thinking of you* and deleted that too.

But the obvious was becoming impossible to ignore. He wasn't just missing her company. He was missing her.

Chapter 27

Jonathan

Saturday, midmorning.

JONATHAN SET his coffee cup on the patio table and sat next to Brandon and his mother, knowing he couldn't postpone the conversation any longer. He'd have to tell them about Paige eventually.

A noisy blue jay squawked a warning from a nearby tree.

He'd rehearsed this conversation about Paige during the flight from Seattle, but now, facing his family's expectations about his personal life, the words felt inadequate.

"Brandon and I had a discussion about various regional markets," Jonathan said. "We both agree that expanding the design business's geographic reach makes sense. It would be a heavy outlay of cash, but the year-over-year profit supports the investment."

Charlotte nodded slowly. "Yes. Brandon and I ran preliminary numbers at the end of the last quarter, before I began thinking seriously about new locations."

"Your global clientele has grown rapidly," Jonathan continued, "especially in the European market. Alternatively, establishing an office in Asia could be a stepping stone to increasing your visibility there."

"London or Berlin, perhaps," Charlotte said. "Or maybe Singapore, or Hong Kong. I'm also continuing to research West Coast locations."

"What about San Francisco or Vancouver?" Brandon said.

"Also good choices. Both are on the list of possibilities," Charlotte replied.

The discussion moved toward the benefits of the various cities, the strength of the industry opportunities, and the ease of setting up offices in various locations.

"I heard a knock at the front door late last night," Charlotte said to Jonathan. "I assume your guest arrived?"

He nodded. "Mmm. It was close to midnight. I expect we won't see her until later."

"So, Jonathan," she said, "how are things going in Seattle?"

"We're getting things done, and the team is great. That said, we're dealing with more assets than we knew about going in, and unless we get more hands or convince management to limit the number of assets, we're going to run into time constraints." He paused. "But we're doing what we can."

"Speaking of the team..." Jonathan hesitated. "I don't know if you remember the woman I dated while I was in grad school, Amelia Preston. Right now, she's at the Rainmere office, and she's the geologist assigned from NorthSound."

"Mm, I remember you talking about her. You were fairly serious about her. Interesting ... coincidence?" Charlotte said.

"Mostly a coincidence. I barely found out she was there before I accepted the assignment."

Brandon frowned. "Working with an ex-girlfriend sounds like a terrible idea."

"I broke up with her when the university investigation began. So, yeah, she hated my guts after, and the first month on the project was rocky. We're talking now, though, and her eyes aren't shooting laser rays at me anymore. Things are improving." Though not in the way he'd expected. His mouth tipped into the start of a smile.

He poured himself a second cup of coffee from the carafe on the table. "About Paige…" Now he was relieved he'd never revealed that Paige had proposed to him.

Brandon perked up. "Are you finally going to get married? Having a married couple at the head of the charity organization would have a lot of benefits. It shows reliability and maturity. The donors would love the look."

Brandon was excruciatingly relentless.

"Stop with the pressure," Jonathan said firmly. He'd made his position on the transition plan crystal clear multiple times already. "Two more years before I take over, Brandon. Not a second before. That's what we agreed. And no, Paige and I are done. I ended it."

He'd planned those two years carefully. Time for him to finish recovering his professional standing outside the family name, to prove he could succeed on his own merits before stepping into the role Brandon seemed so eager to escape.

"What happened?" Brandon said. "You seemed perfectly content together. She's beautiful, and her family connections in this town would lead you everywhere. Seriously, everywhere."

Oh, for fuck's sake.

"What about you? You could get married. The donors would love it just as much," Jonathan said.

Brandon held up his hands and plastered on a sly grin. "Ah, no. I've always said I'm a self-proclaimed bachelor for life. Besides, I'm thinking about…" He paused, seeming to catch himself. "I'm completely dedicated to making the donors' investments worthwhile. For now."

"Well, I, for one, am glad it's over between you," Charlotte said to Jonathan.

Brandon shook his head in disgust. "You're making a mistake, Jonathan. Paige was perfect for this life, for what the Form to Function Fund needs."

"There are more important things to consider than family connections, and you need something beyond 'perfectly content' to sustain and grow a marriage," Charlotte said. She sighed quietly. "I should know. I spent years trying to convince myself that shared social circles and family approval were enough to sustain a marriage. They're not. You need genuine connection, not just convenience."

He hadn't expected her full support right away, but he should have realized she would understand.

Brandon scowled and set down his coffee mug. "Back up and rewind to the part about you working with your ex-girl-friend. The split with Paige isn't about getting back with your ex, is it? You can't throw everything away for someone on the other side of the country."

It definitely wasn't just about Amelia.

"No. I should have broken up with Paige months ago."

"You deserve to be happy. I'm in favor of your seeing Amelia again, if that's what you want to do," Charlotte said.

"It's not like that," Jonathan said.

How could he explain their arrangement without betraying Amelia's trust? The fake-dating contract suddenly felt more complicated. What should he say? He had no intention of lying to his family about his circumstances with Amelia, nor did he care to explain their faux arrangement.

"We're getting to know each other again by clearing up the past," he said. "That's all." Shades of truth and a lie by omission, but it was the closest thing to the truth he could admit to them.

Charlotte smiled briefly and tilted her head in approval. "Sounds like a good place to begin."

Brandon turned toward his mother. "How could you possibly be in favor of this? We need him to stay here and take over running the charity. She lives on the other side of the country."

She studied Brandon with the acute attention she usually reserved for fabric samples.

"You *want* him here," she said flatly. "Besides, you're doing a fantastic job heading the charity organization." Charlotte clicked off her tablet. "The reporter will be here in less than an hour."

Brandon leaned forward, his casual demeanor dropping.

"We need you here, Jonathan," he said again. "The organization needs leadership continuity, and I need..." He stopped himself again. "The timing is more critical than you understand."

A clatter from inside the house interrupted the conversation.

"What was that?" Charlotte said.

Jonathan and Brandon exchanged glances before heading toward the kitchen door to investigate.

Inside, they found Melanie crouched down, searching a lower cabinet, her brunette hair falling forward, partially hiding her face. She looked up sharply when they entered, her blue eyes already narrowed with determination.

"Melanie?" Jonathan said.

Brandon stepped out from behind Jonathan. When no one immediately spoke, he extended his hand to greet the newcomer. "I'm Brandon."

Melanie slowly straightened, weighing what Jonathan assumed she'd overheard. Her gaze fixed first on Brandon, then swept to Jonathan.

Melanie turned back to Brandon and briefly scrutinized his offered hand before finally shaking it. "Melanie Foxx," she said with a note of dissatisfaction.

"How long were you standing there?" Jonathan said slowly.

Melanie shrugged. "A few minutes." Her gaze fixed on Brandon and swept down then up, decisively measuring him. "Long enough to hear your brother isn't an Amelia supporter."

She narrowed her eyes at Brandon. "Let's get something straight," she said. "I'm her extremely loyal friend, and your characterization of the situation is completely unfair. They just went on a first—"

"Melanie, why don't you join us?" Jonathan said hurriedly as he motioned toward the patio table. "I'll introduce you to our mother."

Leaving Brandon behind, she followed Jonathan out to the patio. He briefly introduced her.

"Welcome, and nice to meet you," Charlotte said as she got up from her chair. "Please excuse me, I need to go freshen up before the reporter arrives."

Once they were alone, Melanie took a seat at the table. "Just talking and clearing up the past? What was that?" she asked, then whispered, "I *saw the kiss*, Jonathan. It was a lot more than just talking. Do you have genuine feelings for her? Or are you playing games and stringing her along?"

He needed to keep from digging a deeper hole. And he needed to keep up his end of the bargain with Amelia.

"I'm not playing games. And you're right; it was a lot more than just talking. I ... have feelings for her." He'd always had feelings for her, and not getting too involved was getting harder by the moment. "But it was just a first date." *A pseudo-date*, he reminded himself. "Amelia and I need our space to figure out what's next. I don't want my family getting all worked up about it."

He also needed to keep himself from getting too worked up about it.

Melanie paused, as if considering her position on the matter.

"I believe you," she said finally, "and I can appreciate your perspective after a first date. It's a relief to know you're not deceiving her." Then she narrowed her eyes slightly. "However, if you hurt her because you're not sure what you want, I'll make sure you regret it. Amelia deserves someone who's all in, not someone who's merely managing family expectations."

Warning received.

Chapter 28

Amelia

Saturday afternoon.

AFTER BREAKFAST, Amelia met with the bathroom renovation contractor to review her boss's choices for the upcoming renovations. Once the contractor had started his work, she spent the late morning and a few hours after lunch cataloging the library for Mr. F-O.

Finally, late in the afternoon, when the contractor had gone and the house was quiet again, she stole a few minutes to herself in the living room to read. Curled on the cool leather couch, she spread a blanket over her legs and opened Rebecca's journal.

18 February 1852

The rain has not ceased for nine days now, and our stores of dried corn are nearly gone. Thomas walked three miles through the mud to the Fletcher place yesterday, hoping to trade carpentry work for food, but they have little to spare. Mrs. Fletcher gave him what she could: a small sack of meal and some turnips from her root cellar.

Liza fusses with hunger, and baby Mary cries through the night. I made a thin soup from the turnips and what remained of our salt pork, stretching it as far as I could. We survive on hope and the promise that spring will bring new settlers who need homes built.

A wave of shame swept over Amelia. Things in Rebecca's journal were so substantial and vivid. There were no secrets or fake arrangements. Rebecca and Thomas had simply been trying to survive through harsh realities.

Her phone buzzed with a text from the group chat. Amelia closed the journal and set it on the coffee table.

AUDRA: Hey, I'm trying a new recipe for ice cream. What do you think of adding blueberry flavoring?

AMELIA: I think I need to be a taste tester.

AUDRA: How's it going with your mom? Convinced her to move yet?

AMELIA: Not yet. I talked to her last night. She's having a minor outpatient procedure in a few days. I know it's not a big deal, but I still worry about her.

Amelia had reviewed the medical summary her mom had sent. Warnings and recovery instructions, routine stuff mostly. But one detail had caught her eye in her mom's medical history: *two live births.*

When she asked about it, her mom had brushed it aside. "You know those intake forms. They're always a mess. I'll correct it at my next appointment."

Amelia had always lamented that she was an only child. She

hadn't pressed her mom about making sure the forms were accurate, but she flagged the file for follow-up.

AUDRA: Is she doing okay?

AMELIA: Yeah, nothing too serious. Some kind of enzyme therapy. I'm her emergency contact, so I'll know if anything changes.

Her mom had suggested Amelia get tested too, just to be safe. Another item on her growing summer to-do list.

AUDRA: Hope everything goes well.

AMELIA: Me too. I floated the idea of scaling back or shifting to more remote work to transition to Rainmere. She said she enjoys being busy, that it gives her purpose. Though I think she's less busy now that she's losing students. She assured me she'd figure out her problems on her own.

AUDRA: 😂 You're just like your mother.

AMELIA: I guess so. <sigh>

Amelia's stomach grumbled. She grabbed honey-roasted peanuts, a banana, and iced tea from the kitchen before returning to the couch.

MELANIE: Sorry, just now checking my phone. Been busy with work emails.

AUDRA: You know it's Saturday, right?? I'm always counting down the minutes until I can ditch the lab after a long week.

MELANIE: Stuck here for two extra days. More meetings than expected.

AMELIA: Good news. Well, sort of. My loan came through, but it's a lot less than I'd hoped. I'm worried about affording a decent contractor.

MELANIE: My god, Amelia. Did you know the Fontaine house is HUGE? And gorgeous. The family is being interviewed today for a design magazine spotlight.

AMELIA: I know his mother has money.

Because a con man posing as a suitor had once defrauded her mother, Amelia was always suspicious of a man who seemed wealthy. Was he truly rich, or was he pretending? So when she'd met Jonathan in college, his family's money was something she'd learned to cautiously accept. A man with no money was a red flag for most women, but for Amelia it was the opposite.

MELANIE: So, do you and Jonathan have plans for another date? When you came to pick up the truck, I was too busy packing to ask about it.

Amelia cringed.

AUDRA: I'm dying to know the answer to that, too!

AMELIA: We just had our first date. That's all. Is this another go-round at pitching Leo?

MELANIE: No, nothing like that. The thing is, I overheard Jonathan talking with his family. He wasn't being entirely open with them about you, and I may or may not have cornered him and asked about his motives. Oops. Probably shouldn't have done it, but not really sorry. The lawyer instinct in me took over.

AMELIA: What did he say to his family about me?

She crunched a few sweet and salty peanuts, followed by a bite of banana, and chased it with a swig of her tea.

MELANIE: I only heard part of the conversation. There was something about Jonathan's ex and some talk about the NorthSound office and how he'd met you again.

Amelia waited as the bubbles from Melanie's typing lingered on the screen.

MELANIE: He admitted he has feelings for you.

Amelia's stomach dropped. If Jonathan actually had feelings, their carefully constructed agreement was already falling apart. The whole point of the contract was to prevent exactly this situation.

What should she do? And what kind of "feelings" would be enough to warrant calling off the fake relationship? She wiped her hands with a napkin and pushed the empty bowl aside.

AMELIA: He said that?? Are you sure?

AUDRA: That sounds like a little more than just having fun.

MELANIE: Yes, I'm sure. The worst part is Jonathan's brother wants him to stay in Atlanta to run the family charity fund. So Brandon tried squashing the idea of Jonathan dating you. I don't like his selfish attitude.

Huh. Amelia slumped back into the couch cushions with a groan and tilted her head back to stare at the ceiling. He probably only said he had feelings because Melanie asked, and he was simply holding up his end of the agreement.

Her lips tightened. If she were in his shoes, she certainly wouldn't want to complicate matters by explaining the situation to her own mother.

Her phone buzzed again.

MELANIE: Every time I turn a corner in this house, there's Brandon. Like he knows exactly where I'm going to be. It's so annoying. And his confident, lazy charm completely irritates me.

AUDRA: What is happening? You're usually the calm and collected one.

MELANIE: I know, right? I just can't maintain my composure around him. It's like I've entered the Twilight Zone. 😳

AUDRA: Whoa, this is a first. A guy who unnerves Melanie is a guy I definitely want to meet! Sounds like Jason might have some competition.

MELANIE: Ugh. Don't get any ideas. Jason has nothing to worry about. Brandon Fontaine will soon be nothing but a distant memory in my rearview mirror.

Amelia sighed. The same was true for her and Jonathan. Even if they might have reignited some deeply buried emotional thing from the past, which she wasn't ready for, they lived on opposite sides of the country and both had job and family obligations. They'd be parting ways soon enough.

Which was exactly why the contract was so important—why she needed those boundaries. Either Jonathan was lying to Melanie to maintain their cover story, or he was violating the contract by keeping actual feelings secret.

She opened the text conversation with him and smiled softly at his message from last night.

JONATHAN: Sleep well, Contract Partner. We've got more fake magic to sell next week. And for what it's worth, it was the best fake date of my life.

She began typing. *Ding.*
Amelia inhaled a sharp breath of surprise.

JONATHAN: Melanie asked me a lot of questions today about you and me. I held up my end of the bargain.

AMELIA: How much truth did you give her?

JONATHAN: Enough to keep her guessing and not enough to get us in trouble.

Ugh. So much for irrefutable proof.

AMELIA: Did you tell her you have feelings
for me?

Three dots appeared. Several minutes passed before he finally sent a reply.

JONATHAN: I'd be lying if I denied it.

AMELIA: But did you mean it?

JONATHAN: I meant every word I said to
Melanie.

Chapter 29

Jonathan

Sunday. April 1.

AFTER HIS MORNING shower and shave, Jonathan dressed in
shorts and a light shirt for a day of golf. The interview yesterday
had gotten awkward when he'd accidentally contradicted Brandon's timeline for the charity handover, leaving both of them
irritated. Everything else had gone smoothly, so his mother was
pleased.

From the bedroom closet, he retrieved his sports bag he'd
brought with him. The duffel already held the essentials, all
neatly packed. His golfing shoes, a visor, a tube of sunscreen,
and a pair of clean socks for post-game wear. Still, he double-
checked the contents before he zipped the bag securely shut.

In the kitchen, he scarfed down a bowl of cereal, pushed
start on the coffeemaker, then packed protein bars and two
barely ripe bananas into his duffel.

Next, he loaded a cooler with beer and water. He added a
few energy drinks for good measure, topped it with ice, and
closed the lid.

What was Amelia doing this morning? It was still early on

the West Coast. He doubted whether she was even awake yet. He felt his pocket. Shit. He'd left his phone in his bedroom.

He hurried up the staircase, grabbed his phone from the dresser, and paused. He had another half hour before Drew would show up, so there was time for a brief distraction.

The contract didn't mention texting or pet names. Thank goodness for small favors. He smiled to himself as he changed Amelia's contact name to My Favorite Clause.

> JONATHAN: Good morning. Was wondering, have you started looking for a contractor yet?

He scheduled the message to send later, then hit send.

She hadn't mentioned whether the loan had come in, and he'd been thinking about it as he drifted to sleep last night. DIY Drew might agree to help a long-time friend caught in a bind.

As Jonathan started down the stairs again, tense voices drifted upward from somewhere below. The library door stood ajar. He couldn't make out all the details, but the voices conveyed stress.

A moment later he knew. The muffled voices were Brandon and Melanie. *Odd they're together.* Jonathan paused on the landing. And what were they having a disagreement about?

"You seem to object to every comment I make," Brandon said.

"Amelia is one of my closest friends," Melanie said. Her voice carried something akin to a warning. "And your motives are selfish..."

"...I have a right to be concerned," Brandon said.

Jonathan could only hear pieces of their conversation.

"Oh, no. Don't you dare try to convince me you're against them seeing each other for purely altruistic reasons," Melanie said. "I heard..."

"Fine. I want him running Form to Function, and yes, I see

you both as obstacles. But that's not why I'm against this. He's my brother ... you have no idea how hard he hit rock-bottom when she married someone else."

Jonathan scowled. He shouldn't be listening to this, but he stood transfixed.

"Fine. We can keep our disagreement under wraps," she said. "For the sake of Jonathan and Amelia. It doesn't mean I approve of your position or your attempts to keep them apart. And it won't keep me from supporting Amelia, in whatever capacity she sees Jonathan. And if you try to break them up, I'm definitely your obstacle."

His shoulders stiffened as he continued downward. So, Brandon was actively working against him. But Jonathan hadn't realized Brandon understood how completely Amelia's marriage had destroyed him.

Amelia had a solid friendship in Melanie. And his brother wasn't being a complete asshole about the situation with Amelia.

The front doorbell rang, giving Jonathan an excuse to pass by the library without entering.

He opened the door and let Drew inside. Moments later, Brandon and Melanie joined them in the foyer.

As Drew set down his bag of clubs, Jonathan introduced Melanie and Drew.

"Drew Slater," Jonathan said. "My best friend since college."

"Drew Slater." Recognition lit Melanie's eyes. "You're Audra's contractor friend."

Drew nodded and they shook hands. A grin spread across his face. "Audra talks about me?"

Melanie casually picked up her purse from the hook beside the door and turned toward Jonathan. "My rideshare just showed up. See you all later."

Apparently, she was looking for an escape hatch.

She reached to open the door, but Brandon had already opened it for her.

"Thanks," she muttered.

As soon as Melanie left, Jonathan confronted Brandon. "What the hell were you and Melanie discussing? She's been here for less than twenty-four hours. She's our *guest*."

"Nothing that won't resolve itself," he said dismissively. "I'll handle Melanie differently in the future." He disappeared toward the kitchen.

"I've been dying to ask," Drew said. "You said you asked Amelia out? How did that turn out? And you have to tell me about the dating contract."

Drew was astute, not to mention super nosy. Despite occasional attempts, Jonathan had never succeeded in hiding anything from him.

"We had a casual dinner and hung out together. I told her all about the case and why things went down the way they did. It felt good to set the record straight."

It was the truth. Though he was skating a thin line between the facts and the fake-relationship reality.

Drew's mouth twisted. "And?"

"And ... we had a good time." He wasn't about to mention the knockout kiss that he kept reliving in precise detail. Or his desire to try it again. *Contract partner*, he reminded himself.

"And ... the contract?" Drew was nothing if not persistent.

"Boundaries she needs to be comfortable," Jonathan replied. "And I agree with her."

Drew shouldered his golf bag, still studying Jonathan expectantly.

The details Drew wanted could wait. Jonathan wanted to steer the conversation toward the cottage renovations. Drew would probably lecture him about getting too involved, but he might also jump at the chance to see Audra.

Jonathan bit his lip, then inhaled a deep breath. "I'd like to call in a favor. Cottage repairs."

"Huh. Okay, I'm listening." Drew set his bag down again and shifted his weight. He seemed genuinely curious.

"To make a long story short," Jonathan said, "Amelia needs a reliable contractor to fix the roof on a place she's considering investing in and renting."

"Why not hire someone in Washington?" Drew asked.

"She's worried about affording the repairs, even with a loan," Jonathan said. "It's hard to find a good contractor right now. I need to run the plan by Amelia. But I'd like to know if you're in first."

"I enjoy helping. And getting to spend some time with Audra is a big draw. I could arrange some vacation time. But there's something else I want to discuss first."

Drew's expression turned neutral. "Your dinner was casual," he said. "But your feelings for Amelia in college were not casual at all. And I know you don't like to call in favors." A knowing look crossed his face.

"We have a friendly arrangement," Jonathan said.

"Look, I want to help." Drew studied his face. "But an arrangement? What happens when your project ends?"

Jonathan blinked twice. *T minus two months.* What if ... he *didn't* come back to Atlanta? He shook off the thought and grabbed his duffel bag from the side table.

Brandon reappeared, carrying the cooler Jonathan had filled earlier. "When his project is over, he'll come back from Rainmere, and he'll start learning how to run the family charity organization," Brandon said. "Now, let's go!"

Jonathan's grip tightened on his duffel bag. Two months suddenly felt like no time at all.

Chapter 30

Jonathan

Sunday evening.

Jonathan trailed behind the others into the living room, carrying two wine glasses by the stem.

Melanie had already wandered to the sideboard near the window, where one of Charlotte's lacquered trays sat, its contents perfectly arranged with a stack of coasters, a small vase of peach-colored roses, and a brass monocular.

"Before I forget," Melanie said, turning toward Charlotte, "thank you both for having me this weekend. And for allowing me to extend my stay a few more days. Your home is stunning, and dinner last night was fabulous."

Charlotte nodded graciously. "You're welcome anytime."

Jonathan felt a pulse of anticipation at the reminder. After three days back in Atlanta, he'd return to Washington and to Amelia and the contract they'd signed.

Melanie leaned in and gently picked up the monocular. "This is beautiful. Is it vintage?"

Charlotte looked up from her seat, where she was folding a napkin with sharp corners. "It is. Morocco, 1963."

Melanie turned the monocular over in her hands. "It's heavy. Functional or just decorative?"

"Both." Charlotte stood and crossed to the tray, her heels quiet against the rug. "My grandfather gave it to me when I was a girl. Said it would help me see clearly and know where I was going. Things aren't always what they seem. People, especially."

Jonathan exchanged a glance with Brandon, both of them surprised by the admission.

Melanie raised an eyebrow. "Did it work?"

Charlotte's smile was faint but sincere. "It taught me to ask better questions."

Melanie handed it back gently. "You don't strike me as sentimental."

"I'm not," Charlotte said. Then, after a pause, she added, "But I believe certain objects hold memory."

Jonathan watched his mother's fingers rest briefly on the monocular before she turned away, already smoothing the fabric of a nearby pillow. The moment felt like something she'd allowed them to see rather than something that had slipped out.

Brandon caught his eye, mouthing, wow. Jonathan nodded slightly. They'd both learned early that Charlotte shared her vulnerabilities in small, carefully curated doses.

He was still thinking about the look on her face, about objects holding memory. What memories would he and Amelia hold on to, he wondered, once their arrangement ended?

Chapter 31

Amelia

AMELIA TWISTED her damp hair into a loose bun and shuffled across her bedroom. The spring evening air carried a chill through the open window.

She closed the window and sank onto the edge of her bed. Monday was finally over after she'd put in a twelve-hour day at work, which was miserable after working extra hours Sunday after Lydia's assignment landed that morning. The longest day had barely ended, and already Tuesday loomed with Lydia's impossible deadline.

Her boss's demand for a comprehensive report festered in her mind. A presentation, too, as if the written torture wasn't enough.

Jonathan was visiting family for a long weekend while she and the technicians drowned in work. He'd requested more staff last week, but the request had been denied, of course. Her lunchtime texts to him about the report sat unanswered.

He was probably en route home. She rubbed her temples, attempting to relieve the headache brewing behind her eyes.

Her laptop screen glowed across the rumpled bedding. She opened the spreadsheet titled *Jewell Mansion Projects* and scrolled through the completed items. Kitchen renovations, attic cleanup, bathroom selections—all progressing on schedule.

Her phone pinged.

> MR F-O: See email. I sent you a revised list for April.

Amelia's heart sank. She clicked open the message and scanned the contents. Three new items, and each one was massive. Hardwood floor refinishing. Interior paint coordination. Chandelier replacements.

She clicked on his links to European chandelier makers. Ornate fixtures with price tags that made her cringe. Direct from Germany, naturally. What the heck was a "Baroque-inspired contemporary aesthetic," anyway?

She slammed the laptop lid shut. "You've got to be kidding me." The man's tasks had crossed from demanding to delusional.

She pulled back the covers and slipped between the bedsheets. Inside, the house was silent, while the wind whistled outside and tree branches brushed against the siding.

Most days, she appreciated the solitude and freedom to work without interruption. But tonight she wished for more than texts and emails, someone to talk to about her day, someone to curl up with.

Sleep wouldn't come. She flipped her pillow. Still uncomfortable.

Relax.

Her thoughts drifted to what Melanie had said. Jonathan had mentioned to his family that he still liked her. Then the memory of their kiss surfaced, the warmth of his hand at the small of her back, his lips pressed against hers.

She rolled over, switched on the table lamp, and reached for

Rebecca's journal. Maybe losing herself in someone else's century-old problems would quiet her racing thoughts.

She flipped to where she'd left off: February 1852. Rebecca's family was starving, their farm failing, and all they had left was hope that spring might change things. Amelia closed the journal. On second thought, Rebecca's struggles felt too heavy tonight. She couldn't take on someone else's worries, not when her own thoughts were spinning.

She grabbed her novel instead, a lighthearted rom-com that would help her escape. She'd been on the same chapter for three days. When she reached the bottom of the page, she hadn't absorbed a single sentence. With a sigh, she flipped back and started again.

After a second attempt, she closed the book and stared at the ceiling.

Frustration with Jonathan hit clearly and immediately. So convenient, disappearing when work exploded. Confessing feelings to his family instead of her. What happened to keeping things casual?

The irritation burned for exactly thirty seconds before sensibility kicked in.

She wasn't mad at Jonathan. She was mad at herself. No buffer time built into her schedule. No anticipation of increased workloads. She'd deliberately packed every hour to avoid thinking about personal complications.

To avoid getting involved with anyone.

Amelia turned onto her side, pulling the sheet up around her shoulders. And the worst part was that she couldn't cut any of it from her life. She was relying on the asset project's success to transition from a contractor to a full-time employee with benefits. Additionally, she needed to keep Mr. F-O satisfied to secure three years of significantly reduced rent. And her work-life balance was completely out of whack.

She needed a different approach.

Tomorrow, she'd corner Jonathan about staffing. His job as lead meant fighting management for more people. And the Amherst project had extra staff that could be reallocated. It wouldn't help with the immediate presentation crunch, but it would help with the workload going forward.

Also, Mr. F-O would hear some truth from her. His expectations weren't just unrealistic; they were impossible. He needed to prioritize projects or accept that his timeline wasn't workable.

Yes, tomorrow would be different. She would take control of her situation.

She smoothed the thick comforter with her palm. Maybe her mom had been right all along. She should have built in more personal time. Time to accommodate the unexpected. Time for herself ... and for Jonathan?

No, that wasn't the issue. She'd set clear boundaries for good reason.

But as sleep pulled her under, one thought refused to disappear. The more time she spent with Jonathan, the harder those boundaries would be to maintain.

And that worried her more than any impossible deadline.

Chapter 32

Jonathan

JONATHAN PULLED into the townhome's driveway just after ten, his body tired from the long travel. Crickets chirped softly in the trees. Somewhere far away, an owl hooted as he grabbed his flight bag and the wrapped artwork he'd chosen from his mother's studio.

A rustling sound from the bushes by the front door caught his attention, followed by a thin cry. Jonathan paused, listening. It was probably a raccoon or maybe a fox. A note from the landlord had warned that the area had its share of backyard wildlife drama.

He unlocked the front door of the townhome and pushed it open with his shoulder. Inside, the townhome felt as vacant as he'd left it. No personal touches on the walls or surfaces.

He hung Charlotte's watercolor of Georgia clay and pines in the bedroom and the Lake Lanier sunset oil in the living room. Then he set a piece of Charlotte's sage-colored pottery on the coffee table.

Next came the photos. He set his mother's fiftieth birthday party picture on a side table next to the one with Jessica with her arm slung around Jonathan at her graduation. Then he added Brandon's dog, Poppy, lazing on the porch swing. The family photo by a lake, he placed on his nightstand. Small fragments of his real life in this temporary space.

The crying grew louder, filtering through an open window near the front door. The sound cut through his thoughts. He checked his watch: almost eleven. He should shower and prepare for tomorrow's meetings, not investigate whatever was unfolding outside.

But the crying continued, more insistent. He moved to the window and pushed it fully open. Rustling followed by what sounded like scratching. Definitely an animal, and it didn't sound like raccoons anymore. This was smaller. More vulnerable.

The owl called again, closer now.

"Damn it." He grabbed his phone and headed back outside.

The night had grown cold. Stars scattered across the darkness with a clarity Atlanta's light pollution rarely allowed.

He switched on the phone flashlight, crouched beside the bushes, and pushed aside the lowest branches, directing his light toward the sound.

The beam reflected tiny eyes blinking back at him. Then a second pair.

His breath caught in his throat.

Kittens. Two of them, small and huddled together in the cold dirt. Too young to survive alone. No mother cat in sight.

Jonathan sat back on his heels. His no-pets lease, his 7 a.m. meeting, the fact that he had no supplies and no idea what to do with young kittens at eleven o'clock at night—none of that mattered when another pitiful mew cut through the darkness.

He reached into the bushes.

Chapter 33

Amelia

Tuesday.

AMELIA CLICKED SHUT the pen she'd been using. Midmorning sun streamed through the windows, covering the table in overly cheerful light.

The conference room still smelled faintly of someone's cinnamon muffin, mixed with dry-erase marker and the scent of the new rolling chairs.

She yawned as she gathered her notes from the table. While getting ready for work, she'd noticed dark circles forming under her eyes, evidence of another late night wrestling with overwhelming stress.

"Do we agree on the formula for mineral valuations?" Jonathan turned off his tablet with a soft click and gave Amelia a questioning look.

"Yes," she said.

"Then I think we're finished here," Jonathan said, checking his watch. "Gavin, can you email everyone the revised spreadsheet by end of day?"

"Will do," Gavin said with a quick nod, as he and Patricia packed up their laptops.

Patricia twisted a strand of hair between her fingers. "We might need to consult with the law group again. The environmental offset calculations still need some adjustment." Her gaze lingered on Gavin.

"We can walk through them again," Gavin offered, leaning slightly toward her. "Maybe over coffee?"

The meeting had been productive—asset value calculations, gaps in the archival system, more questions, and some answers— but Amelia hadn't heard a word since Jonathan sat in the seat next to her and put up his first slide about asset categories. She was acutely aware of his presence beside her.

The last two days of twelve-hour shifts while he was in Atlanta had left her running on caffeine and determination. Every muscle in her shoulders ached from hunching over her laptop until midnight. She'd been rehearsing a conversation with Jonathan since 5 a.m., when she'd completely given up on getting any sleep.

Amelia waited as Patricia and Gavin filed out, their shoulders brushing as they passed through the doorway.

As soon as the door clicked shut, Amelia stood and turned to Jonathan.

"We need more staff," she said, her voice tight with controlled frustration. "I can't keep working twelve-hour days. I spent most of the weekend here, Jonathan. All day Sunday. This isn't sustainable for any of us."

Jonathan's expression changed, genuine concern replacing his professional demeanor. "I'm so sorry, Amelia. I know I left you holding everything together."

"The three days you were in Atlanta felt like three weeks." She struggled to keep her voice level. "Lydia dropped the request on us for a full report and presentation by the end of this week. I spent most of the day Sunday pulling together an outline and preliminary data for the report so we wouldn't fall behind."

She pulled out her color-coded project schedule, marked with red deadline flags that hadn't been there last week. "The new timeline is completely unrealistic."

He met her gaze, calm. "I know. I didn't see her email and your reply until Monday as I was about to board the plane. But I worked on the presentation on the flight back. I got in late. I'm sorry I missed sending you an update." His voice was steady. It suddenly made her feel unreasonable for being upset.

Amelia blinked. "You did?"

He slid a thumb drive across the table. "Slides of the market projection analyses, complete with graphs and charts. Presentations are my responsibility."

The wind left her sails.

"You can rely on me to get my part done," he said.

She rubbed the back of her neck and shifted her gaze away from him, looking out the window. "This job is everything to me, Jonathan. If I can secure a permanent position—"

"I know how important this is to you, so it's important to me, too." His expression softened. "I get it. I ghosted you and let you down, and now I'm earning back your trust." He paused and took a deep breath. "I promise, going forward, I'll always bring my A game to whatever we're doing, whatever job or task. You can count on me."

His frankness made something bloom in her chest. Amelia looked down at her notes, abruptly aware of how she'd cornered him for a battle.

"Thank you," she said finally. "But look, it's obvious we need more resources. The Amherst project still has more staff and less workload. We need to talk to management about shifting some staff to our team."

Jonathan studied her for a moment, then reached into his leather portfolio. "I agree. I'll set up a time with Lydia this week."

He pulled out a cream-colored, legal-size envelope. "By the way, I printed a copy of the relationship contract."

"You printed it?" He didn't need to go that far.

Amelia took the envelope, hyperaware of how his fingers lingered against hers, her heartbeat rushing in her throat. The paper felt substantial in her hands, more real and binding than the digital version.

"We're both on the same page," he said.

The physical reminder of their arrangement felt oddly formal, like a hollow business transaction. But Melanie's words from Atlanta echoed in her mind. *He admitted he has feelings for you.* This contract was already compromised before the ink was even dry.

If he wanted more than their casual agreement, he was doing a good job at reminding her of her own boundaries. She hesitated, wanting to ask whether he wanted something deeper than a staged performance.

Beyond the glass wall of the conference room, the techs talked in the shared workspace. Two interns walked by, glancing curiously at them through the glass. No, this wasn't the time or place for that conversation.

"I'll talk to Lydia again about the staffing issue," Jonathan said, breaking the silence. "You've been carrying too much while I was gone."

She nodded, sliding the contract into her binder without looking at it again.

"Thank you," she said finally. "For the help with the

project. And for ..." She gestured toward her binder where the contract lay hidden. "For respecting the boundaries."

Even if those boundaries were becoming harder to maintain with every interaction.

Another intern passed by the glass wall, and she realized eyes were everywhere.

The contract didn't belong with her geological surveys and project reports. Removing the envelope from her portfolio, she made a mental note to slip it into her purse later, for privacy.

"Come on," he said, standing and gathering his materials. "Let's get some coffee. I need to run something by you."

* * *

Thursday, lunchtime.

Amelia had spent the morning reviewing mineral lease valuations and making notes on spreadsheets, so she was tired by the time Jonathan asked, "Lunch?"

They walked a block down to the café, where the booths were always filled with hushed conversations and alternative music floated in the background. The hiss of the espresso machine created a curtain of white noise around their corner table.

When Jonathan returned, he sat across from her and slid a glass of iced tea toward her. "I'm going to take your advice," he said. "I'm going to see Jessica."

Amelia looked up, her eyes widening. She set down her fork. "Where?" Certainly, he wouldn't take another trip already?

He smiled. "She's been in Seattle for the last two weeks. Staying with friends for a few more days. I've been avoiding the conversation. But you're right; I need to fix things between us. It's the perfect opportunity since she's nearby."

The corner of her mouth turned slightly upward as she studied the way his shoulders dipped, his body at ease. He wasn't saying it to convince her or impress her. He meant it. How different from Nate's manipulations.

Without thinking, she reached across the table, placed her hand over his, and gave it a firm squeeze. "I'm glad. Family is important."

She let her hand linger a few seconds too long. He gave her a slight questioning look.

Before she could say more, he glanced toward the café door, at something over her shoulder. Then, before she knew what was happening, he stood and slid into the chair next to her in one swift motion and pulled her into a hug.

The embrace caught her off guard, his chin resting briefly on the top of her head, the woodsy-clean scent of him surrounding her. Confused with his sudden gesture, she stiffened until he leaned in closer and whispered, "Melanie. Behind you."

One hand slipped down around her waist. "Relax into me," he breathed into her ear. A shiver of pleasure ran through her as he gently kissed her cheek, his lips warm and inviting against her face. For a heartbeat, she forgot everything but his arms around her.

"Is Melanie really there?" she whispered against his shoulder, reality rushing back. "She's back from Atlanta?"

"Yes," he murmured, his breath hot against her ear. "I'm not breaking any rules. Even if I sometimes want to."

Her heart skipped a beat, and her breath hitched in her throat. The contract in her purse suddenly seemed undesirable.

"Well, well," Melanie's cheerful voice came from behind her. "Don't you two look cozy?"

Jonathan unwrapped himself from the hug, but his arm remained pressed gently against hers. A reminder of his promise —that she could count on him.

He isn't like Nate, she reminded herself. He showed up, and he listened. He carried his share of the load. Maybe, just maybe, she could trust him not to hurt her this time.

Amelia turned to greet Melanie, her professional smile firmly in place.

Chapter 34

Amelia

Amelia finished sending an email to Mr. F-O: *Reduce or prioritize. Your list for April is too much.*

Her phone showed Jonathan's message:

> JONATHAN: Got a mini surprise for you and some good news. Be there in twenty.

> AMELIA: Remember, no gifts allowed!

> JONATHAN: It's not a gift. I promise. But I think you'll like it.

She typed a quick response about the security guard, then paced the foyer's hardwood floors.

Jonathan's spontaneous hug at lunch yesterday had left her restless. It was for show, of course. Melanie had been watching. But the solid warmth of his arms around her had felt so deeply right.

The contract tucked in her purse clearly spelled out the fake-dating conditions. No gifts. No romantic gestures when they were alone. And no actual feelings.

The security app chimed, alerting her to a car passing through the gate. She smoothed her hands over her sweatshirt and took a steadying breath.

Jonathan appeared at the front door minutes later, holding what looked like a pet carrier. His hair was slightly tousled, and he'd changed from his work attire into jeans and a navy Henley that stretched across his shoulders.

She eyed the carrier suspiciously. "Is this the good news or the surprise?"

Jonathan laughed and nodded once. "It's the surprise." He set the carrier down carefully and opened the top hatch. Two tiny faces peered up at her, one orange tabby and one black with a white patch around its left eye.

"Kittens?" Amelia crouched down to get a better look. "Oh, my gosh. They are so adorable." The black one mewed softly, the sound impossibly small.

"Found them the night I got back from Atlanta," Jonathan explained. "Hiding in the bushes by my townhome. I had a vet check them out. No major issues, just a bit malnourished, and no microchips."

The orange one hopped out to the top of the carrier, wobbling slightly on uncertain legs.

"They need a loving parent," he continued. "And I thought ... well, you mentioned the mansion feels empty sometimes. I thought you might want to foster them? You'd make a great pet-parent."

She gently scooped up the orange kitten, feeling its rapid heartbeat against her palm. "What about you?"

"If you don't want to keep them, I'll foster them until they get adopted. I can't take them back to Atlanta; my apartment doesn't allow pets." He watched her stroke the kitten's head with her fingertip. "I named the black one Pirate. That white ring reminds me of an eyepatch. And the orange one is Treasure."

"Pirate's Treasure." Amelia grinned as she repeated the names together. "I love it." Then she hesitated. With such a busy schedule, she definitely should say no. But the kittens were too delightful.

"The mansion could use some life in it," she said slowly. "And the lease agreement says pets are allowed. But I want to pass it by Mr. Jewell first, as a courtesy."

Jonathan's eyes lit with his smile. "That sounds like a firm acceptance."

Half an hour later, they had set up the mudroom with pet supplies Jonathan brought in from his car. Litter boxes, food bowls, and a makeshift bed out of an old towel she'd found in the laundry room, all neatly arranged for the tiny newcomers. The kittens explored the unfamiliar territory with cautious curiosity.

"Would you like a glass of wine?" Amelia asked, watching the black kitten bat at a piece of lint.

Jonathan arched an eyebrow. "Sounds like a romantic gesture in private," he teased.

Her cheeks heated. "I'm being polite. No romantic gestures intended." Or so she convinced herself as she led him to the kitchen and poured two glasses of pinot noir.

"And the good news is?" she asked.

He accepted the glass, their fingers brushing as he took it from her hands. Her skin tingled at the brief contact. "I told the bosses we need more staff," he said. "I had to negotiate with several managers, but they finally saw it my way and agreed. We're getting one more geologist and another tech starting Monday."

Relief swept through her. Without thinking, she wrapped her arms around him, wine sloshing in her glass. For a moment, she let herself feel the solid strength of his chest and the way his body relaxed then went still beneath her touch.

She stepped back abruptly, heat flooding her cheeks. "I'm ... sorry. That was against the rules."

"Sorry for breaking rule number four?" He raised his glass in a toast. "My pleasure," he said with a sensual lilt.

His expression revealed a hint of hunger that made her stomach flutter before she looked away.

She cleared her throat. "So, when are you seeing your sister?"

"Tomorrow. I'm meeting her at a basketball court, then we're going to lunch."

"Basketball?" After dating for an entire year after college, she really should've known more about his family.

"She's a baller. Division Two college player, almost went pro in Europe." Pride tinged his voice. "It's our favorite interaction. We've always connected better on the court than anywhere else."

Almost went pro. "Okay, I'm impressed," she said. "Come on." Amelia grabbed a plate with a half-eaten chocolate cake she'd bought from the bakery downtown. "Let's sit outside. The sunset from the west porch is spectacular."

The air had cooled as evening settled in; the sun cast brilliant shadows across the lawn. They sat beside each other on wicker furniture. The cushions were still slightly damp after the afternoon rain. Amelia shivered as a breeze rustled the branches of nearby cedar trees.

Without a word, Jonathan shrugged out of his jacket and draped it over her shoulders. His fingers skimmed her neck as he settled the fabric around her, and she fought the urge to lean into his touch. His lingering body heat clung to the jacket, wrapping her in the warmth of him.

"Thanks," she whispered, keenly aware that this gesture,

too, broke their rules. No romantic gestures in private. She didn't want to correct him.

She took a sip of wine instead. "How do you feel about seeing Jessica tomorrow?"

He stared at the horizon, his jaw working silently as the sky deepened from gold into pink hues. "Nervous," he finally admitted, his voice rougher than usual.

She placed her hand on his shoulder, the solid feel of him familiar beneath her palm. "It's okay to be anxious about opening old wounds."

Jonathan looked down at his glass and swirled the wine slowly. "You know my father left when I was thirteen," he said finally. "But I never told you the whole story." He set down his glass.

Amelia handed him a plate of cake and waited.

"Jess and I were always close, but this drove a wedge between us. I've hated how we left things. But I think I was angrier at my father than I ever let myself admit. Jess was younger and saw him differently. And I took that personally."

He paused again, then added, "He walked out one Saturday morning just before the start of Jess's basketball game and didn't come back. No warning. Jess kept looking for him in the stands. It was awful. After he left, I watched my mom hold it together for everyone else. I promised I would, too."

Amelia stayed still. "That's sad," she whispered.

"For years, Jessica defended him. Said he must have had his reasons. That he still loved us. When he missed my college graduation, she made excuses. When he skipped her championship games, same thing." He shook his head. "I couldn't understand it. I couldn't grasp how she could suddenly decide to forgive him when he'd broken her heart worse than he'd disappointed any of us. We fought about it constantly until eventually we just ... stopped talking."

"And now?"

"Now I'm trying to understand that her way of coping isn't wrong, just different. She needed to believe he loved her. I needed to believe he was a monster." He sighed. "Neither version is completely true."

He finally forked a bite of cake.

"I guess I thought hating him was a way of protecting her," he breathed. "But maybe it just made everything harder."

Amelia stroked his shoulder. "You should tell her that tomorrow."

He nodded then looked at her with curiosity. "What about you?" He swallowed a large bite of cake. "What happened with Nate, really?"

The question caught her off guard. She set down her cake plate and took a large sip of wine, her chest tightening. "I trust too easily. That's what happened with Nate." She paused, meeting his eyes briefly before looking away. "Speaking of disappointments, I got another contractor quote I can't afford."

Jonathan accepted the change of subject with a slight nod. "That's the third one, right?"

"Fourth," she corrected. "Apparently, it's a small roof job with a high price tag."

"I might have a solution for that," he said. "I talked to Drew. If you're open to the idea, he wants to come out and do the job. He'll do it for the cost of materials, no labor fees."

"Drew? But he's got his own business in Atlanta." She shook her head. "Coming all the way here? And only charging me for materials? That's way too much to ask."

"If you give the go-ahead, he'll start work in a few weeks," Jonathan said.

"Can I at least pay for his flight?"

He shook his head and smiled. "Drew said he's got a ton of frequent flyer miles to use up."

A mix of relief and excitement washed over her. Without thinking, she hugged him again, and this time she let herself cling to him and the moment.

"It's better news than I could have hoped for," she said. "I don't know how I'll repay him ... or you."

"He's totally on board with it. He enjoys helping people. Plus, Audra's here, and he couldn't possibly turn down the chance to see her."

Understanding dawned. "I should have thought of that." Amelia's smile broadened. She'd been rooting for Audra and Drew to get together for years, but Audra had always held him at arm's length.

Friends, Audra had always said. Then Drew had started his construction business right when Audra got her dream job in Seattle, but they'd remained close as long-distance buddies.

"I worry about you being here alone, Amelia," he said as they separated.

She smiled and picked up her plate. "Well, now I have a one-eyed pirate to protect me." She glanced back toward the house, where the kittens were settling into their new home. "But in all seriousness, don't worry. I'm safe here."

They continued eating the cake and finished their wine, as the sun sank below the horizon.

"This was nice," Amelia said, reluctantly slipping off his jacket and handing it back. That reluctance necessitated reiterating the rules. "But we're getting too close to breaking the fake-dating rules."

"This was a lot better than nice," Jonathan replied, his eyes holding hers. He forked the last bite of his chocolate cake. "Maybe we should try going out on an actual date."

Amelia scoffed, as his suggestion sent a burst of panic through her chest.

She shook her head. "You brought me needy kittens. I fed you cake and wine. That's as close as I get to a real date."

"Why?" His question was gentle, not demanding.

She looked away, focusing on the faint silhouette of trees and the sloping hillside against the darkening sky. "I can't be broken again. I trusted you, and I trusted Nate and got burned so badly I'm still sorting through ashes." She kept her tone even but meant every word. "I'm not strong enough to have a fling then have to say goodbye when you leave."

He didn't argue, just nodded slowly, seeming to accept her boundary.

As she walked him to his car, Amelia's heartbeat quickened with each step. The contract seemed more like tissue paper now, too fragile to protect her from the way he'd looked at her tonight. And too fragile to protect her from her own feelings.

She stood in the driveway long after his car disappeared. The kittens weren't the only charming ones that had found their way into her house tonight.

Chapter 35

Jonathan

Last night's conversation with Amelia lingered in his thoughts as Jonathan parked along a tree-lined curb. He'd told her he was going to talk to Jessica. Time to follow through.

The way Amelia had cradled the tiny orange kitten in her hands. The conflicted look in her eyes when she'd declined his suggestion of an actual date.

I'm not strong enough to have a fling and then have to say goodbye when you leave.

He'd driven back to his townhome with that thought echoing in his mind, wondering if he should have told her he wasn't looking for a fling at all.

He stepped out of the car. The air smelled of fir trees and freshly cut grass. He spotted Jessica the moment he entered the park. Even from a distance, her form was unmistakable. The fluid arc of her jump shot and the precise follow-through that had earned her a college scholarship.

He paused at the edge of the court to watch. The rhythmic thump of the ball echoed in the crisp morning air, a familiar soundtrack from their childhood.

She moved with the same grace she'd had since high school.

Back then she'd outplayed everyone, girls and guys alike. She sent a long three-pointer clean through the net.

Jessica barely glanced over when she spotted him. "Hey," she said, as she quickly grabbed the rebound. "You going to just stand there, or did you come to play?"

She stood at the free-throw line, balancing the ball against her hip, brows raised in a challenge. Her blonde hair was pulled back in a ponytail, wispy strands escaping around her temples. She looked so much like a taller version of their mother.

"Depends," he called back, shrugging off his jacket. "You going to take it easy on me?"

"Ha," she laughed. "When have I ever?" With a quick flick of her wrist, she tossed him the ball.

He dribbled once, twice, testing the bounce. It had been months since he'd played.

She grinned, the first genuine smile he'd seen from her in over a year.

They settled into a light game, just passing and shooting. The ball hit the rim and bounced high. Jessica grabbed the rebound without breaking stride.

Even in a casual pickup game, she moved with natural authority, like she was born to rule the court.

Pivoting, she sent up a clean shot. Swish. Nothing but net.

Her movements were smooth, practiced. His were admittedly rough. But it felt good to move. The rhythm smoothed the tension between them. Muscle memory took over and Jonathan's skills gradually returned.

He dribbled left, testing her defense.

Twenty minutes later, she finished him with a fade-away jumper that would have made her coaches proud.

"Game!" She doubled over, hands on her knees, still breathing hard from the final sprint. "Water break." She grabbed a bottle from her bag, her ponytail sticking to the back of her sweaty neck.

They sat on a nearby bench, both breathing hard. The park was quiet, with only a few joggers and dog-walkers passing by.

Jonathan wiped perspiration from his forehead with a towel.

"Jess, I screwed up, and I owe you an apology," he said, staring straight ahead at the court. "I shouldn't have tried to interfere with your relationship with Roger. I had no right to impose my feelings about him onto you."

She took a long drink of water, then passed the bottle to him. "Where's this coming from?"

"I've been thinking about it for a while. About how I let my own issues with Roger create this ... wedge between us."

"I've missed you, too," she said finally. "Even when I was furious with you."

"I was wrong," he continued. "Your relationship with Roger is yours to figure out. Not mine."

Jessica nodded. "That's all I needed from you." She bumped her shoulder against his. "Apology accepted."

His shoulders dropped with relief. "Thank you." The simple acceptance was a gift.

"So," she said, stretching her legs out in front of her. "There's something else I wanted to talk to you about while we're here." She took her time, then at last said, "I'm thinking about going back to school."

"An MBA?" he asked.

She straightened in surprise.

"Mom guessed your trip was more than just visiting friends," he said with a smirk.

She sighed. "I could never keep a secret from her." She took a sip from her water bottle and leaned back. "I've been visiting programs and talking to people. I want to focus on the business side of Studio Charlotti. The back-end operations, the growth strategy, and the financials. All the stuff Mom hates dealing with. I'm better with numbers and people logistics than mood boards."

"Makes sense," Jonathan said. "You've always had a good head for numbers. So what's the holdup?"

"Mom. She thinks it's a waste of talent to have a Fontaine out of the spotlight and wants to keep me in the client-facing design role." She twisted the cap off her water bottle. "I need help to convince her to hire another designer ... you know how she feels about expanding the team."

He completely understood. Mom had built Studio Charlotti from nothing, and she still wanted control over every decision, every hire. She'd only recently started delegating more substantial responsibilities to Jessica.

Jonathan ran a hand over the back of his neck. "You want me to help persuade her," he said.

"She listens to you differently than she listens to me." No bitterness, just a statement of fact. "Help me assure her that this is the right business decision, not just my personal desire. I want you to be on my side."

He nodded. "I can do that."

Jessica's face brightened. "Really? Just like that?"

"Consider it part of my apology package for being such a stubborn ass." He smiled. "Besides, it's a solid business move. Mom's been turning down clients because you two can't handle the workload. Adding another full-time designer makes sense."

She studied him, head tilted slightly. "What made you change your mind about all of it? A few months ago, you wouldn't even take my calls."

He hesitated. Time was the safe answer, but he didn't want to be vague anymore.

"I've been seeing someone," he said. "Someone I dated in

college. Amelia. We've reconnected, and she helped me see things differently. She called me out for holding a grudge."

He leaned back against the cool bench. "She made me realize I was expecting you to feel the same way about Roger that I do, which isn't fair. And Mom nudged me, too."

"Both smart women," Jessica said, with a hint of approval in her voice. "Think I'll like Amelia?"

The thought of Jessica and Amelia meeting sent a complex ripple of emotions through him. He wanted to share every special thing and every special person with her, but what if he was just setting her up to lose someone else?

"I was thirteen when Roger left," he said. "I wasn't just angry." He paused, bouncing the ball once, then set it aside. "I was scared. It felt like everything I thought I knew just fell apart."

Jessica nodded. "I remember."

"I didn't understand how someone could just opt out of a family. Watching Mom try to hold it together for us, I thought, that's what I had to do too. I stayed angry for her. For all of us."

He looked down at his hands. "I couldn't forgive him because I couldn't afford to. Being angry was easier than being scared."

"I know," Jessica said. Her voice was subdued. "But I was young enough to not be angry and to want to keep the relationship with Dad alive. I tried to appear mad for your sake for a lot of years, but I still remember good times with him. That's why it hurt so much when you made me choose."

He finally understood. He leaned forward, elbows on his knees.

All these years, he'd thought Jessica was betraying the family by maintaining ties with Roger. But she had tried to preserve the remnants.

"I kept thinking you were betraying Mom by not hating

him," he said. "But that was me projecting. I never asked what it was like for you."

She turned toward him. "You didn't have to. I knew how you felt. You got quiet. You got efficient. But I knew you were trying to hold the weight for all of us."

He swallowed against the lump forming in his throat and put his arm around her shoulders. "I thought I had to be the support, the keel, for the family," he whispered. "Are we good?"

She patted his knee. "We're okay now. Just don't make me wait another year to kick your ass at basketball."

Jonathan laughed and kissed the top of her head. "I love you, Jess. Next time, I'm calling you when things get complicated. No more shutting you out."

She squeezed his arm. "I'd like that."

"Good. It's a promise," he said.

* * *

Driving back to the townhome, Jonathan rolled the window down halfway and let the air rush through the car. His chest still felt raw, but in a way that didn't hurt so much anymore.

He thought about Amelia, about the walls she'd built around herself after Nate. And after he'd ghosted her. He'd constructed walls too, around his feelings toward Roger.

Telling Jessica the truth hadn't been nearly as hard as he'd feared.

If he could finally tell Jessica the truth about being scared instead of just angry, maybe he could be that honest with Amelia too, about how he felt. About what he really wanted.

No contract. No clauses. Just the authentic intimacy.

Chapter 36

Amelia

"You seem less on edge the last few days," Amelia said, closing her spreadsheet and studying Jonathan. "Especially given our workload." He looked different this week. Lighter, like something heavy had finally lifted.

"I had a good weekend." Jonathan sat at the adjacent workstation, flipping through a binder of asset evaluations. "Yours?"

"The cutest kittens are invading my space and keeping me sane, but ... Mr. Jewell's renovation demands never end. I'm working through paint selections, but now there's the problem of the rose bushes. He purchased dozens of them, but there are no gardeners available to plant them. They need to get into the ground soon. I'll probably end up planting them myself. Not what I signed up for, but here we are."

Jonathan frowned. "Does he forget you have an actual job?"

"I think he lives on a different planet." She shrugged. "I win a battle here and there, but I think he's winning the war."

Todd, the newest addition to their team, waltzed in with coffees balanced in a box. He placed the first one deliberately on Amelia's desk.

"Latte. Your favorite," he said with a wink.

"Thanks." She kept her response neutral, though she knew he'd made a special trip out to a coffee shop for the latte.

"Has anyone told you how great you look in green today?" Todd said.

Jonathan's expression went stony.

Amelia wasn't sure if he was annoyed by Todd's casual flirtation or by her response. She smiled in amusement.

"I thought maybe we could grab lunch," Todd continued, hovering. "Go over those eastern parcels..."

She politely shook her head in Todd's direction. "No, thanks."

"We're covering those this morning," Jonathan interjected, his tone cool and professional.

After Todd retreated, Amelia leaned forward slightly. "How'd it go with Jessica?" She had intended to ask earlier, but work had swamped them all week.

Jonathan opened his mouth to respond when Lydia appeared in the doorway, her expression serious. "Amelia, Jonathan—conference room."

The rain-slicked windows of the conference room reflected their gobsmacked expressions as Lydia delivered the news.

"Corporate expanded our project scope," she announced. "Besides the overall asset portfolio assessment, they want a complete divestiture plan for the mineral leases we're letting go. Plus, a risk analysis and potential buyer profiles."

"What?" Amelia felt the air leave her lungs in a rush.

"That's an entirely new phase of work," Jonathan said, his voice sounding agitated. "We just got approval to add two people to stabilize the workload, and now we're overloaded again."

"I have no more staff to transfer," Lydia said. "There's talk of extending the deadline, but I can't make that promise."

"An extended timeline." Jonathan paused. "It might be even longer before I return to Atlanta."

His tone caught Amelia's attention. The way he said *Atlanta* lacked the urgency it once had. She couldn't tell whether he was disappointed or relieved.

When Lydia left, Amelia turned to him. "We need a new plan. Fast."

"We'll figure it out," he said.

Amelia checked her calendar. "Today's fully booked ... actually, our schedule is full through the end of next week."

She weighed the professional urgency against personal boundaries. The deadline won.

"Let's have a working dinner tonight," she said finally. "To tackle the scope creep before it overwhelms us."

"Sounds sort of like another maybe-date to me," he teased.

"It's not a date," she said, before realizing it sounded very much like a date. "A working dinner. Just to realign."

A hint of a smile played on Jonathan's lips. "Realigning sounds excellent," he said.

Chapter 37

Jonathan

JONATHAN WATCHED THE RESTAURANT DOOR, checking his watch. The place was nothing fancy. Exposed brick walls, worn wooden tables, scents of lime and fajitas, and decent beer. Perfect.

He'd picked it on purpose. Casual. Uncomplicated. It was a place where two overworked people could spread papers out across an oversized table over a few drinks.

When Amelia walked in, her eyes were still alert despite the long week. He could tell she was determined to figure out a plan.

She'd pulled her auburn hair back and traded her usual blazers for jeans and a white t-shirt. Sliding into the booth across from him, she peeled off her jacket, appearing more relaxed than when he'd seen her at work.

"Sorry I was late," she said. "I had to go home to feed the kittens before our dinner. They're doing great, by the way. Still in the mudroom, but they're almost ready to explore the rest of the house. It's ... nice, actually. Having something alive in there with me."

He handed her a menu. "They make a decent margarita here."

"Sold," she said, already reaching for the cocktail list. "I need a drink after this week."

Jonathan smiled, watching the way her eyes softened. "I had a feeling the kitties would be good company."

"And I'm learning a lot about coordinating food schedules and litter boxes." She smiled and paused. "Not entirely different from managing contractors."

The server came by, and they ordered grilled fish tacos with charred corn.

"So," Jonathan said, unfolding his laptop. "Divestiture planning."

He pulled up the potential client list. "Patterson Industries is looking to expand further into potash and phosphates. We should also research other companies that might be interested in acquiring leases with boron and copper."

During the next hour, they mapped out strategies, determining which research they could delegate.

The restaurant filled around them, Friday night energy buzzing as their plates emptied and drinks were refreshed.

"We need more hands," Amelia concluded, finishing her margarita. "There's just no way around it." After a few more bites of taco, she asked, "What if we hired some temporary contractors? Someone to take over the backlog tasks. Just for a few months."

Jonathan considered. "You're talking about tech-level work?"

"Yeah. Anything that frees us up to handle the divestiture plan without drowning."

He nodded slowly. It was a solid idea. "I'll talk to Lydia on Monday," he said, relief loosening the knot in his chest. "If we frame it as a short-term support role, the expense might get approved."

The server refilled Amelia's water glass and cleared their empty plates. Jonathan closed his laptop. After two hours of work, they finally had a plan.

"We're off the clock now, right?" she asked, already signaling the server. Jonathan nodded, enjoying the spark of fun that lit her expression.

They paid their bills for the working dinner, making sure to tip well for the extended use of the table, then opened a new tab for their personal time.

The alcohol had softened her usual reserve, and a slight flush colored her cheeks. He wished he could savor that look of hers all night long.

Amelia finished her second margarita then ordered something stronger. Her laughter came more easily.

He took another swig of the beer he'd been carefully nursing; at least one of them needed to remain grounded.

"You never told me specifics on how your day with Jessica went," she said. "I've been curious all week."

"It was ... healing, I guess. You were right that I should tell her how I felt about the situation. She deserved to know."

"How did she take it?"

"Good. Better than expected. She listened and accepted my apology." He rotated his beer glass slowly. "We talked about our Dad, too. That was harder."

"I can imagine."

"It felt good to finally say it all out loud." He met her eyes. "Thanks for pushing me to do that. I didn't realize how much I needed to say until I actually said it."

"That's good. Really good." Amelia nodded, her finger tracing the rim of her glass. The restaurant had grown louder, forcing them to lean closer to hear each other.

"What about you?" he asked carefully. "Nate. We've never really talked about what happened to your relationship."

Her expression drifted, and something vulnerable passed across her face. She signaled the server again.

When her next drink arrived, she downed it immediately.

He kept his eyes on her. He waited, watching her trace the rim of her glass.

Finally, she exhaled a long breath, and her shoulders lowered, as though burdened by an invisible weight. "I wanted someone in my life to fill the aching hole you left behind. Nate was handsome and charming and convincing, but he didn't actually love me," Amelia said bluntly.

"Counseling just made it obvious. He didn't want a wife. He wanted funding." She took another drink. "I finally figured out he'd just been using me to fund a new exercise business. That was his reason for getting involved with me. After we married, I cosigned loans with him, then his business failed. I had invested personal money, too."

Her breath wavered. "I tried ... too much, everything. I eventually asked for a divorce to save myself."

"I'm sorry you went through that," he said. The impact of his disappearance was now clearer than ever.

She said nothing more. Maybe she didn't have to. Ten minutes later, she attempted to stand. She swayed.

"Whoa." Jonathan caught her arm. "Let me drive you home."

"I'm fine."

"I'm not putting you in a cab," Jonathan said. "I know Mr. Jewell's estate is guarded by retired Special Forces, but I'd rather not send you home with a stranger." He steadied her again. "I'll drive you."

She muttered something about her car, but he was already pulling her jacket over her shoulders and guiding her outside.

"You can get your car tomorrow," he said.

By the time they reached his rental, she was more giggly than resistant. She leaned against the passenger door, eyes half lidded. "You're warm," she murmured. "I still like you, you know. I probably shouldn't say that."

He clicked the remote to unlock the door. "Noted."

Not exactly the situation he'd envisioned for a confession.

She stepped closer, her forehead near his shoulder. "I wanted ... with Nate," she whispered. "I really tried to make it ... work." She paused, blinking slowly.

He stayed perfectly still, afraid any movement might break whatever trust was happening.

"But he wasn't there for love. Never was." When she looked up, her eyes were glassy and melancholy.

"Let me help you in," he said. He opened the car door carefully and buckled her seatbelt.

* * *

The drive to the mansion was quiet. Amelia leaned her head against the window, her eyes half closed.

The security guard recognized Jonathan's car and waved him through the gate.

In the driveway, Jonathan came around to help her out of the car.

"I'll help you to the porch," he said, crouching slightly in front of her. "Piggyback."

She laughed honestly, a sound he hadn't heard in years, then climbed onto his back. She looped her arms loosely over his shoulders. Her breath was pleasantly warm against his ear as he carried her up the walkway.

"What happened to Nate..." Her voice crumbled. "It was

my fault. Not directly, but..." She trailed off, setting her head on his shoulder.

He set her on her feet at the doorway.

"Key?" he prompted.

She fumbled in her purse, nearly dropping it before producing a set of keys with the door fob.

As he reached for them, she looked up at him, swaying slightly. Then, she was kissing him. Soft at first, then more insistent when he didn't pull away immediately. Her mouth was warm and tasted like lime and everything deliciously her.

Her hands flattened against his chest.

He gently caught her wrists. "Not like this," he said, his voice coarse. For a second, he almost forgot why he should stop. "You'll hate yourself tomorrow. And me."

She stared at him, then stepped back. "I'm sure I'll agree with you ... tomorrow."

He waited until she unlocked the door, stepped inside, and closed it behind her. In the silence of his car, he let out a long sigh and dropped his head back against the seat.

Nate had hurt her, but so had he. He'd walked away from her without explanation. Different damage, but still damage. No wonder she kept him at arm's length.

He'd taught her to expect abandonment, and Nate had completed the lesson. And now she was afraid to reach for something real.

He couldn't blame her.

Chapter 38

Amelia

Saturday.

MORNING SUNLIGHT STABBED at Amelia's senses through the windows and her skull throbbed. She had transformed the library since her arrival. It still smelled of dust and old varnish, but less so.

She'd brought many items down from the attic and filled the built-in shelves with leather-bound books, old ceramic knick-knacks, and framed pictures of stern-faced ancestors she couldn't name. And Rebecca's journals occupied the center shelf, all four volumes.

She winced, retreating to the leather sofa in the shadowed corner with a mug of black coffee. Her stomach felt unsettled, and her tongue was dry no matter how much water she drank.

Hammering from upstairs echoed through the house as the contractors worked on the bathroom at the far end of the south hallway. The noise was not helping her headache.

Amelia reached for her phone, squinting at the screen.

AUDRA: Sorry, coastal cleanup until 3. Will help retrieve your car after.

Great. Stranded with a hangover.

A message from Mr. F-O was waiting when she woke up. He'd thanked her for the work completed so far and agreed that the April task list had ballooned beyond realistic.

For now, he wanted her to focus on making a first pass at paint colors and save the floor-refinishing preparations and chandelier selections for later. At least something was going her way. He also reminded her that the monthly pool service would visit on Monday.

She set the phone aside and yawned.

Last night was a blur. She remembered the restaurant, the work planning, ordering the second margarita, and Jonathan's voice close to her ear. But after that third drink?

She remembered swaying outside. And she'd stumbled through the front door toward the mudroom. One kitten greeted her when she checked on them in the mudroom. At least she'd managed that much before collapsing into bed.

But what had she said to Jonathan? The memory gaps bothered her. She groaned.

A fragment suddenly surfaced. Jonathan had carried her to her doorstep, and his back had felt warm and solid against her body. Her arms were around his shoulders. His gentle refusal when she'd kissed him.

Her eyes shot open, and her face burned. *Ugh!* Had she really thrown herself at him? What else had she revealed in her drunken state?

She sighed and reached for Rebecca's second journal. She didn't want to think about what else she might have said or done last night. Losing herself in someone else's life was a far better idea.

3 September 1852

Thomas was thrown from his horse today and struck his head on a fencepost. His breathing was shallow when we pulled him from the mud, and his eyes would not open. I do not know whether he heard me when I spoke to him.

We brought him home unconscious. Blood seeped through his shirt. My beloved has bandaged ribs and a terrible fever that will not break. The doctor has done what he can, but he says there may be damage we cannot see.

I have not left his bedside. Sleep eludes me as I press my palm to his chest to feel the beating of his heart. I cannot imagine this world without him in it. I pray as I have never prayed before.

Amelia blinked. Her throat tightened. She turned the page slowly.

4 September 1852

He woke briefly, his hand finding mine. His eyes opened just long enough to see me. When the doctor left us alone, Thomas beckoned me closer. "Our love will always bring me home to you," he whispered. "But promise me, Rebecca, that if I die while you are still living on this earth, you will seek happiness and love. That you will live your life to the fullest. This is what I want for you."

Before I could answer, the fever claimed him into unconsciousness again. He sleeps now, his breathing labored. I do not know whether he will survive the night. Our love is my life. Without it, I would merely exist.

Amelia let the book rest on her knees. Her fingers stilled.

Thomas's fierce and selfless love felt like something from another lifetime. Not hers.

She thought of Nate. The memory hit fast. The phone call and the officer's words. *Accident ... no survivors.*

They'd been fighting before Nate had left for the track. About the divorce, his lies, the business loans. She'd said things she couldn't take back. By the time she reached the hospital, he was gone.

The guilt had been instantaneous. If she hadn't pushed for divorce...

A loud crash from upstairs interrupted her spiral. No one sounded panicked and there were no rushing feet. The contractors had probably dropped something. At least they were making progress, unlike her emotional state.

Amelia shut her eyes. Nate didn't deserve to live in her head anymore.

The hammering upstairs stopped, leaving silence. Rebecca's words reverberated in her mind: *Our love is my life. Without it, I merely exist.*

Wasn't that exactly what she'd been doing since Nate's death? She'd been existing, not living. Not out of love, but out of guilt. And that guilt controlled everything.

Enough, enough, enough. She was done hiding behind guilt.

Amelia grabbed her phone. The headache was already fading. She would text Jonathan and thank him for last night. Or suggest coffee.

It was time to live again, without guilt. She placed Rebecca's journal back on the shelf. The cataloging could wait.

Chapter 39

Amelia

AT LUNCHTIME, she ate dry toast and downed three glasses of water before texting Jonathan.

AMELIA: Thanks for last night.

JONATHAN: My pleasure. How are you feeling?

AMELIA: Mostly recovered. Going to plant some rose bushes soon.

Next, she replied to a few emails, including one from Mr. F-O saying he still had no ETA on a gardener to plant the rose bushes.

Two hours later, Amelia knelt in the garden bed to the side of the house, sleeves pushed up, sweat clinging to the back of her neck. The worst of the hangover had passed, and her headache had receded.

The loamy fragrance of overturned soil mixed with the faint sweetness of spring grass. A line of plastic nursery pots stretched along the stone path—thirty antique rose bushes, displaying emerging blooms in varying shades of red and coral, waiting to be planted.

The garden beds she'd prepared stretched along the mansion's south wall, freshly turned soil dark against the weathered stone foundation.

She wiped her forehead with the back of her hand and reached for a trowel. A car door shut out front.

Her phone was in the kitchen, so she'd missed any notifications from the guards.

Jonathan walked toward her, a folder under one arm and a cloth bag slung over the other. She winced. Amelia hadn't expected to see him so soon after last night's embarrassment.

He wore faded work boots, jeans, and a casual blue cotton shirt that stretched across his broad shoulders and chest. The fabric pulled slightly when he moved, revealing the lean muscle beneath. A pleasant interruption.

Amelia's pulse quickened. She'd grown accustomed to seeing him in business attire, but this version of Jonathan stirred something low in her belly.

"I brought the updated presentation draft for Monday," he said, holding up the folder. "Thought you might want to review it before we meet with Lydia."

"You could have emailed it," she replied with a half grin, brushing soil from her gloves.

"Could have." He glanced at the rose buckets. "But then I wouldn't get to check on the bush-kittens." The corner of his mouth quirked upward. "Or see you."

Amelia swept dirt from her knees as she stood. "They're fine. I'm fine. But it's nice to see you." She gestured vaguely toward the house. "I let them out of the mudroom this morning. Pirate climbed the curtains. Treasure watched her like a disapproving parent."

Jonathan laughed. His attention shifted to the garden project. "That's a lot of roses to plant by yourself."

Amelia frowned. "Yeah, it is." She let out a small huff of resignation. "But I think the yard will look terrific once they're in the ground. I get why Mr. Jewell wants to restore the rose gardens."

"You look tired."

"Hangover residue," she admitted. "But I'm functional. And I've had a busy afternoon." She gestured toward the prepared beds.

Jonathan set the folder on a nearby garden bench and pulled work gloves from his back pocket. "I want to help."

"That's not necessary—" She reached for a potted rose just as he stepped forward. Their hands touched, and a jolt of heat shot through her fingertips, raced up her arm, and settled deep in her chest. Her breath caught in her throat.

Jonathan's eyes found hers, darker than usual. "I have no delusions that I'm remotely capable of handling DIY house repairs. But I'm pretty good at gardening and heavy lifting. How about I take over the shoveling duties?"

She hesitated, even as her arms protested the idea of digging thirty holes.

Jonathan didn't insist. Instead, he walked to his car and returned with a post-hole digger. "I came prepared. The hardware guy promised it would make the work go twice as fast," he said. "And we can talk shop while we're planting."

Amelia looked from the tools to the long row of rose buckets, calculating the hours of sweaty labor ahead. "I'd be an idiot to turn down help," she said.

"If we can't have an actual date, at least I can still spend time with you," he said, already positioning the digger for the first hole.

Huh. Amelia smiled at him. What part of this was fake?

They quickly fell into a rhythm.

Working beside him, Amelia noticed Jonathan's every move. The way his shirt dampened with sweat and the flex of muscle in his forearms as he worked the digger. The woodsy scent of him mixing with the earthy garden smell.

He continued to dig holes while Amelia followed behind, placing each rose, backfilling the soil, and tamping it down.

"We should group the assets by small regions in the divestiture plan," Jonathan said, positioning the digger. "Better marketing opportunity than offering individual properties."

"What about grouping by mineral-rights type instead?" she said, carefully spreading dirt around a freshly planted bush.

"Exactly. Bundling makes more sense."

The sun dipped lower as they worked.

Six holes in, Amelia reached past a thorny cane and felt a sharp sting across her elbow. "Ouch. Darn it." She pulled back to find a thin scratch beading with blood.

"Hold on a minute," Jonathan said, setting down his tools. "I've got a travel first aid kit in the trunk."

"I'm impressed," she said when he returned.

"Force of habit. I always carry a kit. Jessica was always getting scrapes and bruises on the court."

He guided her to the bench, where he knelt and cleaned the scratch with an alcohol wipe. She flinched at the sting.

"Sorry," he whispered, gently touching her skin as he focused on applying a bandage.

She looked up at him, only inches away now.

Heat radiated from his body. She could see the slight dampness on his collar. His hand was still resting on her arm—light pressure, steady and warm. Her skin tingled where his thumb caressed her.

"I enjoy working with you like this," she whispered.

His gaze dropped briefly to her mouth. "Is that a confession?" he said playfully.

"An acknowledgment," she said. Her tone matched his. "Today I'm not drunk."

His hand was still on her arm, his thumb tracing small circles that sent excitement spiraling through her body.

"There," he said, carefully smoothing the adhesive. His hand lingered on her arm. He paused and held her gaze for a second longer, then he stood and wiped his hands on his jeans.

They returned to planting, and the conversation shifted to Amelia's plans for the cottage.

"The roof has to be repaired," she said, tamping soil around a deep crimson rose. "Beyond that, I'll wait for Drew's confirmation of the structural assessment before I commit to anything else. The loan will only stretch so far."

"Smart," Jonathan said. "There's no sense in replacing fixtures if the foundation is crumbling."

By the fifth row, the late afternoon sun cast long shadows across the lawn. Amelia stood to stretch her back, surprised to find they'd completed more than half the garden.

Jonathan wiped sweat from his brow with his forearm.

"Thank you for helping," she said when they paused for water.

"I enjoy working with you, too," he said.

He glanced around the mansion grounds. "You know, my sister would love this place. The design is classic nineteenth-century." He hesitated. "This Tuesday, I'm having dinner with Jess. It's her last night in town. I'd love for her to see this place. And to meet you."

Amelia blinked. The invitation caught her off guard. "You want to introduce me to your sister."

"Though that might technically break the rule about not meeting family," he said.

"Rule number eight," she said slowly. "Yes ... it would." They'd already tiptoed into the maybe-we-have-feelings gray zone. Now they were discussing blatantly breaking another rule?

"How about an exception?" he said.

Amelia felt her pulse quicken. They'd already bent several rules. What was one more? Then she remembered her commitment to her friends.

"I can't, though," Amelia said with disappointment. "That evening, I'm having a grill-out with Melanie and Audra. I promised them we'd catch up, and it's the only evening this week we're all available."

He nodded. "Another time, then."

She stared at the freshly dug earth and the rows they'd filled together. It was way more than she would have accomplished on her own.

"You know," she said slowly, "if you and Jessica wanted to join us instead ... I mean, it's casual. Nothing formal, just burgers and whatever salad Audra brings. I've got enough food."

"You sure?"

"Absolutely," she said. "To repay you for your help today."

Jonathan smiled again but didn't challenge it. "Nothing owed. But we'd like that," he said.

They finished planting the southern bed before sunset. As they cleaned and packed away the tools, Amelia felt content for the first time in months, despite the exhaustion.

* * *

Sunday morning.

The warmth of the covers created a tempting cocoon, and Amelia slept in. It was nearly ten when she shuffled barefoot into the kitchen, desperate for coffee. As the machine gurgled to life, she glanced out the window and froze.

Jonathan was in the garden, knees in the dirt, sleeves rolled up past his elbows. The fabric of his shirt stuck to his back, and his muscles were visible as he moved.

He was planting the last of the roses. Alone.

Finishing what they'd started together.

She watched him for a long minute. Something tender and liquid expanded in her chest, spreading through her body like thick honey. Jonathan showed up. He just showed up.

Seeing him working in the garden, caring for something that mattered in her life, sent a rush of desire through her, and it had nothing to do with gratitude.

Amelia grabbed her phone and hurried to the door. She stopped on the patio to snap pictures of the newly completed garden. The roses looked perfect, spaced evenly in the garden along the house.

When Jonathan spotted her, he stood, brushing soil from his jeans. "Morning," he called. "Hope I didn't wake you."

"How long have you been here?" she asked as he approached the patio.

"Since sunrise." He glanced back at his handiwork.

She'd missed the guard notification again. "You didn't have to do that."

He shrugged. "It wasn't about 'have to.'"

He stepped onto the patio, removing his gloves. This close, she could see the flecks of soil on his face, the dampness of his shirt where he'd been working hard.

Without thinking, Amelia reached up and brushed a smudge of dirt from his cheek. His skin was heated from exertion and slightly rough beneath her fingertips. When he leaned into her touch, her breath hitched.

For a moment, neither moved. His eyes searched her face, and she felt the familiar pull between them.

A kitten mewed through the screen door. Amelia nodded toward the house. "Care for coffee?"

"Water," he said with a chuckle. "Finished my daily coffee hours ago."

As she led him inside, Amelia realized Jonathan had given her reliability, something Nate had never provided.

He cared enough to rise before dawn to plant roses that weren't his, for a house that wasn't his. This was what a real partner looked like. Present. Reliable.

Amelia opened a cabinet, grabbed a glass, and filled it with cold water for him. "You have a habit," she said, eyes focused on him, "of showing up lately."

He took a sip then set the glass on the counter. "Only when it matters."

She felt heat rise behind her ribs and spread lower, making her hyperaware of his proximity, the way he was watching her mouth. "You know that makes it harder to keep this fake," she said.

The words hung between them like another confession. Amelia's skin felt too tight; every nerve ending focused on the man standing three feet away.

"Yeah," he whispered. "I know."

For a moment, neither of them moved. The only sound was a kitten's soft paw-steps scurrying into the room.

For a split second, she thought he might close the distance between them. Her lips parted slightly, and she saw his gaze drop to her mouth before the kitten's cry broke the spell.

Jonathan bent to scoop up Treasure, and she climbed onto his shoulder as though she owned him.

"I think she likes you," Amelia said.

"She has good taste," Jonathan replied.

Chapter 40

Amelia

THE SCENTS of lemon marinade and charcoal drifted in the air as Amelia carried a tray of glasses out to the patio.

The sun hung low, tinting the clouds in faint yellows. Treasure and Pirate lounged on a kitchen windowsill, peering out like tiny administrators.

Audra stood near the grill in hot pink shorts and a coordinated tank top, rhythmically brushing marinade over skewered vegetables. Melanie sat nearby, sipping a fizzy drink from a copper mug.

"This place was meant for dinner parties," Melanie said. "You should host more often."

Amelia smiled. "I was thinking the same thing, but I barely made time for this get-together. Free time is in short supply lately."

Audra waved her brush toward the house. "How long until Jonathan and Jessica get here?"

"I told them to be here by six," Amelia replied.

"How are things going between you and Jonathan?" Melanie asked. "What's next?"

"I'm curious too," Audra said, her tone lighter than it had

been weeks ago. "And I have to admit, you seem happier. But why haven't we heard any of the juicy details? It's not like you to keep your besties in the dark ... about anything."

Ugh, Audra was completely right. She'd backed herself into a corner of her own making. Yeah, we faked a date, and now we're seeing each other occasionally, but maybe it's becoming real?

The truth was off the table and sounded ridiculous.

"We're taking things slow," Amelia said finally. "We've agreed to some casual dating, that's all." That was honest. "Besides, he's leaving in less than two months." Also true.

"Seems a little slim on details, but I get you don't want to say much," Audra said. "Speaking of excellent company," she redirected with a mischievous smile, "tell us more about this roof contractor Jonathan found for you."

Another thing she couldn't divulge. Jonathan made Amelia promise not to tell, as Drew wanted to surprise Audra. "He's perfect for the job," Amelia said. "Comes highly recommended."

"And?" Audra prompted.

"And ... he reminds me of Drew. Looks like he walked straight out of a lumberjack calendar," Amelia admitted with a laugh. "Complete with the beard and flannel."

"No way!" Audra's eyes widened. "Sounds like Drew has a doppelgänger."

Melanie's perfectly shaped eyebrow arched. "Is Drew the hot calendar type?"

"I never said Drew was hot," Audra scoffed.

"Mmm," Amelia said, arranging a bowl of fresh berries.

"Drew and I are just friends," Audra insisted.

"Uh-huh," Melanie said. "A very specific, beardy kind of friend."

"We've known each other forever," Audra said, fanning the grill smoke away. "It's not a thing."

"But if it were a thing…?" Amelia prodded.

"Friends who've been dancing around each other for what, seven years now?" Melanie said.

"Eight." Audra's cheeks flushed. "But he's not my type, and there's no dancing going on," she mumbled, then shook her head as if clearing away the thought. "He's good people. I'll leave it at that. Anyway, I'm not the one with a hot man about to arrive for dinner."

"Speak of the devil," Melanie murmured, glancing toward the driveway.

* * *

Jonathan guided his rental car up the winding driveway, aware of his sister's wide-eyed gaze as the stone mansion came into view.

"You weren't exaggerating," Jessica said, leaning forward in her seat. "This place is incredible."

"Wait until you see the interior stone and woodwork," he replied, parking beside Melanie's truck.

As they rounded the side of the mansion toward the back patio, he spotted Amelia, laughing with her friends and completely in her element. Something in his chest squeezed.

She met him halfway across the lawn.

His arms were around her before he had time to consider how she might react. Remembering their audience, he kissed her, intending something brief but convincing.

But when their lips met, he immediately knew he needed more. He pulled her close, one hand on her lower back, the other cupping her cheek as he kissed her. Her mouth softened under his, her fingers curling into his shirt as if anchoring herself to him.

It was a slow kiss. Intentional. The kind that said *we've done this before and we want to do it again.* He deepened the kiss, tasting the cocktail she'd been sipping.

When he pulled back, she stayed close, her hand resting against his shirt.

"Hi," he said.

She swallowed. "Hey."

Behind them, Jessica cleared her throat.

Amelia turned. Jessica gave her a warm smile. "Hi, I'm Jessica. Nice to finally meet you in person."

"You too," Amelia said, stepping back and pushing her hair behind her ears. "I'm glad you could come."

Amelia led them toward the patio, where she introduced Melanie and Audra.

"This place is absolutely stunning," Jessica said, already pulling out her phone. "Would you mind if I take some photos before it gets too dark?"

"Not at all," Amelia replied. "As long as none of the photos are published. The owner is particular about that. Explore all you'd like. There's a beautiful view from the east terrace."

Jessica immediately began documenting the mansion's exterior details. "Mom's going to love these," she commented, zooming in on an intricate cornice. "She's been renovating an estate in New York, and there are great ideas here."

"Your mom renovates houses?" Amelia asked, handing Jonathan a bottle of beer.

"More like she conquers them," Jessica interjected with a grin. "Mom approaches renovation like I approach basketball. All strategy, determination, and absolutely no mercy for anything that doesn't meet her standards."

He watched Jessica as she walked along the patio toward the far side of the mansion, capturing images from various angles.

Fifteen minutes later, Audra called everyone to the table, where platters of grilled vegetables and burgers were being arranged.

"Who owns this place?" Jessica asked when she rejoined them at the table. "It's like something out of a historical homes magazine."

"A client of mine, Mr. Jewell," Amelia explained, passing the salad. "I've never actually met Mr. F-O in person. Our communication is strictly virtual."

"F-O?" Jessica asked.

Amelia grinned and shrugged. "Sorry. It's my nickname for him. Mr. Famous-Owner. He's very private," Amelia replied. "He owns a security consulting firm and is a bit mysterious. I sometimes wonder if he's actually secretly famous. Anyway, as a side gig, I'm his virtual assistant."

Jessica tilted her head thoughtfully. "Jonathan mentioned the renovations are fairly extensive, and the owner's having you photograph everything ... sounds to me like he might be preparing to sell."

Jonathan nodded in agreement. "She's got a good point."

Amelia's jaw slid open. "I don't think so," she said slowly. "His family built the mansion over a hundred years ago. And he just approved a renovation of a guest cottage on the property that I'm going to rent."

"Still," Jessica pressed, "in my experience with real estate, those are classic pre-listing moves. Update everything, document it professionally, and then put it on the market at a premium."

Amelia's fingers tightened around her cocktail glass. Jonathan could see her processing the implications. The cottage renovation, her mom's future, and her extra income—everything tied to the mansion could disappear if Jessica was right.

Beneath the table, he reached for her hand and squeezed. She looked at him gratefully and leaned against him. He draped his arm across the back of her chair, his fingers brushing her arm, sliding into an old but comfortable habit.

"What kind of security work does Mr. Jewell do?" Jessica asked.

"Mostly cybersecurity ... I think," Amelia said. "Though he mentioned his company handles everything from digital protection to physical security systems. I wouldn't be surprised if he has some high-profile clients."

"Interesting," Jessica said.

Jonathan recognized the spark in his sister's eyes, just like when she'd encountered a clever point guard or a new defense strategy on the basketball court.

As dinner progressed, Jonathan watched how seamlessly their worlds blended. Jessica offered a toast and easily engaged with the other women.

Amelia moved between conversations, occasionally catching his eye with a casual smile. She touched him often, her hand on his arm while laughing at Audra's stories, her shoulder pressed against him.

As they cleared plates, Amelia's fingers laced with his when they briefly stepped away to retrieve desserts from the kitchen.

He wasn't playing a part anymore.

"It's nice getting to know Melanie a little better," he said. "And Audra is still as feisty as ever."

"Ha. Yeah, Audra will always be spunky. I love that about her," she replied, reaching past him for dessert plates. "They like you. Audra's already planning to invite you to her next game night."

Her nearness sent a familiar, warm current through his body.

"Jessica's terrific, too," she said. "Her curiosity about everything is infectious."

He nodded. "I agree."

Back outside, as they served Audra's berry cobbler under the glowing string lighting, Jonathan watched Amelia. He couldn't take his eyes off her.

At that moment, he realized he wanted more of this, more of her. A lot more. Not the pretense they'd constructed, but something real.

As the evening wound down and goodbyes were exchanged, Jonathan pulled Amelia close one last time, pressing a slow kiss to the side of her head. "Thanks for tonight. I'll see you tomorrow," he said, soft enough to feel intimate.

"Mmm," Amelia replied quietly.

"I like her," Jessica said as they walked toward Jonathan's car. "She's not what I expected."

"What were you expecting?" Jonathan asked, keys jingling in his hand.

"Someone more like Paige, I guess." She'd named his ex-fiancée deliberately. "But Amelia's different. Genuine and humble."

Jessica buckled her seatbelt and glanced at him. "Whatever you've got going with Amelia, it doesn't look temporary."

Jonathan didn't answer right away. Pieces of the evening replayed in his mind—Amelia's laughter, the warmth of her hand intertwined with his, the depth of their kiss.

"Jon?" Jessica asked.

"It's not," he said eventually. It felt like a proclamation. Just close enough to admit what mattered. He started the car.

"Then you need to figure out what you're going to do about

going back to Atlanta. Because that woman isn't a placeholder, Jon. She's the real thing."

As they pulled away from the mansion, Jonathan gripped the steering wheel tighter. Jessica was right. Everything he'd thought he wanted was in Atlanta, but everything he actually wanted was back in that charming old house with the new rose garden.

Returning to Atlanta had always been the plan. His friends and his job were there. His brother was counting on him to take over the family charity, eventually.

Yet sitting at that table tonight, watching Amelia laugh with his sister, he couldn't shake the notion that he'd rediscovered something worth changing all his plans for.

Chapter 41

Amelia

AMELIA SCROLLED through her camera roll, pausing at the photo from last night's dinner party. Jonathan's smile caught her eye, the passion in his expression as he'd looked at her across the patio table. There had been moments throughout the evening when she'd almost forgotten they were performing.

A photo of Pirate and Treasure lounging in their fuzzy blanket grabbed her attention. Amelia added it to a text to her mom, along with last night's group shot from the dinner party.

AMELIA: Making friends.

She set her phone aside and rinsed her dinner plate. Treasure licked the last bites of wet food from a pair of mismatched ceramic dishes. Pirate had settled nearby on the windowsill, watching Amelia, with her tail curled neatly around her feet.

Amelia breathed a slow sigh of relief. She still had plenty of things to do, but her work-life balance overload situation seemed a bit more under control.

Jonathan had secured management approval for the two temporary contractors faster than she'd expected, and the interviews were already underway. And with Drew arriving soon, the pressure of the roof repairs was finally easing, giving her breathing room she hadn't realized she needed until it had nearly seemed too late.

> MOM: ♥ those kittens are such cuties!

> MOM: I recognize that man in the photo. Is that college-Jonathan? Why in God's name is he there?

Amelia groaned. Her finger hovered over the message before she finally hit send.

> AMELIA: You're right, it is. Turns out, our companies are merging. He lives in Atlanta, but he's here on a 3-month assignment. He explained why he ghosted me, and I forgave him. It's a long story, but it's all good.

Amelia stared at her mother's message. *Why in God's name is he there?* The question mirrored her own confusion about Jonathan's place in her life.

With her dinner finished, Amelia spread out the final paint color selections on the kitchen table for one last review. Jessica's design advice had been invaluable, saving Amelia a lot of time by quickly ruling out colors too dark or cold for the mansion's character.

She settled on soft cream for the main halls with warm slate-gray accents, terracotta for the east wing's accent wall, and sage green for the library trim.

Pirate chose that moment to walk directly across the paint samples, leaving tiny paw prints on the sage green swatch. "Thanks for the quality control," Amelia murmured, easing her away.

She compiled the color selections into an email for Mr. F-O to approve, then hit send.

With the task complete, her mind drifted to the previous evening, to the pressure of Jonathan's hand at the small of her back and the way his kiss felt like much more than a charade.

She'd replayed those moments throughout the day, analyzing them like geological samples under a microscope: the shiver she felt when he'd whispered her name, how his thumb had sketched circles on her wrist when he thought no one was looking. Small moments that seemed too real for a performance.

What would those moments feel like without the protection of their arrangement?

She needed another distraction. Making her way to the living room, Amelia spotted Rebecca's worn leather-bound journal where she'd left it on the side table. Perfect.

Pulling a blanket from a nearby basket, she settled on the couch with the journal in her lap. Treasure jumped up beside her and crouched into a perfect loaf. A few moments later, Pirate joined them, purring softly.

Amelia opened the journal.

Treasure had already claimed the warmest spot against Amelia's thigh, so Pirate sprawled across the journal's open pages. "Really?" Amelia asked, gently shifting her. "Rebecca's love story is that boring?"

Amelia shifted Pirate away from the journal and began reading where she'd left off. Thomas's accident.

15 October 1852

> *Thomas lives.*
> *The doctor says he still has months of recovery ahead,*
> *but I care not. I thought I had lost him to that cursed acci-*

dent, thought I would face this wilderness alone with our children.

The injury has cost us his wages through the winter, but we shall manage. Despite the cold, the cow gives good milk still, and the hens lay enough eggs. The sheep provide wool enough to trade for flour and beans. We will survive. My husband will heal, and my heart is full.

I vow to live in the here and now and make every minute with Thomas count. Each moment together is a gift.

Amelia traced the faded words. Rebecca's relief vibrated from the page. *Make every minute count.*

Rebecca had crossed a continent for love, faced down the harsh wilderness and uncertainty, and knew the difference between surviving and truly living. She wouldn't have settled for a safe, artificial version of love when the real thing was within reach.

Treasure stretched and resettled against her thigh, her purr vibrating louder. Outside, evening sounds of distant traffic and the call of night birds in the trees filtered through the windows.

She thought of her own careful approach to relationships, of the barricade she'd built after Nate's confession that he never loved her, of the safe distance she maintained from anything that might require real vulnerability. She'd chosen the safety of an artificial, short-term relationship, but somewhere along the way, her feelings had become overwhelmingly real.

Worst of all, she'd constructed such an elaborate ruse that she'd cut herself off from the friends whose advice she valued most. Audra and Melanie believed she and Jonathan were already in a real relationship and couldn't help her navigate what she actually faced.

Amelia closed the journal carefully. Rebecca's courage reverberated through her heart with resolve. The fake dating had served its purpose—it had given her time, protection, a way to test herself. But she didn't need that shield anymore, at least not for this next step.

She would ask Jonathan on a real date. Not because of pressure from her friends, not to avoid panic attacks, but because she wanted to see where this could go. No performance, just an honest attempt to find out if what she felt when he kissed her could be something real.

Rebecca had vowed to make every minute count, and Amelia would too. This wasn't about promising forever. But she could be brave enough to ask him on a real date and mean it.

Chapter 42

Jonathan

JONATHAN CIRCLED a cluster of timber parcels on the map, marking the third potential divestiture site they'd identified this week.

Amelia scrolled through notes on her laptop. In the corner, Patricia and Gavin were on a teleconference call, swapping ideas with a financial analyst.

They'd been chipping away at the divestiture plan all week. It was slow progress, but progress. For the last three hours, they'd dissected the various options with methodical precision.

"If we go with the long-term management approach," Amelia said, pointing to a thick listing of leases, "we'll need dedicated, specialized staff." She counted on her fingers. "Foresters, geologists, marketing analysts. Four or five people minimum."

"Better than liquidating everything at fire-sale prices," Jonathan replied, making notes in the margin of his printout. The numbers were finally falling into place, a solution that would satisfy both companies' concerns about responsible asset management.

Amelia was mid-sentence, explaining a draft flowchart of responsibilities, when his phone vibrated on the table.

He glanced at the screen and felt his stomach tighten.

Paige. Shit.

He let it buzz twice more before picking it up. "Excuse me."

He stepped out into the hallway, already regretting the decision to answer. "Yeah?"

"Hi," Paige said. Her tone was too bright. "I wanted you to hear it from me first. Today I accepted a temporary transfer. I'll be working out of the Rainmere office starting next week."

Jonathan paused outside the workroom and stared at a landscape print hanging on the wall. "Say that again?"

"You heard me. Seattle's lovely this time of year. And I think it's time we talked."

"Huh," he scoffed, knowing she'd pulled some strings to get the assignment. "Paige," he said slowly, "what are you really doing?"

"I'm not giving up."

"We broke up, Paige. It's over," he said. "And you've already threatened me once."

"That's not fair," she said sweetly.

"It's accurate." He was losing his patience.

"Look, I think we both said things we didn't mean," she said. "Let's not get into that right now. I just want a conversation. Dinner, maybe. We're still civil, right?"

"I meant every word I said," Jonathan said flatly.

"Unless," Paige continued, her voice sliding into something silkier and dangerous, "you've found yourself some new inspiration out there."

In the background, Patricia called Amelia's name.

"Amelia? The woman Lydia mentioned," Paige said, with a hint of suspicion in her voice. "Come to think of it, didn't you date someone in college named Amelia?"

Jonathan's pulse quickened. Of all the names she could have picked up from the background noise. He should have stepped farther away from the conference room.

His grip tightened on the phone. "She's a colleague. On my team."

"Uh-huh." She paused. "I'll see you next week, then."

The line went dead.

He pocketed the phone and scowled. Fuck. It wasn't the first time Paige had cornered him, but now she was flying across the country to do it in person. And she'd picked up on Amelia's name, for the second time.

He returned to the conference room just as Amelia looked up from her screen. "Everything okay?"

Knowing Paige, she wouldn't be discreet once she arrived. "My ex is transferring to this office," he said.

Amelia blinked. "Oh."

"Temporary assignment ... supposedly."

"You didn't tell me she worked for the company," she said.

"She works at Whitlow Forest Resources, in Atlanta. That's how we met. I didn't think it mattered." He slid back into his seat. "It didn't matter. Until now."

"Is this going to be a problem?" Amelia asked.

Jonathan hesitated. "She's persistent. That's always been her thing." He rubbed the back of his neck. "I'll figure out how to manage the situation."

Amelia gave a small nod, but her expression wavered between curiosity and concern.

Before he could say more, his phone buzzed again. He glanced at his watch as he slipped his tablet into a carrying case. Perfect timing.

DREW: Landed. On my way to baggage claim.

JONATHAN: Heading out now.

He needed to get to the airport before the start of rush hour traffic. "Hey, want to come with me to the airport? I'm picking up the best handyman I know."

She closed her laptop and her lips lifted. "Absolutely. I want to thank him in person."

* * *

In the parking lot, Jonathan unlocked the rental and held the passenger door for Amelia.

She raised an eyebrow as she slid into her seat. "Thanks. Nice touch for a fake boyfriend."

Jonathan closed her door and walked around to the driver's side. "I'm the polite and convincing kind."

On the freeway, the city softened in the distance. The sun was sinking behind the downtown buildings.

"This seems like a date," he said, testing the mood.

"It's not a date." Amelia shook her head. "I wouldn't pick this for an actual date."

He smirked. "But you didn't say you wouldn't go on one."

That earned him a sideways glance. "No, I didn't," she said gently.

"So where would you want to go?" He took a chance. "On our actual date?"

"Tsk." She turned her face toward the window, but he caught the edge of a smile.

"Maybe a picnic by the lake? Or a sunset boat ride," he suggested. "I remember our kayaking trip in college—you enjoyed being on the water."

The sudden memory was unusually intense. A perfect spring day, just the two of them on the river, her laughter carrying across the water as she'd tried to splash him with her paddle. Good times. *Before the investigation fucked things up.*

They reached the airport as the sky tipped further into twilight. Drew stood at passenger pickup, duffel slung over his shoulder, flannel shirt open over a plain white tee. A grin formed as he spotted them, and he waved.

Amelia hopped out as soon as Jonathan put the car in park.

"Look who it is," Drew said, pulling her into a hug. "It's been forever."

"I'm so glad you're here," Amelia said. "I still can't believe it."

Jonathan grinned and gave Drew a firm welcome hug with gentle slaps on the back. "Thanks for being here, man."

They tossed Drew's bags in the trunk and climbed back into the car.

As they pulled away, Amelia asked, "Where are you staying?"

"I'm crashing at Jon's place," Drew said. "For as long as he can stand me."

"And this is really how you want to spend your vacation time?" she said.

Drew shrugged. "You need a roof, and I can help. And your guy here rescued me when I needed it. Besides, Audra's here, and I'm looking forward to surprising her. That's more than enough reason."

Amelia turned to Jonathan. "You're hard to repay, apparently."

Jonathan just kept driving. He wasn't looking for payback. He was building connections, trust, maybe even a reason to stay.

Chapter 43

Amelia

Thursday, early morning.

AMELIA LED THE WAY, the dirt moist under her boots as Jonathan and Drew followed her up the narrow path toward the cottage. The scent of cedar mixed with yesterday's rain. She inhaled more deeply than usual, as if the forest air itself were more potent with Jonathan walking beside her.

Instead of just dropping Drew off for the day, Jonathan walked with them to see the cottage. "And to spend a few minutes with you this morning," he'd said. "I even brought my trail shoes."

Amelia couldn't turn down the offer. She planned to work from home after taking Drew to the cottage, and she was grateful for the morning chat before the rest of a quiet day alone.

"Sorry about the hike," she said as they continued through the forest. "Mr. Jewell is working on getting the side road that leads to the cottages opened up, something about having to modify the security gate."

"For this morning, it's a good change," Drew said. "But I

hope he gets the road open before I need to haul tools and equipment to the site."

Ferns spilled over the trail edges, and the occasional whistle of a bird cut through the stillness. She'd walked this trail a dozen times before, but today it felt different. Hopeful.

Something about this particular stretch of forest made her want to linger, to explore every trail that branched off into the deeper woods. With Jonathan beside her, the usual restless energy she felt outdoors had settled into simple calm.

Drew paused at a gap in the underbrush, crouching to examine something in the dried mud. "What's this?" he asked, pointing to a large impression near a fallen log.

"Bear track," Amelia said, bending closer to study the distinctive claw marks. "Black bear, track's probably a few days old. They're pretty common around here—they come through foraging, especially early morning or at dusk."

"Good to know," Drew said, straightening and glancing around the trees.

"As long as we're making noise during the day, they'll keep their distance," Amelia added. She'd done her research when she first moved to the estate. A small surge of confidence warmed her chest. The forest had felt welcoming, but she'd wanted to understand what she might encounter out here. "It's really only a concern at dawn or dusk, or if you surprise one."

Jonathan's eyes lingered on her as she spoke, with appreciation in his expression.

The forest suddenly felt a little wilder than it had a moment ago, though not in a way that made her want to turn back.

* * *

Fifteen minutes later, she punched in the code on the lockbox hanging from the doorknob. With a soft click, it popped open. The key was cold in her palm.

She surveyed the clearing surrounding the cottage, noting how protected it felt tucked among the trees.

"I appreciate you doing this," she said, glancing at Drew and Jonathan then opening the door. "It's dirty inside, but it has so much potential. I've been here a few times to check the interior. I love the stonework and the picture windows looking out to the forest."

Drew gave a shrug. "Friends help each other. I would have come even if I hadn't owed Jon for making my business a reality."

Jonathan nodded. "We want to help."

Inside, the cottage smelled of old lumber and dust, with a hint of mildew near a worn, seventies-era couch. That would have to go. The rest of the furniture was sparse, with only a dilapidated table and a few chairs left behind by whoever used it last. These would have to go, too.

"Have you told Audra you're here yet?" Amelia asked Drew.

"Planning to call her this afternoon," Drew said. "I hope it's a good surprise for her. And I'm hoping she'll be available to have dinner with me."

She nodded with a smile.

Drew dropped his tool bag and started his inspection, tapping walls and making notes.

Amelia stood with Jonathan near the fireplace, watching Drew work. Standing there felt right, like she belonged in this spot, planning repairs and improvements. "I'm grateful you're here," she breathed.

"I know how much this place means to you," Jonathan said. He turned slightly to face her. "And for the record, I'm not going anywhere without saying goodbye this time. No matter what happens."

She swallowed hard. Something deep in her chest relaxed at the promise. He was leaving, but he wasn't running, hiding, or ghosting. It felt as if she'd been holding her breath for years and was finally able to breathe.

Outside, Drew called to them. "You're going to need more than roofing materials. The drainage is bad along the back side. I can shore it up, but that will extend the timeline."

Amelia and Jonathan drifted toward the open door. "I figured there might be more," she said. "The roof's the priority, though."

"You mentioned a ladder?" Drew said to Amelia. "I need to go up and look, both from the outside and the inside."

A prickle of nerves shivered across her skin. After a few seconds she pressed her lips together then nodded toward the far side of the cottage. "In the shed, around the corner. The lock code is 1889."

Drew disappeared around the side of the house, leaving them in the doorway.

"You okay?" Jonathan said.

"I'm fine. I just..." She looked down, then back up. "My dad ... he died falling off a roof." The memory still made her heart hurt, even after all these years. "He was cleaning gutters. It wasn't even that high up."

She'd been the one to find him. Fourteen years old, coming home from school, calling for him because his truck was in the driveway.

Jonathan stepped closer and took her hand, his fingers intertwining with hers. No words, just a soft squeeze. The simple contact soothed her, and she suddenly realized she'd been shaking since Drew asked for the ladder.

He always knew exactly what she needed.

Amelia took a breath. She hadn't planned on doing this now, but the moment suddenly felt too right to ignore. "Listen," she said. "About us."

Her heart was beating fast, but not from nerves this time. From certainty.

Jonathan raised an eyebrow. "Yeah?"

"I want to say yes. To an actual date." She blurted it, meeting his eyes. "I know you're leaving eventually. I know this is temporary. But I don't want to pretend anymore that what I feel for you isn't real."

He didn't hesitate. "Let's do it," he said, stepping toward her. "We're not committing to forever," he whispered. "Just to be honest about what's happening between us now."

Her breath got trapped in her throat.

"I want to be with you," he continued, voice low. "Without rules. Without pretending. Just you and me."

She nodded, already smiling. "Me too."

His hand found her waist. She could smell his soap, clean and cedarlike, nearly matching the forest air around them. He cupped her face, his thumb brushing across her cheekbone, and she forgot how to think. The gesture felt both new and eternally right.

"Amelia," he whispered, as he touched his mouth to hers.

This kiss was slow, unhurried, and nothing like their previous performances. No audience, no agenda except the pull between them that had been reigniting for weeks.

His lips were tender and sure, moving against hers with patience that made her knees weak. Amelia responded without hesitation. Her fingers slid into the soft cotton of his shirt, drawing him closer.

As his tongue touched hers, she forgot they were standing in a doorway, forgot Drew was somewhere nearby, forgot everything except the fever building between them.

When he deepened the kiss, she made a soft moan. Her pulse hammered so hard she wondered if he could feel it where his hand swept against her neck.

One arm came around her, pulling her against him. She could feel the rapid beat of his heart through his shirt, matching the rhythm of her own.

Amelia laughed under her breath, a little dizzy. "That was definitely not in the contract," she said, leaning back.

"I think we've voided the contract," he said with a coy smile.

Amelia looked at Jonathan. He gently pushed her hair away from her face. It took her a moment to remember how to breathe normally.

No fear. No regrets. Live in the here and now. Make every minute count.

"Yes," she whispered. "Yes, to the real date. Yes to this."

His smile was intoxicating. "Tomorrow night?"

"Tomorrow night."

* * *

Back at the main house, Amelia took off her boots by the front door. Jonathan had changed his shoes and left for the office, while Drew had stayed at the cottage to make a more detailed assessment.

The cats were curled on a sunny window seat in the foyer, twitching in their sleep. Pirate opened one eye for a moment, then closed it again. Amelia settled at the library desk with her laptop.

Before starting her work-from-home day, she opened her text thread with Audra and Melanie.

AMELIA: I think I'm officially seeing Jonathan.

Typing bubbles appeared almost instantly.

AUDRA: Wait. Official what?

MELANIE: What happened to taking it slow?

Amelia sighed and typed more.

AMELIA: I didn't say much earlier because I
wasn't sure it was leading anywhere. Now it is.

AUDRA: I don't know whether to yell at you or
cheer for you. Maybe both.

MELANIE: When does he go back to Atlanta?
Are you okay with that?

AMELIA: I'm going to make every minute
count. At least this time, I know he's leaving.

AUDRA: Are we celebrating? Do I need wine?
Cake? Noise makers?

Amelia smiled, but her fingers hovered for a few seconds before she responded.

AMELIA: Hold the cake, not celebrating yet.
Still processing.

She paused.

AMELIA: It feels good. Scary. But good.

AUDRA: You're allowed to have good things.
Even if they're scary. Plus, you've seemed
more at ease lately. Like you're less worried
about everything.

MELANIE: Audra is right. Full disclosure, I'm still disappointed you didn't try dating Leo, but I'm happy for you.

She typed one last line.

AMELIA: I'm smiling, too.

Amelia locked her phone and opened her laptop to log in to work. She wasn't sure what would come next. But for once, that didn't feel like a reason to back away.

Chapter 44

Amelia

"I CAN'T BELIEVE you chartered this," Amelia said, accepting the crew member's hand as she stepped aboard the eighty-foot schooner.

The smooth deck gleamed and tall masts stretched toward the darkening sky. Floor-to-ceiling windows revealed an elegant salon with cream leather seating.

"It's a new level of experience for me, too," Jonathan said, following her onto the boat. The schooner rocked gently beneath their feet, and he steadied himself against the railing. "I've never done anything like this before."

"What, rented a huge boat?"

"Rented anything this extravagant. My idea of splurging is usually upgrading to first class on a flight."

"Nice to know you're not usually this extravagant," Amelia said.

Captain Saul welcomed them with champagne flutes. "Good evening. We'll be cruising Puget Sound for about two hours. Your table is ready whenever you'd like to be seated."

Amelia turned a slow circle, taking in the upper deck with

panoramic views. The rigging creaked softly in the evening breeze. "This is insane. Gorgeous, but still insane."

A crew member gave them a brief tour. The main salon featured formal seating and a dining table set for two. There was a full galley below, multiple guest cabins, and an upper deck with panoramic views.

"I'm breathless," she exclaimed, tracing the intricate wood trim with her fingertips. "I've never been on anything larger than a fishing boat."

As the schooner pulled away from the marina, Amelia moved to the windows. The city lights were just beginning to blink in the gathering dusk, and the water stretched endlessly in every direction. The large white sails filled as the boat moved with the breeze.

"Being on the water always feels so different from being on land," Amelia said as she watched the wake trailing behind them. "Everything feels more ... open out here. More possibilities."

Jonathan smiled. "I like that. More possibilities."

The chef interrupted with their first course, pan-seared halibut with lemon butter rice. They sat at the dining table as the schooner rocked gently beneath them. The cool evening air drifted through an open window.

"I love it," she said after one bite, "but I feel like I should be wearing diamonds or something."

"You don't need jewels." Jonathan's voice was quiet. "You're perfect exactly as you are."

Heat crept up her neck. He had a way of saying delicious things that made her feel like the only woman in the world.

"So," she said, reaching across the table to touch his hand. "Tell me about your ex-girlfriend."

Jonathan nearly choked on his wine. "My ex-girlfriend?"

"The one who's transferring to Rainmere." She kept her tone light, conversational. "Is her transfer a coincidence?"

Jonathan set down his wine glass and looked out at the water, where the lights of downtown Seattle flickered like scattered stars. "Honestly? I think she arranged it. Paige doesn't believe in coincidences."

"Should I be worried?"

"She has a vindictive streak," he said. "I'm a little concerned she might try to make things difficult for you at work."

Amelia frowned as she considered the possibility. "Only with work?"

"Whatever happens with Paige, it won't change how I feel about you." His response was immediate and firm.

The certainty in his voice made her heart skip a beat. She summoned her courage. "And exactly how do you feel about me?"

"Like I want to rediscover everything about you. Like I want to make you laugh every day." He reached across the table and touched her hand. "Like this might be more than just temporary for me."

Her chest tightened. This was exactly what she'd been afraid of. "Jonathan."

"I know," he said. "I know this is just supposed to be fun. But I want to be honest with you about where I am."

She stared at him across the candlelit table. The schooner continued to sway beneath them in the gentle current. "We only have a month and a half left working together. And then you go back to Atlanta."

"A lot can happen in a month and a half." His gaze locked onto hers.

"A month and a half will go by too quickly," she sighed.

"We're going to make the most of it," he said, his voice resolute. "I promise you."

* * *

Later, as they finished their dessert, the schooner hit a small wake, and they both reached for their water glasses at the same time.

"You look so serious." He took her hand in his. "What are you thinking now?"

She looked down at their joined hands and allowed herself to wish it could always be this way.

Falling for you again would be dangerous. The words stuck in her throat. *But maybe that's inevitable.*

Jonathan lifted her hand and pressed a gentle kiss on the top.

Before she could answer, Captain Saul announced they were approaching the Space Needle, lit up against the night sky. They moved out to the deck, the cool air raising goosebumps on Amelia's arms.

They stood in comfortable silence for a moment. The city lights reflected off the water and the gentle waves lapped against the hull.

"This has been marvelous," she said. "Thank you."

"Thank you for saying yes," he said, sliding one arm around her shoulder.

The schooner's sails fluttered as they changed course, and Jonathan's arm tightened around her.

"About that contract," he said.

"What about it?"

"I think we should revise it," he suggested.

Amelia's shoulders tensed. "Revise it how?"

"Well, for starters, this isn't fake anymore. And since we're actually dating, maybe we don't need a contract at all."

She hesitated and turned to hold the railing again. "I'm not ready to think about that tonight."

"What can you think about?" Jonathan said.

"Right now. This moment. What we have together today." She moved closer and slipped her arm around his waist.

"Just now?"

"Yes. And then tomorrow I'll think about how we are tomorrow." She leaned her head against his arm. "One simple moment at a time."

Jonathan kissed the top of her head as soft light from the schooner's deck lamps came on. "I can work with now," he said. "But are you sure that's enough for you?"

"It has to be," Amelia said.

"Then we're renegotiating our fake relationship into a genuine relationship based on living in the moment."

"I guess we are," she agreed.

They stood quietly, listening to the gentle creaking of the rigging and the splash of water against the hull. Stars scattered across the darkening sky, as the music from the sound system shifted to something slow and jazzier.

Jonathan held out his hand. "Dance with me."

"Here?"

He smiled and nodded. "I want to hold you," he whispered.

She let him draw her close to his body. His hands rested at the small of her back, warm through the thin cotton of her dress. Her palm rested against his chest, and she could feel his heartbeat, steady and strong, beneath her fingers.

They swayed together, barely moving to the soft music. The cool night air carried the scent of saltwater, but all she could focus on was the way her body molded tightly, perfectly, against his.

"This is nice," she murmured, her cheek resting against his chest.

Jonathan pulled her in tighter. "This is perfect."

The schooner heeled slightly as they caught more wind, and Amelia pressed closer to Jonathan for balance.

His hand traced slowly up her back, fingertips finding the sensitive spot where her neck met her shoulder. She shivered and pressed closer, her hand curling into his shirt.

"Amelia." His voice was rougher now, lower.

She lifted her head to look at him, and the intensity in his eyes made her breath catch. His hand moved to cup the back of her neck, thumb brushing along her jawline.

"I want to kiss you," he said.

"Then do," she said, nodding slowly.

His lips met hers, delicately at first, testing. She responded immediately, her mouth opening under his, and the kiss deepened. She slid her hands up to tangle in his hair, pulling him closer. He groaned softly against her mouth, his arm tightening around her waist, drawing her flush against him.

As their mouths separated, her head felt dizzy and her legs unsteady.

"Wow," she whispered.

"We're probably giving the crew an eyeful."

She laughed breathlessly. "Probably."

But neither of them moved. They stayed locked together, foreheads touching, sharing the same air.

This moment in time, with the wind in the sails and his arms around her, was all that mattered.

Chapter 45

Amelia

Saturday morning.

AMELIA WATCHED the sprinklers water the newly planted rose beds as sunlight filtered through the kitchen windows. After spending the morning in the library getting a head start on researching chandeliers for Mr. F-O, she sat at the kitchen table with her laptop.

But her mind kept returning to luscious thoughts about last night's date with Jonathan. His hand on her back throughout the evening, the way he'd looked at her when he said he wanted her to know where he stood.

The two rescued kittens perched on the windowsill, eyes darting between watching her and the birds flittering in the trees outside.

Amelia closed her laptop and headed to the kitchen counter. She wouldn't see Jonathan today; they were both booked. But it gave her an opportunity to think things through, particularly the contract.

Did she still need a contract? Now that they were actually dating, did any of the boundaries make sense?

Her phone buzzed, and her mom's photo smiled up at her from the screen.

"Hi, Mom," Amelia said, tucking the phone between her shoulder and ear.

"How are things going there, honey?"

"Things are good. I got the loan approval for the cottage."

"Oh, Amelia, that's wonderful!"

"And Jonathan's friend Drew is going to help with the repairs. He's a contractor, doing it at cost."

"That's such a relief. I know you were worried about the budget."

"I also finished cataloging the books in Mr. Jewell's library, and now he has me researching replacement chandeliers."

"I'm so proud of you, sweetheart. Which brings me to my news." Her voice brightened. "I've decided you're right about moving to Washington."

Amelia blinked. "You have?"

"After hearing all your suggestions and taking time to mull them over, I've come up with a business plan to keep my music instruction going until I get established in Rainmere. You're right. I can create teaching videos for my existing students and publish a virtual course. And I will gladly accept your help with the technical side."

"That's fabulous! I'd love to help with that," Amelia said. She turned around and leaned against the counter.

What the heck had happened? Just weeks ago, her mother had been resistant to leaving Florida. But before she thought of other questions to ask, Amelia's mind circled back to Jonathan.

"That's great that you're on board with the recording help," her mom said. "I was worried about the technical side, but if you can help me, that's perfect. What else is going on? You sound happier than usual."

Amelia's stomach jumped. "Actually, I'm seeing someone, Mom."

"You finally went on the blind date with Melanie's friend? That's terrific, honey. What's he like?"

"No, Mom." Amelia spoke slowly. "Jonathan. Jonathan Fontaine. You remember him from the photo? We went on a date last night."

Silence stretched across the line.

"Amelia." Her mother's voice shifted from warm to concerned. "Why not date someone local? Someone who could actually build a future with you?" Her mother cleared her throat. "Not to mention, Jonathan cut you out of his life a few years ago. What makes you think he won't do it again?"

"It's not like that. He explained why he left. He was protecting me," Amelia said.

"Protecting you? Honey, that's what they all say. Men who disappear always want you to believe they have noble reasons." Her voice softened. "I just don't want to see you get hurt again. You're finally in a good place. Why complicate things with someone who's just going to leave soon?"

"Because I care about him. And he cares about me. We understand this is just temporary."

"Oh, sweetheart." Her mom sighed. "I know you think you can handle a casual relationship, but you've never been good at keeping your heart out of things. Remember what happened with Nate? I don't want to see you go through that again."

"This is completely different."

"Is it? Nate was never emotionally committed to you. Now you're setting yourself up to fall for someone who's already planning to leave. It's shades of the same thing."

Amelia closed her eyes. Her mother's words hit close to her own fears. "I need to go, Mom."

"Amelia, I'm not trying to upset you. I just want you to be careful."

"I know, Mom. I love you."

"I love you too, honey."

After ending the call, Amelia stared at the kittens in the window. Her mother's concerns echoed every doubt she'd been trying to suppress. Maybe she was setting herself up for heartbreak.

Amelia returned to the kitchen table and opened her laptop again. After the library research, she attempted to gather her thoughts about the contract Jonathan wanted to ditch. She'd started a new list of which boundaries still made sense now that they were really together.

She frowned at her updated list of dating rules. Amelia had decided not to call it a contract anymore.

Rules to keep: No overnight stays. This maintained a significant boundary that prevented domestic intimacy. Keeping work separate from dating life, essential for professionalism. And no social media posts would prevent the creation of a public narrative of a serious relationship.

Time limit, date clarity ... maybe she needed a new rule about acknowledging things would end when he left for Atlanta?

Rules she wanted to drop: No romantic gestures in private. This one had made sense for fake dating but was counterproductive for real dating. *Delete.* The honesty clause was already obsolete since they both had declared their feelings. *Delete.*

The no-sex rule. She highlighted it and hovered over the delete key. Did she want to drop it? Sex seemed like a slippery slope, but...

Before she could completely second-guess herself, she opened the group text with Audra and Melanie.

AMELIA: Hypothetical question. If you were
dating someone you really liked, but you knew
they were leaving town in a few weeks, would
you sleep with them?

MELANIE: Did you already sleep with
Jonathan?

AUDRA: Tell me you slept with him.

AMELIA: We had our second date last night. A
spectacular date. But it's temporary until he
goes back to Atlanta. And no, I didn't sleep
with him. Not yet.

MELANIE: How was the date? I need details.

AUDRA: Forget the date details. Are we talking
about whether to sleep with him or not?

AMELIA: That's exactly what I'm asking. I'm
trying to figure out what boundaries to set.

MELANIE: Are you setting boundaries to
protect yourself, or because you think you
should?

Amelia stared at Melanie's question.

AMELIA: Both? I don't want to fall so hard that
I'm crushed when he leaves.

AUDRA: But are you protecting yourself from
getting hurt, or protecting yourself from being
happy?

MELANIE: I hate to say this, but you might already be in too deep for boundaries to help. The heart doesn't really follow contracts.

AUDRA: Plus, honey, all this forbidden tension might be harder to handle than just being together!

MELANIE: Anticipation can be more overwhelming than reality.

Amelia laughed and nodded to herself. So true.

AMELIA: So you think I should?

AUDRA: I think you should stop trying to control every variable and just see what happens. You like him. He likes you. You're both adults.

MELANIE: What's your gut telling you?

Amelia walked to the window. Her gut told her she was already falling for Jonathan. Her gut also told her that denying herself this chance might be the bigger mistake.

AMELIA: My gut says I'm overthinking this

AUDRA: Listen to your instincts. Sometimes your gut knows best. Or, you know, listen to something a few inches lower.

MELANIE: Whatever you decide, we're here for you. But don't let fear decide.

AUDRA: Temporary isn't necessarily meaningless. Some of the most important relationships are the short ones that teach us what we actually want.

AMELIA: Thanks. I needed to hear that.

MELANIE: Now can we PLEASE get some details about this date?

AUDRA: Was it everything you hoped? Was there another fiery kiss?

AMELIA: It was off the charts amazing. He chartered an entire boat just for us. There was dinner by candlelight, and we slow-danced on the deck.

MELANIE: Wow, he went all out. That doesn't sound like a guy who's thinking temporarily.

AMELIA: Puget Sound was beautiful. We talked for hours and watched the city lights across the water. And kissing him 💗

He'd suggested they get rid of the boundaries altogether. She sighed. She wasn't ready to tell them everything.

AUDRA: What about the kiss?

AMELIA: Let's just say I'm definitely interested in a lot more of the same.

MELANIE: I'm so happy for you. And maybe a little worried, but mostly happy.

AUDRA: Don't be worried. Amelia deserves some romance and a little wild fun.

After saying goodbye to her friends, Amelia stared out at the garden. They were right. Trying to control everything was just fear talking.

Maybe she just needed to trust herself. Trust that she was strong enough to handle whatever happened. Trust that a few weeks of genuine happiness were worth the risk.

Her phone buzzed with a new text.

JONATHAN: How's your Saturday going? Any regrets about last night?

She stared at the message, her heart pounding. Fewer rules, no overthinking. Just honesty.

AMELIA: No regrets. You?

JONATHAN: Only that I let you go home alone last night.

She smiled, excitement spreading through her chest. She deleted "no sex" from the new rules list.

AMELIA: Well, maybe next time.

Chapter 46

Jonathan

Sunday morning.

AFTER RENTING tools and filling his rental SUV with bundles of shingles at the hardware store, Jonathan and Drew entered the back of the Jewell property through the new security entrance and drove toward the cottages at the end of the northern private drive.

Jonathan's shoulders ached from loading shingle bundles that weighed twice what they looked like they should. Drew moved with easy efficiency, hefting materials as if they were featherlight, while Jonathan checked his grip on every load.

Throughout the morning, Jonathan steadied lumber while Drew measured and cut materials. He handed up tools in the precise order Drew called for them and kept the work area organized as debris accumulated. By the time Drew started the actual roof repairs, Jonathan had gained a healthy respect for construction work.

Watching Drew secure the roof, Jonathan felt a deep sense of satisfaction. There was something important about making places safe, about creating shelter. The feeling was strong and calming at the same time.

Audra and Amelia showed up midday with pizza, salads, and freshly brewed iced tea. "We wanted to make sure you're fed," Audra said.

Amelia smiled. "Sorry, there's no beer. You're working on a roof and using power tools." From Amelia's car, they unloaded folding chairs and a card table, as well as a bucket stuffed with cleaning supplies.

Jonathan gathered up an armful of supplies to take to Drew. He watched Amelia set up the table with Audra. She reached to straighten a napkin, and for a split second, he could see it—not this picnic, but a hundred other moments. Sunday mornings. Holidays. The everyday rhythms of a shared life.

Heat spread down through his chest and settled somewhere deep in his stomach. He set down the supplies without realizing it, his hands suddenly unsteady. His breathing fell shallow.

Huh. The realization hit him like a visceral impact. He wasn't just attracted to Amelia. He wasn't just enjoying their time together. This was something else entirely, something that made his throat tight and his future plans feel fragile.

He was growing more attached to Amelia, and he didn't want things to end with the assignment. He didn't want things with Amelia to end at all.

"Lunch is ready, everyone," Audra called out a minute later.

Drew made his way down the ladder. "Besides the roof and the drainage along the outside," he said casually, "there are some plumbing and electrical issues inside that need work, too." He wiped his hands on his jeans. "I'm thinking of staying in town for a month or two, instead of just a few weeks."

"That's way too much, Drew," Amelia said. "I'm so grateful for your help, but I don't want to take you away from your work for so long."

"Stop trying to kick him out. I, for one, have zero complaints about an extended visit," Audra said. She patted Drew on the shoulder.

"I'm waiting for a deal to come through before I need to be back in Atlanta. Besides, we're going to have a slight materials delay. The hardware store didn't have enough matching shingles on hand. They're ordering more, but they won't arrive for at least a week."

Amelia nodded. "What kind of deal?" she asked.

They gathered around the small table Audra and Amelia had set up in the clearing.

"Construction assessment work," Drew said. "I do geological surveys for other companies." Drew wiped sweat from his forehead with a towel.

"Interesting," Amelia said. "I love that you combined your geology background with your interest in construction work."

Drew nodded. "So, what's Brandon's deal lately?" He added two slices of pizza to his plate. "He sure was hot under the collar after our last golf game. Seemed like it was about more than just losing a round or two."

"Brandon wants me to take over running the family charity fund sooner than we agreed. Way more than his usual impatience." Looking at Amelia, he added, "He wants to make sure I come back, and soon."

Amelia turned around in her chair and snapped a few photos of the cottage repairs in progress. "I'm going to send a few photos to my mom."

"How's she doing?" Audra asked. She scooped up a helping of salad. "Since you're renovating, that must mean she's agreed to move? Have the two of you figured out a business direction for her?"

"Yes, she agreed to move," Amelia said. "She likes some of our business ideas. When I told her that the roof repair was happening, she said she's started creating a virtual course. Money from that could help tide her over until she establishes a new student base here in Washington. Completely floored me that suddenly she wants to move. I don't know what happened ... she seemed so hesitant, and now she's full-steam-ahead."

"Hm. I guess you're grateful for the change?" Audra said.

"I am," Amelia nodded. "I know I shouldn't question her change of heart, but it feels like there's something she's not telling me. Like she had some revelation, and she's not sharing what it was."

Twenty minutes later, they finished eating and worked together to clear the table and pack away the extra food.

Drew wandered to the edge of the clearing while the others finished up.

Jonathan slipped his arms around Amelia's waist as she put away the last of the picnic items. He pressed his face into her hair. "I'm glad you showed up today," he whispered as he kissed her gently on the neck. Wanting her was becoming a physical ache.

"Me too," Amelia said.

"This place needs a picnic table," Drew said, surveying the clearing beside the cottage. "And maybe a stone patio."

"Sounds expensive," Amelia said with a slight frown.

"Are you searching for excuses to stay even longer?" Audra said.

"Yes," he said, moving closer to help her lift the supply bucket without being asked. His fingers covered hers on the handle for just a moment before she let go. "Longer to see you."

"Friends forever," Audra reminded him, her tone turning playful.

Audra grabbed the bucket of cleaning supplies from Drew and motioned to Amelia. "Let's get started inside."

Jonathan felt the brush of her fingers against his lower back as she slipped a folded paper into his pocket.

"Our new agreement," Amelia whispered.

His breath caught at the intimacy of her casual but deliberate gesture, and his chest tightened as she stepped away with a quick wink. Jonathan's hand moved instinctively toward his back pocket, wanting to chase the heat her touch had left behind.

"Coming," Amelia said, heading toward Audra and the cottage door.

Drew picked up a bag of tools and started up the ladder.

Jonathan stole a moment to himself to look over the contents of the new dating agreement.

He eagerly scanned the short list: No overnight stays; keep work separate from dating life; no social media posts. Fine, those all made sense.

The last item made his heart drop. Time-limit rule: this relationship ends when Jonathan's Rainmere assignment is over.

He read the line three times, each pass making his heart fall further. Through the cottage window, he could see Amelia wiping down surfaces, her movements quick and efficient. She looked settled here, like she belonged. Like this was exactly where she wanted to be. And she was preparing for him to leave.

He'd hoped she'd encourage him to stay in Rainmere instead of going back to Atlanta. But this time-limit rule? What if Amelia wasn't ready for anything more than "here and now"? His stomach soured. Would she ever be ready?

He folded the paper and slipped it back into his pocket, his mind already working through possibilities. Maybe Steve would have ideas about remote work options. Maybe there was a way to extend the project timeline.

His phone buzzed, interrupting the half-formed plans.

BRANDON: Just found out I got accepted to a leadership program in North Carolina.

JONATHAN: Weird timing. We were just talking about you.

BRANDON: I don't want to know.

JONATHAN: Wait, the same program from after college?

BRANDON: Yes, the same. But this time they accepted me. Vindication is mine.

JONATHAN: Congratulations! Bet Mom's thrilled for you.

BRANDON: I haven't told her yet. I need a plan first.

JONATHAN: Why do you need a plan? Can't you just take time off?

BRANDON: This is an elite program. A year of training. Not full-time, but it's going to affect how much I can do at Form to Function.

Suddenly all of Brandon's pressure for him to stay in Atlanta made sense.

JONATHAN: Did you know when I was in Atlanta? Why the hell didn't you say something? Anything.

BRANDON: Nothing was for sure then.

JONATHAN: A year? When does the program
start?

BRANDON: June 1.

JONATHON: Shit. A little heads-up would have
been appreciated.

There had to be a way.

He'd talk to Steve about alternative work possibilities, about extending the project timeline, about anything that would let him stay. Then he'd figure out how to help Amelia see past that time limit rule. And he'd find a way to deal with Brandon's expectations.

Right now, watching Amelia through the cottage window, only one thing felt certain. He wasn't ready to give this up.

Chapter 47

Amelia

MELANIE SET a bag of donuts and a cup of coffee on Amelia's desk.

"Ooh, donuts!" Amelia said, opening the bag. She inhaled the scent of fresh, warm pastry. "You are a goddess. I could really use a blast of sugar this morning. What's the occasion?"

"Donuts take the sting out of any difficult conversation," Melanie said flatly.

Amelia narrowed her eyes. "Sounds serious. Should I brace myself?"

"Maybe," Melanie said with a half laugh. She glanced at the empty workroom. "Where is everyone?"

"Jonathan is in a management meeting, and the techs are making printouts for tomorrow's presentation."

She and Jonathan had been working on their final presentation for several days. They were both confident that their asset divestiture plans would strengthen the merged company. But management presentations always made her nervous.

"Since we're alone, I've got a few questions." Melanie sat down next to Amelia. "What do you know about Jonathan's recent ex?"

"To be honest, not a lot," Amelia said. She opened the bag and fished out a glazed donut. "I know they work for the same company. And that he broke it off with her. I also know she's transferring here."

"I don't want to be an alarmist," Melanie said. "But you know I've been working with people at Whitlow Forest Resources in Atlanta." She broke off a piece of her cake donut. "I've been hearing some office gossip," she said slowly.

Amelia's donut was soft and still slightly warm. "I usually try to avoid the workplace gossip," Amelia said between bites.

"I know. Me too. But this is important enough, I feel you need to know. As a friend, I need to tell you, since you're getting more involved with Jonathan."

"Now I'm concerned," Amelia said. She wiped glaze from the corner of her mouth with a napkin.

Melanie nodded. "Look, I heard his ex is a bigwig at Whitlow. Her father is the owner." Melanie paused for a moment and took a sip of her coffee. "Her name is Paige Whitlow. As in Whitlow Forest Resources."

Melanie paused, and Amelia washed the last of her donut down with a sip of coffee.

"Rumor has it they were pretty serious," Melanie finally added.

Amelia's stomach dropped. The news was more impactful than it should have been after only two dates.

She slumped back into her chair and wondered why Jonathan had given her the impression that it hadn't been a serious relationship. She sat silently, unsure how to respond.

"I got a memo saying Paige will arrive soon," Amelia said.

"I looked up Paige on the company website, since we have access to both companies' info," Melanie said. "I confirmed that she's the owner's daughter. Maybe it won't matter." She paused. "But the rumors say that she's known for cutting down her enemies. The conversation around the office is she's both beautiful and vindictive."

Amelia didn't want to let this news defeat her. "Jonathan and I have gone out on exactly two dates. I'm not her enemy."

"Yeah, but *he* might be on *her* enemy list," Melanie said. "Look, rumors are just rumors, not facts, but most whispered stories have some underlying truth, even if they are teeny tiny truths. All I'm saying is, watch your back."

"Your lawyer instincts are blinding me right now."

"Good," Melanie said. "You know, he goes back in what, a month? That's one hell of a long-distance relationship."

"My eyes are wide open," Amelia said. "It's a short-term thing ... we have different lives in different places. We've agreed, no commitment beyond now, and the relationship ends when he leaves." She straightened herself confidently. "You and Audra were the ones pushing me to get back in the saddle, and that's what I'm doing. Aren't you happy about that?"

"Yes, it's wonderful that you're getting out there. You're getting your feet wet, but your ass isn't really in the saddle. He's safe sex because he's leaving. No chance for anything real."

Amelia shifted, uncomfortable in her seat. Melanie sounded like her mother.

"Have you heard from Audra today?" Amelia said, deflecting the conversation. "She's been slow replying to my texts for the past few days."

"I think she's got more on her mind since Drew arrived." Melanie closed the top of the donut bag. "She's going to see him at the cottage site for lunch."

"Well, that's interesting," Amelia said. "Wish I had time to dive into that subject. But I've got to get back to my presentation prep. Tomorrow is the big day."

"I'll leave you to it," Melanie said as she patted her friend on the back. She picked up her coffee and headed toward the hallway door.

Amelia considered what her friend had said. Exactly how serious was Jonathan's relationship with Paige? Why would he hide it?

Questions multiplied in her mind. She considered asking him for more details about his past relationship but feared she would appear insecure.

Had Jonathan downplayed the relationship to make her feel more comfortable? Or was Melanie's gossip mill exaggerating the situation? Either way, Paige being both an ex-girlfriend and the boss's daughter shed a different light on her upcoming transfer.

Amelia decided she'd check the company intranet for more info about Paige after the presentation was over. She should at least prepare herself.

The situation suddenly felt loaded with complications she hadn't considered.

She turned back to her computer, forcing herself to refocus. The Paige situation could wait until after tomorrow's presentation. After that, she'd be asking Jonathan some pointed questions about his Atlanta life.

Chapter 48

Jonathan

Friday.

That evening at the Shoyu & Sear-House, Jonathan raised his glass at their reserved hibachi table. Steam rose from the sizzling grill while their chef artfully flipped shrimp and vegetables.

"To the best merger transition team ever," he said. His coworkers all lifted their glasses.

"Thank you all for your hard work over the last few weeks," he continued, "and especially for the extra efforts to get ready for the excellent presentation today. I'm so proud of what we've accomplished together. Here's to increasing achievement in the next month."

Everyone at the long hibachi table cheered and touched their glasses together. *Clink, clink.* Fragrant scents of sautéing Asian food filled the air as their table chef served the meat, vegetable, and rice dishes.

The dinner celebration was a bittersweet triumph. Jonathan leaned back in his seat and took a long pull of his drink.

Their presentation had gone extremely well. The managers

loved the idea of establishing a small, permanent team to manage and sell the less valuable and redundant mineral assets.

But each day they inched closer to finishing their project—and closer to his inevitable return to Atlanta.

As the dinner celebration wound down, one by one, people said their goodbyes, and soon Jonathan and Amelia were alone at the table. Jonathan signaled to the waiter for their bill.

"You know, there's a karaoke place next door," Amelia said with a grin. "Audra and I used to go there a lot after work, but it's been a while. It's a great way to work off stress."

Jonathan nodded and smiled. "I'm impressed. Rainmere's business district is top-notch for a smaller town. Let's do it." He wanted to make her happy and watch her sing and dance into the night. "Just to be totally up front, though ... I can carry a tune, but that's about all I can promise," he said.

Amelia invited Melanie and Audra, and Jonathan texted Drew.

By the time the others arrived, Jonathan and Amelia had reserved a private room at the Karaoke Hall and ordered a pitcher of beer and appetizers for those who hadn't just eaten hibachi.

Jonathan watched Amelia flip through the song selection book, her finger tracing down the titles with focused concentration. It was the same intense expression she'd worn during their presentation that morning.

Though truth be told, Paige's perfect timing this morning had been partly to blame for Amelia's heightened energy. Her arrival at the office just before their presentation was set to start had not helped matters at all.

She'd introduced herself to Amelia and added, "Are you having fun together while he's here? I can't wait for him to come home to Atlanta."

Her words were provocative, vindictive, and well planned.

He was positive that Paige's comments had been enough to sow doubts in Amelia about whether their relationship was completely done.

Amelia had given him several side glances throughout the evening. She mostly seemed calm, but Jonathan was sure she was still mulling over the interactions with Paige.

Fortunately, it hadn't thrown either of them off their game for their presentation.

And his boss had even called to congratulate him. "Terrific presentation, Jonathan. You and your team scored big today." Steve continued to praise their work and the team's solid solutions.

"By the way," Steve added, his voice sounding conciliatory. "I followed up on your transfer questions. Unfortunately, there aren't any job openings at the NorthSound Timber office. And I can't approve any remote work. Upper management won't go for it, at least not right now. We can ask again in a few months."

Not the answers he'd hoped to hear, but being back in Atlanta would offer him a chance to ensure his Career Recovery Program was on the right track and moving forward.

Jonathan's mind flashed back to something from earlier. After the presentation, he'd caught Paige on the phone in the hallway, her voice low and intense. The words "personnel decisions" and "international assignments" had drifted his way before she'd noticed him and smoothly shifted to discussing lunch plans. At the time, he'd dismissed it as corporate small talk. Now, with Steve's definitive "no" on Seattle, the coincidence nagged at him.

Jonathan shook off the burden of both memories—Paige's calculated interference and Steve's disappointing news. The karaoke room's shifting lighting and Amelia's laughter reminded him why tonight was worth celebrating.

Amelia tapped a spoon against her beer glass, bringing Jonathan's attention back to the present moment.

"I have good news, everyone!" Amelia held up her glass. "After our presentation today, my boss offered me a full-time job." Her grin widened. "As soon as this project is over, I'm no longer a contractor!"

Audra and Melanie hugged Amelia and congratulated her.

Jonathan's heart seemed ready to explode. "I'm so, so proud of you," he said. It was another bittersweet moment; he also knew Amelia's ties to Rainmere had just become a lot stronger.

"Let's get this party rolling," Audra said. She selected a fast song then grabbed a mic and Amelia's hand. She motioned to Melanie and offered her a mic. "Come on. You too!"

At the front of the private room, the women sang and danced, jumping and pumping the air to pop music for the next thirty minutes.

Jonathan couldn't take his eyes off Amelia as she moved to the beat, her hips swaying and her hair catching the colored stage lights. When she turned and caught him staring, she beckoned with a crooked finger and a wicked grin that sent heat plunging straight through to his core.

When they finally collapsed onto the couch, breathless and glowing, Amelia handed the mics to Jonathan and Drew. "Guy duet time." She grinned as she leaned forward to grab her drink.

"Are you sure you really want that?" Jonathan asked.

Amelia's brows lifted. "Yes. It's my fondest wish to see you two dreamboats sing together."

"Dude duet, dude duet," Audra chanted.

Melanie joined the chorus. "Dude duet..."

Twenty minutes and several duets later, Jonathan settled next to Amelia on a couch. He leaned in to kiss her, and she cupped his face in her hands, deepening the kiss. Jonathan moaned. "Can we go home now?" he whispered against her neck.

"Not quite yet."

Jonathan gave her a look of mock devastation.

"Are you inviting me to your place?" Amelia asked.

"Yes. I am," he continued, nuzzling her neck.

"Good." She pressed a quick kiss to his jaw. "Because I've been thinking about getting you alone all evening."

She put her arm around his shoulder and leaned her head on his arm. Exactly where he wanted her to stay.

"Drew and Audra look so cute together," she whispered.

He glanced at Drew, talking to Audra, engaged with her every word like they were meant to spend their lives together. "They do," he agreed.

He settled deeper into the couch cushions, Amelia's weight against his side, creating a perfect pocket of warmth and contentment.

He put his hand on her leg with a gentle squeeze. The warmth of her thigh beneath his palm made his pulse quicken. She shifted slightly, pressing closer to him.

"You two look so happy together," Audra said ten minutes later.

"Funny. I said the same about you and Drew just a few minutes ago," Amelia replied.

Audra grimaced and shook her head. "The beer is going to your brain."

Amelia giggled. "I know better. Anyway, we're enjoying the moments we have left. I'm going to savor every minute."

Her comment stung. But every time she mentioned their approaching end, Jonathan's resolve strengthened. Steve's news about no available positions might close one door, but he refused to accept it was the only door.

A half hour later, Audra collapsed into a chair. "I think I'm done for tonight. This was so much fun."

Drew held out his hand to her. "Me too. I'll take you home. I'm good to drive." He'd only had water and soda to drink throughout the evening. Now Jonathan knew why.

"Come to think of it, you both walked in at the same time," Amelia said. "Did you two arrive together?"

Drew nodded, then offered to take Melanie home, too.

Jonathan noticed how Drew's hand remained on Audra's back as he helped her gather her things. She leaned into his touch without seeming to realize it.

Five minutes later, Jonathan held Amelia's hand as they waited for a cab. "About your new list of dating rules," he began, keeping his voice low. "I accept most of your suggestions." He paused, studying her face in the streetlight. "But I'm not fond of the time-limit restriction."

Amelia's smile faded as she turned to face him fully. "Jonathan ..."

"I know we've been busy this week, but this matters too much to ignore," he continued. "We need to talk about it."

Chapter 49

Amelia

WHEN THE CAB ARRIVED, Jonathan opened the door for her. Her mind was busy thinking about what the next few hours would be like, and she barely noticed she was in a cab at all.

In the back seat together, Jonathan slipped his arm around her shoulder and drew her closer to him. She shivered with anticipation as she melted into him.

Jonathan gave the driver the mansion address.

"I thought we were going to your place?" Amelia whispered.

The cab pulled away from the curb and the downtown buildings whizzed by, occasional signs and traffic signals lighting up the night.

"Slight change of plans," he said. "I forgot Drew is staying with me."

Amelia nodded. "Oh." A twinge of discomfort settled in her chest. Going to her place instead of his felt a little too domestic.

The cab driver turned the radio to something romantic and jazzy.

Amelia leaned her head against his chest and breathed in his deep, rich scent. He was still in his work clothes—dark slacks and a white button-down shirt rolled up at the sleeves. Her thoughts ran toward unbuttoning that shirt and what her hands would feel beneath it.

She hesitated. "No staying over," she whispered. Though her heart betrayed her. She knew it would be tough to say goodbye when he left for the night.

"Sure. I get it." Jonathan sighed as he ran his hand gently down her arm. "No worries."

* * *

The cab pulled into the mansion's circular driveway. Jonathan paid the driver and helped Amelia out. His hand rested at the small of her back as they walked to the front door. The night air was crisp against her skin, but his body beside her made her shiver for entirely different reasons.

"It's just you and me and the kitties. If I can find my keys," she said softly, fumbling in her purse. Her hands weren't entirely steady either.

Inside, the mansion felt different, quieter, more intimate with him close to her. Curled up together on the couch, the kittens didn't bother to greet her—a testament to how late it was. Even Pirate, who usually investigated every visitor, merely opened one eye before tucking her head back against Treasure with a soft mew of contentment.

Amelia reached for Jonathan's hand and led him into the kitchen. She flipped on a small set of under-cabinet lights, casting a soft glow across the room.

"Would you like a drink?" she asked, though her eyes never left his face.

"Just you," he whispered, stepping closer. "That's all I need."

She reached up and touched the collar of his white button-down shirt, her fingers brushing against the soft skin of his neck.

"I've been thinking about this all evening." Her voice was barely audible.

His breath caught. "Me too."

She began slowly unfastening the top button of his shirt, allowing her fingers to travel his neckline. Then, the second button. Her fingers trembled with the anticipation that had been building all night.

Jonathan's hands found her waist, pulling her closer, closing the space between them. "Are you sure?" he asked, his forehead resting against hers.

"I'm sure about this," she said, her hands now inside his shirt, flat against his chest, where she could feel his heart pounding. "About being with you tonight."

He cupped her face gently, his thumb tracing her cheek. "Then let me make tonight unforgettable."

Her breath seized, then his mouth was on hers, hungry and demanding. This wasn't the gentle, tentative kiss from their earlier dates. This was passion and need, like months of restraint finally breaking free, for both of them.

The memory of their college nights together had never faded, but this was deeper, stronger than anything they'd shared six years ago.

She finished unbuttoning his shirt, her palms exploring the heated, solid planes of his chest exactly as she'd remembered. He groaned softly and tightened his grip on her waist as her fingertips slipped lower and traced the hot skin of his firm stomach.

"Upstairs," she whispered against his lips, and he followed her out of the kitchen and up the wide staircase toward her bedroom. Her fingers trailed along the banister as his hand stayed steady and firm at her waist.

She paused in the doorway, aware they were crossing a threshold they couldn't uncross.

Moonlight streamed through the windows and lit the room with a soft glow. She reached for the bedside lamp, bathing everything in hazy golden hues. Jonathan shrugged out of his shirt completely, letting it fall to the floor, and she couldn't help but stare at the lean muscle of his shoulders and chest.

"You're so beautiful," he said, his hands sliding up her arms to frame her face. "I've wanted this, wanted you, for so long."

She leaned into his touch, and then he removed her top in one fluid movement. His eyes darkened as they traveled over her lace bra, her bare skin.

"Amelia," he breathed, his voice rough with desire.

She stepped closer, her body molding against his. He pressed his lips to the hollow of her throat. She moaned softly as his hands tangled in her hair.

"I need you," she whispered against his skin, surprising herself with how desperately true it was.

His response was to capture her mouth in a kiss that was pure fire. His hands roamed across her back to the clasp of her bra. "I need you, too," he said against her lips.

"Yes," she breathed, and felt the garment fall away.

His touch was reverent as he explored her newly bared skin, his lips following the path of his hands. She arched into him, gasping as he found the sensitive spot just below her ear.

Amelia breathed in the clean scent of his skin mixed with the faint musky cologne that had been driving her crazy all evening.

"You feel so good," he murmured, his breath hot against her neck. "So perfect."

She'd felt so dead inside after Nate, like winter had settled permanently in her soul. But Jonathan's touch awakened something she thought she'd buried forever, a fierce, blooming sense of being alive.

They moved together toward her bed, with a tangled surge

of exploring hands and mouths. When the backs of her knees hit the mattress, she pulled him down with her, basking in the weight of him above her.

His mouth traveled down her throat, across her breasts, pausing to suck on her tender nipples. A soft moan escaped her lips.

The rustle of sheets and their whispered names filled the quiet room.

Everything about this felt right—his touch, the way he whispered her name like a plea, the careful attention he gave as he worshiped every response her body offered him.

"Tell me what you want," he said, his eyes meeting hers in the lamplight.

"You," she said simply. "All of you."

She shifted restlessly beneath him, seeking more contact, more friction.

What followed was a fierce frenzy of rediscovery and desire. Clothes disappeared piece by piece until there was nothing between them but fever and need and the overwhelming rightness of being together.

Jonathan explored everywhere, relearning every inch of her skin with his mouth and hands until she was trembling beneath him, whispering his name and pulling him closer.

"Please," she gasped, and he needed no further invitation.

She shifted beneath him, guiding him exactly where she needed him, her hands firm on his hips as she whispered, "Like this."

When they came together, it was with an intensity that stole her breath. He moved slowly at first, letting her adjust, his forehead pressed against hers as they found their rhythm together.

"You feel fabulous," he groaned, and she could only respond by pulling his mouth to hers, losing herself in the sensation of being completely connected to him.

She rolled them over suddenly, straddling him with a confidence that made his breath catch. "My turn," she murmured, her hands splayed across his chest as she took control of their rhythm.

They moved together with increasing urgency, her body responding to his in ways that made her forget everything but this moment, this feeling, this man who was making her feel more alive than she had in years.

When release finally claimed them both, it was with a ferocity that left them breathless and clinging to each other in the aftermath.

They lay tangled together afterward, her leg thrown possessively over his, claiming her place against him, listening to his heartbeat gradually slow. His fingers traced lazy patterns on her bare shoulder, and she felt more content than she had in years.

"I want to stay just like this, with you," he said, his hand trailing through her hair. "Not just tonight. I want to wake up with you every morning."

This was what renewal felt like.

As the haze of physical satisfaction cleared, she considered what he'd said. A sense of discomfort seeped through her.

"Don't make me hope for something we both know won't happen," she mumbled, not lifting her head from his chest.

"Amelia—" His hand stilled on her shoulder.

"I just ... know I need to be completely honest with myself about what this is between us." She adjusted her position against him, her head still resting against his chest, and pulled the sheet up slightly, suddenly feeling vulnerable in more ways than one.

He kissed her hand again, his gaze steady and serious.

She felt the weight of secrets between them. And, after what they'd just shared, hiding felt wrong.

And if she was going to ask more about Paige and his past,

she knew she needed to tell him more about hers. "There's something else I want to tell you." She inhaled slowly, then let out a long breath.

"Even though I knew I had to leave Nate, it was hard to put myself first. But I did it. Then there were questions ... questions about how he died. It took the police a long time to declare it an accident. I spent a lot of time wondering if it wasn't an accident, if he did it on purpose, which led to even deeper guilt."

She tilted her head up to catch his gaze. "For months, I felt trapped in the moment of his death, endlessly replaying it. But being with you again ... it's like I'm finally living in the present instead of being haunted by the past."

He held her tighter and kissed her hair softly. "Nate made his own decisions, Amelia. He got into that racer that day. What happened to him wasn't your fault," he said. "I know it was difficult to tell me. Thank you for trusting me."

"But you coming back into my life," she said, "explaining why you disappeared, and reminding me I deserve genuine affection, real honest caring. Even though you're leaving soon, I'm finally finding happiness again."

"What if I weren't?" The question was quiet but steady.

Amelia blinked, lifting her head fully to look at him. "Weren't ... what?"

"What if I weren't leaving in a month? What if I transfer here? To be with you."

She searched his face for any sign that this was just post-intimacy talk, something he'd regret later. And suddenly, her questions about Paige seemed far less important.

"I've been asking about getting transferred to Rainmere," he continued, his voice serious. "I started making inquiries a week ago, Amelia. Before tonight. Before this." He gestured between them. "Because I know I don't want to leave you."

"Jonathan, you're talking about rearranging your entire life."

"I know exactly what I want," Jonathan said.

He was choosing change and growth over certainty. The way she'd had to choose to leave Nate, the way she was learning to choose hope over fear.

Amelia sat up, her defensive instincts kicking in. "I've gotten over the fear of starting a new relationship," she said slowly. "But your life is in Atlanta, and mine is here. Today, or just a month together, whatever we have, it needs to be … enough." She couldn't carry the guilt of forcing him to rearrange his life. What if he blamed her someday?

"Enough?" Jonathan gazed at her, his expression resolute. "After what we just shared, you think this is just enough?"

She closed her eyes against the tenderness in his voice. "I don't want you to go back to Atlanta." She was falling for him all over again.

Hesitating, she almost asked him to stay the night, but caught herself before the words escaped. "I want to hope for more. But it's … difficult."

"Then let me hope for both of us," he whispered, sitting up and kissing her softly. "Let me show you what it looks like when a man stays, and chooses you, every single day."

Chapter 50

Amelia

AMELIA STARED at the laptop screen, the cursor blinking in the empty email draft to Mr. F-O. She'd opened the message twenty minutes ago, intending to select the mansion photos he'd requested, then done absolutely nothing productive since.

The grandfather clock in the corner chimed eleven, with deep notes resonating through the room. Amelia straightened in the thick sofa chair and rolled her shoulders to release the tension that had settled there. The morning sun had shifted, warming the Persian rug beneath her feet where the kittens were sunbathing.

Despite her best efforts to focus on her work, thoughts of Jonathan's hands on her skin and the way he'd whispered her name kept flooding back, making concentration impossible. Jonathan had left around midnight, honoring her no-overnight rule without a single complaint.

The rational part of her brain insisted this was exactly what she'd wanted. No messy morning-after conversations, no domestic intimacy that might blur the lines of their temporary arrangement.

Shouldn't she feel relieved he had respected her boundaries? Instead, she felt hollow, as if something important had walked out the door with him. Her body still pulsed with the lingering sensations of their intimacy. The memory of his touch sent heat spiraling through her even now. Every nerve ending felt alive.

She'd caught herself humming while making coffee, something she hadn't done in years. And now, sifting through photos of the mansion's renovated bathrooms, she smiled for no particular reason.

Even the kittens knew today was different. Treasure and Pirate had followed her from room to room during her morning rounds, purring and brushing against her legs, as if sensing her bright mood and wanting to take part.

Everything felt surreal and wonderful. Jonathan's transfer request to stay in Rainmere, her new full-time position, the fun karaoke, and most of all, the glorious night they'd shared in her bed.

She requested cleaning services for the carriage house. Next, she ordered the chandeliers that Mr. Jewell had approved in time for them to arrive for installation in May.

Amelia knew she still needed to send the slew of photos Mr. F-O had requested.

Her phone vibrated with an incoming text on the group chat.

> MELANIE: Did you go home with Jonathan last night? TELL ALL!

> AMELIA: Last night was … marvelous. And yes, we slept together.

> MELANIE: FINALLY! How was it?

AMELIA: Better than I remembered from college. Way better.

AUDRA: Woo-hoo, you go, girl! I'm so happy for you! No regrets?

AMELIA: None. Except I'm having a hard time concentrating on work. 😄

MELANIE: That's the best kind of distraction.

AMELIA: Are you still seeing Jason?

MELANIE: Yes. He's still interesting. But I might have to take another business trip to Atlanta soon. Gives me a good excuse for taking things slow with him.

AMELIA: More merger stuff?

MELANIE: Some of it. NorthSound has clients in the region, separate from the merger entirely. I'm restructuring contracts that predate the merger talks. Most negotiations I can handle remotely, but a few require face-to-face persuasion.

Amelia opened her photos app and began selecting the best mansion photos for Mr. F-O. She carefully chose pictures of the drive with a perfect angle of the front of the mansion, several of the newly planted rose gardens, and the lawn lined by the old forest. Next, she flipped through images of the house interior.

MELANIE: I saw Paige showed up at the office on Friday.

AMELIA: Don't remind me. I met her too. Right before our management presentation. She made it clear she can't wait for Jonathan to return to Atlanta, implying I was just some temporary aberration.

MELANIE: OMG, how petty. Classic intimidation tactic. She's testing your reaction to gauge the threat level.

She scrolled through interior shots next, selecting images of the kitchen's restored farmhouse sink, gleaming countertops, and one of the indoor pool's mosaic tilework framed in the perfect lighting.

AUDRA: Hey, sorry I disappeared for a sec, been busy! I requested a new work schedule at the lab, which includes some weekend time.

MELANIE: Working on the weekend? That doesn't sound like you.

AUDRA: Just rearranging my schedule, no extra hours involved.

AMELIA: Should I ask Jonathan more about Paige? I don't want to seem insecure about it. But I think I am.

MELANIE: I told you I heard she's vindictive, so be careful.

AUDRA: Sounds like Paige is trying to get under your skin, honey. Don't let her! Jonathan ended things with her for a reason. Trust that.

Amelia completed compiling the pictures and hit send. She

leaned back in the chair as the fabric sighed softly under her weight.

> MELANIE: I've heard there are disagreements happening on the visiting corporate manager team. Politics and personality clashes. Maybe her assignment here won't last long.

> AMELIA: Fingers crossed!

Amelia closed her laptop with a soft click. She pulled her knees up and wrapped her arms around them.

Paige's confident dismissal of their relationship had hit exactly where Amelia felt most vulnerable. But Audra was right.

She decided she would trust what he'd told her. Trust how he looked at her, how he'd made love to her last night with complete attention and tenderness, as if she were the only woman who had ever existed.

Chapter 51

Jonathan

JONATHAN DESCENDED THE TOWNHOUSE STAIRS, the scent of bacon and coffee compelling him toward the kitchen. Last night with Amelia replayed in vivid detail—her soft laughter, the way she'd taken control and shown him what she wanted, how natural it had felt to hold her.

The fake-dating contract felt like a distant memory now, replaced by something infinitely more real and urgent.

The sound of Drew humming off-key snapped him back to the present.

Drew stood at the stove, flipping bacon proficiently. The kitchen smelled like an honest breakfast for once, not his usual grab-and-go routine.

"You need to expand beyond just cereal and coffee for a change," Drew said, cracking eggs into a bowl.

Jonathan leaned against the counter, watching his friend work. "I happen to like my cereal and coffee," he replied.

"That's not breakfast, that's survival mode." Drew gestured with the whisk. "When's the last time you actually cooked something that didn't come from a box?"

"And when exactly did you become so domestic?" Jonathan asked.

Drew chuffed softly. "Remember those cooking shows I went to with Audra when we were in college?"

Jonathan nodded. "I do."

"They inspired me," Drew said.

"I'm going to enjoy the fruits of your inspiration," Jonathan said, as he opened a cabinet in search of plates. "By the way, I've noticed you're spending a lot of time with Audra while you're here."

"We've been hanging out. As friends," Drew said.

Jonathan raised an eyebrow. "Right, friends." The way Drew's face lit up whenever Audra's name came up suggested something entirely different.

Drew plated the eggs and bacon, then paused, spatula in hand. "Actually, I've been thinking about something." He set down the spatula and turned to face Jonathan. "I'm considering moving the base of my business to Seattle."

Jonathan's fork stopped halfway to his mouth. "Why?" The timing seemed suspicious. "Your business is in Atlanta. This is about Audra, isn't it?"

"It's not just about Audra. There are business opportunities here, good ones, and Atlanta has never been my home, not really." Drew set down the spatula and picked up his fork.

"Unlike you, I don't have family obligations anchoring me to one place," Drew continued. "And my business is relatively portable." His parents weren't alive anymore. "I've been doing some looking around here; it's got potential. Washington has its share of environmental consulting needs. And I like it here."

"And Audra is here," Jonathan added, giving his friend a knowing wink.

"Yeah." Drew smiled. "And Audra is here."

"Truthfully, I've been asking about a transfer, so I can't judge," Jonathan said.

"Whoa. I can't believe you just gave me shit about wanting to move here. You're that sure about Amelia?"

"We have a history together. Rekindling something is different than starting from scratch."

"Audra and I aren't exactly starting from scratch," Drew pointed out.

"When the investigation hit," Jonathan said, "I lost everything with Amelia. I will not let another opportunity slip away." He took a forkful of eggs and mixed it with a bite of bacon.

"Seems like a big leap, but I get it," Drew said.

"Anyway, Steve says he'll keep his eyes and ears open, but there's nothing available right now." Jonathan paused. "It's odd. I expected there'd be plenty of transfers going on."

"Maybe there's a freeze on personnel moves while they're waiting for the merger to be finalized?"

"Maybe," Jonathan said with a nod.

As he finished the last of his food, Drew glanced at his watch and pushed back from the table. "I should get my gear together before I head out to the cottage." He carried his plate to the sink, then headed toward the guest room where he'd stashed the additional tools he'd purchased the previous evening.

Jonathan followed him after putting the empty coffee mugs in the dishwasher.

In the guest room, Drew's contractor tools lay organized across the bed—levels, a rolling measuring tape, various screwdrivers, and safety equipment.

"Hand me that drill case?" Drew nodded toward the dresser. Jonathan grabbed the heavy case. There was something satisfying about equipment built to create something solid and lasting.

"Brandon's going to shit a brick if you get a transfer," Drew said casually.

"Yeah, I know. I have to figure out what to do about Brandon." As much as he wanted to be close to his family, he needed to be with Amelia and would push back on his family's demands to be with her. But he didn't want to leave his brother in a bind, either.

"He got accepted into an elite leadership program. It's a year-long commitment, and he'll be traveling to North Carolina regularly for training sessions. That's why he wants me to take over the fund sooner than originally planned."

"Ah. No wonder he's been such a prick about you and Amelia."

"I didn't know about it when I started asking about transfer positions," Jonathan said. "It makes things a lot more complicated."

"The timing sucks, man," Drew said.

"Tell me about it. What would you do about him if you were in my situation?" Jonathan said. "I want to stay here with Amelia, but I also want to help Brandon."

"Family obligations can be tough," Drew said, coiling an extension cord. "Especially when everyone expects you to be the solution to their problems."

"That's exactly it." Jonathan nodded. "I want to do right by Brandon, but I also can't imagine walking away from what I have here with Amelia."

"You know, you're thinking about this like there's only one solution," Drew said. "What if you helped Brandon find and train someone else to take over? You don't have to be the only answer to his problem."

Jonathan shifted the toolbox strap on his shoulder. "Mom's pretty protective about keeping the foundation family-run. I'm not sure she'd go for an outsider."

"Maybe your mom's more flexible than you think. Could you work remotely?" Drew zipped his bag shut. "I run my geological survey business from wherever I need to be. Technology makes a lot possible these days."

"I don't know. Mom and Brandon collaborate constantly, which is why he lives on her estate. The foundation isn't exactly set up for remote work."

"What about a gradual transition?" Drew shouldered his tool bag. "Split time between locations until you figure out something permanent. Give everyone time to adjust." He paused at the door. "Plus, remember, Whitlow Forest Resources isn't the only company out there. And whatever you decide needs to work for Amelia, too. Why don't you just quit Whitlow and go work for the family foundation? You've always planned to do that eventually anyway."

"Because I want to finish what I started." Jonathan leaned against the doorframe. "I spent two years building the Career Recovery Program. It took a lot of convincing to get Paige's father to back it. I had to build a strong business case showing how it reduces legal risk and gives Whitlow first access to ethical, experienced professionals. I want to see it actually work and make sure the first participants get placed successfully. Walking away now..." He shook his head. "It matters to me."

Drew set down the tool bag. "That's solid work. But maybe you could trust that other management would see it through without you."

"Maybe." Jonathan straightened. "I'll think about it."

* * *

Ten minutes later, Drew's rental truck disappeared down the street, leaving Jonathan alone on the front steps. The morning air felt crisp against his face as the impact of his situation settled over him.

Everything about being with Amelia again felt so right.

Inside, he picked up his phone and scrolled to Brandon's contact. He stared at the call button. Time to have the conversation he'd been avoiding.

He needed to find a way to make this work for everyone, but first, he had to convince his brother that the old plan wasn't the only option.

Chapter 52

Amelia

Sunday evening.

Amelia dropped her robe and towel on a lounger and tested the water temperature with her toe. Perfect.

The pool room felt like a sanctuary with its garden-view windows, though tonight the glass reflected only darkness. Underwater lights cast shifting blue patterns on the walls. The air held a familiar blend of chlorine and the faint eucalyptus from the adjacent hot tub.

She hadn't seen Jonathan since Friday night. He'd been putting in extra hours at work, gathering materials for the new contractors he'd just hired for their team. Audra had helped apply the first coat of paint inside the cabin, while Drew continued exterior repairs.

She slipped into the water, letting it soothe her tired muscles. Her shoulders ached from all the cottage painting, and her hands were still stained despite scrubbing. Every muscle in her body protested the weekend's physical labor. Climbing ladders, scrubbing paintbrushes, and hauling supplies.

As she floated on her back, the gentle lapping of water

against the pool edges created a rhythmic backdrop. She'd pushed herself hard all weekend, and her body craved the weightless relief.

Amelia closed her eyes and let herself imagine Jonathan here with her. His broad shoulders cutting through the water. Droplets caught in the soft light as he surfaced near her.

She could almost feel his hands sliding around her waist in the warm water, pulling her close until their bodies pressed together, skin against skin. The thought of his mouth finding hers while the heated spa jets massaged their intertwined legs made her pulse quicken, and heat flowed through her body.

She sighed and pushed herself lazily across the water.

Today was already the first day of May. How had it arrived so quickly? At least she'd gotten the chandeliers ordered. And now she needed to turn her attention to the floor refinishing. She had no idea what preparations were needed, so the first order of business would be to do some research, then hire a contractor.

Satisfied with that resolution, Amelia let her mind wander back to more pleasant diversions. She pictured Jonathan in the spa's bubbling heat, his hands tracing the curve of her waist while steam rose around them. The fantasy felt so real she could almost taste the salt on his skin.

Eventually, she forced herself to finish her swim, though part of her wanted to stay lost in those fantasies.

After a warm shower, Amelia changed into soft summery pajamas and settled into bed with Rebecca's journal. It had been a while since she'd checked in with her historical friend. One corner of her mouth turned upward. Yes, she thought, she felt Rebecca was her friend.

22 August 1853

Disaster came. The fire started so quickly we could barely comprehend what was happening. I smelled smoke first, then saw the orange glow through the kitchen window. By the time Thomas and young Everett reached the barn, flames were already licking through the roof.

We formed a bucket brigade from the well, but it was hopeless. The barn is gone. The damp hay caused the fire. I watched with grief and anguish as months of our harvest turned to ash, saw Thomas's precious woodworking tools, his father's tools, consumed by the hungry flames. Thankfully, the animals were spared.

The following morning, I soothed the children and watched from the window as Thomas stood in the charred remains, his shoulders slumped and his face gray with soot and defeat. We lost everything: the corn, the wheat, the hay we'd worked so hard to store. Even the smell lingered for days, an acrid reminder of how quickly security can vanish.

After this disaster, Thomas and I have agreed that he must leave and take the job in California working as my family's liaison. I have sent word to my dear brother James that we will accept his offer, and Thomas will happily sell goods to the miners there.

We do not wish to be parted, but we need the money, and the opportunity for part ownership in the dry-goods company would give us the security we desperately require.

I will remain here near the Sound, with young Everett and the children. Young Everett is already doing a man's labor on our farm and working for a neighbor as well. To prepare for his absence, Thomas is teaching me how to shoot the rifle.

*I have asked James to send a small advance on
Thomas's pay so we may replace some of our lost farm tools.*

*Though Thomas is now fully recovered from his fall
from the horse last year, I am concerned for his safety on the
journey ahead of him. I can only pray that he will return to
me unharmed.*

*I have not yet faced being alone, but I am gathering my
strength for his absence.*

*The nights will be the hardest. I wake already reaching
for the warmth of his body, and he has not yet left. How will
I bear the emptiness beside me? Yet I must be strong for the
children, for Everett, who tries so hard to be the man of the
house at barely fourteen. Thomas speaks of being gone for
six months, perhaps longer. I pray my resolve proves as
lasting as my love.*

Amelia closed the journal but held it against her chest for a
moment. The image of Rebecca watching her barn burn, then
facing Thomas's departure, made her own fears feel small by
comparison. Yet Rebecca had found the strength to trust in their
love even across the dangerous miles to California.

She turned out her light and sank into the pillows, but sleep
felt far away. Rebecca's words echoed in her mind. She blinked
as a tear escaped and rolled down her cheek.

Rebecca's situation wasn't so different from her own, was it?
Jonathan had his obligations in Atlanta, his family's foundation,
the life he'd built there. What if those obligations called him
back permanently?

The parallel touched deeper than she wanted to admit.
Rebecca had chosen trust over fear, love over certainty. She
would send Thomas away, knowing he might not return,
believing their bond was stronger than distance or danger.

Amelia rolled onto her side. Could she make the same

choice? If Jonathan's work demanded he leave, would she trust in what they were building? Or would she protect herself by pulling away first?

The question felt like a fault line through her chest, threatening to split her open. She'd spent so long building walls around her heart. But Rebecca had faced greater unknowns with nothing but faith and love as her foundation.

Perhaps that was what love really meant. The raw, brave trust that Rebecca had shown. The willingness to believe that some bonds could survive any test.

As her eyelids finally became heavy, Amelia made a silent promise to Rebecca's memory. If a time came when she needed to choose between fear and faith, she would seek the same courage that had carried Rebecca through fire, separation, and an uncertain frontier. She would choose to trust.

Chapter 53

Jonathan

Monday. May 2.

AT 9 A.M. SHARP, Jonathan's entire team received an urgent email announcing a company-wide conference. All the North-Sound employees and the onsite Whitlow staff at the Rainmere office gathered in a large conference room. Although the office was relatively small, the staff still mostly filled the room.

Though the room was bright and modern, there was an air of discomfort. Mass emergency meetings were never a good sign and usually meant employees were going to get laid off.

Lydia and her boss, Todd, stood at the front of the room. Todd stood rigid in his dark suit and muted corporate tie, his polished demeanor a stark contrast to Lydia's approachable, business-casual style.

Paige stood nearby as a management representative of Whitlow, looking as calm and poised as ever.

Todd waited until everyone was present and accounted for. "Unfortunately, the lengthy negotiations between NorthSound Timber and Whitlow Forest Resources have failed to result in a merger agreement," he began.

"Even though the two companies are a good match on paper," Lydia said, "there were differences of opinion on some of the contract terms."

Todd nodded. "And there were concerns about the differences in company culture. NorthSound's collaborative workplace philosophy clashed with Whitlow's hierarchical structure and its family-first promotion practices."

"Because of the decision to end the negotiations, all existing pre-merger projects will be closed down by the end of this week," Lydia said. "Except for a scaled-back version of the asset evaluation project."

Jonathan's thoughts immediately pivoted to Amelia. Would there still be a chance of a permanent job for her? Her face went pale, riddled with concern and uncertainty.

He scanned the room for Melanie. Being a lawyer for the company, had she already known this was coming? She sat near Amelia, her face downturned with disappointment. Maybe she'd had a clue this was coming, or maybe not; he couldn't tell for certain.

At the other end of the room, Paige stood with other Whitlow management staff. She caught Jonathan's gaze with a smug smile that made his stomach churn. Why did she seem pleased about this?

His attention turned back to Lydia as she solemnly surveyed the group. "NorthSound Timber is going to finish the last month of the asset project, though limited strictly to our own leases," she said. "Whitlow team members are being recalled to Atlanta immediately."

Lydia and Todd concluded the meeting by giving insight into how the various teams would be redistributed over the coming weeks and thanking everyone for their efforts and patience.

As people began filing out, Jonathan caught up with Amelia

and Melanie near the conference room exit.

"I can't believe this is happening," Amelia said, her voice barely above a whisper. "Just when I thought..."

"Hey," Melanie placed a hand on her shoulder. "Your job is still good, remember? Lydia said the asset project goes on."

"But only for NorthSound leases," Amelia replied. "The contractors we just hired ... they'll be let go. That feels so unfair."

Melanie's expression darkened. "I knew the negotiations were rocky; there were heated calls about contract terms last week. But I honestly thought they'd work it out. The financials made too much sense."

Jonathan watched Amelia's face cycle through disappointment and uncertainty. "At least you're staying," he whispered.

"For now," she said, not meeting his eyes. Then she looked up again suddenly. "And what about you?"

Jonathan's phone buzzed. He checked the screen.

"Sorry, gotta take this one," he said. "My boss in Atlanta."

He ducked out of the conference room and headed down the hall as he answered.

"I just came from our group announcement, too," Steve said.

"Not exactly what I expected to happen today," Jonathan said.

Steve exhaled, and there was a pause on the line. "Look, I was hoping to wait until you got back to deliver this news in person, but management insists I tell you immediately—"

"What now?" How could things possibly get any worse?

"You're being transferred, effective June first."

Jonathan stopped in his tracks. "Already? Steve, that's great. How did you manage it so quickly? And with the merger fallout, I figured the chances of a Seattle transfer would plummet!"

Without the merger, the closest Whitlow location to Rainmere was its corporate office in downtown Seattle. It was a bit of a commute, but he'd grab the opportunity in a heartbeat.

"No, Jonathan. That's not it," Steve said on a down note. There was another long pause.

Then ... where am I going?

"Steve?" Jonathan slipped into a small, empty workroom and shut the door behind him. "Where's the new assignment?" His voice was edgy, and an anxious knot formed in his chest.

"Brazil," Steve said. His tone was flat.

"Brazil?" Jonathan was stunned. He sank against the doorframe, his mind immediately calculating the impact. He'd be thousands of miles from Amelia, from his family, from any hope of the life he'd been building toward.

If he went to Brazil, he and Amelia would be separated for years. Years! International visits would be problematic. And what the hell would he do about Brandon?

Why would they send him there of all places?

The smug look on Paige's face suddenly flashed through his mind. Not a coincidence. He sat in a conference chair. It groaned under his weight.

"What the hell happened, Steve?"

"I don't know for sure, just that the mandate came from above that you're going to Brazil. I already argued it with my boss, and I tried going through my HR contacts, but there's nothing more I can do."

"There has to be another option. What about the Portland office? Or Vancouver?"

"I already tried asking for West Coast alternatives," Steve said. "It's a firm no-go."

Jonathan was desperate. "What if ... what if I say 'no' to this transfer?"

"I think if you refuse the transfer, there's going to be no way to get a transfer out of Atlanta to Seattle in the foreseeable future."

Fuck.

Steve gave him the usual supervisor spiel for delivering bad news: sorry that things didn't go as you planned, but hang in there, blah blah blah.

"Wrap things up there in Rainmere this week," Steve continued, "and catch a flight back over the weekend. I'll see you at the office first thing on Monday."

He closed his eyes and exhaled slowly, feeling the walls of his carefully planned life collapsing around him.

"I'm going to need to take a few days of vacation time before I come back." His voice was rough.

"Okay, take what time you want," Steve said.

Jonathan ended the call.

The company *had* blindsided him.

If I refuse Brazil outright, they'll never offer me Seattle. But maybe he could negotiate. His mind flashed through what his next steps should be.

Now, instead of just choosing between his family and Amelia, he'd have to choose between Brazil, Amelia, Brandon, and stewarding the Career Recovery Program.

The choice had just become impossible. Refuse Brazil and kiss goodbye any chance of a Seattle transfer—and Amelia. Accept it and lose years with both Amelia and Brandon.

Or he could quit Whitlow altogether. His stomach soured at the thought. Walking away before the Career Recovery Program launch meant abandoning years of work—he'd never witness his framework actually help anyone.

He could take Brandon up on his offer and work for the family foundation, but that came with its own complications. His mother had expectations about how the foundation should be run, and he'd feel constant pressure to be in Atlanta when he wanted to be in Washington.

But if he accepted the transfer, he could lose Amelia even in the short term. A long-distance relationship would be much harder across country borders. He wouldn't feel right asking her to do that.

He took a deep breath and straightened his shoulders. He couldn't sit here stewing forever. Time to get through the rest of the day, somehow.

He made his way back to the team workroom. After sending his vacation request to Steve, Jonathan spent the afternoon reviewing the Whitlow company policies on transfer refusals, then began calling his contacts in other departments.

His last call was the one he'd been avoiding. He stepped outside the building. He needed air for this conversation. He called Paige's number.

She answered on the second ring. "Jonathan." Her voice was warm, almost affectionate. "I was wondering when you'd call."

"Brazil. That was you."

"Me?" A soft laugh. "I'm just a junior manager, Jonathan. I don't make executive decisions."

"Don't bullshit me, Paige."

The warmth shifted, became sharper. "Fine. I had a conversation with my uncle, the one on the executive committee. We discussed how São Paulo needs someone with your skill set. Amazing how these things work out when you know the right people."

His grip tightened on the phone. "You can't actually think—"

"Think what? That a few years in Brazil will give you perspective on us?" Her voice softened again. "Jonathan, sometimes people need distance and time away from distractions and complications to see clearly."

"What we had is over."

"Three years is a long time," she said. "Long enough for college crushes to fade. Long enough for us to reconcile and for you to remember why we worked."

"You're delusional. This isn't going to bring me back to you."

"Maybe not immediately. But I always get what I want." She paused. "São Paulo is a pivot to bigger things for you. Consider it a gift, an opportunity you wouldn't have gotten otherwise. You should be thanking me."

The audacity stunned him to silence.

"See you around, Jonathan."

The line went dead.

Jonathan stood there. His chest felt like it was going to explode with fury and disbelief.

He pocketed his phone and headed back inside. Time to tell Amelia everything.

At the end of the afternoon, he motioned to Amelia. "Let's get out of here," he said, closing his laptop. "Drew's at the cottage tonight. Let's get together at my place. There are some things I need to tell you."

Chapter 54

Amelia

Monday evening.

Amelia stood outside Jonathan's townhome, clutching a paper bag of Korean fried chicken and edamame, still trying to process the day's devastation. The merger failure had left everyone shaken, and Jonathan's invitation for dinner felt like the only solid thing in a world that had suddenly shifted beneath her feet.

He opened the door before she could knock, and the heaviness in his eyes matched what she felt in her spirit. "Hey," he whispered, reaching for the bag and kissing her cheek. "You found it okay."

"Perks of small-town living." She stepped inside, noting how his usually perfect hair was out of place, his t-shirt wrinkled. "You look about as good as I feel."

"Rough day for both of us." He set the food on the kitchen counter and turned to face her, hands sliding around her waist. "I'm glad you're here."

The simple contact unraveled something in her chest. She

melted against him, breathing in his familiar essence. "I still can't believe it's over," she said. "Just like that."

"I know." His hand moved to the back of her neck, his fingers gently caressing her. "Are you okay about your job? Really?"

"In the short term, yes. Lydia was clear about that." She pulled back to look at him. "But what about you? Steve called you back, right?"

Something flashed across his face too quickly for her to identify. "Yeah. We'll figure something out."

He moved to get plates, and she watched the careful way he avoided her eyes. After years of reading Jonathan's expressions, she knew when he was holding something back.

"How long will Drew be at the cottage?" she asked, noting the quiet house.

"He's spending the night there. Wanted to get an early start on the plumbing assessment, since he's still waiting on the extra roof shingles to arrive." Jonathan popped open two beers and handed her one. "We have the place to ourselves."

They settled on his couch with the food spread between them on the coffee table. The Korean fried chicken was perfectly crispy and sauced, the edamame salty and satisfying. A salve for the wounds of the day. As they ate, the merger failure kept replaying in her mind, mixed with the uncertainty of what came next.

"This is good," she said, more to fill the silence than anything.

"You've got more of an appetite than I do." Jonathan's beer sat untouched next to his barely touched plate.

"I'm a stress eater," Amelia reminded him as she grabbed a napkin to wipe the sauce from the side of her mouth.

He ran a hand through his hair. "Amelia, there's something I need to tell you."

The tone in his voice was cold, like a splash of ice water. She set down her beer, suddenly hyperaware of the tick of the wall clock and her own heartbeat accelerating.

"What is it?"

"The call from Steve today—it was about my transfer."

Relief flooded through her. "Oh, thank god. I was starting to think—"

"They want to send me to Brazil."

The words made no sense at first. Brazil. Not Seattle.

"Brazil," she repeated. Her voice sounded strange and distant, disconnected from her body. Brazil wasn't anywhere she could drive to or fly to for a weekend or even imagine affording to visit regularly, if ever.

"Effective June first." His voice was rough. "I'm sorry, Amelia." He set his hand over hers. "I'm so fucking sorry."

The chicken and edamame blurred in front of her as she blinked against the forming tears. June first. Three weeks away. "That's not ... you said Seattle. You asked for Seattle, not a foreign country."

"I know. I tried to negotiate. Portland, Vancouver, anywhere on the West Coast. They're saying no to everything." He leaned forward, elbows on his knees. "If I refuse, I'll never get a Washington transfer opportunity. Never."

She stood up abruptly, needing space, needing air. The couch felt too small, the room too close. "So you're going."

"I don't know. I have to be back in Atlanta on Monday. But I promise you, I'm not done fighting for us."

Monday. One week to decide whether to throw away everything they'd rediscovered. One week to choose between his career and ... whatever this thing between them was that they hadn't even had time to fully figure out?

"Of course you have to go," she said bluntly. "It's your career."

"Amelia—"

"No, it's fine." She was moving now, pacing behind the couch. "It makes sense. Great opportunity, international experience. Your family will be so proud."

"Don't do that."

"Do what?"

"Don't shut down. Talk to me."

She stopped pacing and looked at him. Really looked at him. The man who'd ghosted her when things got complicated. Who'd come back into her life and made her believe this time might be different. The same man who was now going to leave again, just like everyone else.

"What do you want me to say, Jonathan?" she breathed. "That I'm happy for you? That international assignments are amazing career moves? Because they are."

"I'm not interested in making some amazing career move. Please, I want you to tell me what you're feeling."

What I'm feeling. The familiar ache in her chest that she'd carried since she was fourteen years old, preparing to visit her father's grave at the cemetery. It was the same aching hollowness she'd felt for months after he'd disappeared. The same as when the officers gave her the news about Nate's car crash. The crushing weight of wondering if she was somehow responsible for the people she loved slipping away.

"I'm thinking this feels familiar," she said finally.

"What does that mean?"

"It means people don't stay. People always slip away. And there's always a reason." She wrapped her arms around herself. "Being used until you're no longer useful. And sometimes they just ... die."

Jonathan stood up slowly. "This isn't the same thing."

"Isn't it?" She met his eyes. "You're choosing something else over me. Again."

"That's not fair."

"Fair?" A bitter laugh escaped her. "You want to talk about fair? You know what's not fair? Letting me believe this could work."

Amelia pressed her eyes shut. She'd let herself fall for him again even though she'd known something like this might happen.

"I didn't know—"

Her eyes flew open again. "You told me you were asking for a transfer."

"To Seattle! To be closer to you, not further away."

"But it's not Seattle, is it?" It felt as though her heart was cracking open. "It's Brazil. Thousands of miles away. For years, probably."

He stepped toward her, but she moved back. She couldn't let him touch her right now. If he touched her, she'd completely fall apart.

"What is it about me, Jonathan?" The question came from somewhere deep and raw. "What is it about me that makes leaving so easy?"

"Leaving isn't easy—"

"Nate used me for two years, and when I finally had the courage to leave him, he died in a car crash. Maybe on purpose." Her voice was getting smaller, but she couldn't stop. "My dad died when I was fourteen. Just ... gone."

"Amelia—"

"And you. You disappeared without a word. I know now it wasn't really about me, but it felt like it was." She pressed her hand to her chest, where it felt like something was breaking. "You did it so well, so thoroughly that it must have been easy. And now you're leaving again. Different reasons, but the same result."

"It's not that simple," Jonathan said.

"Yes, it is." She was crying now, tears she'd been holding back for years. "I don't get to keep people. That's just how it works for me. Everyone I care about slips away, and there's always a reason it has to happen."

Jonathan's face was stricken. "You think this is easy for me? You think I want to go to Brazil?"

"I know you don't want this. I know this isn't what you planned." Her voice was thin. "But you're still going to choose it. It's probably the smart choice."

"Please stop it."

"Stop what? Being realistic? Accepting that this was always temporary?"

"Stop pushing me away. You are worth everything to me." His voice was fierce now. "You're brilliant and strong and the best thing that's ever happened to me. You're important."

She laughed, but it came out broken. "My track record says otherwise."

He closed the distance between them, hands framing her face. "Your track record is wrong. You are not disposable." He leaned his forehead against hers. "You're not forgettable. And you're sure as hell worth fighting for."

She knew she didn't look convinced. "What are you going to do?"

The question hung between them, biting and desperate. Jonathan's thumbs brushed away her tears, but more kept coming.

"I'm going to keep fighting for you," he said finally. "I just haven't found the answer yet. But I will, Amelia. I'm not giving up on us. This situation is complicated as hell. But I'm going to figure this out."

"It's an impossible choice," she whispered.

"I'm not walking away from you again."

They stood in his living room, holding each other in this

moment that felt like goodbye even though nothing was decided. She could smell his pleasant musky scent, feel the warmth of his skin, and hear his heartbeat against her cheek as he pulled her closer against his chest.

"I'm sorry this became so messy," he whispered into her hair. "I hate that this happened."

"I know." And she knew. She could feel his anguish in the way his hands shook slightly against her back, hear it in the roughness of his voice. This was killing him too.

But knowing didn't make it hurt less.

"What are we going to do now?" she asked.

His arms tightened around her. "Tonight we'll just be together."

She pulled back to look at him. His dark eyes were bright with resolve, his jaw tight with the effort of holding himself together.

At least for tonight, they'd just be here. Together. While they still could hold on to each other.

His expression softened as he looked deeper into her eyes. "Amelia—"

"We don't know what will happen next," she said, her voice barely above a whisper. "If you're leaving for Brazil, then I want tonight. I want to remember what this feels like."

"So do I," he assured her.

She answered by kissing him. Soft at first, then deeper, slipping her tongue inside when his mouth opened beneath hers. Her hands caressed the warm skin at the base of his neck, fingers threading through his hair.

"I need you," she whispered against his lips.

His response was immediate, hands sliding down her back, pulling her flush against him. She could feel his heart racing, matching the frantic rhythm of her own. When his mouth moved to her throat, a soft sound escaped her and she pressed into him, asking for more.

"Here," she breathed, her hands already clutching at his clothes. "Right here."

The couch cushions gave way beneath them as he lowered her down, his frame settling over her. She pulled his shirt free, desperate to feel skin against skin, to lose herself in his hot, solid body.

He pushed a hand under her shirt, running his palm slowly up over her hips, pressing against her stomach before sliding further upward. His fingers ran over her breasts, slipped under her bra and gently squeezed a hardened nipple as his thumb moved underneath. A shiver rushed through her body, and she felt heat tightening between her thighs.

"Amelia," he whispered her name, his voice rough with hunger.

She answered by drawing him down to her, letting the desperate need between them drown out everything else. For now, there was only this, the fierce connection that felt like it could burn away the rest of the world.

They stumbled toward his bedroom, hands roaming, mouths finding fresh places to taste and claim. When they reached his bed, she pushed him down and straddled him, moonlight silvering her skin as she moved above him.

"You feel ... so, so good," she gasped, her hands flattened on his chest, as she slowly rocked against him.

His grip tightened on her hips. "Christ, Amelia. The way you move..."

She leaned down to cover his mouth, swallowing against his

groan as she shifted her angle. "I want all of you," she whispered against his lips. "Every inch."

"You have me," he breathed, his voice breaking as she took him, and he sank deeper inside of her. "God, you have all of me."

Their rhythm built slowly, then faster, desperately seeking her release. She threw her head back and cried out as sensation overtook her. When he flipped them over, pressing her into the mattress, she wrapped her legs around him and pulled him impossibly closer.

"Don't stop," she pleaded, nails digging into his shoulders as he moved inside her. "I want more. Don't ever stop."

"Never," he promised against her throat, his voice rough with passion.

When they finally collapsed together, breathless and spent, she curled into his side, her body satiated.

"That was..." she started, then trailed off, unable to finish her thought.

"Yeah," he agreed, pressing a kiss to her hair.

As their breathing slowed, she couldn't push away thoughts of June first and what it meant. She studied the family photo on his nightstand, the one with Jessica and Brandon on the shore of a lake. His temporary life here, soon to be packed away.

"If you go to Brazil," she said into the darkness, her hand gently tracing the curves of his chest, "how long would you be gone?"

She felt him tense beneath her touch. "Two years," he said slowly, his voice heavy. "Maybe three."

Three years. She'd be thirty-three when he came back. If he came back.

"That's..." she started, then stopped. What was there to say? That three years felt like a lifetime?

"I know," he whispered, his hand stroking her hair. "I know it's a lot."

She pressed her face against his chest, breathing him in. "I can't think about it right now."

"Then don't." His arms tightened around her. "We don't have to figure it all out tonight."

They fell silent again. Outside, she could hear the distant sound of cars passing, normal people living normal lives that weren't about to be completely uprooted.

The silence felt like a promise neither of them knew how to fulfill.

Amelia shifted beside him. The thought of leaving him now felt impossible. A quiet resolve settled over her.

"I'm breaking my rule," Amelia said, pressing closer to him. "I'm staying with you tonight."

He pulled back slightly to look at her, his expression softening with relief. Then he tightened his arms around her again, and she felt some of the tension leave his body. "Good," he murmured, then kissed her forehead. "I want you here."

They made love again before dawn, slower this time, savoring each touch with new tenderness. Morning light eventually trickled through his bedroom blinds, bringing with it all the impossible decisions they still had to face.

* * *

An hour later, Amelia slipped from the bed while Jonathan was still sleeping and quietly gathered her clothes. The merger failure, Brazil, and the impossible timeline all felt too heavy in the stark daylight. She needed space to think, to process what came next.

She was pulling on her jeans when Jonathan stirred.

"Leaving already?" His voice was rough and sexy with sleep. He patted the sheet beside him. "Please stay."

Amelia pushed her arms into her shirt.

"I should get home." She couldn't quite meet his eyes. "Check on the kittens, get ready for work." She slipped on one shoe as she searched for the mate.

He sat up, running a hand through his bedhead hair. "Amelia—"

"You have the rest of the week here, right? To finish up your project?"

"Yeah. I fly out on Sunday."

One more week before everything changed.

"We'll talk later," she said, finally looking at him. The morning light caught the worry in his dark eyes.

"Definitely."

She kissed him goodbye. It was a soft, lingering kiss. Then she let herself out of his townhome.

The drive back to the mansion felt longer than usual, the familiar streets somehow foreign in the early morning light. Everything looked the same, but she felt different. She'd sought comfort last night and had awakened to a completely different world.

Chapter 55

Jonathan

IT WAS seven o'clock in the evening. Jonathan sat on his couch with his laptop and a beer, waiting for the video call to begin. The remains of his meatball sub sat on a plate on the coffee table, with a swirl of marinara sauce where he'd been dipping.

His mind drifted to the night before. The memories sent heat spiraling through him even now, making the distance between Rainmere and Brazil feel impossibly far.

He'd been distracted at work, caught between meetings and trying to wrap up his transition of the NorthSound evaluations, but thoughts of their night together kept breaking through.

Jonathan clicked to accept a conference call with Charlotte and Brandon. "Thanks for setting up the call," he said.

Earlier in the week, when he'd called Brandon, he'd convinced his brother they should share the charity CEO responsibilities, so Brandon would have time to devote to the leadership program.

At first, Brandon had resisted. However, after some detailed analysis and an admission from Brandon that not all of his job tasks required someone in Atlanta, Brandon had agreed to give him the tasks that could be accomplished remotely. And

Jonathan had agreed to visit Atlanta every other weekend for the first several months.

But that discussion had happened before Brazil crashed into his universe. And now things were disintegrating before his plan ever got underway.

"Hi," Brandon said. "Can you hear us okay?"

Charlotte and Brandon were both seated at a glass table that Jonathan recognized from her home office. Design books lined the shelves behind them.

Jonathan gave a thumbs-up, taking in his mother's appearance on screen. Her dark, knowing eyes seemed more vivid through the camera, and her hair—grayer than he'd noticed before—was swept back into a stylish tortoiseshell band.

He heard a rumble in the background. "Sounds stormy down there," he said, settling back onto the couch.

"It just started raining," Brandon replied. "The afternoon storm. You're not missing much."

"Have you given Jessica your blessing yet to go back to school for her MBA?" Jonathan said.

"We're still discussing it," Charlotte said, with a slight, dismissive hand gesture. "She's an adult, and what she does with her career ultimately isn't my decision. I'm not standing in her way, but we're not on the same page with each other. Far from it."

Hm, he'd file that information away for later.

"Well, speaking of family changes," he said, "I wanted to talk about something."

"Brandon told me you want to transfer to Seattle to be close to Amelia," Charlotte said. "He explained the details of your new plans."

"How do you feel about our splitting the responsibilities?" Jonathan posed the question delicately. "And, about me working remotely?"

"Change doesn't come naturally for me," Charlotte admitted. "And this whole virtual technology is a mystery to me. Thank goodness Brandon understands it. But I see the value of it."

Charlotte glanced at Brandon, then back at the screen. She paused, seeming to collect her thoughts. "I'm glad you and Brandon are working together to figure out how to make this situation work for everyone."

Progress. Clearly, there was a possibility she might warm up to the idea.

"Mom and I have talked about it a lot," Brandon said. "So what's the urgent news you've got for us?"

Jonathan took a deep breath. "There's no easy way to say this," he began. "The inquiries about a transfer didn't go as I expected." He braced himself. "They're sending me to Brazil."

Charlotte and Brandon were silent.

Fuck. How did things get so screwed up?

"Instead of a transfer for me to Seattle," he continued, "the merger negotiations failed and they're transferring me to Brazil. I'm currently fighting it, but I think it's a done deal. It's not optimal, but the remote plans with Brandon will still work, I'm sure of it. And there's the Career Recovery Program. I've spent two years building it, and we're set to launch early next year. If I go to Brazil, it could get cut or someone else will have to take it over. I won't be there to see it through."

Charlotte's expression softened. "You've put a lot of yourself into that program, haven't you?"

"It matters to me," Jonathan said. "Helping other people manage the professional fallout that I went through—it felt like turning something terrible into something good. But..." He trailed off.

There was a long pause before Charlotte finally spoke.

"A done deal," Charlotte said deliberately, as though simmering on the idea. "How did Amelia take the news?"

"She's still processing it, I think. I told her we'll figure it out."

Brandon was unnervingly quiet. Jonathan wasn't eager to hear what his brother might say after he digested the Brazil news. It wouldn't be enthusiastic. Of that, he was certain.

"It's wonderful you're trying to make this work with both Brandon and Amelia," Charlotte said.

Relief swept through him. "I was hoping you'd see it that way."

She paused, as though choosing her words carefully. "But honey, I have to ask you something, and I want you to really think about your answer. When you're planning all this remote work in Brazil ... are you doing it because it's genuinely the best solution? Have you really thought about what Brazil means for your relationship with Amelia?"

"I don't understand," Jonathan said.

Charlotte leaned forward, closer to the screen.

"I supported your pursuing Amelia when you were going to Seattle," she said. "That made sense. But Brazil ... you'll be thousands of miles away for years, Jonathan. The remote charity work ... that doesn't change the fact that you won't be able to see Amelia except maybe a few times a year." She blinked and looked away momentarily. "You won't be there when she has a bad day," she said, looking at him again, "or when she needs someone to talk to. You'll miss everything that actually makes a relationship work."

"Mom," Brandon said, setting a hand on her arm.

"No, Brandon," she continued. "Someone needs to say this." She turned back to the screen to face Jonathan again. "I'm worried that all this focus on the planning for the charity—the remote work, the split responsibilities—is a way to avoid facing the real question. Which is: Should you go to Brazil if it means losing her? From my perspective, it looks like you're trying to convince yourself you can have both, when Brazil means likely choosing your career over your relationship."

Jonathan opened his mouth to argue, then closed it again. Charlotte wasn't attacking him; she was pointing out what he'd been trying not to see.

The remote work plan suddenly felt less like an enlightened brotherly compromise and more like elaborate self-deception. He glanced at Brandon's face on the screen, seeing his own uncertainty reflected back at him. Brandon shifted uncomfortably in his chair.

"Actually, there's something else I should probably mention," Brandon began. "The leadership program ... they've already started sending pre-work assignments."

"What kind of pre-work?" Jonathan said.

"Case studies, research projects. I've been working until midnight most nights."

"He's barely been able to keep up with foundation work as it is," Charlotte said.

Jonathan leaned forward, mimicking his mother's posture. "But that's exactly why my remote work will help—"

Charlotte's expression darkened, and he knew her stern but sage advice was about to descend on him.

"Jonathan, think about what you're saying. You'll be starting a completely new job, in a new country, probably with additional responsibilities and expectations. That's overwhelming enough on its own. And now you want to add being Brandon's remote assistant on top of that? Plus, trying to maintain a relationship with Amelia from thousands of miles away?"

She paused, as though giving time to let her point sink in. And it was.

"Honey, that's not a solution," she said. "That's a recipe for failing at something, or maybe even failing at everything. You'll be stretched so thin you won't be able to do any of it well—not your new job, not the foundation work, and certainly not your relationship with Amelia."

He stared at the screen. He'd thought he was being clever. But his mother was right. He wasn't solving anything. He was just spreading himself so thin, he'd fail at all of it.

The choice he'd been avoiding was still there, starker than ever. Brazil and staying involved with the Career Recovery Program as it helped people, or everything else that actually mattered to him. "You're right. About all of it. I thought I had it figured out, but I'm just ... I'm trying to avoid making an impossible choice."

Charlotte nodded slowly. "Sometimes the impossible choices are the ones most worth making."

He took a slow breath, buying himself a moment before she continued. The distant sound of his neighbor's dog barking drifted through the window. Somewhere outside this conversation, life was continuing normally.

"Jonathan, I want you to ask yourself one question before you decide anything. What would you do if you weren't afraid?"

"I'm not afraid," he said. "I'm being responsible."

With the hint of a smile, Charlotte said, "Those aren't always different things."

Jonathan hesitated. He could see the concern on both their faces, the worry that he was making the wrong choice for all the wrong reasons.

"I should go," he said finally. "I need to think."

"Take some time, honey," Charlotte said tenderly. "But don't take too long."

The screen went black, leaving Jonathan alone with his mother's message and the tough choice he could no longer avoid.

Chapter 56

Amelia

AFTER WORK, Amelia set out for a short evening hike along the mansion's wooded trails, seeking solace and hoping to momentarily forget that Jonathan would leave Rainmere in less than a week.

She'd been so busy with all the changes happening at NorthSound—confusion over the merger fallout, projects closing—that she hadn't even taken a break to tell Audra about Jonathan's transfer.

Though Melanie had mentioned it in the group chat, Amelia hadn't yet told them about the Brazil situation. The reality felt too overwhelming to discuss, even with her closest friends.

Breathing in the cool pine scent of the evening helped ground her, soothing away some of the rough edges. The forest wouldn't completely erase the sting of her situation, but it offered temporary refuge.

She followed the northwest trail for twenty minutes before picking up the southern loop that would take her back to the mansion.

As soon as she returned to the mansion, she changed into

comfortable yoga pants and a long cotton tee, then settled on the living room floor to stretch her muscles.

Still tired from her outing, she leaned against the couch and opened her laptop on the coffee table. Time to check the weekend weather forecast and research elevation profiles and conditions of new trail options.

She'd bookmarked two promising loop trails when her email notification chimed with a message from Mr. F-O. *Ugh, not now.* She frowned at the screen and immediately closed the laptop. She was not ready to potentially face another new to-do list from him.

Instead, she reached for Rebecca's journal, opening to the page where she'd left off. Throughout the winter, Rebecca and Thomas had made plans for his journey and exchanged letters with her brother, James.

30 May 1854

> *The Lord tests us in mysterious ways. Thomas departs for California tomorrow, and though my heart feels heavy, I have to believe this separation serves some greater purpose. I have sewn his initials into his traveling shirt and tucked a pressed wildflower from our meadow into his Bible.*
>
> *After the fire, with a small advance of money from James, we purchased seed and essential tools for the spring planting. Yesterday we finished planting crops: wheat as a cash crop, corn for our food and animal feed, potatoes, root vegetables, beans, and onions.*
>
> *Thomas did not want to leave me until the planting was done. Each morning, I will tend these growing things and have faith that our bonds will deepen with distance, like roots reaching toward water.*
>
> *The steamship ticket James purchased in New York for*

Thomas arrived last week in the mail, along with a letter of credit for his initial expenses in San Francisco. Though the sea is not always safe, I am grateful that his journey will be much faster than if he traveled by land.

In San Francisco, James's dry-goods business partner will meet him. The new business sells textiles and other wares. Thomas will serve as James's representative, liaison, and partner. He'll be paid a commission, including a small ownership stake in the company. And Thomas will also provide carpentry work for the stores.

I will anxiously await news of his having arrived safely.

When doubt whispers he may not return, I remind myself that love built on faith can survive any trial. Though miles may separate us, Thomas carries my heart with him, and I carry his trust.

This is not goodbye; this is simply love learning to stretch across distance. I will write as often as I can in my journal as letters to him, and I will count the days not with sorrow, but with anticipation of our reunion.

Amelia closed the journal, her throat tight. Rebecca's strength in the face of separation felt both inspiring and deeply heartbreaking. Rebecca was planning to tend her garden while awaiting Thomas's return.

Amelia was already building walls against Jonathan's departure, rehearsing explanations about how it had been temporary, anyway. But Rebecca had things Amelia didn't—the certainty of marriage, the comfort of children, the promise that Thomas would come back to the life they'd built. Amelia couldn't even be sure what she and Jonathan had become to each other, or if he'd stay long enough to finish it.

* * *

An hour later, with Rebecca's courage fresh in her mind, she knew she couldn't put off Mr. F-O's email any longer. She opened her laptop and clicked on the message:

Miss Preston,

> *I hope this finds you well. I need to inform you I've sold the mansion. This is sudden, but per clause twenty-seven in our contract, I need to exercise the termination option. You'll have thirty days from today to move.*
>
> *I understand this creates an inconvenience, and I apologize for the short notice. The cottage arrangement for your mother remains unchanged since I'm keeping that portion of the property.*
>
> *Please let me know if you have questions.*

William Jewell

The words blurred and her heart plunged. She dropped her forehead into her hands as the reality of another major upheaval hit her.

Jessica had been right about his preparing it for sale. He'd actually sold his family's mansion.

And he'd delivered the news in an email. Seriously? A phone call would have been more considerate. It wasn't as bad as being ghosted, but it stung. Now she needed to find a place to stay, and fast. The timing couldn't be worse.

Amelia took a deep breath and opened her phone. She needed her friends.

> AMELIA: Help! Things are so screwed up. Just found out Mr. F-O sold the mansion, and he's ending my lease. I need to get out of here and regroup.

AUDRA: Come to my place. I'm cooking dinner.

MELANIE: I'm in. I'll bring wine.

Chapter 57

Amelia

Twenty minutes later, Amelia stood outside Audra's apartment building, grateful for friends who dropped everything when she needed them.

Once inside, the scent of sweet chicken sauce with cooked pineapple and vegetables filled the apartment. Audra plated air-fried bourbon chicken skewers over coconut rice.

"Sorry for the last-minute dinner party," Amelia said as she sat at Audra's small dining table.

"Are you kidding? I love an excuse to cook for people," Audra replied, just as Melanie arrived with a bottle of wine and concerned eyes.

"So," Melanie said, pouring wine into their glasses, "what's going on? Your text sounded urgent."

Over dinner, Amelia explained that Jonathan had requested a transfer to Seattle and then how it backfired after the merger fell through.

Amelia took a breath. "He's being transferred to Brazil."

"Whoa, what?" Audra's fork paused halfway to her mouth. "I thought he was trying to stay in Seattle."

"He was. Whitlow's management is sending him to São

Paulo, Brazil, instead. I have less than a week left with him." She set down her fork. "Maybe this is the universe's way of reminding me that people always leave."

"I'm really sorry, honey. That's awful." Audra's face creased with concern and she tapped one glittery fingernail on the table. "It seems so sudden, though. Just out of the blue like that?"

"I'll look into what happened with the transfer," Melanie said, pushing chicken and vegetables off a skewer stick. "Through the merger planning, I've gained some friends in HR at Whitlow."

"Thanks. I'd like to understand what happened," Amelia said, managing a small smile. "Though I'm not sure it matters now. Jonathan's been fighting it—talking to his boss, trying to understand the decision. But apparently, his management is determined to send him to São Paulo." She took a sip of wine. "He says he's hitting a brick wall."

"The move isn't optional?" Melanie asked.

Amelia shook her head. "I don't think so." She let out a slow breath, then took a swallow of the fruity wine and tried to sound upbeat. "An international assignment would be good for his career." It would also likely end whatever was forming between them.

"I should have stuck with my original plan, to keep things simple and temporary." She stabbed at her rice. "The hoping part was a mistake."

"Bullshit," Audra said firmly. "Hoping isn't a mistake. Life just sucks sometimes."

Amelia finished the last bite of rice on her plate. "This is exactly what I needed," she told Audra. "Thank you."

"More wine?" Melanie asked, already pouring. "Besides Jonathan's transfer, how are you handling all the other merger chaos? Are you still worried about your permanent position?"

"Honestly? Everything's so uncertain right now. The

project with Jonathan has gone well, but now I don't know if that'll be enough to secure something permanent."

"Your boss said you've been killing it with this project, right?" Audra said. "I've never seen you more confident about your work."

"Audra's right," Melanie agreed. "Whatever happens with Whitlow, you've proven yourself."

"Now," Audra said, settling back with her refilled wine, "give us some details about the mansion situation. What are you going to do now?"

Amelia pulled out her phone. She found the message and read it aloud, watching her friends' expressions change from confusion to outrage.

"Thirty days?" Melanie set down her glass. "That's barely legal notice."

"It is legal," Amelia said. "I checked the contract. He has the right to terminate for sale. I should have listened to Jessica's warnings about all the renovation projects. She said he was preparing it for sale, and I dismissed her because I didn't want it to be true." Amelia swirled the wine in her glass. "Denial of the obvious."

The three women moved to clear the table, continuing their conversation as they rinsed dishes then moved to the living room.

"The mansion was perfect for what I needed ... space, privacy, and no rent. Everything else near the lake costs a fortune."

Audra scowled. "But how could he just throw you out like that? You signed a lease. It feels so..." She gestured angrily. "Cold."

"It was in the fine print, option to end the lease in the event of a sale. I knew about it when I signed," Amelia said with a small shrug. She sat on Audra's bright blue sofa. "I just figured the chances were so small that I could ignore it. Apparently not."

"I'm so sorry," Melanie said, gently patting Amelia's back. "What a horrible time to get that news, on top of everything else."

"Thirty days to move out. It's such whiplash. One minute I'm coordinating all his repairs and upgrades, the next minute I'm out." She leaned back against the cushions with a long sigh.

"You could stay with me again for a while, honey," Audra quickly offered.

Amelia shook her head. "I love you for offering, but..." Amelia looked around the cozy apartment, remembering their brief roommate phase when she'd first moved to Seattle. "This place is perfect for you, but with both of us plus two kittens? We'd drive each other crazy within a week."

"I wish I had more room," Audra said.

"I've got plenty of space," Melanie offered, "and a splendid view of the city."

"That's incredibly generous, and it would be fun," Amelia said. "But you're twenty-five minutes from the cottages. I want to stay closer to my mom."

"What about the cottage lease? Would you consider moving in with Rachel?" Melanie said. "Any similar fine-print wording?"

"No fine print about that. I double-checked it today," Amelia said with a sigh. "After I realized I don't have any recourse in the mansion agreement. At least something's secure."

She took another swallow of her wine as she realized Melanie's suggestion of moving in with her mother made her uncomfortable. "I'm turning thirty next month. I love my mom, but moving back in with her?" Amelia shook her head. "It would feel like I'm going backward, like I can't handle my life."

"Ah, pride before practicality?" Audra said with a knowing tone. "Doesn't particularly sound like you."

"The cottages are adorable, tucked in that beautiful forest," Melanie said.

"I know, I know," Amelia fidgeted with her glass stem before draining the last drops. "I'm not being rational about this. It's just ... the merger, Jonathan leaving, now this. Why is everything falling apart at once?"

Amelia leaned forward to set her empty wine glass on the coffee table. Her elbow caught the corner of her purse, sending it tumbling from the side table onto the hardwood floor with a soft thud.

"Damn it," she muttered, watching as the contents scattered. Keys jangled. Lip balm rolled under the couch. Her phone slid across the wood.

"I've got it, honey," Audra said, already moving from her spot on the floor to help gather the spilled items.

Melanie set down her wine. "Your purse exploded," she said with a soft chuckle.

Amelia dropped to her knees, cheeks heating as she scrambled to collect everything. "Thanks. I'm not usually so clumsy. This whole day has me rattled."

"You're definitely not," Melanie said, fishing the lip balm from under the couch. "You're just having a day from hell." She paused, holding up a cream-colored envelope that had landed near her feet. "This fell out, too. Looks official."

Amelia's stomach dropped. The fake-dating contract. She'd completely forgotten it was in there.

Chapter 58

Amelia

Her heart pounded as she watched Melanie examine the envelope more closely. Maybe she could deflect, change the subject, get them talking about something else. Anything else.

"Oh, that's just..." Amelia reached for the envelope, but Audra had already moved to look over Melanie's shoulder. The lie died on her tongue. How was she supposed to explain this?

"It's addressed to you," Audra said, her brow creasing as she studied the formal envelope. "From Jonathan Fontaine. Honey, this looks like legal paperwork. What's going on?"

Melanie's eyebrows shot up as she read the back flap. "Dating Agreement?" Amelia witnessed Melanie's lawyer instincts clearly kick in as she took the envelope and studied it more carefully. "Amelia, what kind of agreement are we talking about here?"

"It's nothing," Amelia said, snatching the envelope from Melanie's grasp. But even as she said it, she knew how ridiculous it sounded. Her friends exchanged a look, the kind that said they weren't buying her deflection and were worrying.

She clutched the envelope against her chest, her mind racing. How could she possibly explain that she'd been so afraid of real dating that she'd hidden behind a contract? It sounded pathetic even in her own head.

"Amelia," Audra said gently, settling back on her heels. "What's going on?"

Melanie set down the items she'd collected and moved closer. "We're worried about you. You've had a terrible week, and now there's some mysterious dating contract?"

Amelia looked at her friends' concerned faces and felt the weight of her secrets becoming unbearable. These were her closest friends, who'd dropped everything to bring her dinner and wine and consolation when she'd needed them. They deserved the truth, even if it made her look like a coward.

She took a shaky breath. "Okay. But you're going to think I'm ridiculous."

"Try us," Melanie said.

"Remember when you were both pushing me to go on that blind date with Leo?" Amelia began, still clutching the envelope. "I was panicking about it. Like, freak-out level panicking. And Jonathan ... he offered to help."

"Help how?" Audra asked, though her tone suggested she was figuring it out.

"He offered to pretend to be my date. Just for the evening, so I could tell you guys I was seeing someone and get you to back off about the blind date."

Melanie leaned back against the couch. "You hired him to fake-date you?"

"Not hired!" Amelia protested. "There wasn't any money involved. He just ... wanted the opportunity to explain the past over a meal together, and he understood I wasn't ready to date for real."

"So where did the contract come in?" Melanie asked, her analytical mind clearly working overtime.

Amelia's cheeks burned. "That was my idea. When he

offered to keep up the ruse, I insisted we needed ground rules and boundaries. I was so terrified of getting confused that I needed everything spelled out in writing."

"Confused about what?" Audra's voice had gotten very quiet.

"About whether or not it was real." The words came out barely above a whisper.

Melanie was quiet for a long moment. "So you created a formal agreement to avoid actual dating," she said slowly. "That's ... very you, actually. Practical to a fault."

Audra blinked. "Mmm. Rewind a minute ... panicked?"

"I did try one date a few months ago, but it was a disaster. I ... had a literal panic attack over the appetizers and ditched him. I still can't believe I left the poor guy just sitting there in the restaurant."

"I wish I'd known about the panic attack." Audra's voice was soft, wounded. "I wouldn't have pressed you so hard about dating again. I would have understood. We're your friends."

"I'm sorry about not telling you how bad things had gotten," Amelia said, her voice wavering slightly. "I was afraid."

"Afraid of what?" Audra asked, moving to sit beside her on the couch.

"Afraid of going on a real date. Afraid of having genuine feelings and getting hurt again. And afraid of having another panic attack." Amelia looked down at the envelope in her hands. "After Jonathan ghosted me, then Nate and his lies, I just ... I couldn't handle the thought of opening myself up to someone new. The contract felt safer."

"Oh, honey," Audra said, her anger melting into understanding. "Why didn't you just tell us?"

"Because it sounded pathetic," Amelia whispered. "A grown woman too scared to go on a date. And I'm tired of feeling broken."

"It's not pathetic," Melanie said firmly. "That's grief. It's self-protection. And it's human."

Audra was quiet for a moment, then asked more gently, "When you told us you slept with him ... was that part of the fake dating too?"

"No, that was real," Amelia said, her voice soft. "I didn't have another panic attack, thankfully. And we'd moved past the fake part by then. The sleeping together ... that was because we both wanted to. Somewhere along the way, it stopped being fake."

Amelia sniffed and took a deep breath. "The feelings became real, and now he's leaving for Brazil, and I'm exactly where I was afraid I'd end up, caring about someone who's going away."

Audra squeezed her hand. "But you did it. You let yourself care about someone again. That's huge."

"Does Jonathan know how you feel?" Melanie asked. "I mean, really feel?"

Amelia nodded. "We talked about it. We even let go of the rules and decided to try dating for real. But then this transfer happened..."

For a moment, no one spoke.

"I'm not angry that you weren't ready to date," Audra said finally. "I'm hurt that you felt like you had to keep the truth from us."

"We've been pushing you," Melanie acknowledged. "Maybe too hard. I'm sorry about that. We just wanted to see you happy again."

"I know, and I'm sorry, too," Amelia said. "And I wanted to be ready. I thought if I could just fake it to begin with, maybe I'd start feeling normal again." Amelia wiped her eyes with the back of her hand. "I never meant for it to get so complicated."

"What happens now?" Audra asked. "With Jonathan, I mean."

Amelia's shoulders sagged. "I don't know. He's leaving in less than a week now that the merger's fallen through. Even if we figured out our feelings, there's no time to figure out anything else."

"Have you talked about that?" Melanie asked. "About what you both want?"

"Not really. Everything's been happening so fast. The transfer to Brazil, and now this housing situation ..."

"Maybe that's where you start," Melanie suggested. "Have the conversation about what you both want, even if the logistics are complicated."

"Yeah," Audra agreed. "You spent so much time protecting yourself from getting hurt that you might miss out on something real."

"Okay," Amelia said, taking a deep breath. "First things first. I need to find somewhere to live. Then I can figure out the Jonathan situation."

"The cottage option is still on the table," Melanie reminded her. "It wouldn't be permanent."

"That's true," Amelia said. "I should probably talk to my mom about it. See how she'd feel about a temporary roommate."

"That's the spirit," Audra said with enthusiasm.

"Thank you," Amelia said, looking at both her friends. "For dinner, for the wine, for not judging me too harshly for being a coward."

"You're not a coward," Audra said firmly. "You've been through hell, and you're still trying to figure out how to trust again. That takes time and courage."

Amelia managed a small smile. Maybe Audra was right. Being honest with her friends and with herself was the first step toward not being afraid anymore.

Chapter 59

Amelia

AMELIA WOKE at dawn the next morning. Pirate and Treasure were curled on the bed, pressing against her left calf, softly purring. As soon as the first rays of sun lit her room, she opened her phone to message Jonathan.

She checked the time twice before typing, then deleted and retyped the message before finally hitting send.

> AMELIA: I'll be in at noon, need to work from home this morning to meet the floor refinishing crew. Let's get together after work tonight. I'm ready to talk things through.

Half an hour later, she filled the kittens' ceramic bowls with kibble and a spoonful of wet food for each. "Well, little ones, we're in for some big changes."

As she set down the dishes, Treasure immediately dunked her entire face into the wet food while Pirate delicately sniffed her kibble like a food critic. "Audra would be proud of you, Pirate," Amelia murmured.

She sat at the kitchen table, staring out the window at the

restored rose gardens and beyond to the thick forest. She'd miss soaking in this view every morning.

After a hearty breakfast of overnight oats topped with berries and a sprinkle of cinnamon, Amelia pressed "Call" on her mom's contact.

"Hey, Mom. I've got a few extra minutes this morning before I need to log in to work. Just checking in to see how things are going."

"It's so good to hear your voice, honey. I've been so busy the last few weeks, deciding what things to take with me and what to get rid of … there are way too many decisions to be made, but I'm making steady progress. And at least there haven't been any more cracks appearing around the house lately."

"Can't wait to see you, Mom. And you know I'll be relieved when you're out of that neighborhood and away from the sink-holes." She nestled the phone against her shoulder as she cleared her dishes. Whatever the reason for her mom finally deciding to move, Amelia was thankful.

"It's been too long since we were together," her mom said.

"I know, definitely too long between visits," Amelia agreed. "By the way, there's good news about the cottage," she said. "Drew says it should be ready in less than two weeks. There will be some smaller stuff to do after that, but it'll be completely livable." It was one of the few pieces of good news she'd gotten lately. "He's done a great job. I'm super excited for you to see it." She dried her hands and returned to the table.

"I put a deposit down for movers," her mom said. "I can't believe move day is only a month away." She paused. "Though I suspect packing Sam's toy collection alone will take a full day. That dog has more possessions than some people."

Amelia smiled to herself.

"I can't tell you how wonderful it will be to see you more

often than just major holidays," her mother said. "The cottages are so close to you at the mansion. I feel so grateful right now."

Amelia sighed. "Yeah, Mom, about that..." They might be seeing *a whole lot* of each other. She summoned her courage. It was now or never.

"What is it, dear?" Her mom's voice shifted to a tone of maternal concern, meaning she was reading between the lines. "There's something else troubling you, isn't there?"

"Yeah, actually..." Amelia took a breath. "There's more I need to tell you." She traced the edge of her coffee mug with one finger. "The thing is, Mr. Jewell sold the mansion. I found out yesterday that he's *already* sold it. Fortunately, he didn't sell the cottages, and that part of our agreement with him is solid. No worries about that."

"Oh my goodness," her mom said, her voice soft with surprise. "I didn't see that coming."

Amelia exhaled with a sigh. "Neither did I," she said. "I should have considered the possibility."

There was a long pause between them.

Her mom spoke first, her voice soothing. "So, honey, what does this mean for you? Does your lease transfer to the new owner?"

"I wish it did," Amelia said. She leaned forward, propping her elbows on the table. "But no. My lease is ending in thirty days. I have to move out."

Amelia heard Sam's tags jingling in the background as he moved about her mother's kitchen.

"Have you thought about where you're going to stay?" her mom asked slowly, as though carefully choosing her words. "Maybe with Audra or your other friend ... Melanie?"

Amelia frowned and looked down at the floor.

"They both offered to take me in," Amelia said, "but

Audra's place is tiny, and Melanie lives too far away. I want to stay near you, but the price of renting near Cedarvale Lake—"

"How about staying *with me* at the cottage?" her mom offered with quick optimism. "There's an extra bedroom upstairs, right? I'd love to have you there."

The extra bedroom was small, but it would be cozy. And since Jonathan would be transferring overseas, she wouldn't need much privacy or a big bedroom. A pinch of sadness settled in her chest, as she felt her independence slipping away.

But she needed to save money to repay the loan, and at least she wouldn't worry that her mother was alone. And Melanie was right; it would only be temporary. Then the realization hit her. *Temporary* wasn't at all a given thing in her life anymore.

"Mom, you know I'm really independent," she hesitated, and drummed a finger nervously on the table. "I'd like to have my own place. But living with you, at least for a while, would really help me out. And I can make myself scarce when you've got students over for lessons."

"Oh, dear, we'll make it work. And, speaking of students, I have wonderful news. One of my most talented students will move to your area soon. Her mother just got a position with the university there, so I'll be able to continue her lessons even after I move."

"That's terrific, Mom," Amelia said. Any continuity for her mom was a relief, though it seemed strangely coincidental. She relaxed in her chair for the first time in the entire conversation. "I'm excited for you."

"It makes leaving my other students behind a tad easier. I'm the happiest mom in the world right now." Her voice sparkled with energy. She chuckled. "Though Sam might need time to adjust to sharing his territory. You know how he gets about his favorite spot on the couch."

Sam's territory ... a vision of the huge German shepherd dog chasing the kittens flashed through her mind—his mouth open, tongue wagging, padded feet scrambling everywhere.

"Uh, Mom, how does Sam do with cats? I've gotten pretty attached to Pirate and Treasure."

She glanced toward the corner where Pirate was currently stalking a dust bunny with the intensity of a lion hunting gazelle. "They might be more than he bargained for." She couldn't imagine giving up the kittens now.

Her mom laughed, the sound warm and familiar. "He'll be fine once he realizes they're staying. Sam adapts better than I do, honestly." She paused. "I'm excited about this, Amelia. It feels like the right next step for both of us."

After they said goodbye, Amelia looked down at Pirate, who had abandoned the dust bunny hunt to weave around her ankles, again purring.

"Well, what do you think? Ready for a big brother who's ten times your size?" Pirate chirped once and stalked out of the kitchen, tail high. Apparently, everyone was handling change better than she was.

Chapter 60

Amelia

Amelia pushed through the NorthSound office doors just after noon, laptop bag slung over her shoulder. The morning working from home had been productive, but she wanted to be at the office during Jonathan's final preparations.

His last day.

The thought seeped heavily into her chest as she made her way past the reception desk. By Monday, he'd be back in Atlanta, and from there, who knew when she'd see him again.

The workroom droned with afternoon activity, but Jonathan's desk sat empty. She checked her phone—no messages.

"He's in the conference room with Patricia," Gavin said. "Transition review. Been in there since ten."

"Thanks." She dropped her bag at her desk and headed for the break room. Coffee first, then she'd tackle the mineral assessment reports.

The break room was empty. Afternoon sunlight cascaded through the tall windows. Amelia headed for the coffee station, reaching for her favorite mug, when footsteps clicked behind her.

"Well, hello there."

Something cold prickled at the base of her neck. Amelia turned.

Paige Whitlow stood in the doorway. She was tall and polished, with the kind of beauty that looked effortless but still expensive. Blonde hair fell in perfect waves past her shoulders, and her dark plum silk blouse probably cost more than Amelia made in a week.

"Paige." Amelia kept her voice level, though her hand tightened around the coffee mug. They'd met briefly when Paige had arrived, and this moment gave Amelia the same queasiness. Just as deliberate. Just as calculated.

"Hope you don't mind the interruption." Paige stepped into the room, her eyes shrewd and knowing.

"Not at all," Amelia lied.

"Good." Paige moved closer, her heels clicking against the linoleum. "I was hoping we'd have time to chat before I head back to Atlanta."

"About what?" Amelia set her mug under the coffee maker.

"Jonathan, of course." Paige's laugh was musical and cold. "I imagine he's told you about us."

Amelia's heartbeat quickened. "Some."

"I'm sure he has," Paige scoffed. "Though he has a tendency to ... *edit* the truth when it suits him." She tilted her head, studying Amelia like a specimen under glass. "He forgets to mention a lot of things, doesn't he?"

The machine gurgled behind them, filling the silent void. Amelia forced herself to retrieve the mug with steady hands. "I'm not sure what you mean."

"Of course you don't." Paige leaned against the counter, positioning herself between Amelia and the door. "I'm sure Jonathan mentioned we were engaged for two years. It's not something you easily move beyond, you know?"

The coffee mug slipped out of Amelia's hands. She caught it before it could fall, but hot liquid sloshed over the rim.

"Engaged," Amelia whispered.

"Two years." Paige's smile widened. "I have the most beautiful ring. Three carats, emerald cut. He had it custom designed." She paused, letting the information soak in. "But I suppose he didn't mention that either."

Amelia felt a squeeze in her chest. Jonathan had said they'd dated and that it was over. He'd never mentioned an engagement. Never mentioned that it had been serious enough for custom rings and a two-year commitment.

"I see he didn't." Paige's voice dropped to something almost sympathetic. "How precious. You really don't know anything, do you?" Her tone had turned pungent, with a sickly sweetness.

"I know it's over between you two," Amelia said sharply.

"Really. Is it?" Paige straightened, smoothing her skirt. "I'm transferring to the Brazil office next month. For the same project Jonathan's heading up. We'll be working closely together."

The room suddenly shrank. Amelia set down her coffee mug, afraid her hands would shake if she kept holding it.

"That's ... convenient for you," she managed.

"Yes, it is," Paige said. "You know, there's something about being in a foreign country together, away from all the ... diversions." Her gaze swept over Amelia dismissively. "It really puts things in perspective. I'll help him remember what's truly important."

Amelia scowled and carefully stirred her coffee. "And what's that?" As soon as she said it, she knew she shouldn't have. She was just tangling herself tighter in Paige's web of manipulation.

"History and actual connection. A love that's worth fighting for." Paige pushed off from the counter, moving toward the door. "Jonathan and I have something special. We always have.

The pause between us—it's only a brief hiccup. It doesn't change two years of building a life together."

Amelia's throat felt raw. "He broke up with you."

"Men say things when they're confused or afraid of a longer-term commitment." Paige hesitated in the doorway, her smile razor-sharp. "But they always come back to what's real and beautiful. What's solid. What's ... permanent."

She was gone before Amelia could respond, the strike of her heels echoing down the hallway like gunshots.

Amelia stood alone in the break room. The coffee maker's hiss was the only sound. Her hands were shaking, and she pressed them flat against the counter to stop the tremor.

Engaged. Two years and a custom ring.

The words spun through her mind like a tornado, destroying everything in their path. Jonathan had said they'd dated, that it was over. But engaged wasn't casual. That was planning a future together.

When he told her he loved her, had he meant it or was it a lie? Pretty words to get what he wanted, the same way Nate had lied about loving her right until the end?

Her phone buzzed with a text.

> JONATHAN: The meeting ran long. Grab dinner later?

She stared at the message, her vision blurring slightly. How could he text her about dinner when he'd hidden something this important? When he'd let her believe his relationship with Paige had been unimportant?

Gavin walked through the doorway, stopping short when he saw her face.

"Hey, you okay?" His tone was filled with concern.

"Fine. Yeah. I'm fine." She grabbed her coffee mug, not trusting herself to say more.

"You sure? You look—"

"I'm fine," she said stiffly.

Gavin held up his hands. "Okay, Okay, sheesh, I was only asking." He grabbed a donut from the box on the counter.

She pushed past him, hurrying back to her desk. But she wasn't fine. She was drowning, pulled under by the familiar weight of betrayal and secrets that felt too much like the last year with Nate.

Twenty minutes later, Jonathan emerged from the conference room, his smile fading when he saw her face.

"Everything all right?"

Amelia looked up at him, at his concerned eyes and gentle expression, and felt something essential inside her give way. He looked exactly the same as he had the last time he'd kissed her goodbye at his townhome. But everything had changed.

"Just tired," she said.

He studied her for a long moment, clearly not buying it. But Patricia called his name from across the room. He squeezed Amelia's shoulder before walking away.

Amelia watched him go, her throat tight. Next month, Paige would board a plane to Brazil. She'd be there with Jonathan, with her perfect smile and her custom engagement ring and two years of recent shared history that made Amelia's last two months with Jonathan look like exactly what they probably were —a temporary distraction.

She turned back to her computer screen and blinked against the tears she couldn't hold back. All she could see was Paige's confident smile, hear her voice saying *they always come back to what's real.*

Fine. Let him go back to what was real. Amelia was done with lies and done with being someone's distraction.

Chapter 61

Jonathan

JONATHAN HAD BEEN WATCHING Amelia all afternoon, the sinking feeling in his stomach deepening with each hour that passed. Something was wrong. She'd barely looked at him since he'd returned from his meeting with Patricia, and when she did, her eyes held a distance that made his chest ache.

He'd texted about dinner. She hadn't responded.

Now, as five o'clock approached, he couldn't shake the feeling that he was about to lose something precious before he had even fully grabbed hold of it.

The minute hand hit twelve, and Amelia was already moving. She grabbed her bag, shoved her laptop inside, and headed for the door without her usual goodbye to him, or even to Gavin and Patricia.

Jonathan was on his feet before he'd made a conscious decision.

"Amelia, wait."

She paused, her hand on the door handle, but didn't turn around. "I can't do dinner tonight, Jonathan. I'm sorry."

"What's wrong? Let's talk about it."

"Paige said some things, and I need time to figure out how I feel about them." Her voice was flat, mechanical. It was the same tone she'd used after the merger fell through, but worse. He felt the undertones of her disappointment.

Jonathan's stomach tumbled. He knew Paige well enough to suspect what she might have told Amelia. *Fuck.* He should have gotten ahead of this and told Amelia everything about Paige sooner. "What did she say to you?"

She finally turned, and the look in her eyes stopped him cold. It wasn't anger or hurt. It was resignation.

"I need to go."

Before he could respond, she was through the door and rushing toward the elevator. Jonathan hesitated for half a second, then followed.

The parking lot was nearly empty, afternoon shadows stretching long across the asphalt. Amelia's footsteps were rapid as she made her way to her car, fumbling with her keys.

"Amelia, please tell me what's going on."

She didn't acknowledge him, just yanked open her car door and slid inside. Through the windshield, he watched her insert the key, turn it.

Nothing.

She tried again. The engine made a weak grinding sound, then fell silent.

Jonathan approached cautiously, tapping gently on her window. After a moment, she rolled it down just far enough to hear him.

"Car trouble? Anything I can help with?"

"It's fine." Her voice was tight, controlled. "It'll start in a minute."

"Want me to look?"

"No. I just need it to start."

She turned the key again. This time, nothing happened at all.

Jonathan shifted his weight, placing his hand on the roof. "Amelia, let me help."

"I said it's fine." But her voice was too tight, too controlled, and Jonathan knew she was fighting not to break.

"What happened today?" he said gently.

Through the windshield, he could see her hands gripping the steering wheel, her knuckles white. Amelia hesitated and didn't respond.

"Please roll down the window."

For a long moment, she didn't move. Then the window lowered completely.

"Paige told me about your engagement. Everything you didn't."

Ice shot through Jonathan's veins. He'd been dreading this moment.

"Were you engaged?"

The question struck him like a blow to the chest, driving the air from his lungs. He'd known this moment would come, but somehow he'd thought he'd have more time to explain. To make her understand.

"Yes. I should have told you, but it's over. Paige asked me to marry her, and I said yes because I got caught up in a chance to have a family of my own."

Amelia's eyes closed briefly. When she opened them, the resignation was back.

"Two years?" She asked.

"We were involved for two years, yes. But we were only engaged for two months."

"A custom ring?"

Jonathan's throat felt raw. "Yes. Paige customized the ring herself and sent me the invoice."

"I get it." She nodded slowly, as if confirming something to herself.

"It's not what you think," he responded.

"Isn't it?" She looked at him directly for the first time since they'd come out to the parking lot. "You told me you dated. You made it sound casual, even unimportant. But engaged isn't casual or unimportant, Jonathan. It's planning a future together."

He'd made a huge mistake. "I know I've hurt you by not telling you—"

"Do you? Because from where I'm sitting, you lied to me. You let me believe your relationship with her didn't matter when it obviously did, and that hurts more than you can understand."

"It didn't matter. Not the way you think."

"She's going to Brazil, Jonathan. To work with you," Amelia said. "She told me all about how foreign assignments help people remember what's truly important. How men always come back to what's real and permanent."

Jonathan felt sick. This was exactly what Paige would do. She'd plant seeds of doubt and twist the truth just enough to make it poison. "She's trying to manipulate you."

"Is she? Or is that what you did? Or are you just afraid to admit she's right? Is she just telling me what you didn't have the courage to say yourself?"

"That's not—" He stopped, forced himself to breathe. "Amelia, I should have told you about the engagement. I know that. But I haven't lied about my feelings. What we have is real."

"What we have?" She let out a bitter laugh. "What we *had* was two months of pretending. What you had with her was two years of planning a life together."

"And I ended it."

"Because of me?"

The question caught him off guard. He could tell her it had

nothing to do with her, but they were already standing in the wreckage of half truths and omissions.

"Partly, yes."

"You broke off an engagement with her for someone you'll probably never see again after you leave for Brazil." She shook her head. "Do you see how insane that sounds?"

"It sounds like I fell in love. I realized I never fell out of love with you."

His confession hung between them, desperate and exposed. Amelia's breath caught, and for a moment, her careful composure cracked.

"So you weren't in love with the woman you were engaged to?"

"Not the way I loved you. I thought that was over, so I tried to make something else work."

"Don't," she whispered.

"It's true. I still love you, Amelia. I should have told you about Paige, explained what happened, but I wasn't proud of any of it—"

Tears were sliding down her cheeks now, and Jonathan had never felt more helpless. He wanted to reach through the window, pull her into his arms, and make her understand that whatever Paige had said was wrong.

"It doesn't matter," she whispered.

"How can you say that?" Jonathan felt the ground crumbling beneath him. He was losing her, and he didn't know how to stop it.

"Because you're leaving, Jonathan. In two days, you'll be on a plane to Atlanta, then to Brazil. And she'll be there waiting for you with her perfect smile and her three-carat, custom ring, ready to start fresh with you all over again."

Every word she spoke felt like another nail in his coffin.

She wiped her eyes with the back of her hand.

"I'm considering turning down the Brazil transfer. We'll figure it out." Even as he said it, Jonathan knew how empty it sounded. How could they figure out something when she didn't trust him anymore?

"No." She shook her head. "We won't. Because I can't do this again, Jonathan. I can't be with someone who keeps pieces of himself hidden from me. I can't wait around wondering if you're going to decide she was right, that what you had with her was more real than what we have ... had."

Panic clawed at his throat. She was talking about them in the past tense, like they were already over.

"That will never happen," he said. "Never." He needed her to believe him, but he could see in her eyes that the damage was already done.

"You don't know that," she said. "And I can't take that risk. Not again."

She turned the key one more time, and miraculously, the engine turned over. The sound sliced through him like a blade. She was really leaving. This was really happening.

"Amelia, please don't do this."

"I wish things were different, Jonathan." She put the car in reverse. "But this is where it ends."

He stepped back as she pulled out of the parking space, his hand falling away from the roof. Through the glass, he could see her crying, but she didn't look back.

Jonathan stood alone in the empty parking lot, watching his second chance drive into the distance. The evening chill cut through his shirt, but he barely felt it.

He'd finally told her he loved her, and it hadn't been enough.

Chapter 62

Amelia

AMELIA STOOD in the mansion's foyer, staring at the towers of sealed cardboard boxes that lined the front walls. Each labeled in her neat handwriting: Library: Fiction A–M, Fiction N–Z, Reference Materials, Art Books. A week ago, she'd methodically packed every volume to prepare for the floor refinishing, thinking she'd have the satisfaction of unpacking them once the work was complete.

Now she realized she'd never open those boxes again. Per Mr. F-O's instructions, they'd go straight to climate-controlled storage along with everything else that had made this place feel like a home instead of just an assignment.

She sighed in frustration. She'd been preparing the mansion for sale all along, polishing it to perfection for someone else to love.

The contractors had finished sanding yesterday, leaving behind the sharp scent of wood shavings and the gritty film that had settled on everything. Fine particles still lingered despite the crew's cleanup efforts.

Apparently, the floor refinishing had been part of the sale agreement, another detail Mr. F-O had conveniently forgotten to mention when he'd piled the task onto her already endless list.

Amelia rubbed her forehead, where a dull headache throbbed. The dust wasn't helping, and neither was the suffocating feeling that her entire life was as unsettling as the construction chaos surrounding her.

Sounds of soft mewing broke through her brooding. Treasure appeared from behind a box, her orange fur slightly dulled with dust, followed closely by Pirate, whose white patch looked more gray than usual. Both kittens wound around her legs, purring as if they knew she needed comfort.

"Come on," she murmured, bending to stroke each kitten. She straightened slowly, her back stiff from sleeping poorly. "Let's get out of this mess."

As she climbed the curved staircase, her legs felt heavy. The kittens trailed behind her like tiny, sympathetic shadows. Her bedroom door stood slightly ajar, revealing the stack of empty boxes she'd placed there yesterday, a depressing reminder of how much packing lay ahead.

But tucked on the settee by the window, exactly where she'd left it, was Rebecca's journal. At least she had that.

Amelia passed through the doorway, deliberately avoiding looking at the boxes. Nothing said *unstable life choices* quite like living out of cardboard boxes again.

She would deal with her own displacement later. Right now, she wanted to escape into someone else's struggles, preferably someone who'd faced far worse circumstances than a broken lease and a bruised heart.

She settled onto the velvet settee, pulling her legs up and arranging the soft throw around her shoulders. Outside, low clouds pressed against the window. A light drizzle had streaked the glass, and Cedarvale Lake looked gray and muted through the morning mist.

Treasure curled up against her feet while Pirate claimed the arm of the settee. Both kittens purred softly as she opened the worn leather journal. The scent of old paper carried her back to Rebecca's world of genuine hardship.

At least Rebecca's problems had been real.

14 June 1855

The days pass with a manageable routine, but the nights remain my greatest trial. It has been over a year since Thomas departed for California, and the ache in my chest when darkness falls has not diminished. It is not general loneliness that troubles me—I have Everett and the children for companionship—but the deep yearning for my husband's presence, his steady voice, the comfort of his arms.

Last year's harvest brought disappointment once again. The soil here proves more stubborn than any we knew in New York. It drains poorly in the low places, creating boggy patches that rot the roots, yet turns hard as stone when the summer sun beats down. The clay beneath the surface fights every shovelful, every attempt to coax life from it.

Yet I am grateful for the money James sends from Thomas's earnings. His commission from the dry-goods business provides what our poor harvests cannot. Each month brings a letter with funds enclosed, reminding me that his sacrifice serves our family's survival.

Liza and Mary remind me more and more of Thomas each day, with their long legs and how they weave story-telling into their play.

And Everett has grown into a man this past year. At sixteen, he works with the strength of someone far older. I have noticed him watching young Minna Karlsen when her family comes to town. She is a sweet girl, the daughter of the

Norwegian family who settled near the creek. When she smiles at him, Everett's ears turn red, and he becomes unusually attentive to his appearance.

Each evening, I place a small candle in our front window to guide Thomas home. The light flickers against the glass as I write these words, and I imagine it reaching across the mountains to California, reminding him that his family awaits his return.

Pirate yawned and reached out with one paw as Amelia turned the page.

Treasure mewed plaintively and swished her tail against Amelia's leg. "What is it, cutie?" She glanced down, then back at the journal as she discovered the tattered letter...

20 June 1855
My Dearest Rebecca,

I pray this letter finds you and our precious children in good health and spirits. I write by candlelight in my modest lodgings near Montgomery Street, where the sounds of this bustling city never cease.

The dry-goods business prospers beyond what James and I dared hope. The miners still come seeking supplies, and the influx of newcomers creates a steady demand for our textiles. My carpentry skills prove equally valuable. There is much building as this city transforms from temporary camps to proper brick establishments.

Yet I must speak plainly of the trials here. The streets remain treacherous with mud and refuse, and illness claims lives regularly. Competition among merchants grows fierce, and I witness good men reduced to desperate measures when their ventures fail.

But oh, my beloved, how I ache for you. Each morning I wake, reaching for you, only to find myself alone. Though miles separate us, you carry my heart with you always, and I yours.

Your devoted husband,
Thomas

Amelia closed the journal and leaned back against the settee.

Life without Jonathan would be lonely too. The awareness crept up on her like the gray clouds outside. She shifted on the settee, the velvet cushion suddenly scratchy.

She stared out at the muted lake, barely visible through the drizzle. Mr. F-O had betrayed her trust, stringing her along while preparing to sell the mansion all along. Jonathan had kept the truth about his engagement hidden. Just like Nate, letting her believe in something that was never real.

The rain drummed harder against the window.

Only this time, she had nothing to feel guilty about. She was just lost and alone all over again.

Rebecca was lonely too, wrestling with her own fears about Thomas's safety and return. But even in her uncertainty, she had something Amelia didn't. She had the knowledge that her husband was choosing their separation reluctantly, sacrificing for their shared future rather than moving toward a different life.

She set the journal aside and rubbed her forehead; the headache intensified. Pirate chose that moment to pounce on her shoelace, apparently deciding her brooding needed interruption.

Then her defenses snapped back into place.

If she and Jonathan had tried to make a long-distance relationship work, she would have waited endlessly, like Rebecca, for texts and calls, always wondering when he'd decide she wasn't worth the distance.

Undoubtedly, breaking up with Jonathan had been the right thing to do.

Her phone buzzed with a text.

> DREW: Update on the cottage repairs. Electrical all good, and roof almost done. I can't believe how long it took for the shingles to get here. Will start the plumbing fixes on Monday.

Amelia managed a small smile at Drew's update.

Her mom would be here soon. At least she'd have family nearby, someone who wouldn't leave when things got complicated. Amelia tucked the journal against her chest and closed her eyes, letting the sound of rain against the window wash over her doubts.

Some separations were worth enduring. Others were just postponing the inevitable.

Chapter 63

Jonathan

Saturday afternoon.

JONATHAN CLIMBED the ladder leaning against the cottage roof and set a pile of shingles at the top. The cedar smelled refreshing, unexpectedly comforting.

"Look, I appreciate your help today," Drew said, handing up another bundle of shingles. "But you don't have to be here."

"I'm good," Jonathan said, setting the pile at the roof's edge. "It helps keep my mind off other things."

"Like the fact that you spent this morning packing your Rainmere life into boxes?" Drew sat at the edge of the roof and opened his water bottle. "Okay," he said. "I get it."

Jonathan's feet touched the ground again. "What are you going to do now that I have to leave Rainmere? Sorry you can't stay in the townhome."

"This job will take another few weeks," Drew said. "And the housing change is no big deal. Audra is excited for me to stay at her place." He grinned as though he'd won the lottery.

"Despite my being miserable, I think this worked out in your favor, didn't it?" The corner of Jonathan's mouth twitched upward.

Audra's car rumbled onto the dirt driveway next to the cottage. "Hey, there!" She stepped out of the car and unloaded two bags from the trunk.

Drew climbed down the ladder with a few dark shingles in one hand. His jeans were dusty, and the tool belt at his hip jangled with each step. "Great timing," he called to her. "I just finished the last of the roofing."

"I've got lunch covered," Audra said, heading for the cottage door. "Pasta salad and ranch slaw." She nodded at Jonathan and gave Drew a knowing smile. "And I might have added a few slices of your favorite blueberry lemon cake."

"Have I told you lately that you're wonderful?" Drew said.

"Mm, no, but keep it up and I might leave the leftover cake for you," Audra said with a quick wink.

She disappeared inside with the bags of food and returned a few minutes later, empty-handed.

Jonathan busily sorted copper fittings and PVC joints from the supply box. He noticed Audra was eyeing him.

"You look terrible, which is appropriate," she said.

"You heard." Jonathan looked up at her momentarily.

"I heard," Audra said. As she glanced at his feet, her brows slowly knitted together. "Hm. And your socks don't match."

He looked down and frowned. *Damn, she's right.* They weren't even close. "Everything is a mess right now."

"Amelia texted about the breakup, but she didn't give details."

He continued sorting the supplies. "Is she doing okay?"

"Hard to say," Audra said. "I think she needs time to process before talking."

"When she is ready to talk, she will probably tell you it was because I never told her Paige and I had been engaged."

He should be angry with Paige, but he was too worried about the situation with Amelia to waste any energy on Paige.

"You were what? No!" Audra said.

"It gets worse. Paige is transferring to Brazil, too."

"Oh my god," Audra muttered, as her expression shifted into a scowl.

Drew removed his tool belt. "Food break. I'm starving." He set a hand on Jonathan's shoulder. "This conversation needs beer, but coffee will have to do."

Ten minutes later, they sat around the cottage kitchen table with pasta salad and sandwiches.

"I'm not interested in going to Brazil," Jonathan said. "And I never imagined I'd say this, but I don't want to go back to Atlanta, either."

"That's a big change," Drew said.

"So don't go," Audra said. "It wouldn't be simple, but it's an option."

"She's right," Drew said. "If you're not interested in Brazil, what's really keeping you from saying no?"

"I don't want to give up on our relationship," Jonathan said. "But I can't force her to love me, either."

"This isn't about her not loving you enough," Audra said. "The reality is that Brazil means choosing your *career* over your *relationship*. And she'll see it as you choosing Paige over her."

"You sound just like my mother," Jonathan said. He scraped up a spoonful of pasta. "It feels like Amelia's giving up on us. It feels like ... she's abandoning us ... abandoning me."

"Drama much?" Drew said then softened his tone. "Look, she's not abandoning you."

A hard, achy knot was forming in his chest, just like when his father had left the family. The pain felt old and practiced. He set down his spoon, appetite gone.

"Amelia didn't abandon you," Drew said. "She's protecting

herself. I think maybe she's afraid of trusting her own feelings. And after what Nate did to her, I don't blame her one bit."

"You left out the part about me ghosting her," Jonathan said.

Drew cleared his throat, then took a swallow of his soda. "Yeah, well ... that too."

"Amelia has a lot of baggage left over from both you and Nate," Audra said. "It's diminishing over time, but the wound isn't healed. His not loving her just crushed her."

"I told her I still love her," Jonathan said.

Audra nodded approvingly. "Good move. She needs to hear it, and often."

"Yeah, well, she still broke up with me."

Picking up the dessert knife, Drew nodded toward Audra with a questioning glance.

"Mm, thanks," she whispered. He carefully placed a slice of cake on her plate, then cut a piece for himself.

"Every breakup deserves decent cake," Audra said.

"Give Amelia time to sort this out," Drew said.

"I fly back to Atlanta tomorrow," Jonathan said. "Then I'm taking a few days off to figure things out before going back to the office."

They finished the last bites on their plates.

"I agree with Drew," Audra said, patting Jonathan's arm. "Don't give up yet."

"Okay," he said. "Thanks for the lunch and for listening."

"Time for me to head out," Audra said. "I've got a beach cleanup event tomorrow, and I need to prepare this afternoon." She turned to Drew. "You coming over tonight?"

"Yes," he said with a soft smile. "After I'm done here, I'll shower at Jonathan's then bring my things to your place."

"My couch is all ready for you," she said as they packed up the lunch leftovers.

When Audra had left and they were alone again, Drew gave

Jonathan an overview of the plumbing tasks. "Ready to get started?"

"Yep," Jonathan said, "let's get to it."

Jonathan pulled out his phone and scrolled to Steve's contact. He'd give Amelia time, but he'd also give serious thought to refusing Brazil.

He didn't call Steve, not yet. But for the first time since Friday, he was strategizing a plan that didn't involve a passport.

Chapter 64

Amelia

A week later.

Amelia checked her phone. Her friends had been texting all morning, their messages growing increasingly persistent. The latest round of messages appeared:

> AUDRA: Hey, honey, just checking in. I know you wanted some time to yourself, but after a week of crickets, we're worried about you. Please update us.

> MELANIE: Since it's Friday night, why don't we come over for a visit? I have a new martini recipe I'm dying to try out.

> AUDRA: Ooh, taste testing, yes. I can bring cheese and crackers and some candied nuts.

Her friends meant well, she knew that, but Amelia wasn't in the mood for company. She set the phone on her bed and headed for the pile of boxes in the corner of the room. She needed to stay busy.

She assembled a packing box, securely taped the bottom, and set it in front of the closet. She finally had a smidge of time to pack up her own things in earnest, now that she'd finished boxing up and sending the bulk of Mr. F-O's stuff to storage.

She again glanced back toward her closet. It was full of work clothes, hiking boots, numerous other shoes, and stacks of memorabilia. It was organized, but there was a lot of stuff in there. Apparently, she had a serious problem letting go of old shoes.

She reconsidered her friends' messages and sighed in resignation. Maybe some extra hands would be helpful. She retrieved her phone and opened the group chat.

> AMELIA: Okay, but before we get sloshed on martinis, I need some help packing my closet.

> MELANIE: Deal.

> AUDRA: We've got your back, hon. 🤍

* * *

An hour later, Audra and Melanie arrived at her doorstep. Amelia opened the door and inhaled deeply. Fresh air had never smelled so good after a week of wood stain vapors.

Audra wrinkled her nose. "What's that awful smell?"

"The floor contractors have been busy all week," she said as she led them toward the staircase. "The staining is done, but different rooms on the first floor are in various states of applying the finishing coating."

"Why couldn't Mr. Jewell wait until you moved out to do all of this?"

"An agreement with the buyer, from what he said." Amelia

shook her head, and the corner of her mouth turned downward. "I even slept one night in the library while the staircase cured. The entire house still smells like chemicals."

"I hope he appreciates all your efforts," Melanie said.

At the top of the stairs, Amelia opened her door, and Pirate poked her head out from under the bed, eyeing the newcomers with obvious interest, as if they might steal her favorite hiding spot.

"I've been keeping the kitties up here at night, so they don't have to be shut in the mudroom all the time," Amelia said. "Thankfully, Drew is almost finished with the cottage repairs, at least the most important stuff." Her improvement loan funds were running low, so the timing was good.

They made quick work of the closet, with Audra folding and Melanie wrapping shoes in tissue paper. An hour and a half later, Audra and Melanie began mixing the cocktails on Amelia's kitchen counter.

"Has Lydia told you anything yet about the permanent position?" Melanie asked as she handed Amelia a pink martini that smelled like strawberries and vodka.

"Not a peep," Amelia said. She took a sip of the sweet cocktail, feeling the vodka burn slightly. "But she's been pretty busy with management meetings since the merger fell through."

Audra poured a glass for herself and another for Melanie. "I'm glad you finally wanted to get together," she said. "I have something cool to share."

Amelia set her glass on the counter. "This sounds good."

A sweet smile crossed Audra's face. "I've started taking cooking classes, which is why I changed my schedule at the lab."

"Darn," Melanie teased. "I was hoping it was about having a certain roof contractor as your roommate."

"Shut up," Audra said playfully. "Anyway, you know I love cooking, and I'm really excited to learn different techniques.

And I'm meeting people, too. It's wonderful to have fresh conversations after days alone in the lab."

"That's exciting," Amelia said. "I'm happy for you." She picked up her glass again, and they toasted Audra's new direction. For a few minutes, Amelia looked past her own worries.

Audra refilled their glasses with more of the strawberry-flavored martini, and they sat around the kitchen table.

"Can we talk about the elephant in the room now?" Melanie gently prodded, then took a bite of sharp cheddar on a buttery cracker.

"Are you really just going to let Jonathan walk out of your life?" Audra asked. "I heard the story from Jonathan when I visited Drew at the cottage last weekend."

"What's the entire story?" Melanie said. "I'm feeling left out," she added, with light sarcasm.

Amelia explained the engagement saga, the deception, and Paige's glee over the transfer situation, as well as the breakup details. Maybe it was the week she'd had to mull it over, or maybe it was the martini, but the sting wasn't so harsh when she retold the story.

"He loves you, you know," Audra said. "And he looked like he was going through hell without you. I think you should forgive him."

"He should have told me he was engaged to Paige. And who breaks off an engagement like that? Why did he get engaged in the first place if he wasn't going to go through with it?"

"People get cold feet," Melanie said. "It happens. Better that he didn't marry her if he figured out she wasn't the right person for him."

Audra set down her drink and looked Amelia directly in the eyes. "I love you, honey, but you're not seeing this clearly. This is a trigger for you because Nate lied about loving you. This isn't the same situation at all. Jonathan broke off an engagement that wasn't right for him. Considering that, I'd say he did them both a favor. And maybe ... maybe he was too embarrassed to tell you about it. Breaking off an engagement is not the most flattering look, by a long shot."

"Maybe you're right," Amelia said. "It probably is a trigger for me. And he did say he wasn't proud of how the relationship ended. But also looking at the practicality of it all ... years apart, in different countries, is a long time even under the best of circumstances. We'll barely get to see each other, and Paige is going to be right there with him, working beside him every single day."

"I think you're stronger than you give yourself credit for," Audra said. "And more desirable."

Amelia finished the last swallow of her drink and poured herself another.

Audra pushed the plate of hors d'oeuvres toward Amelia and gently replaced her cocktail with a glass of water. The move was pure mama-bear Audra. "Have some of the cheese and some water first. Maybe you'll avoid a hangover."

"Thanks." Amelia nodded and took a bite of cheese. She chewed her food and shifted uncomfortably in her chair. "I broke up with him, and I'm prepared to see it through."

"Even though the merger fell through, Jonathan's company still has an office near Seattle," Melanie said. "After his Brazil stint is over, he could transfer to Washington. That's still a possibility."

Amelia leaned back in her chair, feeling the cool metal against her back. They wanted her to hope, to believe it could work out. But she knew after his years in Brazil he would end up back in Atlanta working for his mother's company.

"Paige is trying to manipulate you," Melanie said. "Don't let her win. And don't let the stink of Nate's lies continue to dictate your relationship choices."

Amelia mulled that over. What if she was wrong? Paige probably was manipulating the situation.

Maybe Jonathan deserved a second chance, but could she survive three years of wondering if they'd make it? Doubt pressed heavily on her chest.

Her friends were watching her with concerned expressions.

"Look, I'm still not ready to talk to him. But you're both right. This isn't the same as what Nate did or when Jonathan ghosted me." She stared at her water glass. "And maybe I'm letting Paige get in my head more than I realized."

Chapter 65

Amelia

Rain lashed against the windows as Amelia made her way upstairs through the darkness. Her flashlight beam danced across the familiar banister. The power had been out for twenty minutes. Given how the wind was tearing through the old-growth forest around the mansion, it was probably a tree down on the lines.

The backup generator had turned on, but with only enough power to run the security systems, the refrigerators, and a few lights on the first floor.

Power outages were nothing new, but this May storm felt fierce. The rustling of leaves followed the whooshing winds, and the occasional thud of branches against the windows echoed like the footsteps of ghosts roaming forest paths.

Rather than sit downstairs listening to the wind pounding the shutters, she decided to return to Rebecca's journal.

More than a full week had passed since Jonathan had returned to Atlanta, and her workdays felt increasingly empty. No more shared looks during tedious meetings. No more texts about weekend plans. Even her successes felt lackluster when there was no one to share them with.

Amelia paused at the top of the stairs. She also missed feeling his body against hers, as his lips explored every inch of her skin. For half a moment, she indulged and let herself enjoy the memories before brushing them away.

As she passed through her bedroom door, two pitiful mews escaped from beneath the bed. Treasure and Pirate were hiding from the storm. "You've got a perfect place to snuggle tonight, little cuties," she murmured.

She sat on her bed, propping the flashlight against her pillows to create a small circle of light. Rebecca's journals sat on the nightstand. Soon they'd have to join Mr. F-O's other belongings in storage, but for now they were her one comfort. She reached for the third volume, ready to lose herself again in the story.

22 October 1856

> *Last night's storm brought down two trees across the main path to the road. This morning I cleared the first of them myself with Thomas's axe. It felt good to use my strength for something other than just surviving. The Douglas fir took me nearly three hours, but I cut through both trunks cleanly. Thomas always said I had the shoulders for hard work, though Mother with her elitist New York upbringing would faint to see her daughter wielding tools like a farmhand.*
>
> *Liza helped by dragging the smaller branches to our woodpile, and Mary entertained herself by building fairy houses from the bark chips. They've grown so much in the past two years. Liza nearly comes to my shoulders now, and Mary chatters like a jay about everything she sees. Thomas will hardly recognize them...*

The story felt personal, like hazy memories she'd witnessed in some long-forgotten dream.

24 October 1856

> *Working on the second felled tree today, I dropped the axe mid-swing when I saw Thomas's familiar silhouette on the ridge path. He hadn't seen me yet. He carried the weariness of his long ship journey and the walk from town, but there was something in the way he moved, purposeful and sure, like a man who knew exactly where he belonged.*
>
> *My legs carried me down the hill faster than sense would allow. I couldn't stop myself. Pure instinct, like my body knew its match was home before my mind could catch up.*
>
> *The girls heard my shouts and came flying from the cabin. Liza reached us first, then Mary launched herself into Thomas's arms like she'd been waiting her whole life for this moment. We stood there in a tangle of arms and tears and laughter, and I felt whole again for the first time since he left.*
>
> *We talked until dawn, finishing each other's thoughts the way we used to. I'd start telling him about the harvest troubles, and he'd already be nodding, planning solutions before I'd finished explaining. It's everything I could have hoped for.*

Amelia closed the journal and let it rest against her chest. Outside, the storm quieted; the wind settled from a howl to a steady whisper.

Rebecca's joy had been so complete, so whole. The way Thomas had moved with purpose toward home touched something in her soul.

Amelia had never had that with Nate, that intuitive partnership where two people moved as one. She'd loved him, yes, but not with the bone-deep certainty Rebecca described, not with that sense of completion.

Jonathan's words reverberated in her mind. *Not the way I loved you.*

She'd thought he was making excuses. Now she understood. He'd recognized the same thing she was seeing now, the difference between caring for someone and finding your soulmate.

Amelia clung tighter to the journal. "Yes," she whispered. Some connections could survive distance. And perhaps some connections were worth the uncertainty.

The kittens emerged from their hiding spot to curl against her legs. She wasn't ready to pick up her phone, wasn't ready to bridge that gap. But now the possibility didn't feel so impossible.

Outside her window, the rain had mellowed to a quiet patter, and in the distance, the power flickered back to life.

Chapter 66

Amelia

Friday.

AMELIA PULLED her car onto the gravel drive of the cottage and cut the engine. The moment of truth had arrived; she was finally moving in.

For now, she had the cottage all to herself. Drew had said he wouldn't be around today, something about helping Audra prep for another weekend beach cleanup project.

At the porch door, she punched in the code, then propped it open with a nearby stone. She stared inside. With all the windows lining the open living room, sunlight burst in everywhere, giving the interior a cheerful radiance.

Next, she popped open the back hatch of her car and scooped up the first load of boxes.

Amelia set the box of cat toys in the cottage living room. While she'd been packing, the kittens had loved investigating the empty boxes and trying to climb into packed ones. She hoped Pirate and Treasure liked their new home.

Her phone vibrated just as she was picking up a laundry basket full of clothes and shoes from the car. She paused and shoved her hand in her pocket to retrieve it. Wedging the phone between her shoulder and ear, she gathered up another armful of her things.

"Hey, Mom. You caught me in the middle of moving into the cottage," Amelia said, heading back toward the cottage steps. "Just finished emptying a carload of stuff. One more trip to get the kittens and that should be it."

She felt a twinge in her back, a slow ache forming from the repeated trips. Instead of going inside again, she set the laundry basket on the front porch and sat on the top step. "Thanks again for letting me stay with you. I'm grateful."

"It'll be fun having you with me," her mother said. "I feel you're the one giving me a gift."

"When are the movers coming? Are you sure you don't want me to come help you finish packing up?" She stretched her legs and rubbed her shoulder with her free hand. "I could book a cheap red-eye flight."

"No need. I'm doing fine, dear. The movers are coming on Wednesday. And Sam and I are staying with my friend, Kate, for the few days before my flight to Seattle."

"Kate?" Amelia asked.

"I told you about her." Her mother's voice cut out momentarily. Amelia stood and walked to the end of the porch, searching for better service.

"What?" Amelia said.

"She just got hired to teach at a university," her mom said.

"Oh yeah, I remember now." The woman with the talented daughter.

"Kate's been a great help."

"Is there anything I can do?" Amelia asked.

"Absolutely. Once I'm in Rainmere, I plan to play piano for weddings and maybe even theater accompaniments. If you could contact local people ahead of time and promote me, that would really help."

"You got it. I'm on it, like, yesterday!" A dozen contact ideas rushed through her mind. "Wedding planners, local theater directors ... I could set up a website to advertise your services."

And she already had some ideas for cutting the costs of producing her mom's planned video course—

Papers rustling on the other end of the line interrupted her brainstorming.

"Oh, did you see the email I sent?" her mom said. "The realtor says the house will go on the market soon after I move out. I'm excited to see you and have all the moving done, but selling our home is bittersweet. So many memories here with your dad."

"I know," Amelia said. "I have a lot of meaningful memories there, too. But if Dad is watching you from heaven, which I'm sure he is, he'll be relieved you're getting out of there."

"I'm sure you're right," her mom agreed. "At least I know he's always with me. I'll always feel the connection we have in my heart, no matter how many years he's been gone."

Amelia leaned against a support post, feeling the sun-warmed wood against her shoulder. Something tender stirred in her chest. The connection her mom described, lasting through years and loss, made Amelia think of permanence in a way she hadn't allowed herself to consider in a long time.

"Mom?" she said.

"Yes, dear?"

"How did you know Dad was worth the risk? When you first fell in love with him?"

"I suppose I realized having him then losing him would hurt more than anything I could imagine." Her mother's voice grew thoughtful. "But not having him at all would be worse."

A soft breeze rustled through the trees as Amelia shifted her footing.

"How are things going with Jonathan?" her mom said. "And the project you're working on together?"

Amelia paused and let out a long breath, taking a moment to collect her thoughts. She paced, then headed for the door and stepped back inside.

Her mom hadn't been the biggest supporter of her dating Jonathan. And maybe she'd been right to question Amelia's decision.

"Well," she began, "first the easier part ... the merger fell through."

"Oh no, honey. Are you okay? Do you still have your job?"

"Yes," Amelia said honestly. "I'm doing okay. I still have my contract work with NorthSound, and the company continued the asset project, despite the ending of merger talks. But I don't know yet whether I'm going to get the full-time job. Things are kind of fluid in that regard. I hope I'll find out soon."

"Mm. Well, if that's the easy part, I can't imagine the hard part. I'll understand if you don't want to talk about Jonathan."

"It's all right," Amelia said. She walked to the window and pressed her palm against the window frame, watching the early light filter through the trees. "To make a long story short, I broke things off with him after the merger died. We had a disagreement about things he should have told me."

Her voice caught slightly. "But I might have overreacted. Now I'm considering what you said about Dad, how you knew he was worth the risk." She turned from the window. "I think I was so scared of being hurt again that I didn't give Jonathan a chance to explain. And I might have projected some of my biases from the past onto him."

She flipped the latch on the window and slid it open enough to let the cool morning breeze seep through.

"I'm here for you," her mother said. "Always."

"I love you, Mom," Amelia replied. "When you get here, we can talk more about it." Maybe by then she'd know exactly what she needed to do.

She again wedged the phone between her ear and shoulder and grabbed a few boxes for the kitchen.

"I love you more than life." Her mom's voice grew gentle but firm. "Nate shouldn't have lied to you. What he did was ugly, and he didn't deserve you. But not all men are Nate. There are men like your father out there. Men who will cherish you and treat you with honesty."

Amelia sighed as she set the boxes on the kitchen counter. She meant good men like her dad ... and like Jonathan.

"I know," she whispered. She thought of Jonathan's careful attention to her needs, his respectful patience, the way he'd never once made her feel rushed or pressured.

"I hope you find the kind of love your dad and I had. When you find it, never let it go. It will stay with you always, even when life tries to tear it away."

After ending the call, Amelia stood in the quiet cottage, phone still warm in her hand. *Never let it go.*

She had found it. She'd had two beautiful months with Jonathan, and she'd thrown it away because she'd been too afraid to trust.

She sank onto one box, her legs suddenly unsteady. All this time, she'd been telling herself Jonathan had betrayed her trust. But the truth was simpler and more painful. She'd been so terrified of being abandoned again, she'd abandoned him first.

The truth sorted itself out in her mind, piece by piece, like she'd been doing with her belongings all morning. She'd been so afraid of being deceived again that she'd refused to listen when he tried to explain.

She'd accused him of keeping secrets instead of trusting him.

Amelia looked around the cottage, at the sunlight streaming through the windows, at the boxes holding the pieces of her new beginning. This was supposed to be a fresh start. And fresh starts required courage.

She pulled out her phone and started typing before she could change her mind.

> AMELIA: I owe you an apology. And an explanation. Could we talk?

She hit send before fear could stop her. Then she set the phone on the kitchen counter and began unpacking the first box, her hands steady for the first time in weeks.

Chapter 67

Jonathan

Saturday night.

IN THE LIVING ROOM, Charlotte's latest design magazines fanned across the side table, and the soft glow of table lamps created intimate shadows.

Jonathan shuffled the deck of cards several times, then dealt cards around the table.

Jessica reached for another handful of popcorn from the bowl between them. "All packed for Brazil?" she asked.

"Mm," he nodded. Knowing his flight was actually happening the following morning, his stomach had been unsettled for days.

"Are you sure Brazil is what you really want?" Charlotte asked quietly.

"Why are you accepting the transfer if you don't really want to go?" Jessica said, sorting her cards. "You look miserable about it. When did you become someone who does things that make you miserable?"

Over the last two weeks, Jonathan had moved all his belongings from his apartment into a spare room in his mother's house and arranged for the return of his rented furniture. And he'd notified the landlord that he wouldn't be renewing his lease. It all seemed so impossibly final.

His flight to São Paulo was scheduled for ten-thirty tomorrow morning, and he still felt conflicted. He took a large swallow of his drink before sorting his hand.

They each selected three cards to pass to their left.

Brandon laid down the two of clubs. Jonathan followed with a low diamond, Jessica played a club, and Charlotte took the trick with the ace of clubs.

Soon the gin and tonics had loosened everyone up, and the familiar rhythm of Hearts led to straightforward conversation.

"Well," Jessica said, laying down a low heart, "I've decided about school. I want to apply to the University of Washington for the fall."

Charlotte stopped sorting her cards mid-arrangement. "Washington state? I thought you were also considering Emory and staying in Atlanta."

"I was. But the UW program is stronger for what I want to do." Jessica glanced at Jonathan. "Plus, it makes sense strategically."

"Here we go," Brandon muttered, playing his card.

Charlotte's voice carried a patient, negotiating tone. "Jessica, we've discussed this. Having a Fontaine in the spotlight—"

"Mom," Jonathan interrupted, laying down the queen of spades. "You've been talking about expanding into Europe, maybe Asia. That kind of growth requires serious business planning. Market research." He met his mother's eyes. "Jessica's MBA would prepare her for the strategic planning your business needs."

Charlotte picked up her trick, expression shifting from dismissive to thoughtful.

"Exactly," Jessica said. "I'm not trying to step away from the family business. I'm trying to move into the parts that actually suit my strengths."

Jonathan dealt the next hand. "Mom, you've always talked about leaving a legacy. Jessica's not asking to abandon that legacy. She's asking to become the person who ensures it survives and thrives, long after the company outgrows what any one person can manage."

The room fell quiet except for ice clinking in glasses and cards quietly moving. Charlotte studied her hand, wheels turning behind her honey-brown eyes.

"Well," she said finally, "I suppose if you're determined to get an MBA, Washington might provide ... strategic advantages." She looked at Jonathan. "Having two of my children on the West Coast could be useful for business development."

Jonathan's hand stilled over his cards. Two children. She was talking as if his eventual return to Rainmere was a given, not a future maybe. Like she'd been planning for it all along.

Jessica's face lit up. "Really?"

"I'm saying I'll seriously consider it," Charlotte clarified, though her tone had softened considerably.

"And in the meantime," Jonathan said, "you could hire someone to help with client interactions while Jessica's in school. Someone to handle the day-to-day client meetings so you can focus on the design work."

Charlotte frowned slightly. "I'm not comfortable with the idea of bringing in someone who doesn't understand our aesthetic or our standards."

"I could help with the interviews," Brandon offered. "Make sure we find someone who gets the Studio Charlotti vision."

"See?" Jonathan said. "It doesn't have to be permanent. Just someone to bridge the gap until Jessica comes back with her MBA and can handle the backend operations."

Brandon raised his glass. "To strategic advantages and family surprises."

"To family," Charlotte corrected, "even when they insist on complicating things."

Jonathan arranged his cards without really seeing them. Jessica had just made a decision that would change her entire life—choosing what she wanted despite the complicated path.

And Charlotte ... *strategic advantages*. She'd been nudging him away from Brazil for weeks, and he'd been too focused on his mistakes and his Career Recovery Program to see it.

Leaving Whitlow would mean he'd never get to see it launch, never experience his framework actually helping anyone. But the other participating companies were invested, and Whitlow had already committed the resources. Someone else would take it across the finish line.

The irony was obvious—he'd built something to help people recover from doing the right thing, but now he had to do the right thing himself, even if it meant walking away before completion.

Some things mattered more than finishing what you started. Amelia mattered more.

When had he become the person who let a corporation make his choices for him? Jessica was willing to fight for what she wanted. Hell, she was willing to move across the country for it.

He thought about Amelia, completely unaware he was sitting here considering restructuring his future around her. The decision crystallized, clear and inevitable.

He wasn't going to Brazil. He couldn't. Not when everything he actually wanted was in Washington.

"You know what?" Jonathan said, setting his cards face down on the table. "I need to make a phone call."

Chapter 68

Amelia

Sunday. Fourth week of May.

AMELIA STRETCHED IN HER BED, listening to the forest sounds that had become her new morning soundtrack. Birds were calling to each other through the cedar branches, as the distant rustle of something small moved through the underbrush.

Amelia reached for her phone and reread Jonathan's text from last night.

> JONATHAN: Things are moving at lightning speed. Lots going on. Too much for texting, but I'll catch up with you soon.

After reading his message twice more, she opened the small closet to search for clothes, half expecting that same musty smell that had greeted her at the mansion's attic door months ago, old wood and something faintly metallic. But the cottage smelled only of cedar and fresh air. No strange hesitations, no oppressive feelings in confined spaces. Just ... easy. Normal.

She tugged on jeans and a t-shirt, then headed downstairs.

The morning air carried the thick scent of evergreen through open windows.

She surveyed the boxes on the counter.

Two nights in her new home, and she was finally ready to stop surviving on convenience store energy drinks. Yesterday's cold brew coffee from a bottle had gotten her through unpacking the essentials, but this morning called for the real thing.

She started with the box labeled "LATTE STATION— HANDLE WITH CARE" and sliced through the packing tape with her keys. The cardboard flaps sprang open, revealing her coffee maker nestled in crumpled packing paper. Ah, yes.

She unwrapped the machine and found the perfect spot on the counter.

While the coffee maker burbled, she opened each cabinet door to test the hinges then arranged her basic dishes. The smooth movement of well-maintained hardware was oddly satisfying.

After stepping back to admire the functional kitchen setup, Amelia pulled out her phone and settled at the kitchen table with her coffee. Time to update the girls on her progress.

AMELIA: I'm feeling like I belong here.

She attached a photo of her coffee machine and one of the sunlit living room.

AUDRA: 🩶 I'm tired from Saturday's beach cleanup. Loafing today.

MELANIE: No kitties in the pics? Is your mom there yet?

AMELIA: Kittens are still in the bathroom, adjusting to new surroundings. Going to let them out later today to explore. I'll pick up Mom from the airport on Friday.

Amelia took a sip of her second cup of coffee.

AUDRA: Do you miss the mansion?

AMELIA: Oddly, no. I really thought I would. But it's so quiet and beautiful here with all the windows. It's like living in a forest.

AUDRA: Did the stinky smell go away?

AMELIA: lol, yeah, the mansion floors are now gorgeous, and no more stink. Got a few last things to do there for Mr. F-O this week, then my visits there are done.

Before she moved out, she'd sent the last of his furniture and belongings to storage. She'd felt a pang of loss packing Rebecca's journals away, but at least she'd photographed several entries for herself.

AMELIA: Chat later. Gotta set up the Wi-Fi. Service out here is kind of spotty.

She set her empty coffee cup in the sink and headed to the living room.

With the Wi-Fi router in hand, Amelia walked around the cottage, testing different spots before settling on a central location near a living room window.

The ethernet cable connected with a satisfying click, and she plugged in the power adapter.

Back at the kitchen table with her laptop, she chose "Pine

and Piano" for the network name. It felt right for this special place tucked among the trees.

The connection test showed a strong signal throughout the cottage, and she allowed herself a small smile of triumph. The cottage felt more connected now, ready for whatever came next.

> AMELIA: Wi-Fi success! I'm part of the modern world again.

> MELANIE: Spotty service? Any security concerns out there?

> AMELIA: Nope. The cottages are still under surveillance. No surprise there. Mr. F-O arranged with the new owner (Charlie) for the security to stay. The arrangement works out financially for both properties.

The new owner. Amelia was still getting used to the idea.

> AUDRA: So, I think I'm sad. Drew says he's almost done at the cottage. He'll be flying back to Atlanta a few days after Amelia's mom arrives. I'm gonna miss my guy-bestie.

Amelia considered saying something about their friendship and Drew's obvious interest in her, but she decided to keep that for another day.

> MELANIE: Speaking of Atlanta—I've got another business trip there next month. Looks like it's going to happen more regularly. Non-merger clients.

> AUDRA: You staying with the Fontaines again?

MELANIE: Not if I can help it. Going to book a hotel way ahead of time and avoid any chance of colliding with Brandon again.

AUDRA: Seems kind of harsh.

MELANIE: Ha. 😵 Okay, I admit he's sort of good-looking, but we just clashed. Besides, I'm taking Jason with me.

AUDRA: Oh, that's interesting.

MELANIE: Don't get too excited; it's not what you're thinking. Jason has business at the art gallery there.

AMELIA: Still, you're staying together, right?

MELANIE: Speaking of guys being complicated, I've been asking around about Jonathan's transfer.

Amelia scowled at her phone then rolled her eyes. That was a convenient and sudden change of topic. What a lawyer thing to do.

AMELIA: Do I want to know?

MELANIE: From what I hear, Paige convinced her uncle, who also works for Whitlow, that Jonathan would be perfect for the job in Brazil. Subtle revenge. And not something she could or would be fired for, given her family ties.

Amelia hesitated momentarily, then decided to just come out with it and tell her friends where she'd landed emotionally.

AMELIA: After a lot of time of thinking through everything, I've decided to trust Jonathan and give him a chance to explain. And I'm not going to worry about Paige.

AUDRA: Good for you, honey! She does not deserve any of your headspace.

AMELIA: You were right. I don't want to lose Jonathan.

AUDRA: Yay! Sending a hug your way.

MELANIE: Are you going to wait for him?

AMELIA: I read this story recently about a woman who waited a long time for her husband to return to her. It gave me inspiration that I could do the same.

AUDRA: What are you going to do about it? Has he left for Brazil yet?

AMELIA: I'm not sure what we're going to do next. But I told him I'm ready to talk.

MELANIE: Okay, so my next question is not about Leo. Is waiting for Jonathan another way of avoiding moving on to another relationship?

AMELIA: I don't want anyone else. I want Jonathan. I deserve to be happy, and he's worth waiting for.

As the afternoon light softened, Amelia approached the bathroom door where Pirate and Treasure had been adjusting to their new surroundings. Her hand hesitated on the doorknob for just a moment before she turned it.

Two cautious feline faces peered out at her. Pirate emerged first, whiskers twitching as she tested the air, followed by Treasure's tentative steps. They cautiously ventured into the living room, tails held high as they investigated their new kingdom.

Watching them settle into the cottage, Amelia felt something deep in her chest finally relax.

"Good start, little cuties," she said.

This was home now, and soon it would be home for all five of them.

Chapter 69

Jonathan

JONATHAN WALKED down the familiar hallway toward Charlotte's office, his footsteps muffled by the thick Persian runner.

He'd decided. Even after three days, the conversation with Steve was still fresh in his mind, awkward and disappointing, but Jonathan felt only relief about refusing the Brazil transfer.

Everything he actually wanted was here in the States. Well, not here exactly. Three thousand miles west, to be precise.

The memory of Amelia's touch, the way she'd felt in his arms before everything fell apart, sent heat coursing through him. He missed her with an intensity that shocked him.

He'd never felt more certain about anything in his life. He needed to be with her, needed to fight for what they'd started building together.

But first, there was business to handle.

He stepped into Charlotte's office to find Brandon already waiting, looking more relaxed than he'd seen him in months. Charlotte glanced up from her desk, setting down her teacup with a satisfied smile. She sat perfectly composed, in a flowing cream scarf and tailored brown jacket.

"Jonathan." Charlotte smiled, setting aside a stack of papers. "Punctual as always."

"I'm officially ready to accept the CEO position," Jonathan said without preamble. He sat in the chair next to Brandon. "I've thought this through, and it feels right for my next move."

Charlotte didn't say anything.

"I'm committed to the foundation's mission," he continued. "Launching the next generation of creators in design and architecture feels meaningful, and now that I've left Whitlow, I'm ready to step into the role."

Brandon's shoulders sagged with relief. "Thank god." He closed his laptop and turned to face Jonathan. "I was going to burn out trying to do both jobs at once."

"That's exactly why we need this transition to happen smoothly," Charlotte said.

Jonathan pulled a summary sheet from his portfolio and set it on Charlotte's desk. "I've researched the logistics for remote work. Video conferencing technology, project management software, quarterly visits to Atlanta for board meetings and strategic planning. It's entirely feasible."

He wasn't asking permission.

Charlotte put on her readers and flipped through his documentation, eyebrows raised. "Thorough." She paused and stared up over her glasses as though studying him.

He was taken aback. The last time they'd discussed the possibility of remote work, he'd just found out he was going to Brazil, and Charlotte hadn't been so receptive.

Brandon leaned forward with interest. "You don't seem surprised, Mother."

"I'll travel quarterly," Jonathan said, more confident than he'd felt in years. "Plus additional trips as needed for major events or donor meetings. Technology handles the day-to-day operations."

Charlotte scrutinized the papers with the same focus she brought to her design projects. "The transition timeline?"

"We can begin the transition work right away," Jonathan said.

"I can shift to an advisory capacity immediately," Brandon said, genuine excitement creeping into his voice. "I'm barely keeping up with foundation responsibilities as it is."

"Two-week job overlap for knowledge transfer," Jonathan added. "I'll need to wrap things up in Atlanta, but I want to be back in Rainmere as soon as possible."

Charlotte set the folder aside and walked to the window, her expression thoughtful. "I'm impressed by your research and planning. But before we make this official, I have something else to show you."

She returned to her desk and pulled out a stack of photographs. "You know I've been considering expansion opportunities for both Studio Charlotti and the foundation. Last month I decided on West Coast market penetration."

Jonathan glanced at the photos and froze. His blood went cold as he recognized the stonework, the elegant lines, the sprawling grounds. Mr. Jewell's mansion.

Charlotte's expression softened. "When I saw Jessica's photos of the house design, I fell in love. I researched the property's history carefully, including its significance to the current occupants and the previous owner."

Jonathan's heart clenched. The mansion sale. Amelia had lost another piece of stability because of his mother's business decision.

"It was you who bought it? But why? Are you going to flip it for a profit?" She'd done it many times before. His mind raced. "Amelia might think I orchestrated this somehow. That I manipulated her."

He sank into a chair, running a hand through his hair. It was something he hadn't anticipated. One more reason Amelia might think he'd abandoned her when things got complicated.

"Because," Charlotte said, "I believe this creates an opportunity. The property includes extensive grounds, a carriage house I'm turning into guest suites, and office space that would be perfect for a West Coast hub. For both businesses."

She paused. "You could even host donor events there for the charity."

Jonathan looked up sharply. "You want me to live there? In the Jewell mansion?"

"It's no longer the Jewell mansion," Charlotte said with mild amusement. "I want you to consider it, but the choice is yours. The foundation will benefit from a Pacific Northwest presence. There's significant wealth in the tech sector, potential for major donors and partnerships. And Studio Charlotti has been fielding inquiries from Seattle and Portland clients for years."

The pieces clicked into place with immediate and stunning clarity. His mother had orchestrated this entire scenario.

"You've thought of everything," he said.

"I've thought of what serves everyone's best interests." Charlotte folded her hands in her lap. "The foundation gets visionary leadership and geographic expansion. Brandon gets his freedom to pursue his own path." She paused, studying Jonathan's expression. "Studio Charlotti gets market presence. And you get to be where your heart is pulling you."

Brandon grinned. "Mom always did like chess more than checkers."

Charlotte pulled employment contracts from her desk drawer. "These formalize everything we've discussed. Salary, benefits, remote work arrangements, travel expectations."

"Remote work? So you were already on board with the idea of my working remotely," Jonathan said.

"Yes," Charlotte said. "Brandon and I had discussed it in

broad terms before. And I'll admit to having done some research of my own since then."

He should have seen it coming.

"She's presenting a deal you couldn't possibly turn down," Brandon said with admiration. "I'm taking leadership notes as we speak."

Jonathan stared at the papers. Signing these meant leaving the corporate world entirely, committing to the family business, and betting everything on a future in Washington. With Amelia. If she'd have him.

The enormity of what he was putting on the line became real. Amelia had ended their relationship. Wanting to apologize differed greatly from her wanting him back. He was preparing to move his entire life across the country for a woman who might not take him back.

But looking at these contracts—thinking about being with Amelia, the foundation's mission, and the work they could do together—he'd never felt more certain about anything. This was right. This was where he belonged.

He picked up the pen.

"One concern," he said, pausing before signing. "How are we planning to handle the mansion situation with Amelia? She can't think this is some elaborate manipulation."

"Carefully." Charlotte set the contracts aside. "With complete transparency about the timeline and my motivations. She'll understand that this decision benefits everyone involved."

Jonathan signed his name with bold strokes across both contracts. "I hope you're right."

Brandon reached across to shake his hand. "Welcome to the next best step in your life, little brother. For both of us."

As Jonathan handed the contracts back to Charlotte, clarity flooded through him. He was officially CEO-elect of the Form to Function Fund, and he was moving to Rainmere. He was going to fight for Amelia, for the relationship they'd begun, for the life he could see so clearly when he imagined their future together.

He had no idea whether she'd take him back.

But every piece of his life felt like it was falling into exactly the right place. Now he had to convince Amelia this was right, too.

Chapter 70

Amelia

Wednesday.

It was a typical morning at the office. Well, the new typical, Amelia realized. The last few weeks had been quieter since the Atlanta team had left. The remaining NorthSound staff were back to their pre-merger, relaxed pace.

Amelia remained in the workroom with Patricia and Gavin as the asset project work continued to progress.

While updating her color-coded project schedule, she realized she needed to completely redo the timeline, now that the scope had narrowed to just NorthSound assets.

Patricia set a coffee cup next to Amelia's keyboard. "Thought you might want this," she said. "Unfortunately, the bagels are already gone." She paused at the door. "Oh, and I'll have that revised spreadsheet to you by end of day."

"Thanks," Amelia said with a smile. "Effort appreciated."

She glanced at her phone again, hoping for any word from Jonathan, then forced herself to put it away. She thought again about his last message, saying things were moving at lightning speed and wondered what exactly was happening. Things with work? Things with Paige? What kind of things?

After reviewing the remaining asset portfolio list, she methodically checked each one against her priority list, then turned her focus back to updating the timeline.

Two hours later, Lydia poked her head into the workroom. "Hey," she nodded toward Amelia. "I need to talk to you. I've got to run to a meeting now but come to my office after lunch so we can chat."

Oh shit. She'd spent the last few weeks keeping herself busy through every moment of work, trying not to focus on the fact that she didn't know if there would still be a permanent job offer for her or not.

Being a contractor paid the bills, but it wasn't the endgame.

* * *

After the longest lunch hour of her life, Amelia stepped into Lydia's office.

"Close the door for me, please?" Lydia asked.

Wondering if that was a good sign or a bad sign, she shut the door behind her as Lydia motioned for her to sit down.

Amelia sat across from her boss. The standard office rolling chair suddenly felt very uncomfortable, and she shifted in her seat.

"I've got good news, Amelia," Lydia said, leaning forward. "First, let me congratulate you. Your work on the asset project was excellent. With all the turmoil over the merger collapse, I couldn't let you know sooner, but now I can offer you a permanent position with NorthSound Timber."

A wave of relief washed over Amelia. So much of her life over the last year had hinged on this moment. Her goal was finally coming to fruition.

"And ... management still thinks divesting older and less productive assets is a smart move for us, so we're extending the project. We'd like to hire you as the new team lead."

Team lead. Feelings of pride and accomplishment bubbled in her chest. Her eyes felt full.

Lydia slipped a small piece of yellow paper across her desk. "This is what we can offer for your starting salary if you accept. And of course there are benefits as well."

Amelia read the handwritten amount. It was more than she could have hoped to start.

"I'm so, so grateful for the opportunity," Amelia said, blinking to hold back the tears. "Yes. Yes, absolutely, I accept."

Lydia smiled and held out her hand. "Welcome to the company."

Amelia stood and shook Lydia's hand. Finally, something big—the best kind of big thing—had gone her way!

For the next fifteen minutes, they discussed logistics, and Lydia explained the next steps of paperwork and the HR process.

"I should have asked sooner, but I'd like to take Friday off," Amelia said. "My mom's moving here, and I'm picking her up at the airport in the morning."

"Record it as a compensation day. I'll approve it. Take Monday too if you want the time. You've earned it, for all the extra hours you've put in lately." She paused.

"There's ... something else I think you should know about," Lydia began. "You know Whitlow Forest Resources transferred Jonathan Fontaine to Brazil."

"Mm," Amelia nodded. "I heard. But that doesn't have anything to do with me."

Lydia hesitated, picking up her tablet and sliding it into a leather portfolio jacket. "Jonathan resigned from Whitlow on Monday, effective immediately."

"What?" The word came out as barely a whisper. Amelia felt the blood drain from her face as the meaning sank in. Her shoulders sagged as though someone had just loaded a weighted backpack onto them. She gripped the arm of her chair to steady herself.

"His boss called me yesterday, wanting to know if I knew what Jonathan was planning. Of course, I said no, absolutely not. Normally, I wouldn't have said anything, but the two of you seemed to get close while he was here—"

"He resigned?" Amelia said. The information stunned her. *Why?*

Amelia's mind was spinning, trying to make sense of what Lydia had just said. No wonder Jonathan told her things were moving swiftly for him.

"He's not going overseas?" Amelia finally whispered.

"So, you didn't know," Lydia said, looking away for a moment, then returning her gaze to Amelia. "Apparently, Jonathan's going to work with his family's business. Steve was completely surprised, too."

Amelia's mind shot through the implications. The family foundation was based in Atlanta. Jonathan had always talked about eventually working there, but she'd assumed that was years away.

"No," Amelia replied. "I ... had no idea."

Lydia thanked her for her time and congratulated her again before suggesting Amelia visit an HR contact.

Amelia left Lydia's office and headed back down the hallway toward the workroom. She walked slowly, her mind still reeling from everything Lydia had told her. The hallway seemed endless.

Part of her wanted to feel relieved. A clean break, no messy long-distance complications, no waiting around for someone who might change his mind.

But instead, she felt empty. Their last conversation had been that awful fight in the parking lot, and now that might be their last memory of each other.

Jonathan loved Atlanta. He'd told her that back in March. His friends and family, his neighborhood, the lifestyle. She'd heard it in his voice when he talked about going home.

And now he was taking over the foundation, the one based at his family's estate in Atlanta. The role he'd been committed to taking on eventually, the one that meant staying with his family.

He wasn't coming back to Washington. Not in two years, not ever.

She was glad he wasn't going to Brazil, and glad he'd found a way to stay with his family instead of being sent overseas alone. Amelia wished he'd told her he'd resigned. But since she'd broken up with him, she wasn't exactly in a position to complain about his lack of communication.

Back at her desk, she pulled out her phone and texted Jonathan.

> AMELIA: I heard you quit Whitlow. Is everything okay?

With a nervous swallow, she pressed send.

She couldn't let their story end with that terrible fight in the parking lot. Whatever happened between them in the future, she owed him an honest apology for how she'd handled everything.

And maybe, if she was being completely honest with herself, she needed to see him one more time before accepting that they were really over.

Knowing in her heart it was the right thing to do, Amelia opened her phone again and began searching for a cheap flight to Atlanta.

Chapter 71

Amelia

Saturday afternoon.

AMELIA CHECKED the time on her phone.

"Mom?" she called toward the upstairs. "Audra will be here in less than five."

"Be down in just a minute..." Light shuffling noises along hardwood floors filtered down from above.

Things were changing in a hurry. Sam sat near a window, surveying the forest. For now, Amelia had tucked the kittens safely away in her bedroom, but she knew they'd have to meet the German shepherd dog soon.

She reread Jonathan's last text. He'd sent it three days ago.

JONATHAN: I'm sorry I didn't tell you myself. I've taken over the charity CEO position from Brandon. We're working through a fast transition, and it's a lot to handle. I'll find you as soon as I come up for air.

Find you ... as if he'd lost her, and he needed to locate her, not just reach out when he had time.

Audra's red convertible rumbled into the drive, and Amelia headed for the door. Her mom came down the steps, her soft-soled shoes quiet against the hardwood.

As she reached to open the front door, Amelia grinned at the faint, familiar scent of her mother's lavender hand cream.

Outside, her mom hugged Audra. "So good to see you again," Audra said as she opened the front passenger door for Rachel.

"We picked up some gourmet local picnic treats," Audra said, "then I dropped off Melanie at the park to get things set up."

Amelia settled into the seat behind Audra and buckled her seatbelt.

The convertible's engine hummed as they wound around Lake Cedarvale's shoreline. Afternoon sunlight bounced on the water's surface like flecks of gold. Amelia's mom leaned against the open window, taking in the view of sailboats dotting the lake and the tree-lined slopes surrounding it.

* * *

At the park, Melanie had secured a perfect waterfront spot at a bench and set out a small folding table.

From a paper bag, Audra carefully unpacked chicken salad wraps and delicate, sugary pastries.

Melanie motioned for Amelia's mom to sit in the middle of the bench next to her, "in the place of honor."

"Group time!" Melanie said. She snapped a few photos with her phone. "How are things going?" she asked Rachel.

"Going well, I think," she said. "Though I'm tired from moving, flying—well, from everything, actually."

"How do you like Rainmere so far?" Audra said.

"It's lovely here, but it'll take me a bit before I feel established. There's a lot of unpacking to do. I'm eager to be done with it and to dive back into teaching. And the cottage will feel a lot more like home once the piano arrives."

"Amelia said you're going to be playing at some events until you have a few more students. What kinds of events?" Melanie asked.

"Oh, yes," her mother said as she accepted a wrap and set it on her plate. "In my younger days, I played the piano and the organ for many weddings. Hopefully, the local theaters might need an occasional substitute for plays and musicals, too."

"I've got a list of leads on substitute accompaniment opportunities," Amelia said, "and two coordinators have booked her for late June weddings."

"Weddings are such a treat, watching couples begin their lives together." Her mom's expression turned wistful. "Though I always fight back a few tears at weddings. They make me miss my husband, Sam. Still love that man to pieces."

"I'm confused," Melanie said, her brows creasing together. "Isn't your dog's name Sam? I'm sorry if I've mixed up the names."

Rachel smiled with a soft laugh. "You haven't mixed up anything, dear. I miss my Sam so much I named my dog after him. I'm not sure what that says about me, but I still love saying his name. Have to say, I talk a lot to both of them."

She turned to Amelia. "Speaking of extra work, are you still going to continue as Mr. Jewell's assistant?" her mom asked. Over the last few days, Amelia had already told her friends and her mom about her new job. "Do you even need to do that now that you're full-time at NorthSound?"

"Mr. Jewell is coming back to Rainmere soon, though I'm not sure exactly what 'soon' really means for him. And he's asked me to help him with getting another cottage repaired.

Maybe he's going to live there? Same thing I've been doing for him. We had some back and forth about how I've got less time available, but I'll help as much as I can. At least for now."

"Do you want to do it?" Audra asked.

"Or do you simply feel an obligation to him?" Melanie said.

Amelia shrugged. "Old habits are hard to break. I like to keep busy. But yeah, I guess I also feel a twinge of obligation, which is weird since he did abruptly end my other lease."

* * *

Fifteen minutes later, they'd finished eating and begun putting away the food. Melanie clicked a few more group photos, framed against the backdrop of the afternoon lake.

A line of ducks swam along the shoreline, and a passing rowing crew practiced their synchronized rhythms. The water lapped gently against the dock pilings below them, and a light breeze carried the scent of pine across the lake.

Eventually her mom asked, "How are things with you and Jonathan?"

Amelia hadn't mentioned Jonathan's resignation.

After explaining that he wasn't going to Brazil, and how he was working for his family in Atlanta, she studied their concerned expressions.

"There's no waiting two or three years for him to transfer to Seattle," Amelia concluded. "He ... isn't coming here."

"I'm so sorry, honey," Audra said.

Her mom wrapped her arms around Amelia and squeezed tightly.

"Are you sure about all of this?" Melanie said, with a questioning look. "He hasn't said he's staying in Atlanta. All you know is that he's going to work for his mother's charity."

"Jonathan loves living in Atlanta; he told me that several times. And there's a reason Brandon lives at his mother's estate."

The family dynamics alone would keep him there, even if he wanted to leave.

"I'm getting on a flight to Atlanta late tonight," Amelia said. "I'm going to apologize to Jonathan in person and say goodbye. The right way." Even a red-eye ticket was expensive, but with the confidence of her new employment status and using the last of her free miles bonus points, it would be worth every penny.

The plan sounded impulsive when she said it out loud, but it was the only way she could think of to make things right between them and get the closure she needed.

"You're just going to show up?" Audra said. "Who does that?"

"That's what I said when she told me her plan," Rachel said, shaking her head.

"Why not wait until Jonathan has time to talk through it with you?" Melanie said. "Maybe he's got other options in mind."

"I've thought this through. I miss him, and I want to apologize to him in person. Mostly I don't want him to talk me out of coming," Amelia admitted.

"It sounds like you might be in love with him," her mom whispered. "When you find it, you just know. Like the love I found with Sam. If you're lucky, it's the love that lasts a lifetime, or sometimes longer."

Her mother was right. Her chest tightened, and her hands stilled in her lap.

She was in love with Jonathan. Not a casual attraction or merely physical desire, but the deep, soul-soaking kind of love that made her understand why her mother still talked to Sam fifteen years after losing him.

But she couldn't burden Jonathan with that knowledge, not when he was trying to do the responsible thing for his family.

The knowledge sat heavy in her stomach. Three months ago, she would have run from this feeling. Now she wanted to protect it and protect him, even if that meant keeping it to herself.

Going to Atlanta wasn't about changing his mind anymore. It was about loving him enough to let him go.

She wanted to tell him she loved him. God, she wanted to. But what was the point when he was tied to Atlanta and she'd just accepted a full-time position in Washington? Saying it wouldn't change the geography between them. It would just turn goodbye into something more painful than it already was.

She turned to Audra. "Can you get Jonathan's apartment address from Drew?"

"Drew said Jonathan moved out of his apartment. Preparation for moving to Brazil," Audra said.

"Mm," Amelia nodded her head. "I suppose he'll move into his mother's estate house now."

"I've got you covered," Melanie said. She opened her phone and began scrolling through her contacts. "I still have Charlotte's address from my last Atlanta visit. If you're going to go through with it, at least I can make sure you knock on the right door."

"I don't know, honey," Audra said, twisting a strand of hair around her finger. "Surprises like that can backfire pretty spectacularly. But ... I sincerely hope it goes okay."

Melanie clicked to send the contact information to Amelia.

Audra shifted on the bench, tucking one leg underneath her.

"I have some news, too," Audra said. She picked at the edge of her napkin, then looked up at her friends. "I'm considering quitting my job and pursuing my dream of becoming a chef."

Amelia hesitated. Cooking classes were one thing, but quitting a scientific career to be a chef was something entirely different.

"The restaurant industry is a challenging business," Melanie said carefully.

"I thought you loved studying the ocean," Amelia said. "You took the job here specifically so you could work with renowned ocean geologists."

"I know," she said, her voice trailing on a sad note. "I still love the ocean more than ever, but working isolated in the lab all day is just too lonely. No decisions made yet, just thinking through options. For a happier direction."

"We're here for you," Melanie said.

"Yes, we are," Amelia agreed, hugging her friend tightly. "I'm sure you'll figure out what's right for you."

"By the way, how was it living with Drew?" Amelia asked with a tiny grin, as she leaned back against the bench. "Anything you care to tell us?"

"Fine. It was fine." Audra said. Her voice pitched slightly higher, her hands suddenly busy rearranging the empty food containers. "Just convenient having someone around to split the grocery bill, you know? Nothing more complicated than that."

"You're overexplaining. Since when do you care about splitting grocery bills?" Melanie said. "Tell us more."

Audra scoffed. "It was nice to have a friend to talk to after a long day at work. That's all. Anyway, he flew back to Atlanta this morning. My tiny apartment is back to being all mine."

"Fast dodging of the question," Melanie said.

"He told me he's coming back for a visit next month," Amelia offered. "Said he's going to build a picnic table for us. I'm not positive, but I think it may just be an excuse to visit Audra."

While they packed away their picnic remnants, Amelia

couldn't help thinking, *some things end, but new things always begin.*

In a few hours, she'd be on a plane to Atlanta. She'd tell Jonathan she was sorry. The rest would stay locked in her heart. It was time to go home and pack for the hardest conversation of her life.

Chapter 72

Amelia

Saturday night.

IN HER WINDOW SEAT, Amelia cracked open the shade to peer outside. It was dark, approaching midnight, and her eyelids were heavy. She closed the shade again.

The magnitude of her decision to go to Atlanta was at the forefront of her mind as she watched other passengers filing down the center aisle.

When the doors closed, a safety video began.

A flight attendant casually showed how to use the emergency oxygen masks and life preservers. Amelia nervously adjusted her seatbelt again, then fidgeted with her phone.

Once the presentation ended, she began scrolling through photos to find Rebecca's journal pages to take her mind off the imminent takeoff.

She paused in her perusal as the plane turned, taxiing toward the runway. The passenger next to Amelia, a woman her mother's age, selected something to watch from a long list.

The opening scenes of *Titanic* flashed on the screen. She couldn't hear the sound, but the sad melody of bagpipes played in Amelia's mind. She tilted her head at the woman's very romantic movie choice, which didn't at all match her practical appearance.

Amelia looked away, back to the journal's May 1857 entry, and touched the screen to enlarge the text. The plane shook on liftoff. Several passengers turned their lights out and the dull roar of the plane smothered the few quiet conversations.

She decided she was too tired to read. Looking out the window at the landscape below, she watched as the plane ascended in the moonlight and gently turned away from the Cascade Mountains.

Two dings chimed as the plane reached cruising altitude. A fuzzy announcement declared larger electronics were now allowed.

She closed her eyes, still imagining the soft *Titanic* theme music, as she drifted to sleep.

* * *

Sometime much later, Amelia awoke to a darkened cabin and the images of musicians playing on the deck of the Titanic.

The ship will sink, Amelia thought. It wouldn't be long. The woman beside her seemed thoroughly absorbed.

Amelia rubbed her eyes and slowly rolled her shoulders. She opened her phone again and returned to the pictures of Rebecca's journal.

22 May 1857

> *Having Thomas at home these past months has filled
> my heart to overflowing! The dark days of waiting and
> worrying while he was in San Francisco feel like a distant
> memory now. This morning, he surprised me with wild-*

flowers he picked with little Mary and Liza on his way back from checking the horses.

The bouquet was full of purple lupine and white trillium that he knows are my favorites. He tucked one behind my ear and kissed my temple, whispering that I am more beautiful than any flower that ever bloomed. How can one woman be so fortunate in love?

The farm near Puget Sound brought us little profit, despite our best efforts. But Thomas's venture in San Francisco has immensely improved our fortune. We now have enough coin to purchase proper farmland on Cedarvale Lake, where the soil runs rich and dark. Thomas speaks of the timber there, and the vast water, and I find myself dreaming of the cabin we will build together.

We will begin building next month. Thomas has already sketched the rooms. It will have a proper kitchen with a large hearth, and two bedrooms upstairs with windows facing the morning sun.

Everett will move with us and build his own cabin. He has become such a capable man these past years, helping me keep our farm running while Thomas was away. And now the two of them work side by side as equals. I watch them plan and build together, and my heart swells with pride at how far we have all come.

I cannot imagine facing this new adventure without Thomas by my side. Those two long years apart taught me that no amount of gold could replace the warmth of his presence. After so much uncertainty, it feels like we are finally planting roots that will grow deep and strong.

Amelia smiled a little at Rebecca's joy, but then she felt a pang of sadness.

She glanced again at the movie playing next to her. Jack was dying in the water, beside Rose. They hadn't had a choice. They had no chance of saving their love. Love eternally lost.

The woman watching the movie dabbed her eyes several times with a tissue.

For a moment, Amelia wondered if she was doing the right thing. Should she be fighting harder?

She shifted in her seat, then found the second photo of the journal from 1859. She hesitated, hoping Rebecca's happiness would continue. It would be difficult to process if things didn't turn out well at Cedarvale Lake. But surely they had?

15 August 1859

> *I can hardly contain my happiness as I write! Our son Tommy toddles about the cabin now, getting his chubby hands into everything. At fifteen months, he shows his father's determination and his uncle Everett's mischievous spirit. He follows little Mary and Liza everywhere, tumbling after them with such determination that they giggle and clap their hands for him.*
>
> *Everett has become quite the young man at twenty and is to marry sweet Minna Karlsen come October. Her family has been our salvation this season. It was her father, Henrik, who suggested we try dairy farming. Thomas was skeptical at first, but the Karlsens have shared their knowledge freely, and we now have six fine cows and a bull.*

Another baby! Little Tommy. And Everett's engagement. Their happiness seemed complete.

She glanced away from the screen momentarily, out the window again. The plane flew above the clouds, which hid the ground below. The endless darkness and the din of the plane soothed her.

Our cabin sits on a gentle rise above Cedarvale Lake, and through the tall firs we can glimpse the water sparkling in the daylight. Thomas chose this spot without hesitation, though we'd never seen it before. When I asked what drew him here, he said only that it felt like coming home.

There is small game for hunting and a stream nearby where we draw water for the house.

Down at the shoreline of the lake, Thomas built a simple wooden dock last spring where he can pull in his fishing boat. Little Tommy squeals with delight when his papa carries him down the path to the water's edge.

Some evenings, when our work is done and Tommy sleeps, Thomas and I sit on that dock and watch the sun paint the sky. I think of those early years, the fear and uncertainty, the months apart when I wondered if this life would break us.

But love has a way of making all hardships worthwhile. We are prosperous now. But much more than that, we are together, and that makes us truly rich.

Amelia closed her phone, still thinking about Rebecca's life reflections. *Love has a way of making all hardships worthwhile.*

Her throat tightened as she thought about Rebecca and Thomas choosing each other again and again, through failed farms and long separations, through uncertainty and fear. They had refused to give up.

She swallowed hard. Here she was, flying toward Jonathan to say goodbye ... to give up.

She leaned her head back against the seat, letting out a shaky breath. On the screen beside her, the *Titanic* credits were rolling, and the woman next to her was dabbing at her eyes again.

Amelia turned to look out the window. Below the clouds, Atlanta was getting closer with each passing minute.

The first city lights appeared through breaks in the clouds. She pressed her palm against the cool window. Her reflection stared back at her in the dark glass.

And she knew then for certain that saying goodbye to Jonathan was going to be much harder than she'd imagined.

Chapter 73

Amelia

Sunday morning arrived with the kind of sticky warmth that made Amelia's wrinkled travel clothes cling to her skin. At nine o'clock, Atlanta's humidity hung in the air like a damp blanket, so different from Washington's cool spring rain.

The rideshare driver had the air conditioning running full blast, but it did little to cut through Amelia's exhaustion. She'd barely slept on the red-eye flight, and now her eyes burned as she stared out the window at unfamiliar streets.

Amelia paid the rideshare driver and made her way to the front door of the Fontaine home, only her small backpack over her shoulder. It would be a quick visit. Her return flight was scheduled for later the same day.

As she approached the elaborate front porch, she recalled Melanie's description, and it fit to a tee. The modern cream-colored stonework and beautifully manicured gardens looked like something out of a magazine spread. Charlotte's design aesthetic was even more impressive in person.

Twenty-four hours ago, booking the red-eye had felt brave and necessary and like a good idea. But standing outside the mansion, her shoulders aching from lack of sleep, her throat dry from recycled airplane air, suddenly she wasn't sure.

She needed to see him. She wanted to see him. The practiced apology she'd rehearsed through every time zone scrolled through her exhausted mind. *Jonathan, I'm sorry. I should have trusted you.*

Her hands trembled as she smoothed her wrinkled shirt. She was exhausted, nervous, and scared all at the same time. And she probably smelled like airport and desperation.

She inhaled a large breath, then let it out slowly. She'd been preparing her apology speech for the last twenty-four hours, through the airport, on the plane, in the rideshare. She knew exactly what she needed to say.

If she could just see his face. If she could just make him understand.

She finally summoned the courage to press the doorbell.

The good-looking man who opened the door was tall, but a few inches shy of Jonathan's colossal frame. His jaw was layered with short, neatly trimmed dark hair, and he appeared comfortable in a soft shirt and jeans. Until he saw her. Then something flickered across his face. Surprise? Concern?

"Hi," she said, trying for a smile despite how wrung-out she felt. "I'm Amelia Preston." It was awkward. She felt awkward. *God, I look like I slept in these clothes. Because I did.*

"Are you Brandon?" she asked, trying to keep her tone cheerful even as her stomach knotted. "I'm looking for Jonathan. I just came from the airport. From Seattle. I took the red-eye." She was babbling now, from exhaustion. "I know I should have called first, but I really need to see him."

"Yes," he said smoothly. "I am Brandon. It's a surprise to meet you, Amelia. Jonathan has told me about you." He gave her a questioning look.

Brandon's hand hesitated on the doorknob, and for a

moment she thought he might close the door. Then his expression softened to something that looked almost like pity, which made her stomach drop.

"I'm sorry, but he's not here." Brandon shifted his weight and glanced over his shoulder into the house. "He's…" He cleared his throat. "He's traveling for work."

She froze. *Not here.* She'd flown across the country, and he wasn't even *here.*

Her vision blurred. She had to blink hard against the sudden sting of tears. "Oh."

Brandon's jaw tightened, as if he'd made a difficult decision. "Listen, you look exhausted. Why don't you come in for a minute? Let me get you some water."

"I don't want to impose—"

"You're not." He stepped back and held the door open wider. "Please."

The foyer was even more impressive from the inside, with soaring ceilings and a curved staircase. Everything in coordinated shades of cream and beige with mauve trim and impeccably designed. With her disheveled clothes and airport smell, Amelia felt out of place.

Brandon led her toward what looked like a kitchen, his movements slightly stiff. "When did you get in?"

"About an hour ago. I came straight here." She accepted the glass of water he handed her, grateful for something to do with her shaking hands. The cool liquid helped her dry throat, but it couldn't wash away the sick feeling of failure.

"That's … quite a gesture." Brandon leaned against the counter, arms crossed, studying her with an expression she couldn't quite read. He looked like he wanted to say more, stopped himself, then tried again.

He ran a hand through his hair, looked away toward the windows. "Jonathan's not in Atlanta," Brandon said. "He's…"

Another pause. His fingers drummed once against his bicep before he stilled them. "He's away on business for the foundation."

"When will he be back?" The question came out desperate. She hated how she sounded, but she was too tired to care about pride.

Brandon's gaze slid away from hers. "I'm not sure." The words came out too quickly, too rehearsed. "But Amelia..." He looked at her again, and his expression shifted to genuine concern mixed with something else. Guilt? "Whatever made you fly all the way to Atlanta ... maybe the solution isn't here. Maybe you should go home. To Rainmere. And wait to see what happens next."

The careful emphasis on *Rainmere* felt deliberate.

What an odd thing to say to someone you've just met. He was sending her away.

She tried to read his shifting expressions. Was he telling the truth? Or covering up for his brother? The thought made her chest ache.

"Is he ... hiding from me?" The words came out barely louder than a whisper, and she hated the vulnerability in them. *Please say no. Please.*

"Definitely not," Brandon's response was immediate, emphatic. He uncrossed his arms and took a half step toward her. "He's working for Form to Function, just like he always promised." He hesitated and shifted his position stiffly. "Amelia, for what it's worth, he loves you. He's told you that."

The tenderness in his voice made her eyes burn again. She looked down at the water glass in her hands and watched the condensation slip onto her fingers.

"Listen." Brandon set his own water glass down carefully, not quite meeting her eyes. "I wish I could be more helpful, but this really is between you two." He walked toward the foyer, and she had no choice but to follow. At the door, he paused, his hand on the frame. His knuckles were white.

"You should head back to Rainmere." He said it slowly and deliberately. "And trust me when I say the timing will work out."

Amelia stared at him, stunned. His insistence, the careful way he kept emphasizing Rainmere, the guilty set of his shoulders, none of it made sense. "I don't understand."

"I know." His face held real sympathy. "Take care of yourself, okay? And Amelia?" He waited until she looked up at him. "Jonathan's lucky to have someone willing to fly across the country for him. Remember that."

The door closed with a soft click, leaving her alone on the elegant porch.

Amelia stared at the closed door, her exhausted mind trying to process what just happened. Brandon knew something, that much was obvious. The way he'd carefully avoided her eyes, the deliberate emphasis on certain words, the guilt written across his face.

She considered ringing the doorbell again, to demand real answers. But her hands were shaking too hard, and she was too tired to fight. What would she even say?

Should she text Jonathan? At this point, there was no surprise left to ruin, just her own humiliation to document.

Amelia pulled out her phone with trembling fingers, opened his contact, and stared at the screen. The cursor blinked in the empty message field, waiting. But what would she even say? *Hi, I'm standing outside your family's house like a stalker because I needed to apologize in person, but you're not even here, so I probably look pathetic?*

No.

If Jonathan was truly away on business, a text wouldn't accomplish what she'd come here to do. She needed to see his face when she apologized. Needed him to see that she meant it, that she was sorry, that she—

That she loved him.

God. She'd flown three thousand miles, finally realized she needed to tell him she loved him, and still couldn't say it.

Amelia slipped her phone back into her pocket and forced her feet down the front steps. Each one felt heavier than the last. The elaborate gardens that had impressed her moments earlier now felt like a mockery of her impulsive decision to come here.

This was Jonathan's world. Mansions and family estates and people who always knew the right thing to say. And she was the woman who could barely afford the plane ticket she'd just bought, standing on a porch in wrinkled clothes, chasing someone who wasn't even here.

She pulled up the rideshare app on her phone and requested a car back to the airport. The wait time showed four minutes. Four minutes standing on this perfect street in front of this perfect house, feeling like a complete fool.

While she waited, she rehashed the conversation with Brandon and searched for clues she might have missed. His careful word choices. The way he'd kept emphasizing Rainmere. That look of guilt.

Trust me when I say the timing will work out.

It felt like empty reassurance. The kind of thing people said when they didn't know what else to offer, when they wanted you to leave so they could stop feeling uncomfortable.

The car arrived within minutes. As Amelia settled into the backseat, a familiar heaviness settled over her. It felt like defeat.

She'd flown across the country to apologize to the man she loved, practiced her speech a hundred times, and gathered every ounce of courage she possessed. And for what? An awkward five minutes with his brother and a glass of water.

At least she'd tried. When Jonathan eventually learned about her visit from Brandon, he'd know she'd made the effort. That she'd been willing to look foolish, to be vulnerable, to chase after him despite everything.

That had to count for something, even if they were heading toward goodbye.

The car pulled away from the curb, and Amelia watched the façade of the Fontaine mansion and its perfect, manicured gardens disappear behind them. Her apology would have to wait, and the closure she'd been seeking felt just as elusive as ever.

She leaned back against the seat and pulled her phone from her pocket, checking whether she could reschedule her flight. Every minute in Atlanta felt like prolonging the failure.

Time to go home and figure out how to move forward without him. But as she pulled up the airline app, her vision blurred again. This time, she let the tears fall.

Chapter 74

Jonathan

JONATHAN SPREAD donor profiles across the small desk, cross-referencing giving histories with foundation priorities. His laptop displayed the presentation he'd been refining since five a.m., incorporating everything from Brandon's crash course on major donor gift-cultivation strategies.

The late flight had been brutal, as they hadn't touched down until nearly midnight. But Charlotte had insisted on the early start. Three major meetings today: a tech executive couple at 10:30, lunch with family foundation trustees, then an afternoon estate tour, and more donor meetings throughout the week. Years of Charlotte's relationship-building had led to this moment, and the foundation's West Coast expansion depended on these conversations.

He adjusted his tie and reviewed his notes one final time. His phone buzzed with donor confirmation texts: the Hendersons running early, the Roths asking about environmental metrics. Standard logistics, but Jonathan felt an uncomfortable pre-pitch adrenaline.

He was reaching for his blazer when his phone buzzed with a call. His brother's picture popped up on the screen.

"Hey, Brandon," Jonathan said. "I've got exactly three minutes before Mother and I have to leave. We've got a donor meeting."

"You've barely been gone two days and Amelia showed up at our door," Brandon said.

Jonathan's hand froze halfway to his blazer. His chest tightened with a sharp mix of hope and panic. "What? Why would she go there?"

"She was very eager to see you," Brandon said. "I don't know for sure why, but I don't think she was planning on staying long. Said she'd just come from the airport, and all she had with her was a backpack."

"What specifically did you say to her?"

"The truth," Brandon said. "That you're not here, and I had no idea when you'll be back. I wasn't going to lie to her, but I also didn't want to spoil your secret."

Jonathan absorbed what Brandon was saying.

"I very diplomatically encouraged her to go home," Brandon continued. "She just left here. You owe me one. I don't enjoy delivering bad news to a pretty woman, especially when it's not my news to deliver. Hopefully, she'll be on her way back to Rainmere tonight."

"Thanks. I'll take care of it," Jonathan said. She was looking for him, but he hadn't been there for her. His stomach sank. The thought of her flying across the country, only to find him gone, made him feel like he'd failed her all over again.

He hesitated. "How did she seem?"

"Exactly as you'd expect," Brandon said. "She looked pretty dejected when I sent her away. Made me feel like a schmuck."

"Shit," Jonathan muttered. "Look, I've got to go. Thanks for the call."

Jonathan hung up. *Fuck.* He didn't have time to call her. He opened her contact, still titled MY FAVORITE CLAUSE, and smiled as he typed.

> JONATHAN: I have client meetings all day. Will call you later tonight so we can catch up.
> There's so much I want to share with you. Have a safe trip back to WA.

The office door abruptly swung open, and Charlotte stuck her head inside, interrupting his texting. "We've got to go now, Jonathan," she said with a decisive tone. "We can't keep them waiting."

Jonathan clicked his phone closed and hastily pushed it into his pocket. "I'm ready," he said, as he reached for his blazer and his portfolio. "Let's go."

Chapter 75

Amelia

AMELIA WAS glad to be home, even if the trip hadn't gone the way she'd hoped. She pulled her backpack closer to her chest, still feeling the sting of embarrassment from showing up at Brandon's doorstep unannounced.

Melanie parked her truck in the cottage driveway and cut the engine.

"Thanks again. I really appreciate you picking me up," Amelia said.

"No problem. Lucky you could get an earlier flight."

"Want to come in and have some late dinner?" Amelia asked.

"I'll have to take a rain check," Melanie said. "I need to go home and review some preliminary contracts for an early morning meeting." She frowned. "Hey, where's your car?"

"Mom borrowed it for the evening. She went to see a play at the local theater."

"Good for her, stepping out already," Melanie said.

Amelia unbuckled her seatbelt, then checked her phone again. "Still no word from Jonathan."

Her finger paused above his number. A little knot of worry seeped into her chest. *He wouldn't ghost me again, right?*

The question stuck like a thorn in her heart, as memories of unanswered texts and sleepless nights from five years ago threatened to surface.

"It's too soon to worry," Melanie said. "He's on a business trip. Likely, he's very busy."

"You're probably right." Amelia leaned her head back against the headrest. "Brandon was polite about my showing up on his doorstep, but I felt like an idiot. I was so flustered, I didn't even say thank you for inviting me in or giving me water or anything."

"Don't beat yourself up about it," Melanie said sympathetically. "You said you're exhausted. Here, I can give you Brandon's number if you want to call. Maybe he can reassure you that Jonathan is still busy?"

"You've got Brandon's number?" Amelia's eyes narrowed as she lifted her head and slowly turned to face Melanie. "I could have sworn you said you don't like the guy."

Melanie sighed with a tiny scowl. "I don't." She pressed "share" to send Brandon's number to Amelia. "Jonathan gave me Brandon's contact as a backup when I was visiting last time. Don't ask me why I haven't deleted it yet. I really couldn't answer that. Probably because I don't think enough about him to remember that I have his contact info."

"Thanks," Amelia said.

"Call Brandon, get some reassurance."

"That seems a little pesty."

"Ha," Melanie huffed. "Brandon deserves to be pestered."

Amelia chuckled softly and opened her door.

The cool, damp air brushed against her arms. The surrounding forest was obscured in the quiet darkness. She inhaled deeply, letting the cedar and rain-soaked earth fill her lungs. The forest felt different tonight, expectant, as if holding its breath.

She shivered as the drizzle intensified.

"I'll think about it," she said. "Thanks again for the ride. See you at work." Amelia closed the truck door.

She waved back toward Melanie as she climbed the wet cottage steps. The truck lights swept across the trees as Amelia pressed the code, unlocking the front door.

A large nose bumped against her hand as she opened the door, and the kittens both meowed enthusiastically. Sam whined as he pressed his head under Amelia's hand.

She set down her backpack. "Wow, look at you three all together. Friends already?" She rubbed Sam between the ears, then knelt to greet Pirate with a few quick pets. "What a greeting."

Treasure sat tentatively a few feet away. Sam carefully wound his way between the kittens and headed for the couch.

Amelia wandered into the kitchen to feed the animals, hoping a normal routine would relieve her restless energy. Her hands shook slightly as she checked the food bowls her mom had already filled.

Amelia considered giving Jonathan more time to respond. Should she call Brandon? Melanie was right; Jonathan was probably very busy. Still...

She glanced at the clock her mom had hung on the wall, shaped like a cute red teapot. Eight o'clock. It was eleven in Atlanta, too late to call Brandon.

Amelia climbed the narrow stairs to her bedroom, each step heavier than the last. She peeled off her travel clothes, took a quick shower, and pulled on soft cotton pajamas. But even the simple comforts couldn't diminish the churning in her stomach.

Every nerve ending felt raw, exposed. She wanted to pace,

to run, to do *something* other than sit here wondering and waiting.

* * *

She settled on the couch with a blanket, opposite where the kittens had cuddled up to Sam, and tried to work herself up to texting Brandon.

> AMELIA: This is Amelia. I know it's late, but can I call you? I'm worried about Jonathan.

> BRANDON: Yes, it's all right. I'm still awake. How did you get my number?

She let out a sigh of relief and pressed call.

"Hello again, Amelia," he said. His voice seemed tired.

"Melanie had your number. She suggested I call you," Amelia said.

Brandon groaned.

"I want to apologize for showing up at your home so unexpectedly this morning."

"Thank you, but that's not necessary," Brandon said. "It was fine. You make it back to Washington all right?"

"Yes, I did," Amelia said as she pulled the blanket up higher around herself. "About Jonathan ... he said he would contact me soon, but that was several days ago. I don't want to contact him again if he's really busy."

But there was the thing about having been ghosted once. Amelia's stomach soured at the thought.

Brandon inhaled a big breath and exhaled slowly. "I can't believe he put me in this position." There was a silent pause. "I don't want to spoil the surprise," he said finally, "but it isn't in my nature to mislead."

439

"Surprise?" Amelia said. She straightened herself as the blanket pooled in her lap.

"I told you the truth when I said I don't know when he's returning to Atlanta. The point is, he's there in Rainmere."

The phone nearly slipped from her suddenly nerveless fingers. Her heart hammered against her ribs as the revelation sank in. Jonathan was in Rainmere, had been here the whole time, while she was flying to Atlanta like an idiot.

Why didn't he tell me himself? The thought stung momentarily before being swept away by the larger discovery.

"That mansion of yours. Our mother bought the house from Mr. Jewell. He's there."

"*That's* his business trip? Jonathan is ... here?" Amelia blinked and almost dropped her phone.

"Yes. She and Jonathan arrived yesterday. He plans to stay there. Permanently."

"But why?"

Brandon sighed. "Isn't it obvious? Because you're there. And yes, he's been extremely busy. He and my mother had meetings with several very wealthy potential donors today, and there are more meetings lined up for later this week. But Jonathan should be the one to fill you in on the rest. I've already said enough."

Charlotte Fontaine bought the mansion.

The pieces clicked together with startling clarity. She'd been spiraling about unanswered messages. And he'd been quietly rearranging his entire life to be with her.

She couldn't decide if she should be upset because her life had been uprooted from the mansion or grateful that Jonathan was *here* ... and permanently.

"Thank you," Amelia said, her words barely more than a whisper.

"Today was crunch-time for Jonathan. I'm sure you'll hear

from him soon," Brandon said. "Everything will be fine. Good night, Amelia."

Amelia set the phone down with trembling hands, then pressed her palms against her cheeks. Her skin felt flushed despite the evening chill seeping through the cottage windows.

Jonathan was back in Rainmere, and he'd come back to be with her.

What am I going to do?

She stood abruptly, and the blanket tumbled to the floor. Every instinct in her screamed to go see him immediately.

Amelia looked out a window at the darkened forest, raindrops tapping lightly on the glass.

No car. She couldn't drive there.

Despite the cold and darkness, Amelia decided in a heartbeat to go to the mansion to see Jonathan. She needed to tell him exactly how she felt about him, face to face.

Logic tried to intervene. It was night, it was raining, and she had no car. But logic had no place here. This was about something deeper, something that pulled at her soul.

She didn't even bother to change out of her pajamas. Instead, she just threw on a coat and then reached for her boots. The hiking boots felt sturdy and reassuring as she laced them over her pajama pants.

She didn't care how she looked. This couldn't wait for a convenient time or perfect circumstances.

Flashlight. In the kitchen, she opened the drawer where she kept all her tools and emergency supplies and grabbed her flashlight.

Then she hurried out the door.

Chapter 76

Jonathan

JONATHAN COLLECTED the last of the brandy glasses from the library, stacking them on a serving tray as Charlotte gathered abandoned cocktail napkins from side tables.

The evening had stretched longer than expected, but informal drinks after dinner had sealed legitimate connections rather than mere transactional networking.

He loosened his tie and followed Charlotte to the study, where she opened her laptop on the antique mahogany desk. The rich scent of leather-bound books filled the tranquil space.

The sooner they finished debriefing, the sooner he could call Amelia. Midafternoon, he'd realized he'd forgotten to click "send" on his last message to her, but the donor meetings had demanded his complete focus.

"Well, that went better than I'd hoped," Charlotte said, pulling up her notes document. "The Hendersons are definitely interested in funding the digital design bootcamp program, and the Roths want a formal proposal for sustainable design scholarships."

Jonathan settled into the leather chair across from her,

tapping to open his tablet. The faster they wrapped this up, the better.

"Mrs. Henderson asked three follow-up questions about mentorship programs," he said. "That's a good sign." He scrolled through his notes, comparing his observations with Charlotte's meticulous digital list. "And Dr. Roth mentioned wanting to tour the coworking spaces we've established for young designers."

They continued working through each conversation systematically, Charlotte adding details to her strategic notes file.

As Jonathan leaned back in his chair, the day's professional accomplishments shifted to more personal reflections. With the first round of donor meetings behind them, he finally had breathing space to process everything that had happened.

"Tonight, working here felt right," he said, "and the donors loved the house." Charlotte had orchestrated this entire scenario, but tonight it felt less like strategy and more like a gift.

Charlotte closed her laptop and studied him. "When I saw Jessica's pictures of Amelia's rented mansion, I knew I had to buy it. It wasn't on the market, but I gave Mr. Jewell an offer he couldn't refuse." She paused, watching his reaction. "I was thinking the mansion would be an exquisite wedding gift for you and Amelia."

Jonathan's fingers paused over his tablet screen. "A wedding gift? The entire mansion?" He'd assumed she'd bought the property for business expansion, and his relationship situation was convenient timing. "Amelia broke up with me, remember? What if she says no?"

Charlotte leaned back in her chair. "I fully intend to establish a West Coast hub here for both businesses, but I've always believed the best investments serve multiple purposes." Her voice softened. "And frankly, I'd rather see this house filled with family than just used for business offices and quarterly board meetings."

A familiar surge of excitement mixed with unease landed in Jonathan's chest. Charlotte was discussing wedding gifts, and he and Amelia hadn't even had their reunion conversation yet.

The CEO position, the mansion purchase, and now wedding gifts. The magnitude of his grand gestures suddenly felt overwhelming, even to him. How would Amelia respond to all of this? Would she see genuine commitment, or would it look like manipulation?

Here he was, planning their entire future. Drew's relationship advice had always been to start with dinner and a movie, *something normal*. Instead, Jonathan had rearranged his entire life, and his mother had bought the mansion.

"You're having second thoughts," Charlotte observed.

Jonathan ran his hand through his hair. "Not about the foundation or moving here. But maybe I'm getting ahead of myself again. It's a bad habit. And all of this," he gestured around the room, "might be too much too fast. I should focus on rebuilding my relationship with Amelia, not overwhelming her with grand gestures."

Charlotte smiled knowingly. "Jonathan, sometimes grand gestures are exactly what's needed to show serious intent. You're not that graduate student planning elaborate opera dates anymore. You're a man making carefully considered life decisions."

His eyes widened in surprise. He'd never told her about the opera tickets.

"Brandon mentioned it years ago after a golf game with Drew." She chuckled gently. "Your brother thought it was hilarious that you researched Wagner before you'd even taken Amelia for coffee."

Jonathan felt heat rise in his cheeks. "Right. Well, I'm trying not to repeat that pattern."

"This isn't the same thing." Charlotte leaned forward. "You're not planning a first date. There's a difference between getting ahead of yourself and thinking strategically about what you want."

Jonathan checked his phone. Past nine, but not too late. "Now that we're done summarizing today's meetings, I need to call Amelia."

Charlotte flashed a perceptive smile. "I think that's an excellent idea."

"And I want to see her first thing in the morning, before she normally leaves for work." The plan crystallized as he spoke. "I've made her wait too long for this conversation."

His phone buzzed with a text message. Brandon's name appeared on the screen.

> BRANDON: Amelia called me. I couldn't keep the truth from her any longer. She knows you're at the mansion in Rainmere.

Jonathan stared at the message. His carefully planned morning conversation evaporated.

Chapter 77

Amelia

AMELIA STEPPED out of the cottage into the night, her hiking boots softly thumping on the gravel driveway. Rain droplets tapped against her coat hood as she pulled it up, the sound sharp in the stillness.

Nine o'clock, and it was already dark and overcast, hiding any moonlight.

The forest loomed around the cottage like a living wall, impenetrable beyond her flashlight's glow. Every shadow could hide anything. Any sound could be danger.

She mentally catalogued all the rational reasons this was a terrible idea: alone, at night, in bear country, with weather deteriorating.

Pulling her phone from her coat pocket, she squinted at the screen. Eighty percent battery, plenty of charge. But she knew service was spotty in the woods. *Shit.*

Amelia shoved her phone back into her pocket, dismissing the idea of delaying any longer. Urgency vibrated through her body like electricity, stronger than her fear of the dark forest.

Jonathan needed to know she was wrong about everything, that she was ready to trust love again.

Chilly rain struck her face like tiny needles as she turned from the driveway onto the dirt road. It was uncomfortable but somehow cleansing. Each drop seemed to wash away another layer of doubt. Her flashlight beam bobbed ahead of her, a small circle of safety in the vast darkness.

She hurried, her damp pajama pants swishing against her legs with each stride.

She knew this was crazy. She was wearing striped cotton pajamas under a raincoat, trekking through the forest at night in the rain to tell a man she loved him. If Audra could see her now, she'd either cheer "Go get him!" or demand to come along as backup.

But it felt right. Righter than anything had felt since she'd lost Jonathan years ago.

The dirt road stretched ahead, her footsteps muffled by the softened earth. Overhead, the sound of rain on leaves created a steady rhythm, punctuated by distant water running somewhere in the darkness. The scents of cedar and damp soil hung heavy in the moist air, intensified by the rain.

Rain trickled past her hood and into her shirt, and her hands grew cold and wet in the steady drizzle. The temperature was dropping too. Her breath misted visibly.

She checked her phone again. Almost no service. Amelia pushed the phone back into her coat pocket.

The wind intensified and the tall firs creaked and swayed overhead. Their branches rustled like hushed conversations, and raindrops fell steadily, pattering against her hood in a regular cadence.

This recognizable route felt like a lifeline. She'd walked this road so many times that muscle memory could guide her even in the dark. This time, no one else was dictating her direction. This was her choice, her path, her decision to trust again.

She reached the trail entrance, where the dirt road intersected the forest path to the mansion. The same route she'd taken when exploring the estate grounds, hiking to the cottages, and to reach the chapel.

The words were already forming in her head. She'd tell him she loved him, that she'd been wrong to doubt him, that she wasn't afraid of the real connection between them. By the time she reached his door, she'd know exactly what to say.

The rain came down harder now, with fat drops gleaming in her flashlight beam. She felt her boots slipping along the wet earth.

* * *

Twenty minutes later, rustling exploded from the bushes beside the trail. Branches cracked.

Amelia stopped abruptly.

More branches crunched. A musky odor drifted on the wind. Something wild. Something big. Adrenaline flooded her system. Bear? Maybe coyotes?

The rustling came from multiple directions now, closing in fast. She swept her flashlight beam through the woods, catching glimpses of movement but nothing clear enough to identify. Her hands shook, and the light beam jumped.

There was something else too, something that made her skin prickle. The path ahead felt wrong. Her body wanted to turn away.

Run. Every fiber said run.

A branch snapped very close. Twenty feet? Fifteen? Too close.

Panic overrode everything else. Amelia ran. She crashed through wet underbrush, her flashlight practically useless as she fled in terror.

Moss-slicked logs suddenly appeared in her path, forcing

her to scramble around them. Low tree branches caught at her coat, and hidden root systems threatened her every step.

Then something strange happened. Even as she ran blindly, an odd, inviting sensation guided her along certain paths. When panic wanted to send her left toward an open trail, something inside her pushed right, toward denser trees. Following that warm sensation felt safer than fighting it.

Then she felt it again—an inexplicable hesitation, an internal voice shouting *stop!*

Amelia skidded to a halt just as her flashlight beam exposed a steep drop. She was on the edge of a hidden creek ravine. One more step would have sent her plummeting onto the rocks far below.

Her heart hammered as she stepped back and pressed her palms against the rough bark of a nearby cedar. Listening again to the drops tapping on her hood, she inhaled several deep breaths to steady herself. She'd come far too close to serious injury.

How had she known? Was that her own voice?

Amelia looked around. Nothing looked familiar anymore. She was lost.

* * *

She chose the path that looked easiest, downhill through a gap in the trees. If she was going to be lost, she'd be lost on her own terms. Three steps in, her boot snagged on a tangle of roots. She pitched forward, hitting the rocky ground hard.

The impact drove the breath from her lungs. Her hands scraped against rough and gnarled fir bark, her knee struck a stone with a spike of pain, and a sharp ache shot up her shin where it smacked into a hidden stump.

She groaned and rolled onto her side, lying still for a few moments before reaching to retrieve her flashlight.

Sweeping the beam over herself, she assessed the damage. Her pajama fabric was torn, and there was blood on her scraped palms. Her knee throbbed, and her shin was bloody and raw.

Her wrist ached when she moved to right herself. Definitely painful, maybe sprained.

She struggled to stand, shifting weight off her tender ankle.

The rain was intensifying to a genuine downpour, and the temperature continued to drop. Cold fear seeped into her mind like an unwelcome invader, sapping her strength.

She felt a pull, the same internal compass sensation that had saved her from the ravine. Pain and exhaustion forced her to surrender. She couldn't keep running from her instincts, couldn't keep fighting what her gut had been trying to tell her all along.

The rain created a melody she could follow, each surface producing distinct sounds. Under her feet, the moss-covered ground felt softer than bare earth, giving her more information she hadn't noticed before.

When she stopped forcing logical navigation, one direction seemed clearer than the others. Not visible exactly, but it felt right. She had confidence about which way to go, despite having no landmarks she could name. The trees no longer felt threatening but protective, as if the dense canopy was sheltering her from the worst of the rain.

This felt exactly like learning to trust Jonathan. Scary but right.

Each step following her instincts helped to build her confidence. The rain seemed to lessen as branches parted more easily in certain directions.

She was making progress, understanding the forest, moving with purpose instead of wandering in panic.

Her ankle still throbbed, but she worked with the injury rather than fighting it. She tested each step, finding her balance, accepting the slower pace.

A few minutes later, golden light filtered through the trees ahead. Amelia stopped short as the mansion windows became visible through the darkness.

Jonathan.

She caught her breath, still favoring her injured ankle. Her pulse raced.

Rain dripped from her torn pajamas. Scraped, muddy, and bleeding, she knew she must look like a disaster. But a fire bloomed in her chest. She'd made it.

The forest had led her home.

Chapter 78

Jonathan

THE DOORBELL ECHOED through the mansion's grand foyer at the same moment Jonathan's phone buzzed with a security alert. He glanced at the screen, frowning at the notification.

SECURITY GUARD: Subject identified as Amelia Preston crossing property on foot. Appears injured. Proceeding to the main house.

What the hell? Injured?

Jonathan was already moving past the library and toward the front entrance. His heart hammered against his ribs. What was she doing walking across the property at night? And how badly injured?

He yanked open the front door.

Amelia stood on his doorstep. Jonathan's breath caught in his throat.

She was a mess. Was she in her pajamas? Her pants were torn and muddy; her raincoat was dripping water onto the stone porch. Scratches covered her hands, and there was blood on her palms.

Her hair hung in wet tangles around her shoulders. But she was standing, her chin lifted, her eyes bright and shining at him.

"Jesus, Amelia." The words came out rough and uneven. "You're hurt. Come inside."

"I ran through the forest to get here." She said it as if it were the most obvious thing in the world, as if she had always arrived at his doorstep in the middle of the night, drenched in blood and soaked through.

Jonathan stepped back and urgently gestured for her to come inside. His eyes swept over her, taking in the blood and scrapes with growing concern. "Let's take care of you and get you warm and dry."

The massive door clicked shut behind her, and suddenly they were alone in the foyer's warm light. Water dripped from her coat onto the polished floors, and Jonathan could see she was shivering.

She limped slightly as she moved, favoring her right ankle.

"I ... ran to see you," Amelia said, and Jonathan could hear a tremor in her voice.

"Jonathan, who's visiting at this hour?" Charlotte's voice came from the library doorway.

"It's Amelia," Jonathan said over his shoulder.

Charlotte appeared in her business attire, her expression shifting from curiosity to concern as she took in Amelia's condition. "Oh, my goodness, dear. What on earth happened?"

"I got a little lost," Amelia said, exhaustion creeping into her voice for the first time.

Charlotte moved to Amelia's other side, immediately reaching out to steady her. "Jonathan, get her out of those wet things. I'll get some bandages and—"

"Mom," Jonathan whispered. "I've got this."

Charlotte studied them both for a moment, then smiled. "Of course." She nodded and rubbed Amelia's shoulder. "It was good to finally meet you," she said, then headed back toward the stairs.

She collected a small suitcase that had been sitting by the banister. "I'll take my things upstairs. In the morning, I'll move to the carriage house," Charlotte said, "and give you two some privacy."

"You don't have to—" Amelia started.

"Nonsense. You came all this way to see my son, and frankly, it's your turn. I've been taking up all of his time since the second we arrived." Charlotte's smile was gracious. "And we'll have plenty of time to get acquainted properly tomorrow."

She disappeared through a side hallway toward the back door, leaving Jonathan and Amelia alone.

"Your mother seems lovely," Amelia said quietly.

"She likes you already." Jonathan reached for her coat. "Let me help you out of this."

She winced as she lifted her arms, and he saw fresh blood seeping through the torn fabric of her pajama sleeve.

"Christ, Amelia, you're really hurt." His hands were gentle as he helped her out of the wet raincoat. "Help me understand what's happening."

"I realized I needed to tell you something," she said. "Urgently."

She looked up at him. Despite the scratches on her body and despite the exhaustion in her eyes, her voice was steady. "I love you, Jonathan."

All the air left his lungs.

"I love you," she repeated, stepping closer. "I should have said it before. And I should have trusted you, trusted us. But I was scared, and I let fear make my decisions."

Jonathan stared at her, this fierce, stubborn, extraordinary woman who had just run through a forest in the dark to tell him she loved him.

"You ran through the forest at night to tell me you love me." He couldn't suppress the amazement in his voice. "Do you have any idea how much I love you? How long I've waited to hear you say those words?"

Her lips curved in a small smile.

He cupped her face, tilted it up gently, and kissed her. Her lips were warm against his, responding despite everything she'd been through to get here.

"But first, I think we should probably patch you up," he said.

"Before I bleed on your mother's floors?" Amelia quietly joked.

Jonathan swept her up in his arms, careful of her injuries, and carried her toward the library.

"I can walk," she protested faintly, but she didn't struggle.

"Your ankle is hurt."

"It's just a little tender," she whispered.

"Amelia." He set her down gently on a leather sofa. "Let me take care of you."

She looked at him for a moment, then nodded and leaned back without arguing further. He disappeared into the adjoining bathroom, returning with his travel first aid kit, several clean towels, and a bowl of warm water.

He knelt in front of her, taking her injured hands in his. Her palms were scraped raw, embedded with bits of bark and dirt.

"This is going to sting," he warned, dampening a clean cloth.

She sucked in a breath as he began cleaning the wounds, but she didn't pull away. "Brandon told me you're staying here permanently," she said.

"I am." Jonathan rinsed the cloth, his touch gentle as he worked. "I signed on at my mother's foundation. We're establishing a West Coast hub here in Rainmere."

"Because of me?"

He looked up at her, and his hands stilled. "My decision to be here is because of you. Because of us. Because I want to begin my life with you."

Tears gathered in her eyes. "Jonathan, I—"

"I love you too," he whispered, returning to cleaning her wounds. "I never stopped loving you. And I know I never will."

"I know." Her voice was barely audible. "I was just too afraid to let myself believe it."

He moved to her shin, rolling up the torn fabric of her pajama leg. The scrape was deep but not serious, though it was still bleeding.

"What happened out there?" he asked, dabbing antiseptic on the wound. "And why didn't you drive here?"

"My mom borrowed my car for the evening. She sold hers before the move. It was old, and it wouldn't have been worth paying to ship it." Amelia cringed as Jonathan cleaned around one knee. "And I fell. Got lost in the forest. There were animals." She flinched as he cleaned another cut.

"After I got lost, the forest felt ... different," she continued. "Like I could sense which direction was right, even in the dark."

Jonathan glanced up at her, his expression curious. "You could sense it?"

"I know it sounds strange. But when I stopped fighting that feeling and started following it, I found my way here." Her fingers touched his face. "To you."

He caught her hand, pressing a kiss to her palm, careful of the bandages. "I'm glad you found your way to me. And I'm glad you weren't more seriously injured."

"Jonathan." Her voice was stronger. "I came here to tell you I love you, but I also came to ask you something."

He sat back on his heels, looking up at her. *She ran through the forest in the dark to find me. This incredible woman chose me.* Whatever she wanted to ask, he already knew his answer would be yes.

She took a deep breath, her hands shaking slightly as she reached for him. Her fingers threaded through his hair, and she leaned closer until they were breathing the same air. Her eyes searched his face as if memorizing every detail.

"Marry me," she whispered.

Jonathan felt his heart stop, then start again, pounding so hard he was sure she could hear it.

"Amelia—"

"I know it's crazy. I know I'm sitting here covered in bandages and mud, probably looking like something that crawled out of a swamp." She leaned forward, her hands framing his face. "But I've spent years being afraid of taking risks again, afraid of getting hurt, afraid of loving you the way I've always wanted to love you. I'm done being afraid."

"You're asking me to marry you." After everything they'd been through, she was the one making this leap. His hands slid up to frame her face, mirroring her touch.

"I'm asking you to marry me." Her thumbs traced across his cheekbones. "I'm asking you to build a life with me. I'm asking you to say yes to forever with me."

Jonathan closed the last few inches between them, his mouth finding hers in a kiss that was desperate and tender and full of five years of longing. She tasted like rain and earth and everything wild, and when she kissed him back, he felt everything he'd been holding back rush forward.

"Yes," he breathed against her lips. "Yes, Amelia. Yes to everything."

She laughed, the sound bright and breathless, and kissed him again. This time, her arms wrapped around his neck, pulling him closer. He was certain the quivering of her fingers against his skin had nothing to do with cold or exhaustion.

He moved to sit beside her on the sofa, dragging her onto his lap, mindful of her injuries. She leaned into him with a soft sigh and tucked her head against his chest.

"I can't believe you ran through the forest in the dark to propose to me," he murmured into her hair.

"I can't believe you moved across the country for me."

"For us," he said, his arms tightening around her. "I moved here for us."

She pulled back to look at him, her eyes brilliant. "So we're really doing this? We're really getting married?"

"We're really getting married." He cupped her face in his hands, still trying to believe this was real, that she was his. "Though next time you want to have a life-changing conversation, maybe we could try it when you're not bleeding."

"Where's the fun in that?" She smiled and kissed him again, slowly and sweetly this time. She slipped her hands under the back of his shirt, her palms tender against his skin as she pulled him closer.

Outside, the rain continued to fall, but inside the mansion's warm embrace, Jonathan held the woman he loved and knew he was finally, completely home.

"I had to get lost to find my way back to you," she said against his skin. "To us."

Chapter 79

Amelia

August.

AMELIA STOOD at the edge of the mansion's back terrace, watching the chaos unfold on the lawn below. Early afternoon August warmth surrounded her as the dry air carried sounds of laughter across the expansive lawn.

Music drifted from the strategically positioned outdoor speakers, creating the perfect backdrop for an unexpectedly competitive Bottle Topple tournament. Charlotte had thought of everything for the engagement party.

Is this really my life now?

She watched Jonathan's Atlanta family spontaneously mingling with her small circle of family and friends. Charlotte adjusted her mother's chair to catch more shade without even being asked. The casual, motherly gesture made Amelia's chest tight with gratitude.

A year ago she was alone after Nate's accident; now she was surrounded by people celebrating her future. The contrast was overwhelming in the best possible way.

"Come on, Drew!" Audra called from her position near one

of the telescoping poles. "You keep saying construction work gives you steady hands."

Drew wound up dramatically, frisbee balanced in his grip, while everyone offered contradictory advice.

"Aim left!" Jonathan said.

"No, right!"

Melanie motioned toward the poles. "Just throw the thing!"

He let it fly with theatrical precision, and the disc sailed completely wide of the bottle perched atop the pole. The entire group erupted in groans and laughter.

"Steady hands, my ass," Brandon said. He grinned as he left to retrieve the frisbee.

"He's still ahead of you," Charlotte called mildly from her position keeping unofficial score on a napkin.

"Not for long," Brandon said. Amelia caught the way her mother smiled at the easy family dynamic.

Rachel stepped up for her turn, and Amelia moved closer to watch, catching the middle of her mother's conversation with Jessica. "I finished producing my advanced virtual piano course last week," her mom was saying as she lined up her shot. "With Amelia's help, of course. Now I just need to build a website."

"I could help with that," Jessica offered immediately, bouncing slightly on her toes. "I'm no expert, but I've been working on updating the Studio Charlotti website. Web design is actually kind of fun."

Rachel beamed. "Really? That would be wonderful, honey."

Jonathan's family so instinctively embraced hers. The ease with which Jessica had offered to help. It was all significant.

When her mother's throw went wide and she stumbled backward laughing, Jonathan was there immediately, steadying her with the automatic care he'd show his own mother.

She'd always had a family. *Now I have a clan.*

"Audra, whatever you did with that harvest salad with the

candied pecans," Charlotte said as she approached the group, "it's absolutely divine. I've had three helpings."

Audra flushed with pleasure. "Thank you. Actually, that's why I'm taking my own advice about getting off my behind and doing something with my dream. I signed up for evening classes at the culinary institute. Real training, not just weekend introductory classes."

"Good for you," Melanie said, reaching for her frisbee. "When do you start?"

"Do you have a taste-testing waiting list?" Jonathan said.

Audra smiled and nodded. "September. I'm not quitting my lab job yet, but..." She shrugged, looking pleased with herself. "I have to start somewhere. And occasionally you have to take your own advice, right?"

"You always give exceptional advice," Amelia said. "I'm certain you'll be glad you followed it."

Drew's face lit up. "I am so proud of you." He pulled her into a quick, enthusiastic hug. "Your cooking is already amazing. Now the professional world is going to find out, too."

"Speaking of stepping out in new directions," Drew continued, one arm still loosely around Audra's shoulder. "I'm not moving my business to Seattle just yet. But I'm going to try taking on a few clients here. See how it goes."

"Smart move," Jonathan said approvingly. He tossed a frisbee, barely missing the bottle on the leftmost pole. The bottle wavered but stayed upright.

"And it'll give me a reason to visit regularly." He gave Audra a slow wink.

"Besides, there's always something that needs fixing around this place," Jonathan said. "And you know how my mother loves to redesign. Occasional contract work will always be available here."

The current round ended when Jessica knocked a bottle

clean off its perch, sending it tumbling to the grass with a satisfying thud. Everyone cheered.

Audra corralled the group toward the lunch spread she had arranged on the terrace.

"How is Mr. Jewell doing?" Charlotte asked as they filled their plates.

"He's moving into cottage four, but it's going to be a while," Amelia said, adding a slice of focaccia bread and a spoonful of basil pesto to her plate. "He's making major upgrades first. And the field behind it? Turns out it's his archery range."

"Archery?" Jessica perked up. "That's so cool. Can he teach people?"

Amelia laughed. "I have no idea, but I can ask."

"Why would a wealthy guy like that want to live in a cottage?" Audra said.

"I suspect he was planning on *eventually* selling the mansion; Charlotte just got to him before he could put it on the market. And, honestly, I don't know why he's moving to the cottage."

After lunch, they drifted around the terrace. Some dropped onto the steps, others claimed chairs and balanced dessert plates on knees and side tables. The animated lunch chatter dissolved into quieter, intimate discussions.

When Charlotte and Rachel settled into adjacent chairs nearby, Amelia listened to their conversation with quiet joy.

"It wasn't easy raising kids on my own," Charlotte said. "Especially when I was trying to build a career at the same time."

Rachel nodded. "Some days the balance seemed impossible for me. But look how they turned out." She gestured toward Jonathan, who was helping Brandon gather empty plates. "You should be proud."

"I am." Charlotte's voice was sincere. "And I'm thrilled that

Jonathan chose someone with your daughter's strength. It takes courage to open your heart again after a loss."

"He makes her happy," Rachel said simply. "That's a huge part of what I want for her."

Amelia made her way across the terrace to stand with Jessica near the drinks station. "Does this feel like home now?" Jessica said, gesturing at the mansion. "I know you rented here before, but now it's truly your home. It's like something out of a fairy tale."

"It still doesn't feel real sometimes," Amelia admitted. "What about you? Are you excited about school?"

"Terrified," Jessica laughed. "I'm excited to start UW's international business program and it's a perfect for Mom's expansion plans, plus I'll be closer to you guys when I start in the fall, but..." She bit her lip. "It's been a while since I was on a campus, and I'm older than most of the students will be."

"I can understand that might be uncomfortable," Amelia agreed. "But I'm sure you'll do well. And you'll have Jonathan and me nearby if you need anything."

"Do you mean that?"

"Absolutely. We're family and we're here for you whenever."

"Thank you. That means more to me than you know." Jessica's satisfaction was visible. "I didn't want to assume, but I was really hoping we could be the family that actually shows up for each other."

As teams reformed for the final rounds, Melanie and Brandon found themselves paired together through a process of elimination.

"I suppose we can be on the same team. If it's absolutely necessary," Melanie said with cool politeness.

"I'll try not to slow you down," Brandon replied with equal

courtesy. The tension of unsettled business in his voice was subtle but undeniable.

"Jonathan mentioned that the leadership program keeps you very busy," Melanie said. "How generous of them to let you out."

Brandon scoffed. "Yes, they let me out," he said with a sarcastic grin. "Even leadership programs allow weekends. I'll be back in North Carolina Monday morning."

Audra cleared her throat and picked up a Frisbee. "All right, who's ready for the next round?"

Melanie joined Amelia at the drinks station during the next team changeover. "Have you set a date yet?"

"Late spring," Amelia said, her voice brimming with optimism. "That should give us enough time to make all the arrangements."

"I'm delighted to be a bridesmaid. And Audra will shine as your maid of honor."

Amelia squeezed Melanie's hand. "It wouldn't be the same without the two of you by my side."

Melanie's phone buzzed. She glanced at it with an annoyed expression. "Mom finally texted back about my promotion, despite the merger fallout. She said, 'Contracts aren't as challenging as real legal work, but good job.'" She gave a wry smile. "Twenty-seven years old and I'm still wanting to impress them."

Before Amelia could respond, Charlotte appeared on Melanie's other side.

"Some parents have very narrow definitions of success," Charlotte said gently. "What matters is that you're establishing something meaningful for yourself."

Melanie blinked in surprise at the support. "That's ... exactly what I needed to hear. Thank you."

"I've offered to help with venue decoration through Studio

Charlotti," Charlotte said to Amelia. "Whatever you need for the wedding."

"That's generous," Amelia said. "I can use all the decorating help I can get."

"We're family now," Charlotte said. "And I will love every minute."

Amelia had to look away before she started crying happy tears.

She excused herself and made her way across the terrace, drawn to the quiet spot where Jonathan stood watching the end of the final game.

They watched Audra and Drew compete in perfect partnership, anticipating each other's moves, celebrating successes, and commiserating over misses.

"Do you think they'll ever get together?" Jonathan asked, slipping his arm around her waist.

"Audra says no," Amelia replied, leaning into his firm body. "But look at them."

They watched as Drew steadied Audra for her throw, and she landed a perfect hit that sent the bottle spinning to the grass. Their embrace stretched beyond simple congratulations, both of them holding on as the hug appeared to drift toward affection.

"We found our way together," Jonathan said. "Maybe they will, too."

"We did." Amelia felt a flutter of gratitude for second chances and for stubborn hearts that refused to give up. "It feels so complete and perfect, having everyone together."

"This is how I always wanted family celebrations to be," he said. "Chaotic and full of laughter, with people who actually care about each other."

After years of feeling like her family was shrinking, Amelia realized it was finally growing again. The thought came with a familiar pang, a brief wistful moment wishing her dad were here. He would have loved Jonathan.

She had a fleeting thought that Rebecca would have understood this joy too, the rightness of choosing love over self-protection.

"I love you," she said simply.

"I love you too," he said, pressing a soft kiss to the top of her head.

Charlotte clapped her hands together as the final round ended. "All right, everyone, time for cake and champagne! This is an engagement party, after all."

Everyone moved toward the beautifully decorated cake table, where Charlotte and Audra had arranged flutes of champagne and sparkling cider.

Audra brought out her phone for spontaneous family photos, capturing all the happy moments of people mingling with drinks and cake.

"Come here," Charlotte said, pulling Amelia aside while the others were enjoying their cake. "I just want you to know how happy I am. I'm gaining another daughter, and you're a wonderful addition to the family."

Amelia's throat tightened with emotion. "I'm so grateful for how you've welcomed us. Both of us."

"Thank you for making my son smile like that again," Charlotte said, as she set one hand on Amelia's shoulder.

As Charlotte turned to check on other guests, Amelia caught sight of her mother approaching Jonathan near the champagne table. She moved closer to listen.

"You're exactly what Amelia needed," Rachel said to Jonathan. "Thank you for taking such good care of her."

"She takes care of me too," Jonathan replied. "That's how the best partnerships work."

As the afternoon wound toward evening, people began the

gradual process of saying goodbye, though nobody seemed to want to go. There were promises to get together soon with many lingering hugs, and Rachel accepted Charlotte's invitation to visit Atlanta.

Finally, Amelia and Jonathan found themselves alone on the front steps, waving farewell as cars disappeared down the winding driveway.

"Ready for part two?" Jonathan asked, taking her hand.

"Always," Amelia said, and meant it completely.

The afternoon had been perfect, but she was ready for the intimacy that would follow, just the two of them that evening, together, planning the rest of their lives.

Chapter 80

Epilogue

AMELIA WOKE SLOWLY, awareness returning in slow, delicious layers. Jonathan's warm body curved behind hers, his arm heavy across her waist. His gentle breath stirred the hair at her neckline. She savored the solid weight of him pressed against her back, and the lazy contentment that came from a night of thorough loving.

Sunday morning light filtered through the bedroom windows, casting golden hues across their bed. A subtle change in his breathing told her he was awake, followed by a gentle movement of his fingertips tracing shapes across her bare shoulder.

"Good morning," she whispered, sliding deeper into his embrace.

"Morning, beautiful." His voice was rough with sleep and satisfaction. Amelia shifted to face him, and she shivered as his lips brushed the sensitive hollow of her throat. "How did you sleep?"

"Like someone thoroughly exhausted me." She slid her hand across his chest, moving her body into closer contact, more of his heated skin against hers. Sensations of desire stirred low in her belly as she met his warm, heavy-lidded gaze.

"Good," he said, his fingers stroking smooth circles across her back. "I love waking up with you."

She ran her fingers along his chest and then curved around a firm nipple, marveling at how perfect the casual intimacy and easy touching felt, the way her body exactly fit against his.

She sighed contentedly against him. "What time is it?"

"Early enough." His hand slid down to rest on her hip. "I may have a surprise for you."

"Oh?" She raised an eyebrow, her interest piqued. "What kind of surprise?"

Instead of answering, he reached over to the nightstand and took up his tablet. "I've been doing some research."

Amelia pushed herself up on one elbow, curiosity cutting through the haze of his touch. "Research on what?"

"Wedding venues." He clicked to display a document with pictures of venue links and notes. "Spring options in the Pacific Northwest."

Her breath caught. The thoughtfulness of it, the realization that he'd been actively planning their life together, made her chest tight with love. "Jonathan..." She scrolled through the pictures. "You collected all this?"

"I couldn't help myself," he said, clearly pleased. "April still feels right?"

"April," she said, leaning over to kiss him, soft and lingering. "When everything's beginning to bloom. Like us."

For a while, they lay tangled together, the portfolio spread between them. The venues were impressive. He'd selected intimate gardens, historic inns, even a waterfront location with windows overlooking Puget Sound.

"A boat wedding?" She said, grinning at one clipping. "I love that you included boats."

"Or maybe a lakeside ceremony," he said, fingers tangled in her hair.

"Mm, sounds lovely. Your mother offered Studio Charlotti resources too." Amelia settled against his chest, the portfolio forgotten as she absorbed her contentment.

"We'll figure out the family balance." His voice was soft against her hair. "Some help, some things just our choices."

Jonathan's phone buzzed on the nightstand. He glanced at it. "Text from Steve. Says the Career Recovery Program preparations are going well. On track for launch in January." He set the phone aside, his arms tightening around her. "Someone else will get to see it through, but it's going to help people. That's what matters."

When he kissed her, it was soft but certain, and she felt the promises in it. Different from last night's desperate passion, this was deeper, carrying the peaceful assurance that they belonged to each other.

"Let's try something," Jonathan said eventually, pulling her closer.

"What?" But she was already moving, letting him arrange her between his legs, her back against his chest.

"Future dreaming." He wrapped his arms around her from behind, resting his chin on her shoulder. "What do you think we'll be doing next Christmas?"

She leaned into his embrace, looking out at their grounds through the windows, pressing her back against his chest. "Married eight months by then."

"Hosting Christmas here," he added. "Our first as husband and wife."

"Your mom decorating the mansion; my mother playing piano for holiday concerts." She grinned. "Maybe Drew and Audra will be engaged by then."

Then she turned and positioned her legs on either side of him, snuggling her lower body tightly against his.

He took her face in his hands and pressed his lips to hers, passionate and familiar, yet still discovering. She laughed softly and pulled him down with her as she settled on her side, her head sinking into a pillow. Their bodies fit together with practiced ease.

"I can't wait to marry you," she whispered against his mouth.

"Spring can't come fast enough," he agreed, his hands sliding over her skin reverently. "But right now, I want to show you exactly how much I love you."

His mouth moved to her throat, and she arched beneath him. "Jonathan..."

* * *

Thank you for reading *The One Who Ghosted Me*. Want to know how Amelia and Jonathan's story began?

Download *She's Off Limits*—the exclusive prequel novella—and discover the moment they first fell for each other.

Grab your FREE copy here:
https://dl.bookfunnel.com/cizie86n5c

QR code for the exclusive prequel novella, *She's Off Limits*,
by Erica Devon. Download your FREE copy today!

Book 2 - Coming Soon!

Coming Soon: Melanie & Brandon's Story

Melanie Foxx doesn't believe in soulmates. Brandon Fontaine definitely doesn't believe in past lives. Forced to team up for Amelia and Jonathan's wedding-venue challenge, they clash over everything—except their inconvenient attraction.

But when old family wounds collide with eerie flashes of "we've been here before," they'll have to choose: repeat the same heartbreak ... or finally rewrite the story their souls keep trying to tell.

Acknowledgments

Thank you to my husband for providing the greatest support an author could ever hope to find. I'm incredibly grateful to you for holding my hand and my heart through the seemingly endless years toward publication, and for being there to share our wonderful life together every single day. Thank you to my two adult children, who mean everything to me. To all of my other family members for their support and encouragement, thank you!

A huge thank you to my editors, Karinya Funsett-Topping, Jessica Kendall, Julie Miller, and Shannon Barefield. From early drafts through the finished product, I couldn't have completed this book without all of you and your sage advice and talents. You are invaluable!

Thanks to my writing-sprint partners and especially my Texas author friends, you've inspired me and made writing a joy.

To every reader who takes a chance on my books, I cannot thank you enough for stepping into my world. 🩶

Reading Group Questions

1. Amelia and Jonathan's story is a second-chance romance—they reconnect five years after he ghosted her in college. Do you think his reasons for disappearing were understandable? Was his ghosting forgivable, or were there better ways he could have handled the situation?

2. Forgiveness plays a huge role in this book—Amelia had to forgive Jonathan for leaving, but she also had to forgive herself for feeling responsible for Nate's death. Which act of forgiveness do you think was harder for her, and why?

3. Jonathan is thoughtful and careful, while Amelia is direct and practical. How did their personality differences create both conflict and chemistry? What moments showed them complementing each other best?

4. The physical intimacy between Amelia and Jonathan builds gradually throughout the book, from hesitant touches to the passionate epilogue. How did their physical relationship reflect their emotional journey? Did the pacing feel natural?

5. Forgiveness is the central theme of this book. Beyond Amelia forgiving Jonathan and herself, where else did you see forgiveness play out in the story? (Think about family relationships, friendships, or self-forgiveness.)

6. Which scene or moment hit you hardest emotionally? Was there a particular conversation, revelation, or quiet moment that stayed with you?

7. This book balances emotional depth with fun, lighthearted moments—lawn games, banter, engagement party chaos. What was your favorite playful or funny scene? How did those lighter moments enhance the overall story?

8. The merger failure threatened both Amelia and Jonathan's jobs, and Jonathan's potential transfer to Brazil created geographic pressure on their relationship. How did these external obstacles affect their romance? Did the "real world" conflicts make the story feel more grounded?

9. Jonathan created the Career Recovery Program to help others who face career setbacks after doing the right thing— something he experienced firsthand as a whistleblower in graduate school. When he resigned from Whitlow to stay in Washington with Amelia, he walked away from the very program he founded. Meanwhile, Paige used professional threats and personal manipulation to try to control his choices. Did Jonathan's willingness to leave behind his own creation make his commitment to Amelia more powerful? How did Paige's antagonism affect your view of their relationship?

10. The mysterious Mr. Jewell (or 'Mr. F-O' as Amelia nicknamed him) was Amelia's long-time employer, providing her with work and housing at the mansion—until he unexpectedly sold the property to Charlotte, forcing Amelia to move out with only 30 days' notice. What did you think of this secretive employer? How did the mansion sale affect your view of him? Were you surprised by Charlotte's role as the buyer?

11. The cottage renovation and Amelia's role managing the estate created a sanctuary for her healing. How important was the setting—Rainmere, the mansion, the forests—to Amelia's emotional journey?

12. We get glimpses of other potential couples in this book—Audra and Drew's growing closeness, and the tense dynamic between Brandon and Melanie at the engagement party. What are your predictions for these relationships? Which couple are you most excited to read about next?

13. Some readers noticed unusual elements in the story—the metallic smell Amelia encountered in the attic stairwell, the forest seeming to guide her during her desperate night run to reach Jonathan, her inexplicable connection to Rebecca's journal entries, and the intense feeling of 'rightness' with Jonathan that went beyond normal attraction. Did you pick up on these hints? What do you think they might mean for future books in the series?

About the Author

Erica Devon writes contemporary romance with humor, heart, and happily-ever-afters in settings that range from mountain wilderness to elegant estates. After 20 years as a geologist and computer scientist, she brings authenticity to stories of second chances and fated connections. Between writing sessions, you'll find her hiking Colorado trails, binging K-Dramas, or hanging out with her supportive husband and family.

Website & Newsletter Signup: www.ericadevon.net
Instagram: @erica_devon_author
Facebook: Erica_Devon_Author

Join My Reader Community

Thank you so much for reading *The One Who Ghosted Me*.

I hope Amelia and Jonathan's story brought you joy, hope, and maybe a few happy tears.

If you'd like bonus scenes, behind-the-scenes extras, and early updates on the next Fontaine Family book, I'd love to stay in touch.

You'll be the first to hear about new releases, special promotions, and exclusive bonus content available only to subscribers.

Thank you for supporting my stories. It means the world. 

—Erica Devon

Join my reader community:
www.ericadevon.net

QR code for www.ericadevon.net